SHATTERED HEART

THE DONNELLYS
BOOK THREE

DOROTHY F. SHAW

PRAISE FOR DOROTHY F. SHAW

"*Unworthy Heart* reminded me of what I love about the romance genre."—The Book Tart

"*Unworthy Heart* by Dorothy F. Shaw made me think, made my heart happy, made me tear up and made me sigh in happiness. Shaw combines heat with heart almost flawlessly. I cannot wait for the follow-up books in this series."—Romance Novel News

"I fell in love with the series from book one…Grab your copy and buckle up for the ride. Dorothy Shaw doesn't do anything halfway."—Beyond the Valley of the Books on *Defensive Heart*

"Holy smokes, can Dorothy Shaw write a freaking awesome sex scene…"—Wicked Good Reads on *Defensive Heart*

"*Defensive Heart* by Dorothy F. Shaw is a good read which gives credence to the statement that opposites do attract."—Harlequin Junkie

"Even though there is plenty of sex in *Shattered Heart*, the author does not neglect the storyline at all – packing it full of romance, danger, trauma, healing, laughs, and the Donnelly family."—Crystal's Many Reviewers

"*Shattered Heart* is an emotional tear-jerker of a romance that had me reaching for the tissues on more than one occasion."
—Romance Novel News

"Wow! What a sexy, steamy story that kept me reading from the first page."—Crystal's Many Reviewers on *Stripped Bounty*

"If you are into vanilla, forget this book! Characters larger than life and sex to die for. Dorothy F. Shaw painted a canvas that is both intriguing and close to hardcore."—Amazon Reviewer on *Stripped Bounty*

"Epic story! Rosie and Badger are amazing characters that pull you into the story. The sex is HOT and the ending is perfect!"—Book Addicts PR on *Stripped Bounty*

"I was blown away by how easily the story was told by Dorothy F. Shaw"—CeeriJays Smexy HotReads on *A Few More Rules*

"*A Few More Rules* (a femdom novella) is a super-hot romance that sets the foundation well for a probable HEA between Rig and Beth. This story is a winner."—Romance Novel News

"WOW!!! This erotic, sensual short story will have you panting for more! These two beauties are more than fang bangers. The dark world of lust and sex will feed any appetite you desire."—Bookaholic and More Blog on *Playtime*

"I like books that grab my attention so much that I read a line and end up gasping or commenting out loud... and this one did just that - a few times! I'll definitely be reading it again."—Goodreads Reviewer on *Playtime*

"True to Dorothy Shaw's form, *Avoiding the Badge* is full of everything I love about her writing."—Amanda at Wicked Good Reads

"I liked the way the author brought about the truths that they had been keeping from each other, and I really enjoyed the steps that the two characters took in order to overcome the troubles in their path."—Amazon reviewer on *Avoiding the Badge*

"*Redeeming the Badge* is a second chance romance that is hot as Hades and with a backstory that will twist your heartstrings." —Amazon Reviewer

"This is a tale of love and heartache, dealing with some tough issues such as infertility, endometriosis, and miscarriage. It will tear at your heartstrings and make you believe in true love." —Amazon Reviewer on *Redeeming the Badge*

"Jeff and Tish are a good couple with incredible chemistry that makes you jealous. I can't recommend this series enough." —Amazon Reviewer on *Trusting the Badge*

"*Trusting the Badge* is a quick read for readers who enjoy a focus on relationship building, characters with tragic backstories, and some steamy moments." —Amazon Reviewer

"It was written in a way that I got very emotional reading it, most books don't make me cry. This one did."—Amazon reviewer on *Jaded Heart*

Shattered Heart

The Donnellys Book 3
© 2019 Dorothy F. Shaw

A crush is just a fantasy. The real thing packs some serious heat.

When Cynthia Donnelly lays eyes on her high school crush at her brother's wedding rehearsal, she regrets her self-imposed, one-year moratorium on dating. If possible, he's even hotter now than when they were teens.

Back in school, Shane made a point to ignore his best friend's cute, sassy little sister. Now that she's grown into an incredibly sexy woman full of Irish spunk, resisting her is out of the question. Besides, in his book, all "hands-off" rules have expired.

One sizzling night together should have been enough. Instead, the heat rises, tempting Cyn to take a chance on a long-distance relationship and making Shane consider pulling up stakes and moving back to L.A.

Cyn's recently dumped ex, however, has other ideas. His quest to get her back escalates into violence, shattering Cyn's faith in herself, and in anyone else of the male persuasion, and leaving Shane with his work cut out for him to repair the damage—or lose his shot at a once-in-a-lifetime love.

DEDICATION

This one's for you, Mommy.
For everything you endured and survived…
And for everything you taught me.
I'm strong because of you.
Thank you for that.

ACKNOWLEDGMENTS

Shout-out to my beta readers: Sunnie Andrews, Trenda "TBird" London and my cousin, Sherri Zak. Thank you so much, as always, your feedback was invaluable. To my cousin, Lisa Ruiz, for her medical scene assistance. To Anthony Garcia for the U.S. Marine details and LAPD scene advisement. And to one of my best friends, author Sidda Lee Rain. Thank you for being the only eyes I had on this while it took shape! You saved my bottom for sure! #TheBraIsOff! #RedHairDontCare!

One I forgot to mention in Defensive Heart, book 2, is author Shawna (Thomas) Guzman… Chica, I could thank you a thousand times, plus a thousand times more, and it would never be enough. You took me by the hand and molded, shaped, taught and then, with a soft heart but firm hand, taught some more. I could not have made it this far without you. I still have so far to go, but I will forever be grateful for you.

**Added with 3rd version re-release: Special thanks to Sunnie Andrews (badass aspiring author and friend) for being an awesome PA and proofreader/beta reader. And fetching coffee and getting my ass to signings ALMOST on time. <3

CONTENT/TRIGGER WARNING

<u>Trigger Warning</u>: *This book contains a physical assault of the heroine by her ex.*

Buckle up for a bumpy emotional journey with the characters as they fall apart and then slowly find their way to healing, and to each other. You might get angry or tearful along the way, you may even get frustrated, but as is with any good love story, it'll be worth it in the end.

PLAYLIST

Garth Brooks - *To Make You Feel My Love*
Tarra Layne - *Difference*
The Chicks - *Baby Hold On*
A Thousand Horses - *Smoke*
Kenny Wayne Shepherd - *Slow Ride*
Edwin McCain - *I'll Be*
Big & Rich - *Save a Horse (Ride a Cowboy)*
Tarra Layne - *Beautiful Day*

CHAPTER ONE

"Oh my God, Maiya! You look fucking incredible!" Cyn Donnelly scrambled to her feet and ran to her future sister-in-law's side. She smiled in awe of how beautiful her brother's future bride looked in her gown. "I thought it was gorgeous when you settled on it a few months ago, but now that it's been fitted? Yeah…*in-fucking-credible.*"

"I can't even…" Maiya cupped her hands over her mouth, tears breaching the edges of her eyes, and gazed at Cyn in the large mirror in the bridal shop. She swished the tulle skirt from side to side. "I can't believe it's me."

"Cynthia, please…language." Cyn's mother, Roseanne, frowned at her as she came to Maiya's side, too. "Maiya, you look perfect." She stroked her hand down the back of Maiya's hair. "An absolute angel, honey."

Maiya stroked her fingertips over the strapless sweetheart neckline of the gown and then smoothed her palms down the beaded and sequined bodice. Cyn rolled her eyes at her mother, then took Maiya's hand in hers and nodded. "Mom's right, you're an angel."

"A tattooed angel, maybe?" Maiya giggled.

"Those are the best kind, especially in a mermaid gown that shows off all your amazing curves. Ryan is gonna pass the hell out when he sees you coming down the aisle." Cyn squeezed her hand.

"Do you really think he'l—"

"Crap! I'm late! Where is she?" All three women turned around to see Jodi, Maiya's best friend, come barreling around a rack of wedding gowns, blonde curls billowing behind her before skidding to a halt. "Oh sweet Jesus and the Blessed Virgin…" Jodi pressed her hand to her chest. "Maiya, you're an angel."

"That's exactly what we said, too!" Cyn laughed.

Jodi stepped in front of Maiya. "I don't doubt it, Cyn. It's like she fell from heaven or something. Turn around, Maiya. Let me see the back."

"Oh my God, stop!" Maiya pressed her hands to her cheeks. "You guys are totally embarrassing me now." With a laugh, Maiya rolled her eyes and turned around, facing the mirror again.

"I'm going to have them bring out your veil, too." Mom stepped away.

Settling in the seats behind them, Cyn watched as Jodi doted on Maiya, a giggle or two bubbling up in all the excitement. Ryan and Maiya's wedding was this coming weekend, and Cyn couldn't be happier for them. A little over a year ago, her brother had met a woman who made everything in his life make sense, and in the process, his precious son, Jacob, would finally have the mother he so deserved.

For lack of a better word, it was a fairy tale. And although Cyn knew life wasn't really like that, Ryan and Maiya came pretty damn close. Sure, they argued. Sure, they got on each other's nerves—after all, they were as opposite as two people could get. But in the end, they connected and, in Cyn's book, that equaled happy. She sighed and rested her chin on her fist. If only she could be so lucky.

Her mother returned and placed Maiya's veil on the back of her long, thick red hair. The tulle hung to her lower back, turning an already perfect dress into an absolutely perfect ensemble. Maiya beamed, staring at herself in the mirror, and then her tears made another appearance. Jodi hugged her best friend, and Mom held Maiya's hand.

Yup, happy was exactly what this was.

Cyn's phone chirped from her purse, the text tone letting her know exactly who it was before even having to check the screen.

> Carlos: Not gonna make dinner.

> Cyn: Are you serious? Carlos, this is really important to me. Why can't you be here?

> Carlos: Something came up at the office.
> Sorry. Will text later if anything changes.

She didn't bother replying. Her boyfriend was blowing her off…yet again, and even if he really did have a valid reason, it didn't matter because there was *always* some excuse, some reason why he couldn't do whatever he might've committed to doing with her. Guaranteed, he wouldn't text her later either, even if something changed.

Closing her eyes, Cyn swallowed down the golf ball-sized lump of disappointment in her throat. She and Carlos had dinner plans with her other brother, Jimmy, and his girlfriend, Sonja. The couple had arrived last night from New York with Sonja's daughter, Casey. Ryan and Maiya were coming, too. It was supposed to be the six of them, but now, because Carlos was a grade-A flake, Cyn would be the fifth wheel at the table with four other happy people. Damn him.

For the life of her, she couldn't understand why she put up with his shit. Yeah, the sex was decent, but that was beside the point. It wasn't about the sex for her. Worse, for the last few months, the only time the man showed up for her was when his dick was hard, but even that had tapered off. At least before, she could tell herself it was worth it. But now? Cyn took a moment and thought back to the last time they'd actually had sex…two weeks ago? Wow.

"Cyn, you've got that look on your face again. And your phone's in your hand. Not a good sign."

She looked up from the screen at Maiya and sighed. "Yeah, I know."

Maiya put her hands on her hips. "He's not coming, is he?"

"No." Cyn slid her phone back into her purse and stood. "But it doesn't matter because today is your day, and we are *not* talking about my drama." She kissed Maiya's cheek.

"Roseanne? Can you please order your daughter to dump this dude? Please?" Maiya pulled her veil off and handed it to Jodi.

"Sweetheart, I wish I could. You know as well as I do, my kids do what they do, and I let them because if I didn't, they'd never find their way. Cyn knows I don't particularly care for Carlos, and she also knows no one else does either. But she's going to have to learn in her own time."

"That's what I always say, Roseanne. We're raising adults, not babies. Best they learn their lessons in their time." Jodi raised a hand in the air. "Not that y'all need me to put my two cents in. You've raised ten, but I'm just saying it's nice to know I'm going about it the right way."

Agitation prickled the skin on the back of Cyn's neck. *Learn in my own time, whatever.* She crossed her arms and cocked one hip to the side. "Excuse me, but I'm standing right here."

"And?" Maiya laughed. "Whatever. Not like it's a secret how we all feel. Carlos is an asshole—sorry, Roseanne, for cursing—and you deserve better, Cyn. Now help me out of my dream dress, and let's go get our nails done." Maiya turned and headed for the dressing room.

Cyn glanced at her mother, who was wearing a smile

wider than the Grand Canyon. Jodi was, too. *Awesome.* With an exasperated sigh, Cyn followed after Maiya. "Fine."

Yeah, Carlos was an asshole, she knew it. But Cyn still loved him. Eventually, when it got painful enough, she'd let go and walk away. She just wasn't there yet.

CHAPTER TWO

Shane Conlon parked his rented SUV in the driveway of his oldest friend's house. It felt like forever since he'd seen Joey Donnelly, and really, it had been. Serving his country, combined with never coming home to visit even years after, tended to have that effect on his most cherished relationships. Shane grabbed his large duffel bag from the trunk and approached the front door.

Before he'd made it up the first step, the door flung wide open, and Joey walked out onto the stoop. "Holy shit, look at those gray hairs. You're getting old."

With a laugh, Shane approached him. "Backatcha, bitch."

Joey clasped Shane's outstretched hand and pulled him into an embrace. Goddamn, it was good to be home.

His best friend pulled away and clapped Shane on the shoulder. "So fucking glad you're here. You've been away for too long, Shane."

"Tell me about it." Shane ran his hand over his close-cropped hair and blew out a breath.

"Come on, I got some people I want you to meet." Joey grabbed Shane's bag and ushered him into the house.

He followed Joey through a quaint living room and

beyond into the kitchen. A very pretty woman with long, curly, almost black hair sat at the kitchen table, feeding an equally pretty child who was in a highchair.

"Stephanie, this is Shane." Joey smiled.

She wiped her hands on a towel and stood. "My God, this is the infamous Shane Conlon? I'm so happy to finally meet you!" She approached him and, with no hesitation, pulled him into an embrace. "Welcome to our home."

Shane wrapped his arms around her and knew, without a doubt, why Joey had fallen head over heels in love with the woman. "I don't know about the infamous part. I will say, finally meeting the woman who tamed Joey is definitely a pleasure." He pulled away and smiled at her. Her brown eyes sparkled with amusement, and he couldn't help but wholeheartedly adore her in the span of a nanosecond.

"And this little dolly is the boss of the house. Madison, meet Uncle Shane," Joey said.

The small child in his best friend's arms had the same curly, dark hair as her mother and a face just as pretty. "Wow!" Shane ran his hand over the back of his neck. "Wow, Joe, she's beautiful. Of course, because she takes after her mother." He winked at Stephanie as he stepped over to Joey and the baby. "How old is she?"

"She's just coming up on ten months. Not walking yet, but crawling everywhere." Joey kissed his daughter's cheek. "Isn't that right, Madi?"

The baby babbled some sort of baby speak Shane wasn't able to understand but found cute as hell as she patted her daddy's face with her little hands. Shane ran his fingertips over her tiny arm in utter amazement that Joey was a father. And a husband. A beat of regret rolled through him. He'd missed so much being away. Saying he was glad at the opportunity to come home and really spend some time was an understatement. "She's beautiful. Just…beautiful, Joey. I couldn't be happier for you."

"Can I get you something to drink? Eat?" Stephanie touched his arm.

"I grabbed a quick bite on my way from the airport, but coffee'd be great if you have it."

Stephanie laughed. "If we have it? Coffee's the main staple in this house. There's always a pot made, and if there isn't, then someone's in trouble." She moved to the cabinets and pulled down a mug. "Cream and sugar?"

"Got it. Just black, please, ma'am."

"Hardcore." She nodded.

"It's the Marine in him." Joey placed Madison back in her highchair and filled the tiny spoon with whatever yellow mush the child had been eating when they'd walked in. "Have a seat, man. Tell me what's new." He fed the baby a mouthful.

Shane took the seat on the opposite end of the table from his friend, still amazed at the scene before him. "Well, since I got back from Afghanistan, I took advantage of my construction experience. Finally obtained my contractor's license and have mostly been doing remodels and home additions." Stephanie set a cup of coffee in front of him and then took a seat. He smiled at her. "Thanks."

"All those years serving paid off. So, you're doing well? Making a good living, I take it?"

"Damn good, I'd say. The best part is being back in the States. I tell ya, we really don't know how good we have it until we spend some time in a country where people aren't free."

"I can't even imagine." Stephanie shook her head and then sipped her coffee. "Thank you for your service, Shane. I'm honored to have you in our home."

"The honor is all mine, ma'am. But you're welcome." He nodded.

"Okay, enough with the ma'am. You're making me feel old." She laughed.

"Sorry, some habits don't go away. You may have to adjust." He winked.

"Hey, I echo Steph's sentiments. Even if you do have a few gray hairs." Joey chuckled. "Make yourself at home."

"Thanks, man. It feels great to be here." Madison let out a squeal and blew some raspberries, spitting baby food all over Joey. Shane burst out laughing.

"Madi! Oh, baby doll." Joey looked at the splatter on his shirt. "Guess this just made the laundry pile." Madison giggled before blowing another round of raspberries, and Shane laughed harder. "Daddy's gonna get you for this. You just wait." Joey stuck out his tongue at her, and the baby giggled again.

"Welcome to my world." Stephanie tossed Joey a towel as she laughed. "I'm thinking she's done eating." Stephanie stood, wet a washcloth and wiped the baby's face and hands. "Go change, Joe, and maybe you boys can go sit out back. I need to get her in the bath."

After pulling his wife down for a kiss, Joey got to his feet. "Grab your coffee, Shane. Head out through the slider. I'll be out in a second. I want to hear all about life in Texas."

"You got it." Shane stood and headed through the sliding glass door off the kitchen area while Joey went to change his shirt. There wasn't much to tell, really, but he'd give Joey as much as he could. Shane was more curious about what'd been going on in his best friend's neck of the woods.

He'd missed so much, and considering he'd finally made it home to help his mother with some upgrades on her house, Shane wanted to know all about what the Donnelly family had been up to while he'd been away.

God, everyone had grown up and, being Joey's best friend, Shane had spent the majority of his elementary, middle and high school life at their home. Spending family time with the Donnellys felt more like coming home than when Shane visited his own mother.

CHAPTER THREE

Cyn dropped her keys onto the kitchen table and tossed her jacket over the back of one of the chairs. Dinner with her brothers and their significant others had been wonderful—of course, after she'd given the typical excuses of why Carlos wasn't with her, she'd endured the pity in everyone's eyes because they knew, yet again, he'd let Cyn down. Regardless, she'd settled in with her family and had a nice meal.

Smothering a yawn with the back of her hand, Cyn made her way through the hallway to her bedroom, ready to strip down and let some hot water beat on her neck. She and Maiya had gotten really close over the last year, but Sonja, Jimmy's girlfriend, had been the real center of Cyn's attention. The woman was beautiful but had a layer of formal polish on her that had surprised Cyn. Sonja definitely wasn't the type of woman she ever thought Jimmy would end up with. But as the night wore on, Cyn watched how Jimmy and Sonja interacted—which was to say, they bickered, joked, poked, prodded and teased each other so much so that Cyn was in awe and had to shove aside an unwelcome spike of jealousy that kept poking her in the stomach.

She was happy for her brother—both of them—but hell if she didn't wish she'd found what they had.

With one last glance at her phone, Cyn stepped into the shower and washed the day away. She loved Carlos and missed him all the time. Tilting her head back, the water ran over her hair. He just wasn't there for her. Like, ever.

He had been in the beginning when things were fresh and new. But shortly before celebrating one year together, he'd become distant and then, eventually, emotionally absent.

Heaviness settled in her chest as Cyn wrapped her hair in a towel and pulled on her robe. No matter how hard she tried, she ended up in this same place with all her relationships. Alone and lonely, while her heart remained committed to a guy who never truly committed to her.

With Carlos, she'd begged, cried, yelled, talked, demanded and then yelled some more. And it'd gotten her nowhere except alone. Every so often, he'd cast bait, usually right when she was about to leave his ass, and Cyn would latch on hook, line and sinker. For a year out of their two years together, she'd been playing this cat-and-mouse game with him, and the lack of real connection in the relationship had worn out its welcome for sure.

Cyn shed the robe and pulled on a pair of yoga pants and a tank top. There was a quart of ice cream in the freezer with her name on it and some work she needed to catch up on. Just as she settled on the couch, Ben & Jerry's "Boom Chocolatta" in one hand, client schedule in the other, her cell rang.

Seeing it was Carlos, she set the schedule down and picked up her phone. "Hey there."

"What are you up to, baby?"

"Just on the couch. Wishing you were here."

"How was dinner?"

Cyn frowned. It always felt so deliberate when he ignored her little mentions of missing him or wanting to see him. But again, his work kept him pretty busy, so maybe he wasn't even aware he was doing it. She let out a sigh. "Dinner was nice. I wish you'd been there. I got to meet Sonja, Jimmy's girlfriend. I really think you'd like Jimmy. Celia is home too, but you've met her before. Anyway, how was your work thing? Get that all taken care of?"

"Yeah. Pretty much." The sound of him yawning came through the receiver. "What's her story?"

"Who? Sonja?"

"Yeah."

"She's a single mom. Criminal defense attorney in Manhattan, and from what I can tell, she's very refined."

"Refined?"

"Yeah." Cyn laughed. "I dunno, she's just really formal and precise. Totally not Jimmy's type. It's kinda funny, actually, seeing them together. But he's happy, I guess, so whatever."

"Sounds about right."

Cyn waited before replying, hoping he might mention wanting to see her. Something…anything along the lines of, "Hey, I miss you, why don't you come over?" Or "I'm coming over, I need to see you" would do. When the silence stretched longer than Cyn could bear, she broke it. "So, I miss you."

He cleared his throat. "Miss you too."

"Do you?" She rose from the couch and headed for the kitchen.

"I said so, didn't I?"

Cyn placed the ice cream back in the freezer. "Yeah. It's just…"

"Just what?"

She sighed and pressed her fingers to her forehead. "I feel like it's been forever since I've seen you, is all."

"Just been busy, baby."

"Always busy, Carlos. Seriously, I get it. My business of planning corporate events isn't all photo booths and dunk-the-CEO games, you know? I'm beyond busy, too, but come on."

Frustration and sadness peppered her tone. Hating how whiny she sounded, Cyn cleared her throat and continued. "I mean, I have an appointment first thing tomorrow morning with a client in North Hollywood, but I still make time for us."

"I get it. Look, I'm about ready to collapse into bed, but we'll find some time soon."

Cyn's heart fell, and she swallowed past the lump that'd formed in her throat. Asking for attention felt gross on too many levels. Most times, she managed to bite her tongue and *not* ask to see him. But sometimes, in moments of weakness, she'd take her chances and ask.

And right now was a moment of weakness. The dinner with her brothers and their plus-ones had poked at her loneliness in a big way. Being single was one thing, but being lonely while in a relationship was entirely another. With a deep breath, she placed her bet on his answer. "How about I come over now and crawl in bed with you?"

He sighed. "Where's your appointment in the morning?"

"North Hollywood."

"All right. I guess if you're at my house, you'll be closer to your appointment, so it makes sense for you to stay here."

The lump made a reappearance, and her heart got heavier. He didn't want her to come over because he wanted to see her, or at least if he did, he didn't say it. Instead, he gave a reason of convenience. "That's not really a good reason."

"Sure it is."

"No. Not really, but whatever."

"Cyn, why does there have to be a reason anyway? Just grab your stuff and head over. But fair warning, I may be asleep by the time you get here, so hurry up."

Cyn walked to her bedroom. "Fine. I'm packing a bag now. See you shortly."

"Okay. Text me your ETA when you get in the car."

She rolled her eyes and grabbed her overnight bag from the closet. "Of course."

"See you soon." He disconnected the call, and Cyn tossed her phone on the bed.

The situation sucked, and she loathed always being the one to ask and press for time with him, but at least she'd see him tonight, even if it was spent sleeping. She pulled her toiletries bag from the cabinet in her bathroom. The stupid thing was always ready to go. And she had a steady supply of travel-sized bottles. God forbid Carlos let her keep any of her things there. That'd be far too much like she was moving in or something—as far as he was concerned, anyway. But really, she wasn't. It would just be freaking easier to not have to drag shit back and forth and simply have shampoo, conditioner and body wash there. Maybe a toothbrush, too.

When she was finished topping off what she was missing in the toiletries bag, Cyn grabbed a change of clothes, stuffed them in the duffel and slid on her flip-flops.

She tossed her bag across the front seat of her four-door Jeep Wrangler, started it up and texted Carlos, letting him know her twenty-minute ETA. With a sigh, she backed out of her driveway.

Things weren't perfect, not even close, but she'd take what she could…for now.

CHAPTER FOUR

SHANE KNOCKED ON THE FRONT DOOR OF HIS CHILDHOOD home and waited. Most people had a key to their parent's home, especially if it was the same one they'd grown up in. But not Shane. And definitely not *his* mother. She'd changed the original locks on the house long ago, probably four times over since, but once he'd left home, he'd never been given a key again. Hell, every time there was a new man in her life, the doorknob probably got replaced.

The door swung open, and there she was… Her shoulder-length blonde hair was curled at the ends to perfection, framing her beautiful, nearly wrinkle-free face. The makeup was a bit overdone, but that was always the case with a former Texas high school debutante/pageant queen. She stepped onto the front stoop and pulled Shane into an embrace. "Darling, it's so good to see you!"

He patted her back. "Good to see you too, Mom."

She backed away and ushered him into the house. "Did you just get in?"

His mother kept moving, obviously on her way to the kitchen, and Shane followed. "A few hours ago." He glanced around, noticing the new furniture and decor in the various rooms, and couldn't imagine what on earth needed updating. Everything looked pretty damn updated to him.

"Oh, I see. At Joey Donnelly's, then?" She moved to the kitchen island. "Can I get you something to drink?"

He took a seat at the table. "Water's fine. And yes, I was at Joey's."

"That's nice. How is he? My goodness, must be awkward seeing him after all this time. I'd heard he'd gotten married." She brought him a glass of water, complete with fresh ice from the freezer, and set it on the table.

Shane shifted in the chair and chose to ignore her presumptuous statement as his mother took the seat to his right. "Joey got married a couple of years ago. He and his wife, Stephanie, just had a baby."

"So many children in the Donnelly family. Always amazed me. I never understood why anyone would want that many kids. There must be endless amounts of grandchildren now. That Roseanne was definitely made for having kids. I tell you, you'll never hear me complain about not being a grandmother yet. I just can't picture it. Of course, Derrick has grandchildren, and they come over once in a while." She leaned close to him. "I usually schedule my hair appointment and spa treatments on those days." With a chuckle, she patted the side of her hair. "Of course, Derrick hasn't quite figured out the connection, so don't tell him." She smiled, and Shane didn't miss the devious glint that had sparked in her eyes as she raised her cup of tea to her lips.

He just looked at her. This was his mother, the woman who never really wanted to be a mother, to begin with, and was never afraid to make that fact known. And now, she had no issue expressing her disdain for grandchildren. Plus, she'd pretty much insulted Mrs. Donnelly, which poked so many of Shane's nerves it wasn't even funny.

Because she'd never really wanted kids—something his mother never hid from him—Shane's relationship with his mother had never been great. After his father passed, when Shane was fifteen, it'd gotten worse.

It was exactly the reason why he spent as much time as he could with the Donnellys. Mrs. D was a saint as far as he was concerned. Their home, though a bit chaotic because of all the kids, was a far better place to be. During his childhood, he'd had more peace there than anywhere.

Shane took a long gulp of his water, drowning the words he wanted to say. His mother would make a horrid grandmother. He couldn't even imagine her playing with kids. God knows she'd never played with him. Giving himself another second to get his anger under control, he swallowed another mouthful of water, managing to not choke on his agitation and set the glass down. "I'll be sure to make a note."

"Oh, a note! Yes, thank you, darling. That reminds me." His mother rose and moved to her purse. When she came back to the table, she held a small sheet of paper in her hands. She set it down and slid it over to him. "Here are the things I need you to work on while you're here."

Shane read it over. It was a very detailed list of everything she wanted done—complete with little drawn boxes he could check off when he'd finished each item. Controlling *and* anal, the perfect combo… Not. He looked at her. "Great!"

She cleared her throat and pointed to the list. "As you can see here, there's quite a few things. Do you think you're capable, or will you need to hire some professional help?"

Shane bristled, and once again—though he had no idea how—he shoved it down. "No, Mom. I think I can handle everything on here."

"Wonderful!" She clapped her hands together. "Derrick should be home any minute. You'll stay to meet him, won't you?"

Shane wanted to meet this new guy as much as he wanted a hole in his skull. In an effort to keep the peace, he forced a smile. "Of course. I'm always happy to meet the flavor of the month." *Shit...* The comment rolled out before he had a chance to stop it. He mentally braced himself. She'd either ignore it or lose her blonde mind. No telling which.

His mother's smile didn't falter. Guess she was going to ignore the jab. Lucky him. Her practiced grin actually stayed in place longer than even he was used to. Frozen, as if her face was carved from marble. But she blinked a few times, rather rapidly, and the vein in her forehead might've bulged just a little. He had to give her credit. She had that fake expression down pat. Years of teen beauty queen practice paid off. In full.

As the silence stretched, Shane's guilt kicked in. Maybe he'd actually hurt her feelings. He cleared his throat. "Sorry."

"Whatever for, darling?" She looked away and sipped her tea, eyes still blinking away.

Things never got any easier between them. Of course, Shane didn't help the situation much when he said shit like he'd just laid down. Plus, being such different people only made their relationship harder. Shane was more like his father, and it always felt as if his mother resented him for it, more so after his father died.

No matter what Shane accomplished, he never felt like his mother was proud of him. Not when he excelled at school or sports or even in the damn Marine Corps. If he'd died in Iraq or Afghanistan, and the military had delivered the Medal of Honor to her, Shane was sure it wouldn't have been enough. He glanced at her as he took another drink of water. Being born had been his only crime. Shane let out a sigh and shifted in his seat. There wasn't much he could do about his life sentence.

"Charlene, where are you, gorgeous?"

"In the kitchen!" His mother jumped from her seat and

had a compact mirror pulled from her purse checking her lipstick faster than Shane could track.

Shane frowned, watching her primp. "You look fine, Mom."

Derrick had arrived. Oh joy.

CHAPTER FIVE

Cyn curled her feet beneath her on the couch and turned on the television. It was Saturday night, and she hadn't heard from Carlos all day. She could've gone dancing with Angie, but opted for ice cream and a juicy, cry-her-eyes-out chick-flick instead. Cyn had texted Carlos a few times, receiving no response. She'd also called once and gotten his voicemail, but hadn't left a message—why bother? There wasn't anything to say. Apparently, he'd gotten busy, probably with work or some other bullshit excuse he'd make.

Regardless, everything was more important than her, so right now, she was all about the fuck it and fuck him attitude.

Flipping through the pay-per-view listings, her phone rang. Glancing at the screen, she saw it was Carlos and in one motion, swiped the screen and pressed the device to her ear. "Hey."

What she got back was the furthest thing from a reply, but instead, a lot of muffled sounds in her ear.

"Carlos, you there? Can you hear me?" No response, just rustling…until she heard a woman's voice in the distance.

Next was a woman giggling. *What the fuck?* And then Carlos's muffled voice, "Come here, baby. No really. You got something there. Let me get it for you, sweet thing." More giggling, followed by a very distinct "Mmm" sound.

"Oh, hell no!" Cyn stood, and the remote slipped from her lap, landing on the floor with a thud. "Carlos!" No response—except for more rustling sounds, plus another moan.

This was not happening. Could *not* be happening. Except it was.

"Carlos, you mother-fucking-cocksucker!" Rage flowed through Cyn like hot lava as she stormed to the kitchen. "I can hear you, you asshole!" How could he do this to her? Better question was, how *long* had he been doing this to her? No wonder they hadn't been spending time together. No wonder they hadn't been having sex either! He was so very obviously banging someone else.

The phone disconnected. Cyn pulled it from her ear and stared at the screen. Her whole body felt hot, yet her blood ran ice cold through her veins. Carlos had blown her off and ignored all her texts because clearly something *had* come up—that something being his dick. Cyn may've been blind—or choosing to be blind—to what he'd so obviously been doing, but that didn't make her stupid. She was, however, a very pissed-off woman who was about to show him exactly what happened when her temper was invoked. She'd been holding tight to one final straw, and the asshole just broke it.

Cyn put on her sneakers and headed out the door to Carlos's house. When she arrived, she parked—purposely blocking in his bullshit poor man's Mercedes in the driveway. She stalked up the cement walkway toward his door, her anger making every inch of her skin itch. She raised a shaky hand to the door, clenched it into a fist and pounded.

No answer.

Of course, there was no answer. The bastard was probably already fucking the chick Cyn heard on the phone. Cyn pounded again and didn't stop pounding until the door finally swung open.

"What the fu—"

"Exactly! You sonofabitch!" Cyn pushed past him into his living room.

"Hang on, baby." He grabbed her by the arm, halting her.

Cyn jerked out of his hold. "Hang on to nothing. Where is she, Carlos?"

"Who?"

"Ugh, you are *such* an asshole!"

"Um…"

Cyn whirled around to find a petite redhead standing at the edge of the hallway. "Her!" She pointed at the woman before glaring back at Carlos. "Who the fuck is she, and what the fuck—" Cyn looked back to the redhead and propped her hands on her hips. "What the *fuck* are you doing in my boyfriend's house?"

The woman's eyes went wide, and her mouth dropped open.

"Baby, it's not what you think."

Cyn glared over her shoulder at him. Was he seriously going to deny what she was seeing with her own eyes? Her temper went into overdrive, and fury raced through her like a raging river. There was no fucking way she was going to stand there and listen to this bullshit. "Not what I think? Really? Have you lost your fucking mind?"

CYN SAT on Ryan and Maiya's back porch, rocks glass full of Jameson in hand, bawling her eyes out. But she'd done it. She'd finally ended it with Carlos. And it'd gone down with a bang.

Maiya lit a cigarette and blew out a stream of smoke. "Honey, he's a douchebag, and I know it's cliché to say, but you're better off without him."

Cyn took a swig of booze and then sniffled. The alcohol burned on its way down her throat, warming her insides but doing nothing for the chill that had settled in her bones. "I know." She shrugged and stared into the golden liquid. "I mean, yeah, it's cliché, but it's true. Bastard doesn't deserve me. God, I can't believe he brought her home to his place. *And* tried to deny anything was going on!"

"I honestly don't know how you didn't go all Lorena Bobbitt on him." Maiya drew on her smoke. "Hell, I would've."

Cyn blurted a laugh through her tears. "Damn, now that's funny. Definitely the Italian in you." She shook her head. "No, I didn't cut off any appendages, but I did lose my shit like some kind of crazy person. Especially after he was all, 'Oh baby, it's not what you think. Don't go assuming.' Because, yeah, hearing his sleazy ass over the phone while he fondled whatever body part of hers he could get his grubby hands on, plus catching him with her in his house, would definitely be a big fucking false assumption on my part that he was screwing her."

"Ugh, gross." Maiya frowned. "I'm so sorry, sweetie."

"Thanks. I'm not. It was bound to happen sooner or later." The tears were back, which was stupid because she shouldn't be crying. Instead, she should be relieved. Cyn wiped her cheeks, but within seconds, they were wet again. She finally knew, finally had some definitive closure, and now she could move on. Except, move on to what? Another asshole?

For whatever reason, Cyn had a habit of picking the same guy over and over again. They might've had a different name and face, but they were all the same. Emotionally unavailable, almost always dishonest and totally disrespectful.

Cyn didn't get it. What was it about these guys that they kept finding her? Or, maybe the better question was, why was *she* finding and also falling for them? She leaned back in the lounger and sighed, swirling the liquid in her glass.

Maybe she did get it. After all, *she was* the common denominator.

Her parents had such a good marriage, not perfect by any stretch, but all things considered, they were happy. It wasn't as if Cyn didn't have examples all around her for how a relationship should be or what it could be. She did. Fuck's sake, all three of her older siblings were happily married too. Even Jimmy, the one who refused to open up to anyone after his ordeal with his ex-bitch-girlfriend, Gina, had found happiness again. So, why couldn't Cyn?

"Earth to Cyn. Talk to me, honey."

Cyn glanced over at her brother's fiancé. "I'm sorry, Maiya."

"And just what the hell are you apologizing for?" Maiya stubbed out her smoke in the ashtray. "You haven't done anything wrong."

"I have shit-poor timing. That's what I've done. The last thing you need a week before your wedding is to be dealing with my drama." Cyn stood.

"Uh-uh, no. You don't get to do that. We're friends, Cyn. And I love you to fucking bits, so sit your ass back down and talk about it as much as you need to. Besides, that's what family does, right? They're there for each other no matter what. At any time. And at any hour." Maiya pointed a finger at her. "I have your family to thank for teaching me that. So, don't go feeling bad because you're having drama. Your drama is welcome anytime, honey."

"Shit." Cyn buried her face in her hands as she burst into tears again. In the next moment, Maiya had her arms wrapped around her, and Cyn sank into her embrace. "I don't get it. I just don't get it."

Maiya smoothed her hand down the back of Cyn's head. "Don't get what, honey?"

Cyn pulled away and sniffled. "Damn, I need another tissue."

"Hold the snot, I'll grab you one." Maiya ran inside and brought a tissue back out for Cyn. "Here, sweetie. Blow. Then tell me what you don't get."

Cyn sopped up her face and nose and tried again. "I don't get why I keep picking these guys. I mean, I get it." She sat on the edge of the lounge, and Maiya sat beside her. "I get that it's me that's picking them, but what I don't understand is why."

"Well…" Maiya shrugged. "You got a broken picker."

"A what?" Cyn wiped her nose.

Maiya smiled and rubbed Cyn's back. "A broken picker." She held up one finger, bending and straightening it. "Your picker's broken. And that's why you keep picking creeps to date. I should know, mine was broken for *years*."

"All right, but…" Cyn stared at her fingers. "Why? I mean, it's not like my family is all fucked up or that I come from a broken home— No offense." She nudged Maiya's shoulder.

"None taken. But who knows why, Cyn. I guess that's something you need to figure out. Maybe once you do, you can un-break it."

"You think I should stay single for a little while?"

"Might be a good idea. Give yourself a break from men for a bit. It sure can't hurt."

Cyn blew out a breath and then took another sip of her drink. She looked up at the stars decorating the sky. "A relationship moratorium?"

"Okay. Yeah, that's definitely a term you could use. It's also a song by Alanis Morissette, but whatever." Cyn snorted a laugh, and Maiya giggled, too. "Take a few months and spend some time working on you. Maybe pour your focus on your business."

"A year."

"Whoa! A year? You're going to stay single for a whole year?"

Cyn swallowed the rest of her drink. "Yeah. You think I can't do it?"

"Shit. A year? No sex? You're a braver woman than me." Maiya lit another cigarette.

"Yeah. A year. No sex." Cyn nodded. "I'm doing it…or not doing *it*, to be specific."

Maiya smiled. "All righty then. From this day forward, I now dub thee celibate!"

"Ooh, that's a scary word." Cyn scrunched up her nose. "Like I'm a nun or something—hey! There's an idea."

Maiya laughed. "No. That's a very bad idea. Besides, you'd have to cover your adorably cute hair under a habit. And start praying the rosary and shit."

"Nuns don't wear habits anymore." Cyn laughed.

"Whatever. Either way, you're not nun material. Plus, the clothes aren't flattering." Maiya smiled.

"True. But I'm serious about the moratorium. I'm doing this. I'm staying single for a year." She nodded. "I think I need another drink. I think I'm going to need a lot of drinks. Maybe if I stay drunk for the next three hundred and sixty-five days, the time'll just fly by."

Maiya laughed again and took Cyn's glass from her hand. "One more Jameson coming up. Just remember to pace yourself. Oh, and I'll get the guest room ready for you. No way you'll be driving home tonight, Ms. Celibate."

Cyn watched Maiya disappear into the house as she stretched out on the lounge again. She had no idea what she was doing, but she was willing to try. She'd had enough shitty relationships to last her a lifetime. Taking a year off to figure out what her issues were and to fix them was a scary but necessary thing to do. It would be a process and definitely not something for the faint of heart. But Cyn could do it. As a Donnelly, stubbornness was in her DNA. And she was definitely stubborn enough to follow through.

CHAPTER SIX

Apparently, Shane had arrived in town just in time for Ryan's wedding. In true Donnelly fashion, they'd insisted he attend. Which also included the bachelor party. He sure as hell wasn't going to say no. Which was why he was now at the wedding rehearsal, sitting in the middle of a pew in the back of the church they'd all attended when they were kids, while the entire wedding party scurried around up front as the priest and the wedding planner directed them to their proper places to stand. What a circus—but definitely a fun one.

As entertained as Shane was at the familiar chaos, his focus kept gravitating toward one person in particular: Cynthia Donnelly. Blowing out a breath, he stretched his arms out on the back of the pew. The last time he'd seen Cyn, she was still in high school. Christ—he cringed and glanced at the crucifix. *Whoops.* He blessed himself and focused on Cyn again.

She had been two years behind Joey and him in school, and Shane remembered always finding her cute. But in a "she was his best friend's little sister and off-limits" kind of way. She'd sure grown up since then.

She was still cute and probably still off-limits—except now

it was in a "sexy, petite and curvy in all the right places" kind of way. His exact kind of way, to be specific. Damn, was he really sitting in church lusting after his best friend's little sister? Shane shifted in the pew and adjusted the rapidly rising hard-on in his jeans. Yep, he sure as hell was. Cynthia Donnelly had grown up, and Shane liked what he saw. A lot.

A tall, slender blonde took a seat at the end of the pew in front of him. Jimmy came running over to her, bent and kissed her cheek and then said something in her ear too low for Shane to hear. The woman placed her hand on his cheek as she laughed. Jimmy glanced up and caught Shane's eyes. "Oh wow. Shane?"

Shane got to his feet and moved to them. "Live and in person." He extended his hand. "How ya been, Jimmy?"

The blonde turned around and faced him as Jimmy shook his hand and pulled him into a brief embrace. "Damn good, man. Wow, it's good to see you. I found out last night you were in town. It's been what? Sixteen, seventeen years?"

Shane stepped back and smiled. "Pretty much. Since I lived here anyway. I've popped in for a few visits here and there, but yeah, seventeen years. I hear you've been making a name for yourself with your art."

"Giving it hell." Jimmy smiled, shaking his head. "God, it's fucking great to see you, bro."

"James, watch your mouth. We're in a church," the blonde whispered as she smoothed her hand up the back of her pulled-up hair.

"Yep, and you're Jewish. I'm sure Jesus will forgive both of us." Jimmy laughed, and the blonde scowled at him, then rolled her eyes.

Shane covered his mouth, stifling his own laughter. "You haven't changed one bit, Jimmy."

"Nah. No fun in that. Anyway, Shane, this is my beautiful woman, Sonja. Sonja, meet my brother Joey's best and oldest friend."

Sonja stood and extended her hand to him. "Now that we know everyone's religion, and I'm thoroughly mortified, it's a pleasure to meet you."

Shane shook her hand. "Ma'am." He nodded. "Pleasure. Please don't be embarrassed. I've known this guy his whole life."

"Damn straight. Awesome you're gonna make the wedding. You're coming to the bachelor party tonight, right?" Jimmy wrapped his arm around Sonja's waist.

"Wouldn't miss it. I'm staying with Joey and Stephanie, so where he goes, I go."

Jimmy cocked his head to the side. "Not staying with your mom?"

"Hell no." Shane chuckled. "I'm doing some work on the house for her, but I'm not staying there. We get along much better when we don't share space. You know that."

"Some things never change, huh? Sorry to hear." Jimmy nodded.

"Jimmy, get your butt over here! You're holding up the rehearsal."

Jimmy looked over his shoulder, and Shane followed his gaze. Cyn was standing in the middle of the center aisle, hands on her hips, annoyed expression on her face. Shane laughed. "Some things never change is right."

"Yup, she's still bossing us around." Jimmy kissed Sonja on the cheek. "Better get back before she comes over and grabs me by the ear. We'll catch up later."

Sonja resumed her spot in the pew. "You're welcome to join me."

Shane took her up on the offer and slid next to her. "Thanks."

"Personally, I think I'd enjoy seeing Cyn grab him by the ear. But maybe that's just James's sick sense of humor rubbing off on me." She grinned.

Shane chuckled. "I've seen it. Trust me, it's pretty funny. So, how long have you and Jimmy been together?"

"It's been a little over eight months now. I think." She tilted her head to the side, a thoughtful expression on her face. "We can't agree on an official date, but technically, we met almost a year ago."

Shane fixed his gaze on Cyn, watching every sway of her hips as she bounced back and forth between the bridesmaids and the groomsmen. "Sounds like there's a story there."

"Oh, I'm sure James will fill you in tonight. He *loves* to tell people all about how we met and what a pain in the ass I was. He says it's our love story."

Cyn bent over to gather the bouquets of flowers for the bridesmaids, her full ass on perfect display. Shane blew out a breath and lost all train of thought. Damn, what he could do with that ass. He ran his hand along the back of his neck and blew out another breath.

"Looks like you've got a story you're wanting to write." Sonja laughed.

Shane dragged his gaze away from Cyn and all her delicious curves and focused on Sonja. "I'm sorry, what was that?"

She raised a single brow and nodded her head in Cyn's direction. "The expression on your face is priceless right now."

Shane's face got hot. She'd caught him gawking, and obviously, there was no point in denying it. "I've known her since she was a little girl in pigtails."

"Yes, but now she's a woman."

"Yeah." He ran his hand along the top of his head. "She sure is."

Sonja crossed her arms and let out another chuckle. Shane snorted and bent forward, resting his elbows on the back of the pew in front of him. Cynthia was *all* woman. Wrapped in a pair of tight blue jeans and a white tank top that hugged her very ample chest and tiny waist. Yeah. *Alllll* woman.

Regardless, Cyn was still Joey's little sister, and Shane would do his very best to keep his hands to himself. But that didn't mean he couldn't look. He was a disciplined Marine. A damn good soldier. But he was also a hot-blooded male, and *not* looking just wasn't going to be possible.

CYN RAN around the front of the church, helping the wedding planner get everyone in order. And was completely distracted by the fact that Shane Conlon—God help her and be still her racing heart, Shane-fucking-Conlon—was sitting in the back of the church. Staring at her like she had a target on the front of her shirt. It was the sole reason she'd gone into director mode and was pretty much trampling over the wedding coordinator and bossing everyone around. Jeez, she must look like some kind of control freak from hell.

Why in God's name was he in town? Near as Cyn could figure, it'd been about seventeen years since she'd last seen him. And about fourteen years since she'd thought about him. Prior to that? Well, Cyn had thought about Shane Conlon daily. He was her grade-, middle- and high-school crush. As a teenager, she'd followed him around like a pathetic little puppy whenever he was at their house, which was pretty much every day. Joey hated her tagging along and, most times, ran her off, so instead, she'd just hang back in the shadows and spy on them.

Shane had been a to-die-for, hot-as-hell teen boy. His brown hair a little too long. His blue eyes a little too bright. And his devil-may-care attitude far too appealing. But the dimple in his chin, God, if that dimple didn't just beg to be kissed. She'd always wanted to press her lips against it.

"Cyn? What next?" Jimmy asked.

Gah…focus, Cyn! "Um… I think we need to run through

who's doing the readings, right?" She glanced at the wedding coordinator, hoping for an answer.

"Yes, I have Angie down for the first reading," the woman said.

"Present and accounted for." Angie stepped up to the lectern, her black knee-high boots accentuating her already long legs.

Free to return to her memory stroll through the neighborhood of Shane, Cyn took a breath and glanced over at him. Yep, he was still staring. At the beginning of her junior year of high school, Shane had shipped off to boot camp. And that was that, except she pined over him for the entire year after. She'd even written him a few letters the first few months after he was gone, but he'd never replied to any of them. By the time she hit senior year, she'd moved on, forgetting all about Shane—as much as anyone could forget their childhood crush anyway.

And now here he was, all tall, buff and tanned. More gorgeous than a man had any right to be…with his now-close-cropped brown hair and bright blue eyes. Eyes that wouldn't stop staring at her. And his dimple, she swore the freaking thing was calling her name.

Cyn's entire body felt like it was boiling in a pot of hot water. Her stomach had tied itself into a knot, and she was sweating. Nice. How sexy was that? Good thing she'd worn a tank top that day; sweat stains on a T-shirt were in no way attractive. That's assuming he even found her attractive. Maybe he was staring because he wasn't sure who she was? People changed a lot in seventeen years. He hadn't, not really, but she had. In more ways than one.

Mary stepped beside her, nudging Cyn's hip. "What's up? Are you feeling okay? You look a little pale."

"What? Oh," Cyn wiped her brow. "Yeah. I think. Well…" Her tongue felt like it was coated with rubber cement.

She crossed her arms and glanced over her shoulder at Shane again.

Mary followed her gaze. "Ohhhhh. I see." Her sister laughed.

"Don't go there, Mary. I'm in no mood."

"I'm not going anywhere, but by the looks of it, you sure seem to be."

"So what? It's not a big deal. I mean, really, look at him. All fine as hell. Even you can't deny that."

"Oh, believe me, I love my husband, but I'm not blind or dead. That man is one hundred percent grade-A prime beefcake."

"Way to objectify." Cyn snorted. "Sadly, you're right."

"And you're single. Wonder if he is, too." Mary wagged her brows.

Her sister Celia came up beside them. "What're we talking about?"

"Boy stuff." Cyn brushed her bangs away from her eyes and winked at Celia. "Doesn't matter, Mary. I'm staying single. Besides, I'm currently nursing a broken heart."

"Very true, honey. You doing okay?" Mary touched Cyn's arm.

"Take it from me, girls suck just as much. Sorry, Cyn." Celia kissed her cheek and walked away.

The subject change was welcome, though the topic wasn't one Cyn wanted to get into. "I'll be fine."

It was true. She would be fine. The initial sting of finding Carlos with another woman had settled into a dull ache, and she was actually starting to feel relief. Odd thing was she figured she'd be more broken up than she was, and it made her realize she should've ended things long before she had.

It was amazing the things a person found themselves tolerating simply because they'd gotten used to them, built a resistance. Sadly, Cyn had grown accustomed to not being treated well—in truth, she'd taught every single guy in the last five years how to treat her. It'd become the norm, being treated badly, and she was disgusted with herself for allowing that kind of trash in her life.

She glanced at Mary to find her staring at her, concern evident in her eyes. "Truly, Mary, I'm fine. I'll be fine." Cyn forced a smile and stepped away from her. She didn't need to be mothered by her older sister; that's what Mom was for. Not that she was looking for mothering, either. Cyn had made a decision the other night while talking with Maiya, and Shane Conlon be damned, she intended to stick to her guns.

Moratorium was the name of the game. And she wasn't going to deviate from the plan.

Cyn stole another peek at Shane and immediately regretted it. He was mid-stretch, his large arms over the top of his head, biceps bulging as he flexed, arching his back. His gaze was locked on her the whole time, and as he dropped his arms back to his sides, the corner of his mouth tilted into a delectable grin. A bolt of lust shot through Cyn, and her skin burst into a tingling blaze. She groaned and wiped the bead of sweat trickling down the side of her neck.

Damn. Timing was a bitch with a capital B.

CHAPTER SEVEN

Later that night, Shane stood at the bar, bottle of Bud in hand, as Ryan got the full-on stripper treatment on stage. Poor guy was tied to a chair in the center as four strippers danced around him, rubbing their various body parts over his face, chest and lap. Shane chuckled and tilted the bottle to his lips. Ryan looked like he was ready to die of embarrassment or bolt for the nearest exit. Maybe both.

The rest of the guys—Donnelly brothers, brothers-in-law and friends—circled the stage, hooting and hollering and throwing dollar bills onto the stage. In addition, Celia, eighth in the Donnelly birth order, was with them. Shane remembered when she'd been born, for fuck's sake.

Apparently, she was gay—something Shane hadn't been aware of until she'd gotten into the limo with them. At the moment, Celia was over in the corner of the bar, receiving a very personal lap dance from a bleached-blonde stripper with enormous breasts. The stripper was *Playboy* hot, so he sure couldn't blame Celia for handing over cash for the boob-treatment. To each their own, he guessed, but he couldn't see wasting his money.

Shane just wasn't a strip club kind of guy. He had no problem hanging with everyone there, but he'd keep his dollar bills in his pocket. In less than an hour, they'd be meeting up with the girls at another dance club. Cyn would be there, and Shane was biding his time until then.

Damn, if he couldn't peel his eyes away from her that evening in the church. He'd even caught her staring back at him a few times, but she'd never come over to say hi. He wasn't sure why, but he planned on asking her as soon as he got the chance. Maybe he'd get lucky, and they'd play a few country songs, and he'd be able to persuade her to dance with him.

Ryan was finally freed from the confines of glittery stripper boobs and G-strings and let off the stage. Man, the guy looked relieved, and Shane felt relieved for him. Shane jerked his chin in Ryan's direction, signaling him to come over. He wanted to buy him a shot or three. Joey walked with Ryan, arm slung over his little brother's shoulder. When they arrived, Shane signaled the bartender. "Ryan, you need a shot."

"Jameson. Make it a double, please." Ryan scrubbed his hands over his face. "Goddamn, I'm covered in glitter. Maiya's going to have a field day with this."

"She the jealous type?" Shane ordered a round of shots and another beer for himself.

"Hell no. I mean, not like that. She'll just tease the hell out of me the rest of the night. She knows full well she owns my ass and has nothing to worry about."

Jimmy stepped up to them. "Right? Maiya's more like the kind of chick that'll say, 'Go ahead and let them chickadees get you all worked up, and I'll take you home and reap the benefits of it.' Am I right, Ry?"

"Pretty much." Ryan chuckled.

Joey grabbed one of the shots the bartender delivered. "Stephanie doesn't really care either. She pretty much goes with the 'don't ask, don't tell' method. But you know the girls went to a male strip show tonight. And you also know that, unlike us, they get to touch and grope and do pretty much whatever the hell they want to those poor guys."

Celia stepped up to them with a huge smile on her face. "I get to grope all I want, too."

"Yeah, well. The benefits of being a gay chick in a titty bar. If Andy were here, she'd be boob-deep, too." Jimmy laughed and looked to Joey. "Poor guys? My ass. Those fuckers are probably making bank shaking their asses in those banana hammocks."

"Okay, brain bleach, anyone?" Shane laughed and raised his glass.

"I think I just threw up a little in my mouth." Celia raised her glass, too.

"Try and contain it, Celia." Joey smiled and faced Shane. "Shane, so fucking psyched you're here. Truth, man."

Ryan raised his shot. "Definitely. So, who's calling the toast?"

"I got this." Jimmy grinned, holding his glass high. "Health to the men, and may the women live forever!"

"Sláinte," Shane said with a nod. They all tapped the bottom of their shot glasses on the bar top and then tossed them back. Shane placed his glass upside down on the bar and then clapped his hands together. "So, about the ladies. What time are we meeting up with them again?"

Joey grinned. "Shane, you got a look in your eye I've seen a few too many times. Who's got your attention?"

"What? Nahh. No one. All good. Just curious." He leaned against the bar, doing his best to douse whatever Joey saw in his eyes. Shit. Damn. Fuck.

Celia rested her arm on Jimmy's shoulder. "This should be interesting."

"Sonja and me had a sweet little chat after dinner." Jimmy rubbed his hands together, grin firmly in place.

"Did you, now? What about? Or should I say, who?" Joey

nodded with his eyebrows raised, and his lips quirked in a similar grin.

Shane shifted and tilted his bottle to his lips. Fuck him, Sonja had caught him staring at Cyn, and she'd spilled it all to Jimmy. He should've figured. "Come on now."

"Seems our boy here might have his eye snagged on Cyn."

"Not cool, Jimmy." Shane ran his hand over his hair. "Cyn's like a sister to me." *Fuuuuckkk!*

"Back up. Let's not get crazy." Joey set his beer on the bar. "She's my sister, not yours. But yeah, when we were kids, we were all like siblings to you, so I get it, but we're not kids anymore." Joey gripped Shane's shoulder. "Cyn's a grown woman. And you're a grown man. And it's a free damn country. You've done your part to ensure that, I'll add. What happens between you two is none of my business."

Shane blew out a breath. "Joey, it's not like that. Really."

"Doesn't matter if it is or isn't. I'm taking the Stephanie approach: Don't ask, don't tell." Joey leaned close. "Just… Cyn's nursing a broken heart right now, so don't fuck with her head. Cool?"

Damn, Shane needed to get this convo reined in quick. Yeah, Cyn did it for him—in a big way, but that's where it ended. He wouldn't disrespect the Donnelly family, especially Joey, by going there with her. It was a code he honored and cherished. No way on earth he'd fuck that up. "Joey, you're my brother, blood or not, and I respect you more than I could ever put into words. I got no intention of fucking with anyone's head. Get me?"

"I got you, man. But seriously, if your eye's on Cyn? I trust you. You're my best friend, and I love you, man."

A lump rose in Shane's throat, and he swallowed it down into the pool of guilt taking up space in his stomach. Considering how hard his dick had been while in church, Joey was lending Shane more credit than he should. It didn't matter that he was all but giving him his blessing to go for Cyn, either. Shane wasn't going there.

"Ladies, please. Hug now, and let's move to the other bar." Jimmy propped his hands on his hips. "The smell of champagne in this place is getting to me. And I'm ready to see my sunshine."

"I was going to ask if anyone needed a tissue. Christ's sake, that was deep." Celia rolled her eyes, laughing, and nudged Shane with her hip.

The banter from the younger brothers, as well as Celia, was enough to break the emotional moment, and they all laughed, but Joey still held Shane's eyes a moment longer before nodding at him. Fucking hell, Joey was being serious, encouraging even.

Didn't matter.

Shane was *not* going there.

No matter that they were adults, and Cyn was ringing all his bells. No matter that he hadn't stopped thinking about her since he laid eyes on her that morning.

No matter. Not gonna happen.

CYN HAD JUST GOTTEN done stuffing another dollar bill in the all-too-good-looking and built-like-a-freight-train stripper's tight boxer briefs when Maiya brought her another shot of Patrón. How many had she had now? Three? Four? Who the hell knew—better yet, who the hell cared? She was having a fantastic time, thoroughly enjoying the rippling mass of muscles in her face. She grinned up at the dancer, and he shot her a wink. The dancer prior to him had picked her up, raising her so high her freaking crotch was level with his face as he urged her legs over his shoulders—like she weighed no more than a feather. She definitely weighed more than a freaking feather, but he hadn't seemed to notice.

Was Shane that strong? Cyn licked her lips. A dangerous line of thinking, but in Cyn's half-drunken state, her imagination went into overdrive, and all she could think about was Shane doing the same to her, except she'd be naked. A groan slipped out, and Cyn fanned herself.

"Yep, that's exactly what I'm saying. These guys are fucking *hot!*" Angie tossed back her shot and wiped her mouth with the back of her hand, and then perched a dollar bill between her cleavage and come-hithered one of the dancers with a crook of her finger.

Cyn laughed. "They sure are." If Angie only knew what she was really thinking... She glanced over at Sonja. "You doing okay, Sonja? You want another drink?"

Sonja smiled and held up her empty shot glass. "If I do another shot of Jäger, James will tan my backside for sure." She giggled. "Did I just say that out loud? I did, didn't I?" Her eyes went wide, and she covered her mouth.

"You sure as hell did. I gotta say, I never want to hear about the depraved sides of my brother, but wow, that was kinda hot—as long as I put the fact that it's my brother you're talking about out of my mind!" Cyn busted up laughing.

"I'm so sorry. Really. Oh my lord." Sonja brushed her hair over her shoulder.

"Oh hell, chica. Don't be." Maiya smiled. "Jimmy has a wild side, but so does Ryan. Sorry, Cyn, you're gonna need to cover your ears." She laughed.

Cyn cocked her head to the side and pursed her lips. "I wonder what kind of side Shane has."

"I knew it! Girl, I knew you were checking him out today," Jodi, Maiya's best friend, said. "Tell me all about that hunk of gorgeous man."

"Not much to tell, really." Cyn looked over at Angie, who was sandwiched between two strippers.

"Like hell, there's not much to tell." Mary sipped her drink.

"Shut it, Mary."

"Nope. Deal with it, brat." Mary stuck out her tongue at Cyn, then turned to Jodi. "Shane is Joey's best friend. They've known each other since grade school. Really, he's family to us. But, Cyn here, she's had a crush on Shane from kindergarten to damn near senior year of high school."

Jodi set down her drink. "Ooh! Sounds juicy. Tell me more. Did you ever hook up with him, Cyn?"

Ugh, damn her sister for digging up old bones for the second time today. Cyn was doing everything she could think of to put him out of her mind—rather unsuccessfully—but she was still trying. "No. He barely knew I existed back then. And I'm sure nothing's changed."

"I beg to differ." Sonja hiccupped and then laughed. "He couldn't keep his eyes off you at the church today. I swear he had to be burning a hole in your back; he was staring so intently. That man may not have known you existed when you were kids, but he sure knows you exist now."

Cyn wanted to crawl under the table and die. Just die right there. This was crazy, and Sonja was wrong. There was no way in hell Shane Conlon was interested in her. Just no way. Yeah, he'd been staring, and she'd felt his gaze on her like a physical touch the whole time they were in church, but that didn't mean it meant anything. Did it? *Oh shit! Shit, shit, shit!* "He couldn't—" She groaned. "There's just no way."

Maiya laughed. "Well. I guess there goes your nice little vow."

"What vow?" Jodie asked.

Maiya cringed. "Damn. Sorry, Cyn. The booze is talking."

"It's okay. But I think I'm going to need another shot." Cyn wiped her sweaty hands down her thighs. This wasn't exactly something she wanted to share with everyone, but per usual, nothing in her family stayed a secret for long.

Damn, she was so screwed—which was exactly what she was trying to avoid being. Cyn blew out a resigned breath.

Celibacy sucked, even more so when it came to missing out on the chance of going to bed with the guy she'd fantasized about for her entire teenage life.

CHAPTER EIGHT

SHANE STEPPED INSIDE THE DIM BUT HUGE COUNTRY DANCE club. He glanced around the vast space—Christ, it was the size of a small football field—and followed the rest of the crew in search of their ladies. *Theirs*, not his. Shane didn't have a lady. He was single and had been for years with every intention of staying that way—but he'd be a fool to deny that he was definitely searching out Cyn. In spite of the convo with the boys at the strip club, he'd been desperate to get another glimpse of her all night, hopefully a little closer this time.

Cyn was nowhere to be found when everyone had joined up. Concern that she might've headed home instead of joining up settled like a brick in his stomach, but he wasn't about to ask where she was. She'd looked so fucking hot earlier in the church he practically considered going to confession for all the dirty thoughts he'd entertained as she flitted around in her tight jeans and tank top—both accentuating her fine ass and equally fine breasts to perfection. She had to be there somewhere.

The rest of the group headed off to the mechanical bull set up on the other end of the bar. Shane turned in the other direction and rounded a set of tables, scanning the dance floor in hopes of finding Cyn, when he ran smack into her.

"*Oooph!*" She gripped the front of his button-down shirt.

He grabbed her arms, steadying her. "Shit. Sorry, girl. You okay?"

She gazed up at him, her body against his, her grip still tight on the fabric of his shirt…and then she licked her lips. *Holy fucking shit.* Lust hit Shane in his gut like a sledgehammer, and his dick went rod-hard in his jeans. She did it again, and as he watched the tip of her pink tongue run along her bottom lip, it was all he could do to not bend down and follow its path with his own tongue. And just that fast, all his protestations from earlier evaporated. He was so screwed.

She smiled, a hazy, dreamy expression in her eyes. "It's *really* good to see you, Shane."

She'd definitely been drinking. Shane ran his hands down her arms and onto her tiny waist. "I gotta say, it's real good to see you too, Cyn."

Cyn smoothed her warm palms down his chest to his sides, glancing to where her hands had traveled and then back to his eyes. "It's been a long time."

"I'm starting to wonder why I stayed away so long." He pulled her a little closer, knowing full well his hard-on was pressing against her stomach. Her eyes went wide, and she licked her lips again. *Fuuuuckkk!*

She smiled, just a slight curl to her perfect lips as if she knew the effect she was having on him. "Why *did* you stay away so long?"

"Lots of reasons, but that was before I knew what I was missing out on in doing so." He focused on her lips, then returned his gaze to her eyes. Yep, totally screwed. What a shit he was.

"Oh yeah? And what were you missing out on?" She slipped her hands under the edge of his shirt and pressed her fingers into the flesh of his sides.

"Girl..." He blew out a breath. "Dayyumm." Shane resisted the urge to grab her ass and pull her tighter against him. But only barely. "I was missing out on you, Cyn." Fuck it. Booze and desire were driving, and the train just jumped the track. He slid his hands lower and cupped her full ass in his palms. "And this. I was missing out on this, too."

Cyn raised a brow and pursed her lips as she shook her head. "I think... Did you... I mean..." She giggled and cut herself off by clearing her throat.

Jesus, she was cute. He grinned and moved his palms up to her lower back. "What's that?"

She tilted her head to the side. "Shane Conlon, did you just make a pass at me?"

He glanced away but quickly focused his gaze back on her. "Yes, ma'am." He nodded. "I believe I did."

"Wow! Shock the shit outta me!" She slapped his upper arm. "Really?"

He frowned. "Why should that shock you? You're damn sexy. And I'm not blind, Cyn."

"Yeah, but..."

"But nothing—actually, but everything. Your ass is sexy too."

Her eyes went wide. "I guess I just never thought...you know—" she shrugged, "—that you ever noticed me before."

"Hell, we were kids. Plus, seeing as though you're my best friend's baby sister..." It was his turn to shrug. "Meant you were kinda off-limits."

"So now I'm not off-limits? Is that it?" A coy smile arched her lips, and his fingers ached to touch them.

Instead, he smoothed his palms around her sides, loving how her tiny waist flared into full hips. "Well, if I abide by the friend code, it means you're totally off-limits." There went the E-brake and, along with it, her smile. Damn. For the life of him, all Shane wanted was to put that pretty arch back on her lips. Garth Brooks's "To Make You Feel My Love" echoed from the club's sound system, and Shane sent up a silent prayer of thanks. "Dance with me?"

That gorgeous smile came back even brighter than before. "You dance?"

"Yes, ma'am. I sure do. Think you can keep up?" He let her go, took her hand and tugged her toward the dance floor.

"Oh, I know I can keep up just fine. It's a slow song, after all." Cyn laughed, and it carried over the loud music, rippling over his skin.

When they reached the floor, he turned to face her, raised their clasped hands, and wrapped his other around her waist and pulled her against him. "You can two-step, right?"

"Wait, what?"

With a chuckle, he started moving, urging her backward with the sway of his body and shuffle of his feet. The song was perfect to move with her to. Shane had no idea if she'd ever danced a two-step before, but he was betting she'd catch on pretty quick. She stumbled a bit, but he held her tight and kept them in time. As he figured, within a few beats, she caught his rhythm and synced her steps with his. "Atta girl. You got it."

She glanced down at their feet, smiling. "Wow."

Yeah, wow was right. Shane rounded the floor with her, his hand pressed tight to her lower back, her full breasts pressed even tighter to his lower chest. Even with the significant difference in their height, she fit against him perfectly. He drew in a deep breath, and her sweet scent wound its way into his lungs, making him dizzy with desire.

He gazed down at her. *Shit, bad idea.* The swell of her cleavage above her low-cut silver top was a target for his eyes. Another dangerous temptation. His dick thought it was a great idea, thickening further behind his zipper. He turned her, keeping her tight against him, and her brown eyes sparkled from the lights in the club and what he hoped was excitement, and then she licked her lips again.

It took everything he had in him, but he jerked his eyes away from her mouth. "Cyn, you keep licking those fine lips of yours, and I'm going to end up kissing you."

She arched a brow and grinned, a devious glint in her pretty brown eyes.

Yep, screwed. Fuck!

***

Cyn's body tingled from head to toe as Shane danced her, slow and easy, around the dance floor. He wanted to kiss her. Which was bad—very bad, because she desperately wanted to be kissed. With his big body pressed against hers, she let herself pretend, if only for a few minutes while the music played, that there was no Carlos, no horrible track record because of her broken picker and, for fuck's sake, no self-imposed moratorium.

Before she'd run into him—literally—she'd been half-drunk. Maybe whole-drunk was more accurate. But now she felt stone-cold sober. Sober enough, she was unable to deny that the man, who smelled better than chocolate ice cream, had been her unattainable dream. The one forever in the "what if" category. The very one that she swore, if she ever got the chance—the freaking opportunity, she'd take it in a hot second. And now he wanted to kiss her.

What the hell was she thinking? This was Shane-fucking-Conlon! She was taking her goddamn chance; it was likely the only one she'd get. Cyn licked her lips again, and he groaned. A thrill raced through her, and lust pooled in her stomach. "What if I want you to kiss me?"

"I'd say you've been drinking." He turned them.

"So have you." She ran a fingertip down the side of his neck.

"You're playing with fire." He gazed down at her with his lips pressed tight together, and the muscles in his jaw twitched.

"Nobody has to know. More specifically, Joey doesn't have to know."

He sighed through his nose, and his hand on her lower back slipped around her waist and gripped her tight. "Killing me."

"I'd rather be kissing you."

He steered them off the dance floor and walked Cyn to a far corner of the bar, turned her and backed her against a wall. "You think that'd be enough?"

The cool panel of the wall against Cyn's back sent a chill racing over her skin. Shane dropped her hand and framed her waist in his big palms. He was so much taller than her and built like a truck, towering over Cyn, blocking out everything around her. Cyn gazed up at him as she ran her hands up his muscled chest and over his broad shoulders. With a slight grin arching one corner of her lips, she tiptoed up and circled the back of his neck with her palms, tickling the edge of his close-cut hair with her fingertips.

Their lips were only a breath away; their bodies pressed tight together. He was hard; she felt the line of his cock against her stomach like a brand on her skin. "Do it, Shane. Kiss me."

"It's not going to be enough." He grazed his lips over hers.

It was a bare whisper of a touch, nothing more, but filled with so much heat, Cyn's entire body ached for him—for more. "Do it."

"Cyn—"

Screw it. Cyn gripped the back of his neck and jerked him to her lips. His mouth came down over hers, and his warm tongue swept inside, and—Oh sweet baby Jesus—he was right. Cyn arched against him, and Shane's grip tightened on her hips, pulling her tighter to his hard body.

She deepened the kiss and knew this one taste wasn't going to be near enough.

SHANE'S BODY WAS LOCKED, loaded and ready to fire. Cyn's soft curves were molded against him as he devoured her mouth like a starving man. She tasted sweeter than anything he ever remembered having on his tongue before. Plus, she kissed like a woman on a mission. Like she knew what she wanted and wasn't going to stop until she got it.

They'd both been drinking, and he knew carrying on like this with her was a bad idea. Hell, laying his hands on her to begin with had been a bad idea, but once he had her in his arms, he couldn't help himself. He'd told her he needed to abide by the friend code, but in truth, he'd said it more for his benefit than hers. Shane really did want to respect Joey. He'd meant everything he said to his best friend, but goddamn, she was lighting his fire in such a big way he didn't think he could stay away from her.

Her tongue stroked over his bottom lip, and then she nipped it. He groaned and pressed her against the wall and, without another thought, smoothed a hand up her side to one perfect, full breast. Just a little more, a few more minutes. Just...*fuuuuckkk!*

This was too good. She was too hot. Shane wanted inside her. Like, right fucking then.

He broke from her lips and ran his mouth over her jaw and down the side of her sweet neck. "You taste so damn good." He still had her breast in his palm and couldn't stop himself from squeezing the firm flesh. Wanting more, he ran his thumb over the tight peak of her nipple through her shirt.

Cyn scraped her blunt nails up the front of his zipper, grazing his prick through the denim. "Don't stop."

"Girl..." He nipped her collarbone and tugged the low neckline of her shirt down just enough to reveal more of the perfect swell of her breasts. "Told you." He swiped a finger inside her bra and found her nipple. "Told you it wouldn't be enough."

She gasped and gripped his dick through his jeans. *Holy shit.* Shane growled and rolled his hips, pressing against her palm.

"Too late now." She caught his mouth again and slid her tongue between his lips.

Shane was ready to explode, his dick throbbing as she rubbed her palm up and down the outline of his shaft. He cupped both of her tits, squeezing them, and then pinched her nipples through her thin top and bra. She whimpered, and he swallowed it down, devouring her mouth. The kiss got hotter, wetter, deeper, and his head spun.

Her taste filled his bloodstream, and her lips and tongue stole his breath. Every inch of his skin came to life…for her.

How in the hell had he not realized this raging chemistry existed between them before? Worse, now that he'd found it, he wasn't sure he could go without it again. If Shane had known—damn—if he'd known this was what he'd have with Cynthia Donnelly, he would've grabbed hold of her seventeen years ago and not let go.

But now he did know. Of course, the problem with that was he couldn't unknow. The bell had been rung, and without a doubt, he was going to have this woman. He was going there —sure as fuck many more times than just once.

CHAPTER NINE

Cyn gripped the thick ridge of Shane's cock through his jeans and whimpered into his mouth. Between her tits being squeezed tight in his big hands and the play on her nipples, Cyn thought she might actually have an orgasm. Fucking hell, he was building her up, and fast. Her tits were her greatest weakness. She loved them played with. Pinched, grabbed, fucked—Oh God! His dick felt huge in her palm, and now she couldn't get the image of what all that thickness would look like sliding through her cleavage. She gasped. "Shane."

"Anything." He nipped her bottom lip and squeezed her tits again. "Anything you want."

Anything, huh? She gazed up at him through a haze of lust. "I want this—" she gripped his shaft, "—fucking between my tits."

He clenched his jaw; that muscle in his cheek flexed again, and she wanted to nip at it with her teeth. Jesus, that was hot. Then he growled. "Your place."

It wasn't a question; it was a command. And holy fuck, because they were still in the bar, one she was happy to follow. The tequila had her acting all footloose and dignity-free. In her opinion, there was nothing worse than a drunk chick making out in a bar, yet here she was, doing just that.

Cyn glanced to her left and right. At least no one saw them, or she hoped. Shane was so big, and she so short, Cyn was pretty sure he'd blocked anyone's view of what was going on between them. She drew in a deep breath and licked her lips. Fuck, he tasted good. "Meet me out front in five."

"You and that tongue." He groaned. "As much as I hate to ever utter these words, you might want to let go of my cock."

"Shit!" Cyn glanced down at her hand. Yep, there it was, attached to his prick like it'd been glued there. She laughed and let go. "Five minutes."

He nodded, and she ducked under his arm, heading for the front bar. Cyn had no idea where her family was, and she prayed with each step that she wouldn't run into them. She pulled her phone from her back pock—

"Hey! There you are." Maiya grabbed her arm.

"Here I am!" Cyn grinned.

Maiya wiped under Cyn's bottom lip with her thumb. "Jeez. Your lipstick is smeared. And you look a little—oh my fucking God! Were you with Shane?"

Cyn's eyes went wide. *Shit!* She had no idea what to say. Normally she was quicker on her feet than this, but her brain had apparently short-circuited due to fierce contact with Shane's tongue, body, cock and hands. *Dammit!* Plus, Maiya had a gift of reading people, like she was reading Cyn right now. "Um..."

Maiya crossed her arms. "Cyn, really?"

"Well..." Cyn shrugged. "Can you blame me? I mean, look at him! He's just so—"

"Ya know what? You're right. Do it. Go for it. Fuck it, or him," Maiya giggled, "but make it good because you're going back to your moratorium first thing in the morning." Cyn opened her mouth to make another excuse, but Maiya cut her off. "No, honey. Don't. It's okay. I love you, and it's your life, and yep, he is just so… Mmm. Far from me to begrudge you a few long-awaited orgasms." Maiya grinned. "Go have fun."

"I love you, too." She gave Maiya a kiss on the cheek.

Free to go, Cyn navigated the crowd toward the exit—a little hitch in her step and sway in her hips while Big and Rich's "Save a Horse (Ride a Cowboy)" played. Just as she reached the doors, she requested an Uber car from her cell. When she stepped outside, Shane was standing off to the left, leaning against the building, leg bent with one booted foot propped on the wall behind him.

Big muscles, narrow waist and thick legs waiting just for her. All he was missing was a cowboy hat pulled low. Cyn shook her head. Good God, he was fine…the man was *far* too fucking fine, and it took her breath away. A beachboy turned cowboy, and she was going to ride him until the freaking sun came up. Giddy-up!

Shane felt her before he saw her. As he glanced at her, he cursed himself a thousand different ways because he was doing this. There was no way he wasn't doing this. A better man would've stopped long before it started, but at that moment, Shane couldn't be a better man. He'd just gotten a taste of something he'd never had in his life, and at his age, with all he'd survived, a person didn't pass an opportunity such as this up. "You ready?"

"I called for an Uber."

"A what?"

She laughed, and the sweet sound went straight to his still-rock-hard dick. Cyn stepped closer, shoving her phone in her back pocket. "It's like a cab, but less expensive and much cleaner."

"How much time till it gets here?" He tugged her in front of him and ran the tips of his fingers over her cleavage.

With a moan, she licked her lips and pulled her phone from her pocket again. After studying the screen, she looked up at him. "Four minutes."

He bent his head. "Gimme that tongue." Cyn snaked out her tongue and licked over his top lip. His dick jerked behind his zipper, and he grabbed her ass, hiking her against him. "I got uses for that tongue."

"Oh yeah?" She rolled her hips. "Me too."

Shane took her mouth again in another frantic clashing of tongues and teeth, sucking the taste of her down like she was air for him to breathe. The fire between them got hotter. Intense, chaotic and out of control. Getting her out of her clothes and getting between her legs was mission-critical. His dick was about to explode, and based on what she'd said in the club, he'd be exploding, at least the first time, all over her delectable tits. He dived his fingers into her hair and jerked her head back. "I want inside you."

Cyn moaned and rubbed against him. A car pulled up in front of the bar, and she let him go and checked her phone. "That's our ride. Come on."

With his hand in hers, Shane let Cyn lead him to the sedan. They slipped inside the backseat, and she confirmed the address with the driver. Before they'd even pulled out of the parking lot, she'd shifted in the seat and was licking and sucking at his neck. Goddamn, she was blowing his mind, and in the best possible way. Cynthia Donnelly, all petite and perfect curves, had her hands, mouth and tongue all over him. Was she crazy? Wait. Shit… "Cyn?"

"Yeah." She nipped at his earlobe.

Fuck him, he was about to throw some cold water on their flames. "How much did you drink tonight?"

She giggled. "A bunch. Why?"

Fuck. "Maybe we should reconsider this."

She jerked away like he'd burned her. "What?"

"Come on now. Don't look at me like that. You know

why." Damn, he couldn't believe he was doing this, but it was important.

She slid away from him. "How much did you have to drink tonight?"

"A bunch. But I'm sober now."

"And so'm I."

"But, Cyn… I just want to make—"

"Hey, listen." She brushed her hair out of her eyes. "I appreciate you looking out and wanting to do the right thing…making sure I'm not too drunk to know what I'm doing or make a competent decision. But, honey?" She moved close again and curled her hand behind his neck. "I'm good. And I know exactly what the hell I'm doing. So, shut the fuck up and kiss me, Shane."

All he could do was smile at her. Yeah, they were two consenting adults, and true, he wanted to make sure she was in her right mind and knew what she was doing. He might be weak in this moment and failing as far as the vow he'd made to himself and her brother, but he wasn't a fool or a dickhead. He'd known this gorgeous creature her entire life, and he cared about her. Shane wanted to do right by her…even if it meant *not* getting to sink between her thighs and her extremely unbelievable tits tonight. He could be patient; he could wait.

In the dim shadows inside the car's interior, Cyn bent her head and laid a kiss on him that made everything in his body go tight—tighter than it already was. He was glad he'd taken the time to ask if she was good. But goddamn, when he realized she was, relief blazed through him like a speeding bullet, and as soon as she got them inside her place, he planned on getting inside her. Shane was going to devour this little petite firecracker and couldn't wait to be burned by every single one of her sparks.

CHAPTER TEN

CYN STRUGGLED WITH THE KEY IN HER FRONT DOOR LOCK AS Shane snugged up behind her—his hands roaming from her tits, down her sides, to her ass and back up again. "Fuck," she breathed and tried again. "Got it!"

As soon as her feet were over the threshold, Shane spun her in his arms and kicked the door closed behind him. "Mine."

Had he just said "mine"? And was that a growl? Cyn didn't have time to think about it further because he spun her again, picked her up and pressed her against the solid wood of the door. She wrapped her legs around his waist, and he ground against her center. "Holy fuck." She clawed at his back, wanting desperately to feel his skin.

Shane yanked her silver top down and ran his tongue over the top of her breast. "Said something about me fucking between these?" With one hand on her ass, he hiked her higher and tugged her bra cup down with the other, revealing one tight nipple. "Oh, girl. Dayyyumm!" Dipping his head, he bit the pink nub and then sucked it deep into the heat of his mouth.

Cyn's head snapped back, and she cracked the back of her

skull on the door. Fuck if she cared, though, because while he was sucking her nipple, he was also rolling his hips, grinding against her clit.

He pulled away from her breast and cupped the back of her head. "You okay?"

She laughed. "Yeah, just put my tit back in your mouth and keep moving like you are because, holy shit, I'm gonna come."

A sly grin spread across his lips. "Not yet, you're not."

Cyn circled his neck with her arms and rolled her hips. "Betcha I am."

"That so?" He nipped her bottom lip.

"Guaranteed." She giggled. "I'll even let you watch."

"Girl…" He yanked her away from the door and laid her down on the hardwood floor in the foyer. Nestled between Cyn's spread thighs, Shane rested his bulk on his strong arms planted on each side of her head and gazed down at her. "You'll come when I say you can, and I'll still watch."

Excitement barreled through her. Well, well, well… Shane Conlon was a bit of an alpha. Considering his former U.S. Marine status, she wasn't too surprised. She preferred her men to be on the aggressive side, so win for her.

As a woman who ran her own business, having someone else be in charge in the bedroom was just fine and dandy by her. And considering this was only going to be a one-time deal, Cyn was more than pleased to have hit the alpha male lottery. Jackpot, baby! She'd get her fill of Shane Conlon, he'd go home, and she'd go back to her self-imposed celibacy.

She was banking on tonight being enough to tide her over because she'd be getting herself off to the memory for the next year. Cyn ran her hands beneath his shirt and up his sides. "You like to be in charge, don't you?"

"Maybe." He bent his head and nipped her chin. "Let me guess, you prefer it the other way around?"

"Nope. But I do want this freaking shirt off you."

He rose off her and knelt between her legs. "Ask nice, and I'll consider it."

Oh wow. Her whole body clenched. Cyn licked her lips. Oh yes, she'd hit the fucking mother lode. "Please take your shirt off, sir?"

"Sir?" His eyes flared, and he groaned, then unbuttoned his shirt. "You're gonna be the death of me, aren't you?"

"Let's hope not." She giggled. When he parted the two halves of his shirt, Cyn raised her hand to touch him, but remembering her manners, she stopped. His chest and abs were sculpted to perfection. Bare of any hair, except a small trail leading from his belly button, she couldn't wait to run her tongue over both. Tanned to perfection, too—and not from some tanning bed either. It was pure sunshine that'd kissed his flawless skin. "How about Sergeant? That work? May I touch you, Sergeant?"

"God Almighty." He shook his head and grinned. "Call me what you want, but take your shirt off first. Bra, too."

"Absolutely." Cyn tugged her top off her head, tossing it to the side. She arched and unhooked her bra. After pulling it away, she cupped both breasts in her hands and squeezed them together. Shane stared at her, lust stamped all over his face. Cyn smiled and pinched her nipples. "Like what you see?"

"Love what I see. Tell me again what you want me to do with them?" He bent forward, resting on his arms again, but not letting his body touch any part of hers.

Cyn ached to feel his weight between her legs again. She also ached to touch the rippling muscles of his upper body. He was pure power, and she wanted to play with every bit of it. "I want you to fuck my tits."

Shane growled as he rose to his knees again. He grabbed her hands and placed them on his chest. "Gonna slide between them real soon. But first, you may touch all you want."

Hot damn! *And hell yes, another growl!* She liked the way the rumble of it vibrated straight to her core. A lot. Cyn sat up and first smoothed her palms up and over his round shoulders. He had a tattoo on each upper arm: an American eagle with the American flag billowing in the background and a grim reaper holding a scythe on the other. She liked those, too.

Gliding her hands down his chest, she spread her fingers and smoothed her palms over each muscled pec. Cyn was petite, yes, but the sheer size of him made her hands look incredibly small. She circled one flat areola with a fingertip, then scraped her nail over the nipple as it hardened. She licked her lips and gazed up into his eyes. "You're fucking beautiful. A goddamn Adonis."

"That mouth of yours? Gonna fuck that too."

"Yes, please." Cyn's panties were soaked, and every time something dirty came out of his mouth, her clit throbbed. She was so going to fuck his brains out tonight. A few times. And then maybe once more for good measure. Cyn moved her hands down the ridges of his abs until she reached the lip of his jeans. She caught his gaze, asking silent permission. He nodded, and she tugged open the button and pulled down the zipper.

"Something you want in there?" Shane got to his feet and kicked off his pants. With a devious glint in his eyes, he slid his hand down his boxers and arranged his dick.

The head was now peeking out from the waistband, beckoning her. She got to her knees in front of his thick thighs. "Uh-huh. Badly. So, so badly."

"Ask nicely."

Oh, good God, she was the one that was going to die. She had no idea he'd be like this. And fuck yeah, it was working for her. Really working for her. "I need to suck your cock. May I, please?"

SHANE STARED down at the woman perched on her knees before him, listening to things come out of her mouth he never in his wildest dreams could've anticipated. Every muscle in his body was strung tighter than a suspension wire, and his prick was weeping for attention. Literally. "Take it, girl. Take what you need."

She licked her sensuous lips, tugged the waist of his boxers down and snaked her tongue over the wet head of his cock. A moan came out of her that went straight to his balls, and with gritted teeth, he cupped the back of her head in his palm.

She glanced up, and the spark in her brown eyes socked him square in the gut. "Fuck, you taste good."

Shane let out a breath. "All for you."

With her lips curved into a small smile, she pushed his boxers farther down and lowered her mouth onto his cock, taking him deep. Then deeper—to the back of her throat, and Shane had to gulp for air because the wet heat of her mouth felt so fucking good, he thought he might pass the hell out. *Fuuuuckkk!* Ten years in the Marines, two tours in Iraq, plus the years in Afghanistan as a contractor and never, ever had he come close to passing the fuck out. Yet, here he was.

She moaned and pulled him from her mouth, and ran her tongue down his shaft. Cyn licked over his balls, sucking the skin, teasing with her teeth. The look on her face was another punch in the solar plexus. Her eyes were closed as she took what she wanted. There was no mistaking that look. Shane had never witnessed it in his life, but there was no denying it.

Cyn loved what she was doing.

The caveman inside him roared, pounding his proverbial chest, and Shane's hand flexed in her hair.

Cyn's lids fluttered open, her thick lashes framing her pretty brown eyes to perfection. "So fucking good."

Before he had a chance to respond—to tell her how hot she was or to say anything at all—she swallowed him to the back of her throat, drew him out, and swirled her tongue around the rim and then took him deep again. Shane's head fell back, and tingles danced over his skin. "Jesus. Fuck. Goddamn!"

She moaned and continued as Shane lost his mind, and the room went hazy around him. When the fuck had head ever taken him to his knees? But that's exactly where he was headed if he didn't get a grip on himself. He glanced down at her, ready to pull free just as Cyn fisted his shaft at the base and popped him free of her lips. "Fuck my mouth, please?" She licked the head. "Please?"

Holy hell. Time to get that grip he needed. Shane blew out a breath, cupped her chin in his palm and tilted her head back. "I want between those luscious tits of yours."

"Mmm." She took her full breasts in her hands. "These?"

"Those." He pulled her to stand. Considering the difference in their height, he needed to change their location. He glanced to his right and spotted the couch. Not gonna work. Kitchen table might work better. "C'mere." He muscled her up, and she let out a giggle. "Arms and legs around me." Shane moved toward the back of the house. "Kitchen this way?"

Cyn pulled her lips from his neck. "Yeah. Kitchen? Why the—"

Bingo. He found exactly what they needed and plopped her ass down on a raised window seat along the back wall. He gazed down at her. "Compensating for our difference in height."

"Wow." She took his cock in both hands and stroked him. "Lick between my tits. Get me nice and wet, so you slide like silk. Fuck, you feel so goddamn good in my hands. Tasted so good on my tongue, too."

"Thought you didn't want to be in char— Oh fuck! Yeah…that feels." He blew out a breath. Cyn was working him good, and the fact that he hadn't come yet was a goddamn miracle. She let out another giggle, and he felt it ripple deep in his gut, as much as he felt her hands stroking his dick.

"I don't. Just making sure you know what I like."

"And need?"

"Yeah." She smiled, and again, he lost his breath.

"Whatever you need, you get." Taking her breasts in his hands, he bent and licked between her cleavage, his tongue tingling from the salty sweat coating her soft skin. Unable to deny himself, Shane moved to one nipple, sucked it, bit it, then moved to the other and gave it the same attention. She moaned and kept at his dick. His balls tightened, and his orgasm crept up his spine. "You keep working me like that, and I'm not going to make it between your tits. I'll just end up coming all over them instead."

"Ha! Nah…you're good, honey." With her eyes locked with his, she urged him forward, took her breasts in her palms, and he slid between the full mounds of flesh.

Shane shifted his hips, drawing back and gliding forward again. The warmth of her skin surrounded his shaft, and the wetness allowed him to glide with ease through her cleavage. He wasn't a small man. By any stretch, and that wasn't him being arrogant it was just truth.

He couldn't drag his eyes away, and his mouth had dropped open as he panted for breath. If Shane thought he'd lost his mind before, he was dead wrong. The sight of his thick cock being swallowed by her tits, her tiny pink nipples poking between her fingers as she held him in place, and the feel of all that heat surrounding him drove Shane off the edge. "Are you shitting me?"

"Fuck yeah, baby. Feel that? Give me more. Come all over my tits." She gazed at him, slaying him with the desire in her eyes.

Yup, goner. Done for. Lost.

Shane's orgasm hit like a ton of bricks, and the first spurt shot from his prick like a bullet, landing at the base of her throat. "*Fuuuuckkk!*" He pumped his hips, his cock jerking, his semen shooting between her cleavage and up onto her neck and chin.

Cyn snaked her tongue out, licking what she'd drawn from him. With a hiss, she let him go and promptly sucked the head between her lips. Shane finished in the back of her throat, with her hand wrapped tight around his shaft, moaning and pumping her fist until she'd sucked every drop from him.

Unable to speak and barely able to breathe, Shane braced himself on the window behind them. About ready to collapse, he rested his forehead against the cool glass. She'd let his cock go, pressed her lips to his stomach, and trailed her fingers over his lower back.

When the feeling returned to his face, he made an attempt at speaking. "Never..." *Christ.* He shook his head, drew in another breath and tried again. "Never been like that before. Ever."

Cyn's fingers tightened on his sides. "Is that a good thing?"

"Girl, I can barely stand. What do you think?" He chuckled.

She laughed against his stomach. "I think...how's your recovery time? I want more."

To Shane's surprise, his cock stirred, and he laughed harder. Yeah, total goner. Done for. Lost.

CHAPTER ELEVEN

Cyn found herself back in Shane's arms, her legs wrapped tight around his hips, being carried down the hallway to her bedroom. He apparently liked carrying her, and she had to admit, although it was a bit primitive, she kinda liked it too. He'd also not stopped kissing her either. And she also had to admit, she more than kinda liked that.

Her back hit the bed, and Shane came down over her, his lips never leaving hers. He framed her breasts in his big hands and tweaked her nipples. Yeah, she kinda liked a lot of things. *Gah!*

"Gotta get inside you." He stood and lost his boxers.

Her gaze was locked on his hard prick. Long, thick and angled up toward his belly button, almost touching it. He was perfect. Shane Conlon had been blessed in a way that most men only dreamed, and he was all hers for the night. She'd had him in her mouth, between her tits and now—God help her—she'd have him in her cunt. If her luck held out, a few times. She removed her jeans. "Yes. Like, right fucking now."

He climbed onto the bed. "Demanding little thing."

Cyn laughed, leaned to her side and retrieved a condom

from the nightstand drawer. "Yeah, well, it slips out on occasion. Especially with your delicious cock staring right at me."

He held out his palm, and she handed him the condom. He tore open the package and rolled the latex down his gift from God. "I should put you over my knee."

Cyn's eyes went wide as her body went up in flames. He could spank her all he wanted. She hoped like hell he would. "That's not a threat, Shane."

"Damn…" Shane shook his head, grabbed her by the ankle and slid her toward him. He angled down between her spread thighs and licked through her bare slit, then slipped two fingers inside her. "Ain't nothing better than a bare, hot and tight pussy. Sweet honey, too." He glanced up at her, and Cyn gasped and grabbed the bedsheets. "Nice and smooth. Might just make you wait a little longer because yeah…your taste." He slid his fingers from her channel, pressed his thumb to her clit and snaked his tongue to her opening, dipping it inside.

Cyn was so on edge from everything they'd already done, her orgasm bubbled up like a tidal wave. "Shane!"

"Come for me." He dove two fingers inside again and sucked her clit.

"Oh fuck. God! Yes!" Cyn slammed her head back on the pillows and exploded. Her climax tore through her, sending tingles over her skin while her pussy clenched and spasmed around his fingers.

"Yeah, that's what I was looking for." He licked through her slit again.

Cyn raised her head, her breaths sawing in and out of her, and stared down at him. Shane had the most obvious expression in his blue eyes. One that could only be perceived as sheer pride in what he'd drawn from her so quickly. He'd earned it; she'd gone off like a freaking stick of dynamite. "Feeling pretty pleased with yourself, cowboy?"

He chuckled as he licked his lips. "Any reason I shouldn't be?"

Cyn stifled her laugh but couldn't keep a grin from surfacing. "Not saying."

"Uh-huh. Might have to paddle that ass anyway." He rose and climbed over her, settling his hips between her spread thighs.

Cyn was more than grateful he'd put the condom on earlier because she was beyond greedy for him. "Told you—" the head of his cock pressed to the mouth of her pussy, "—unngghh!"

"Told me what?" He slid the tip in.

Cyn moved her hands down his back to his ass and grabbed hold of the firm flesh. "That's not…ahh fffuuucc—" Shane drove his dick the rest of the way inside her, and Cyn forgot what she was saying.

He pulled back and slid deep again. "What was that?"

A hard breath rushed out of her. Full—she was stuffed full of his cock, her cunt rippling around his thickness as her body tingled from head to toe. He was propped on his forearms, his eyes boring into her with such intensity she thought she might spontaneously combust. Cyn swallowed and gazed up at him. No words were said, and neither of them moved. Something passed between them in the silence of her bedroom, and Cyn ignored it. She had to. Instead, she shifted her hips beneath him. "Fuck me, Shane. Please?"

"Anything you want, Cyn. Anything." He lowered his head, and kissed her and then thrust his hips forward.

As his pelvis rubbed back and forth against her clit, his shaft slid within her channel. Holy shit. Her body tightened, and Cyn moaned into his mouth, tangling her tongue with his. She raised her knees higher, dug her heels into the bed and shifted her hips in opposite time with his. And fuck, it was good. Mind-blowing good. He dove his fingers into her short hair, tilted her head back and licked down her chin to her neck.

She moved with his thrusts, her orgasm rushing up fast as her channel clenched around his shaft. Cyn couldn't stop it, or her need for more of him, as his thickness drilled inside her, and he worked her clit at the same time. She smoothed her palms down his back, his ass and up again—the feel of the muscles rippling beneath his skin with each shift of his body sent additional pleasure ripping through her. "Fuck. God, don't stop!"

"Tight. So fucking tight. Your pussy is squeezing me like a glove." Shane growled against her neck, gripped one of her thighs, raising her knee to his side, and rolled his pelvis harder. "Feeling that slick cunt of yours. Come for me again, Cyn." Shane pushed himself up onto his fists and drove into her with such force the top of her head hit the headboard.

Cyn reached back and grabbed the iron scrollwork in the wooden frame. With the added leverage, she arched her back, rolling her hips. "I can't... Oh my God..." Her second orgasm broke free, and Cyn lost her breath on a silent scream. She bit down on her bottom lip, and wave after wave rolled through her as her clit pulsed and her pussy clenched in rapid spasms around his hard shaft.

Shane kept at it. "Give it to me. Fuck, yeah. Yes! So damn good."

Before she'd even caught her breath or could see straight, Shane reared up and flipped her over, and she was face-to-face with her mattress. *Uh-oh!* He yanked her hips high, ran his fingers from her clit through her slit and then his palm landed on her ass cheek. *CRACK!*

"Oh fuck!" Tingling heat spread from the spot he'd slapped. Panting, Cyn turned her head and moaned. And then he slapped the other side with an equal amount of fervor. It stung. A fuckton. But in the most delicious way.

Shane smoothed his rough palm over both spots, then

trailed his fingers between the cleft of her ass, stroking over her anus. A sound came out of Cyn she would've never thought was her own, and her eyes glazed over.

"Want me here tonight?" He pressed the tip of a finger against the puckered opening.

"Yes." She arched, raising her ass higher. "Want you any way, all ways, please." She wasn't a woman who normally liked anal. She'd tried a few times in her past, but being petite, it never seemed to feel right or work for her. Shane's cock was huge, and she should be scared at the thought of him even trying. But in that moment, she was so gone in a hazy orgasmic bliss and desperate to have more of him, she'd even take him there.

"Mmm. Girl, gonna be the death of me." He moved his hand, and she felt his cock sliding through the folds of her pussy. "Not yet. But I do plan on making this sweet cunt come for me a few more times."

She whimpered and curled the sheets tight in her fists. Most guys bragged. Were all talk. Most guys *tried* to do what Shane just vowed. And most guys failed.

But Shane didn't brag or try *or* fail. Shane delivered.

The head of his cock dragged over her clit before sliding, with one solid thrust, into her cunt. The swollen crown grazed her G-spot on his entry. Cyn closed her eyes and let out a ragged moan. Sweet Jesus! There wasn't a doubt in Cyn's mind that by the time he was done with her, Shane would make good on his vow, and she'd orgasm more times for him than she ever had in one night for anyone else.

SHANE STARED down at the heart-shaped ass pressed to his pelvis. Damn thing was full, round, and the closest thing to perfect he'd ever seen. He wanted to take Cyn's ass, almost had. But tonight wasn't the night for that. There'd be others.

But goddamn, so fucking tempting, especially when he'd stroked over her tight hole, and she arched further, pressing against his fingers.

"Shane, please?" She shifted her hips.

"Shh…I got you." He smoothed his palms over her backside where he'd left his mark. Gripping her hips tight, he drew his dick out and drilled back in. Hard. Her ass cheeks jiggled each time his pelvis bounced against her, and Shane had to bite the inside of his cheek to keep from losing his mind.

She arched, rolling her hips. "Oh fuck! Oh fuck, yes!"

"Slide your hand down and rub your clit." He gritted his teeth and powered into her. Fuck, she was magnificent. Shane's balls tightened, his orgasm ready to break free. But not yet, first her. Always her.

With every thrust into her, she moaned, groaned and whimpered. Each sound she made was music to his ears as they climbed in octaves. Her cunt clenched around his shaft, and he growled. "Fuck…" He sucked his thumb into his mouth, wetting it, then slid it through the cleft of her ass. "Keep working that clit for me." Shane pressed his thumb into her asshole.

Cyn screamed, arched her back and slammed against him. Her pussy squeezed his dick as she came, shouting his name, rocking against him and taking what she wanted. He was happy to give it to her. Shit, he was happy to give her anything she wanted. Shane bent over her, his chest tight to her back and let himself go—pounding into her with reckless abandon.

She reached between her legs, caught his balls in her palm and squeezed. That did it. "Fuuuckkk!" Shane's orgasm hit, and as it did, he clamped her shoulder between his teeth. Panting through his nose, his cock jerked over and over inside her. He closed his eyes and drowned in the waves of his climax, the spasms from her tight cunt milking him and the feel of her petite body beneath him.

When his body finally settled, he slipped from her channel

and rolled to her side. At some point, Cyn had collapsed to the bed. Though he wasn't sure when that'd happened. He brushed her hair away from her eyes. "You okay?"

She nodded. "More than okay." Her voice was a bare whisper with a hint of a rasp threaded through it.

He propped himself on an elbow and trailed his fingers down her spine. "Not done with you yet."

"Damn, Shane." She smiled. "Really?"

"Yeah. Really." He kissed the tip of her nose before rolling away and off the bed in search of the bathroom. After a quick cleanup, he returned. She'd pulled the sheet over her and was curled on her side, eyes closed. Jesus, she was petite yet fit him to a T.

He'd always been attracted to taller women; considering his size and height, it just seemed to work better. But so far with Cyn, when they were lying down—and he was buried deep inside her—their difference in height and size didn't matter.

He slid in the bed beside her, and she opened her eyes, scooted closer and laid one of her knock-'im-on-his-ass kisses on him. Shane curled an arm around her back and pulled her tighter to his chest. Yeah, so not done with her yet. He rolled to his back, taking her with him, his mouth still fused to hers.

Cyn broke from his lips and kissed down his jaw to his neck. "Not done with you yet either." She grazed his shoulder with her teeth and licked her way down his chest, sucking and nibbling at his skin as she went.

"Good to know." Shane sucked in a breath when she found his nipple and bit it. He cupped the back of her head and then ran his fingers through her soft hair.

"You smell so good." She pressed her face to his abs. "Taste even better." She moaned and circled his belly button with her tongue.

He gripped the back of her hair and tugged. "Cyn…"

"Mmm?" She licked down the line of hair leading from his naval to his pelvis.

"Cyn…"

"Mmhmm?" She licked over the rapidly growing head of his cock.

Shane jacked his head back onto the pillows and hissed through his teeth. "Oh my…fuck!"

"Shhh." She sucked the head between her lips.

Shane sucked in another sharp breath and glanced down at her. Regardless of the dimness of the room, it was easy to see she had her pretty brown eyes trained on him and her lips wrapped tight around his dick. As crazy as it sounded, she looked like a fucking angel—with maybe a tiny set of devil horns adorning her short crown of chestnut-colored hair.

She closed her eyes as she took him deep into the haven of her mouth, and his prick swelled, full and hard. He moaned, his hips thrusting up on their own. But he refused to take his gaze from her. She was magnificent, sucking his dick. Shane knew he'd never forget how he felt and how she looked at that moment. Ever.

Cyn worked him with her mouth, teeth and tongue—sucking and licking, nipping and teasing. He could've come again for her—but like before, not yet. First her. Always her…

———

CYN HAD a mouthful of Shane's cock, when suddenly she was lifted by her arms, spun around and laid out flat on top of him, facing the opposite direction. She'd started to protest, but his dick was in her face, so she was happy about that, but then she felt it. Him. His lips. *Good God!* Shane dragged his tongue through her folds, and her body went loose and tight at the same time. *Good. Fucking. God!*

Doing her best to get herself back on track and suck him until he lost his mind, she grabbed him by the base of his shaft and slid him back in her mouth. At the same time, Shane dragged a finger, or maybe a thumb, she couldn't be sure, through her very wet pussy and then pressed it into her ass. His cock popped from her mouth. "Oh *fuck!*"

"Swear to God, gonna have this ass. Someday, gonna have it."

"Shane…" Her words sounded breathless, her voice a bare whisper as a shiver raced down her spine. With his tongue buried inside her pussy, he worked her with his fingers. Cyn's channel clenched, her clit pulsed, and her ass burned, but in the most decadent way—all of it building her back up.

But it was his words…his words had done the most to cause her orgasm to come rushing to the surface. Cyn swallowed and tried to focus on his cock. She didn't want to come yet. She licked down the shaft to his ba—*CRACK!* The flat of Shane's palm landed on her ass cheek, and Cyn's head jerked up. "Holy shit!"

He growled and yanked her by the hips. "Need this pussy." In the next breath, his mouth was on her clit, sucking hard. Two fingers drove into her channel, and his thumb pressed back into her ass.

Dammit, now she couldn't reach his cock to continue sucking. Cyn licked her palm, extended her hand and gripped his shaft. She got one stroke in before Shane flicked her clit with his tongue, nipped it with his teeth and, curling his fingers, hit her G-spot. Fuck, she was going to come. She was going to come so hard she might split in two. "Shane!"

He pressed deeper into her ass, stroked in and out of her cunt and sucked her clit—he didn't stop or slow, granting her no mercy. Cyn squeezed the head of his cock, and he growled but didn't take his mouth from her. The rumble from his growl vibrated through her, and the ball of heat building in her stomach got bigger. She moaned and rocked her hips, riding his face with no shame at all.

Unable to focus on his gorgeous prick, she let it go and

smoothed her hands down his sides. She buried her face in his abs and let him take her exactly where he wanted her to go, which was apparently orgasm heaven. She was going to come, just a little more— *Oh God!*

Shane curled his fingers again and pressed them against that sensitive spot inside her, sucked hard on her clit, and pulled his thumb from her ass. Cyn held onto to him as a wave of pure sexual heat blazed through her...and then his hand landed on her butt cheek so hard it brought tears to her eyes.

Cyn's orgasm hit with a force harder than the palm of Shane's hand, and she let out a guttural moan that she sucked back into her lungs and released again. The waves of her climax rolled through her, one after the other. On and on until she'd lost all sense of anything but his body beneath her and his hands and tongue. Shane...his scent, his feel, his everything.

The room spun around her, and she realized she was moving again. Shane had turned her, settling her astride his hips. The length of his cock positioned along the seam of her sex. Cyn dragged in a ragged breath and, without thought, rocked her pelvis forward and back, gliding her slick folds over his shaft. "Oh fuck. Fuck, that's good." She bent forward and kissed him, rubbing her tongue over his, tasting her juices mixed with the heady flavor that was all him. Pleasure blazed through Cyn like a wildfire. "Need another condom," she breathed against his lips.

"On it." Without shifting from beneath her, he stretched his long arm to the nightstand and pulled another condom from the drawer. He tore the package open. "Lift up, babe."

She did as he asked—her ass in the air and her lips to his throat. When he was done, he ran two fingers over her asshole again, then urged her back down. Cyn let out a gasp when she felt the solid head of him at the mouth of her pussy. Sitting upright, she gazed at him as she slid down his cock, taking him fully inside her. "Shane Conlon, you could become an addiction."

"I'm game." He gripped her ass cheeks, spreading them apart, then raked his fingertips down her thighs. When he reached her knees, Shane raised his arms and placed his hands behind his head. "Ride that prick, girl. Let me see those gorgeous tits of yours bouncing and begging me for attention."

She giggled. "All I'm missing are some boots and a hat."

The corners of his mouth curved into a devilish grin. "That can be arranged." He popped his hips. "Come on now, move that fine ass of yours."

"Giddy-up." She cupped her tits in her hands, tweaked her nipples before moving her palms to his chest for balance. Cyn rolled her hips, rising and falling onto his prick, losing her breath each time she was stuffed full of thickness. Heat swirled low in her tummy. She'd never had stamina like this. How many orgasms had he drawn from her already? Three? Four? Christ, she'd lost count. Figuring there was no way in hell she'd come again, Cyn closed her eyes and rode him at a slow and easy pace, rolling her pelvis on each downward slide.

Shane moaned through each of his deep pants for breath. "That's it. Ride my cock like you own it. Fuck, let me taste those sweet nipples."

Cyn curled forward. Shane met her halfway and took both breasts in his hands and squeezed. She gasped and licked her lips. "I love my tits played with."

"Happy to oblige." With her full breasts in his palms, he pressed them together and switched from one nipple to the other, sucking, biting, and sucking again.

Using his shoulders for leverage, Cyn bucked her hips forward and back a whole lot faster than she'd been just a moment before. The play on her tits was going to drive her over the edge again. Plus, in this position, her clit was getting plenty of stimulation. Good God, she was definitely going to come again. "Yes! Shane, fuck!"

Shane released her breasts, gripped her hips and slid her back and forth against him. "Give it to me, Cyn. Come all over my dick again." He kissed her hard, then pulled away. "So fucking sweet. Your cunt is so goddamn sweet, I can barely stand it."

Cyn's orgasm hit, and she threw her head back, yelling so loud it echoed around the room. Before she'd had a chance to even think about recovering, Shane rolled them, rose to his knees, and jerked her legs up over his shoulders.

And then he fucked her. Like he'd been doing, yet different. Harder. Faster. In a completely primal way.

Shane pounded into her, and her pussy clenched again— the tingles from her last mind-blowing orgasm still alive and well and pulsing in her clit. God, but he was fucking amazing to see. The veins in his neck stood out, his jaw was clenched tight, and his lips were pressed in a firm line.

All she could do was hold on to anything she could reach. His arms... The sheets...and finally, the headboard. He fucked her like a wild man, and she took all he wanted to give her and enjoyed every fucking minute of it. "Come for me, honey. Let me feel that big cock pulse inside me."

"I got something better for you. Fuck—"

"Yeah?" She rocked her pelvis, meeting his thrusts. "Give it to me."

"Hell, yeah. Here it comes." In one motion, Shane jerked from her channel, ripped off the condom, and took himself in hand. He bent forward, stroking his length.

Hot ribbons of semen spurted over her belly and tits. Cyn's eyes went wide as he pumped his fist up and down...her skin tingling everywhere he marked her. Caught in the web of the heady moment, she smoothed the hot, creamy fluid over her body, moaning as she did. She actually might've lost her mind because…without thinking, she spoke. "Oh my God. I love you!"

Whoa! What the fuck, what?

CHAPTER TWELVE

THE NEXT EVENING, CYN STOOD AT THE FRONT OF THE church, bouquet held tight in her hands, beside her sisters and Jodi, the matron of honor, as her brother Ryan and his soon-to-be wife, Maiya, exchanged vows. It'd been less than twenty-four hours since her night of mind-blowing, unfuckingbeliev-able sex with Shane, and she couldn't get the memory out of her mind.

She stifled a yawn—still tired from the prior night's party and extra-sexual activities—and glanced over at Shane. He was sitting in the pews about four rows back, focused on her brother and Maiya, clad in a navy blue suit, pale gray shirt and burgundy tie. Basically looking too gorgeous for words.

"I, Maiya Anne Rossini, promise to cherish, to hold, and yes, even sometimes obey…but only in the bedroom…"

Cyn barked a laugh. Ryan threw his head back, his laugh loud and filled with love. All their friends and family laughed, too, though there were a few gasps. Leave it to Maiya to crack everyone up as she committed her life to Cyn's brother. God, she adored Maiya. She was perfect for Ryan and for Jacob, too.

Cyn focused on Maiya's profile as her future sister-in-law

stared into Ryan's eyes, his hands clasped in hers. "To do the dishes when you cook. To read Jacob bedtime stories. To be the best wife I can be. Ryan, I vow to love you for all the days of my life and with all that I have inside my heart and soul. But I also vow to let you love me in return." Maiya slid Ryan's wedding band on his ring finger.

A few tears escaped down Ryan's cheeks, and he nodded, his gaze roaming over Maiya's face. He leaned in and kissed her. That was more than Cyn could take. She blinked, trying for all it was worth to save her makeup, but it was no use. Wetness coated her cheeks, and she sucked in a harsh breath. Witnessing the raw beauty of what her brother and so many others she knew had pushed Cyn to a place where she was caught between absolute happiness for her brother and a stifling longing for her own slice of happiness.

The priest cleared his throat and, with a smile, leaned close to Ryan and Maiya. "We're not to that part yet."

The whole church started laughing again, and it was enough, thank God, to pull Cyn back to the moment, which was right where she was supposed to be. Today wasn't about her. Or her relationship drama. She glanced over at Shane again, but this time, he was looking straight at her. Her breath caught in her throat, and her stomach tightened.

She couldn't fully decipher the expression in his eyes, but could tell that among whatever else he was thinking, lust for her was present. Sex with him had been something out of a dream. They clicked in a way most people only wished for.

Shane knew her body, knew how to make it sing. She had no idea how, just that he did. Cyn had had at least six orgasms. Six! Who the fuck had six orgasms in one night? She shifted on her feet, and the ache in her hips she'd been trying to ignore all day made its presence known.

And then, at one point, she'd told him she loved him. Cyn cringed and looked away from his intense stare. For fuck's sake. He'd let it slide, being gracious enough not to call her out on it, thank God.

"I, Ryan Matthew Donnelly, promise to cherish, to hold, to respect. And when you don't obey…" he grinned, "…in the bedroom, of course—to make you glad you didn't."

More gasps and laughter from the crowd. Cyn swore she caught a "God forgive my children" from her mother.

"Right on, that's what I'm talking about!" This from Jimmy.

"I'm holding you to that," Maiya said to Ryan.

Unable to contain her amusement any longer, Cyn bent forward, clutching her stomach, laughing. This was just too awesome.

Ryan continued with a smile. "I promise to do the dishes when it's your turn to cook. To always do the yardwork and kill the spiders in the house." Then his expression turned soft and gentle. "To support you in being the mother Jacob needs. And to be the best husband I can be. Maiya, I vow to love you for all the days of my life and with all that I have inside my heart and soul. But I also vow to never let you down, to be stubborn and diligently bust down your walls whenever fear gets the best of you, and you *accidentally* put them up." He slid the diamond wedding band over Maiya's finger.

Maiya leaned forward to kiss Ryan, and the priest stopped her. "Hang on. We're almost there." More laughter, but as the priest continued, the church fell silent again. "Let us humbly invoke by our prayers, dear brothers and sisters, God's blessing upon this bride and groom, that in his kindness he may favor with his help those on whom he has bestowed the Sacrament of Matrimony." The priest placed his hands over both of their heads and prayed the marital blessing out loud. When he finished, the entire church responded with the obligatory "Amen."

The priest stepped back from Ryan and Maiya. "It is before their most cherished friends and family, in accordance with the laws of the state of California, and before the Father, the Son and the Holy Spirit that I bless this union between Maiya and Ryan." He spread his arms wide. "I pronounce you husband and wife. Now—" he winked at them, "—Ryan, you may now kiss your bride."

"I got this!" Ryan turned and cupped Maiya's face in his palms and kissed her. And kissed her. And then kissed her some more.

The whole church rose to their feet, clapping. And still, the kiss went on. Maiya wrapped her arms around Ryan's neck, her body plastered against his as they took what each other gave, holding tight to one another.

Cyn let out a sigh, swiped the tears from her cheeks and glanced over at Shane. He was clapping, a broad smile showing off his perfect, white teeth. Then he slid his eyes her way, and his smile got wider. *Damn...* Cyn licked her lips. She wasn't supposed to have more than one night with him. She couldn't. And shouldn't...but what if they both happened to accidentally stumble into a coat closet at the reception hall and had a quickie?

"Ladies and gentlemen, may I present, for the first time ever, Mr. and Mrs. Ryan Matthew Donnelly!"

Cyn jerked her eyes back to her brother and new sister-in-law. Ryan and Maiya had turned to face the congregation, their clasped hands raised in the air. Jimmy urged Jacob forward, and little man scooted around the front of his parents. With a big smile, Maiya bent and wrapped him up in her arms.

It was official. Ryan, Maiya and Jacob were a family. Makeup be damned, Cyn's tears flowed like a river. Her brother deserved this. Jacob deserved it, and Maiya did too. They deserved the happy. Tons and tons of it. Warmth spread through Cyn as she smiled through her tears. Today was a good day.

CHAPTER THIRTEEN

Shane stood with his back against the bar in the reception hall, Jameson in hand, as guest after guest filed in. The wedding had been beautiful; then again, most were. But a Donnelly wedding even more so.

Glass to his lips, about to take a swig of his drink, he saw her. Shane paused, holding his breath and watched as she rushed in, a pile of bouquets in her arms. She began arranging them, one by one, in front of each place setting on the head table. Once done, Cyn turned and ran back to the entryway of the hall. Just before she was out of his sight, she snagged one of the waitstaff by the arm and spoke into his ear. She turned, pointing to each table, nodded her head and, poof, she was gone.

Cyn owned a small corporate event planning business, and even though Ryan and Maiya had hired a wedding planner, Cyn likely had her fingers in as many of the details of the wedding and reception as she could. Shane swirled the golden liquid in his glass and took a sip. Man, oh man, he couldn't shake the images of their night together from his mind. Not that he was trying, really. She'd been so fucking perfect—each curvy inch of her and for every minute they'd spent together.

He'd slept with her in his arms, and for the first time in forever, he'd actually slept through the night. In the morning, things felt a bit off…almost as if neither knew what to say to each other or where to go from that point. But really, what did a person say after waking up next to the person they'd just had completely unexpected, earth-shattering, newsworthy sex with? Shane had no idea. Thus, the morning had been awkward.

They'd both been drinking. However, they'd been sober enough to know what they were doing—heaven and hell, did Cyn know what she was doing? Shane groaned as the images of his dick in her mouth played through his mind. He blew out a breath and smoothed a palm over the top of his head.

A waitress approached with a tray of hors d'oeuvres. Shane snagged a bacon-wrapped something, thanked her and popped it in his mouth. Just as he swallowed, the DJ's voice sounded over the low classical music filtering through the space. It was time to introduce the wedding party, as well as the bride and groom. He downed the rest of his whiskey and moved to a spot where he'd get a better view of Cyn.

Shane watched as bridesmaids and groomsmen, eight of each, including the matron of honor and best man, were introduced. The DJ announced Ryan and Maiya, and they entered. The crowd clapped and whistled as the couple moved to the dance floor for their first dance.

Norah Jones's "Come Away With Me" played as Ryan danced with his bride. After a few moments, the DJ announced for the wedding party to join the couple in their dance. Shane watched as Cyn moved to the floor, her youngest brother Mark, one of the groomsmen, her partner. Shane couldn't wait to dance with her again. As soon as he had a chance, he planned on getting her back onto the floor. Maybe, if he was lucky, her bed.

Cyn threw her head back and laughed, her bright smile warming Shane straight to his toes. He wanted to make her smile like that all the time. *Shit.* Shane shook his head and blew out a harsh breath. Jesus, how in the hell had he gotten this spun on her so fast? The sex was fucking phenomenal, but it wasn't like he was staying in town for long. Jesus, he needed another drink. He'd only rolled in to lend a hand to his mom, get some things upgraded on her house, and roll right back out.

When he got to the bar, he ordered another Jameson and kept his back to the dance floor. He needed to get his head screwed back on straight before he was screwed…literally. He chuckled and sipped the fresh drink. Getting screwed was exactly how he'd gotten where he was right then—all hung up on a woman he couldn't keep and probably never should've touched.

"May I join you?"

All thought of what he shouldn't have done fled his mind, and Shane turned to face Cyn. Her sweet voice sounded better than any singer he'd ever heard. He smiled. "Thought you'd never ask."

A small smile arched her lips, and she touched the front of his tie. "We match."

We sure as hell do. He glanced down at her hand on the burgundy fabric. "We do, don't we? I hadn't thought about it until now."

"Well, Maiya wanted us in bright red, but Jodi convinced her to go with burgundy instead. I think it was a good choice, though the red would've been beautiful too." She smoothed her hands down the bodice of her strapless gown.

"I think you'd look beautiful no matter what color you were in."

She dipped her chin, and with blushing cheeks, the smile he'd give everything he owned to see appeared.

Shane placed his finger under her chin and tipped her face up to him. "Breathtaking when you smile like that." Goddamn, he wanted to kiss her.

Cyn licked her lips and placed her hand on his chest. "I want to kiss you."

"Yeah? I want to be kissed." Shane leaned in, ready to taste her again, but Cyn moved her fingers to his mouth.

"Not a good idea. And definitely not here."

He frowned, not quite sure what to make of her statement. "I don't understand."

"I know, but I'll explain later, okay?"

"Ohh-kayy. I guess." He stepped back from her. Nothing like a cold bucket of water being dumped over your head.

"Come on, don't look at me like that. There's a ton of people here and I can already see my mother waving at me. We'll talk later. Promise."

"All right, Cyn." He bent and kissed her cheek. "Save a dance for me?"

"You got it." She smiled and stepped away.

Shane stayed where he was, watching as she disappeared into the crowd. The vision of her incredible ass and hips in that dress was perfection. But the sight of her walking away from him, in general, was one he didn't much care for.

A WHILE LATER, Cyn glanced over from the dance floor to find Shane at the bar with her brothers, Ryan in the center, of course. They were doing shots, calling out Irish toasts one after another. Having Jimmy in town was always awesome, but seeing Shane among her brothers, especially Joey, made Cyn's heart clench. He fit in with them—but then again, he always had.

All her siblings, including her parents, saw Shane as family. But not Cyn. Cyn saw him as a dream. She'd swooned over him in the innocent way all adolescents did over their crushes. When she'd reached high school and puberty, all innocence was lost, and she fantasized nonstop about him. Cyn had gone on numerous dates during those years. Even had a few steady boyfriends…and she'd compared them all to Shane. When they kissed her, rather than Cyn's focus being on them, she'd wonder what Shane kissed like—what his lips would feel like or how his hands would feel on her body.

Looking back on it now, it was a pretty shitty way to be, but what the hell did she know? She'd been young and foolish, plus a tad obsessed with Shane, to say the least. And he'd never ever, not even once, looked at her as anything other than a kid. Sure, he used to tug on her ponytail or tease her, but her brothers did that same stuff, too. Thinking about it, she supposed he could've been flirting with her in that odd way kids flirted. There certainly was one way to figure that out for sure.

Cyn moved off the dance floor, claiming she needed a drink, and walked in his direction. She sure knew what he kissed like now. Definitely knew how his lips felt and his hands. She knew pretty much what every inch of Shane Conlon felt like. And, considering she was rocking a decent buzz from the champagne, she wanted to feel him again.

She stepped up to Jimmy and nudged his hip with hers. "Whatcha doing, boys?"

"Coming to chaperone us, like always?" Jimmy grinned at her. "You want a shot, Cyn?"

"Definitely *not*. And definitely *yes*."

"Huh?" one of Ryan's friends asked.

"That's just 'Cyn speak'. Hang around long enough, and you'll pick up on it." Jimmy held out a shot glass filled with what Cyn assumed was whiskey.

"Hanging around wouldn't be a hardship by any stretch." The guy raised both brows and gave her an appraising smile.

A small grin tugged at the corners of her mouth, and then she downed the shot in one swallow. Was this dude really gonna try and throw some game her way? She didn't even know his name. Cyn leaned between the men, flipped the glass over and set it on the bar top, not missing the glare Shane was directing at Ryan's friend. Oh boy. Wrong place, wrong time, but…damn if seeing him get the slightest bit jealous didn't make her go all soft inside as a tingle rose between her thighs. No denying it, the possessiveness of it turned her on, in a major way.

However, she needed to put a stop to things now before booze started talking and an all-out Irish brawl began. Cyn crossed her arms and stared at Shane. He still had his eyes trained on the guy, and if looks could kill…yeah. She rolled her eyes. Hello, testosterone anyone?

"Come on now, boys," Joey said.

Jimmy let out a devious chuckle. Cyn cleared her throat. Shane either didn't hear her or was ignoring her, still mad-dogging Ryan's friend.

At that point—Phil? Frank? Whatever the fuck his name was—realized Shane was locked on him. "Hey, whoa. What'd I say?"

"How about them Dodgers?" Cyn's brother-in-law, Camden, said.

"Ahem!" Cyn reached through the circle of testosterone and grabbed Shane by the arm. "S'cuse us, boys." She dragged Shane away toward the back hall where the bath-rooms were.

"Shit, Cyn," he called from behind her.

She glanced over her shoulder as she walked. "Shut it."

"Hey, now."

Cyn stifled a giggle. She'd poked the alpha on purpose, wanting to keep him riled up, and it'd worked.

SHANE'S SKIN itched from the flow of anger racing in his veins. Man, that fucking guy, looking at Cyn like he had a shot in hell of having a go at her. Screw him. Cyn was Shane's woman, even if she didn't know it yet.

To make matters worse, Cyn had dragged him away from the group like he was some kind of misbehaving child. To add a cherry on top of the shit sundae he was being forced to eat, she'd just told him to shut up. Not cool. Not even in the same building as cool. "Don't tell me to shut up, Cyn. Ever."

She spun around so fast he had to grip her arms to keep from running over her. "I did not say shut up. I said, shut *it*. There's a difference."

"Really? How do you figure?" Shane propped his hands on his hips.

"Because I said there is." She tiptoed up, gripped the back of his neck and slammed her lips against his.

Shane groaned into her mouth and then wrapped his arms around her tiny waist, picked her up and walked toward the end of the hall. She pulled from his lips and licked down his neck, and Shane held her tighter. "Damn, girl. My dick is so fucking hard right now."

"There's a coat closet at the end of the hall. I think there's a lock on the door." She nipped at his earlobe. "I'm soaked through my panties. Fucking hell, that was hot, you getting all bent out of shape at that guy." She giggled and then moved back to his lips.

"You're not pissed?" he said against her mouth.

She tilted her head back. "Does this feel like I'm pissed?" She bit his bottom lip. Hard.

"Ouch…kinda?"

"Ya big baby." She laughed and nuzzled his neck.

He might have to paddle her ass for that. Shane opened the bottom half of the Dutch door, stepped inside the closet and set Cyn on her feet. "Gonna be like that, is it?"

"Ha. Did I bruise your ego?" She closed the bottom and top half of the door. He heard the lock click in place, and then she turned to face him.

The expression in her eyes sent a bolt of lust straight to his throbbing dick. He popped the button on his pants and slid down the zipper. "Make it up to me."

Cyn pulled up the hem of her dress and got on her knees in front of him. "With pleasure."

Before Shane had a chance to say anything else, Cyn had his dick in her mouth. All his breath oozed from him on a low moan. The sounds of her slurping, as she drew him in and out of her mouth, had his balls drawing up tight. Unable to take his eyes away from the top of her head, Shane thrust his hips forward. His fingers itched to grab hold of the soft strands and fuck into her mouth, fast and rough, but he didn't want to mess up her hair. Instead, he smoothed his hand over the back of her head and applied some pressure. "Goddamn."

She moaned, pulled him free of her lips and licked down the shaft to his balls. With her gaze locked on his, she sucked his sac, then licked back up his length to the head. Cyn swirled her tongue around the rim. "You want to fuck my mouth, don't you?"

"Hell yeah. But I want inside that tight, wet cunt, too."

She snaked out the tip of her tongue and licked the bead of arousal oozing from the tip. "Which do you want more?"

"Both. I'm all about equal opportunity." Shane gripped his shaft in his palm and swirled the head around her lips and chin. "Love being in this hot mouth, but right now, I'm about to bend you over that bench over there."

She raised a single brow. "Do it."

"Patience." He slid the swollen head between her parted lips—his fist keeping her from taking him any deeper. Cyn closed her eyes and moaned, sucking so hard Shane's knees went weak. His orgasm came rushing to the surface, and before he lost it and spurted down her throat, he pulled away.

Okay, he was wrong...to hell with patience. He needed inside her pussy now.

Cyn's entire body was clenched tight with desire. Shane's scent flowed through her system, and his flavor coated her tongue, making her crave him more. She couldn't get enough of sucking his prick—completely out of character for her—but since he was only allowing her to suck the head, the lack of full access made her feel like a caged animal. So, in return, she was blowing his mind…by blowing his cock.

Shane groaned, and his fingers twitched in her hair. Yep, totally blowing his gorgeous mind. Before she had even a second to mentally pat herself on the back, Shane yanked his dick away and pulled Cyn up by her arms, lifting her to her feet. The room spun around her, and she found herself set down in front of the bench. Cyn glanced over her shoulder at him. "I wasn't done yet."

"Neither'm I. Get that dress up over your ass."

She smiled, never taking her eyes off him. As she gathered up the fabric, raising the dress over her backside, she bent forward. Shane pulled his wallet free of his back pocket and removed a condom. After rolling the latex on, he moved behind her. "This ass of yours. Mmm." He smoothed his palms over the curve of her butt cheeks. "So fucking fine."

Cyn reached between her legs, moved her panties aside and pressed two fingers inside her wet channel. "Want you inside me."

"Raise your ass higher for me." With a groan, he slid his fingers between her legs, connecting with hers. "Been thinking about being inside your sweet cunt all day."

Cyn knelt on the bench, grabbed the back of it and raised her ass higher. "Me too. I got so worked up thinking about you this afternoon, I had to get myself off in the bathroom before the wedding."

Shane dragged his fingers from her swollen pussy to her

asshole, coating the tight hole with her wetness. "Did you come hard for me?"

Cyn gasped and bent lower. "You know I did." Every time he touched and teased her ass, her body lit further, like a livewire. She wanted him to take her ass. She wanted him to take whatever he wanted. "Fuck me, Shane. Please…"

The blunt head of his cock pressed to the mouth of her pussy, and Cyn bit her bottom lip.

"This what you want?"

"You know it is," she breathed and pressed back against him.

"Take it, girl."

Cyn shifted farther back, and the head slipped inside her channel. "Fuck, yes. More, honey." A low groan slid past her lips as she was filled with the thick length of his cock.

He bent forward and nipped her ear. "Gonna be hard and fast, so I suggest you brace."

Hell yes! Damn right, she'd hold on because she knew he meant it. With a tight hold on her hips, Shane drew back and drove into her. Cyn gripped the back of the bench. "Oh God!" She gritted her teeth while Shane rocketed into her with sharp thrusts, his hips slapping against her ass. And Cyn died and went to heaven.

Reaching between her legs again, she found her clit and rubbed. Bolts of pleasure skipped down her spine as her climax built, and Shane's grip tightened on her hips.

"So tight, wrapped around my dick like a glove." He slid a hand between her legs and covered her fingers with his own. "Rub that clit for me. Help me make you come all over my prick."

Shane's tone and choice of words wove through Cyn's mind and body like a symphony. Christ, the words alone were nearly enough to make her come. She'd always said, "Turn on my mind, and you can have my body." Shane had managed both…to perfection. Her channel clenched, and her clit spasmed.

She was close, ready to tip over the edge. And then he slapped her ass. He shifted somehow, which changed the angle of his dick, sending him deeper and hitting her G-spot. "Holy shit! Yes! Shane, don't stop… Fuck!"

Shane moved his hand from between her legs, and he pushed two fingers into her mouth. "Suck them."

Cyn groaned, suckling his fingers, knowing it was his way to help her keep the noise level down. They sure as hell didn't need to get caught having wild monkey sex in the coatroom at her brother's wedding, for God's sake.

"Getting close. Goddamn." He grabbed on to her ass cheek with his free hand, his other now covering her mouth, and slammed into her so hard her teeth chattered.

Cyn panted through her nose, her muffled screams loud in her head as she took him deeper with each thrust. Her climax hit, and Cyn's cunt clenched tight around his shaft. As her orgasm rolled through her in endless powerful waves, her clit spasmed with little zings of pleasure.

"There's my girl. Giving you mine now." Shane slammed into her one last time and came. His shaft jerked inside her with each pulse of his orgasm. "Fuck yes. So good."

Breathless, Cyn fell forward onto her elbows. So good was right. Jesus, how the hell was she going to give this up? Sex with Shane was so fucking epic that every experience she'd had prior to him paled in comparison. And the idea that she'd ever experience this kind of intensity with anyone else was not something she could even fathom.

He'd changed everything. Every. Goddamn. Thing for her and she had no idea what to do next.

Shane ran his palms over her shoulders, down her back and to her ass. "You're like a drug, Cyn." He pulled from her channel. "Honestly, I'm not sure what to make of that."

Already caught in the same web of confusion, Cyn went with the safest response she could think of. She glanced over her shoulder at him. "Nothing to make of it. Good sex is good sex."

"If you say so." With a chuckle, he bent and kissed her shoulder before stepping back.

Cyn got her panties back in place and arranged her dress. "You disagree?"

"Not saying that." He did away with the condom in the trash can by the door. Peering into it, he laughed. "Let's hope no one notices that in there."

"Here." Cyn pulled a couple of tissues from an open box on a side table and covered the evidence of their little romp. "That should do it. So what *are* you saying?" She ran her fingers through her hair.

Shane hooked her around the waist, pulled her close and kissed her. She melted against his hard body, entangling her tongue with his. Kissing Shane was another thing he'd changed for her. She found she wanted and could kiss him for hours, days, even—again, out of character for her. Cyn broke the kiss and gazed up into his pretty blue eyes. "Was that an answer?"

"Best one you're gonna get right now." He kissed her forehead and then stepped out of the coatroom.

Cyn took a seat on the bench. She'd settle for the kiss instead of an answer. God only knew what he would've said. She traced her lips with her fingertips, and a shiver ran down her spine. Kissing had always been a gateway drug, a means to an end. Not something she craved. Not something that had her thighs lighting on fire. But with him, none of those old norms applied. Christ, she'd been daydreaming about kissing him all day.

And it didn't matter. It didn't.

Who am I trying to convince exactly?

He was leaving, and she was going to get used to being single.

But Jesus, once-in-a-lifetime chemistry, didn't seem to give a crap about any of what was supposed to happen and sure had piss-poor timing.

CHAPTER FOURTEEN

"I'm telling you, Angie." Cyn smoothed some sunscreen on her nose. "When he kisses me? Good Christ, I can't stop thinking about it."

Her sister Angie glanced over from the edge of the pool in Cyn's backyard. "Stop! You're freaking me out. The more you talk about it, the more it sounds like one of those kisses I've read in romance books. You know, the kind that don't happen in real life. Like ever. Except it's happened to you and shit…I want to be kissed like that. Just once."

"I think it's awesome," their younger sister Celia said from one of the pool floats. "But yeah, gotta say I'm jealous too. A kiss like that? I'd love to find a woman who could set me on fire that way, too."

Cyn got to her feet, grabbed her bottle of beer and took a seat on the edge of the pool. "Watch what you wish for, little sisters. I kinda wish I didn't know." She swirled her feet in the water, focusing on Celia. It was cool having her in town for the wedding, and Cyn loved having her at the house for the day.

"What do you mean?" Celia asked.

"What I mean is, what if I never find it again?" She took a swig of her beer. "What if, when I finally get done with my year of staying single, I spend the rest of my life kissing a bunch of toads in search of that same feeling I got when Shane kissed me?"

"Now, that's some depressing shit right there. Way to go, now you're really bumming me out." Angie laughed. "Wait… Year of staying single?"

Cyn cringed. She hadn't shared her plan with Angie yet, and now Celia was going to hear about it, too. "Haven't had a chance to tell you. Or you, Celia."

"Uh-oh." Angie pulled herself out of the water and grabbed a towel.

Cyn stood and followed her sister to the lounge chairs. "It's not that big of a deal."

"Wait for me. I don't want to miss this." Celia slid off the float and got out of the pool, too.

"You single for a year is a big deal, Cyn." Angie wiped her face with the towel and stretched out on one of the loungers.

What the hell? The statement kind of stung. "Why do you say it like that?"

Celia grabbed a towel and ran it over her short, spiky, black hair, then pulled one of the chairs over. "It's not that big of a deal, Ang. I've been single for a year before."

"Celia, believe me, it's a big deal for Cyn. And, Cyn, I say it like that because…" Angie sipped her beer. "I've never seen you without a guy at your side."

"That's not true." Cyn frowned and lay back on the cushion.

Angie chuckled. "It *is* true. You just don't want to admit it."

Celia sipped her beer. "Sorry, Cyn, but I think she's right."

Cyn smoothed her palm down her thigh. "Fine. Maybe it's a little true. But that's my point. I decided last week, after I caught Carlos cheating, that I was done with men for a while."

Angie shifted and adjusted her bathing suit top. "Okay, yeah, but a year?"

"Why not a year? Listen, Maiya and I were talking that same night. After I cried my eyes out, we came to the conclusion that I have a broken picker. I keep picking the same kind of asshole over and over again. And I don't know why. It doesn't make any sense. I mean, look at Mom and Dad; they have a great relationship. So do Katie, Mary and Joey. I'm sure Ryan will have one too. So, yeah, why the hell can't I have one? Shit, even Jimmy's in a state of relationship bliss." Cyn motioned to her other sister. "Hell, Celia's even had bliss before."

"I'm currently without bliss at the moment, so don't lump me in with the success pool." Celia shrugged.

Angie shaded her eyes from the sun with one hand. "Look, I don't have the greatest track record either, but I've had a few decent guys. Celia, you were dating that sweet girl for a few years in college, and you two ended things on good terms, if I remember right. I guess the difference is I dump their asses when it's not working. Cyn, *you* stay. For, like, *wayyyy* too long. Why do you do that?"

"Again, that's my point. I don't know why." Cyn sighed and took another swig of her beer. "Maybe I'm relationship defective?"

Angie laughed. "No, you're not."

Cyn laughed, too. "Seriously, Ang. I must be."

"Come on, don't be such a baby. No one's *truly* relationship defective. You're just a little...bent, maybe." Celia chuckled.

Cyn gazed out over her pool. "What's really odd is I don't even care anymore that Carlos cheated on me. I mean, don't get me wrong, at first I did. I was devastated—hence the crying jag and Jameson consumption at Maiya's. But somewhere through that and the following days, I just—" she shrugged, "—let it go, I guess."

"I wonder if Shane's magic kisses have something to do

with that." Celia raised her brows and tipped her head to the side.

Cyn gave the idea some thought. "I don't know. Maybe? They're definitely a bonus." She grinned but quickly sobered. "I do know that I had reached the end of my rope. Finally just done with Carlos's shit. Him fucking around behind my back only gave me more reason to leave."

Angie flicked a bug off her leg. "You know what, maybe I should stay single too. I can be your wingman. We'll hit the clubs. We'll shop. We'll do all sorts of things—wait, can we have one-night stands?"

"No." Cyn laughed again.

Celia stopped herself before taking a swig of beer. "Harsh."

"What? Why not?" Angie blinked.

"Because one-night stands, if they're any good, turn into more than one night. And then you find yourself craving that fucker and end up in a freaking coat closet getting banged doggie-style over a bench."

Angie's eyes went wide. "Hello? TMI!"

"Oh, please." Cyn waved at Angie, and Celia burst into a fit of laughter. There was no such thing as TMI where Angela was concerned. Cyn's younger sister had done all sorts of crazy shit with guys. "You probably already had sex in that same closet."

Angie sat straight up, a shocked look on her face. But then broke into a huge smile and winked. "Yeah, I did. Last summer."

"Slut." Cyn giggled.

Celia shook her head. "Oh my God. You two are killing me."

Angie pulled her long, dark hair out of its ponytail. "Takes one to know one."

Cyn adjusted her bikini straps. "Yeah, yeah. So, you really want to do this with me?"

Angela tied her hair back up. "Sure. But you know, if a kiss comes along like the one you had with Shane, I may have to bail on you."

"I totally want weekly updates on how this goes." Celia ran her hands over her hair.

"Done, Celia. And fine, Angie, I guess I'll take you while you're available." Cyn laughed and raised her beer bottle. "Here's to a year's moratorium."

Angie frowned. "Mora-what?"

"Moratorium: A temporary suspension or prohibition of an activity. In this case, of men."

"Oh. Got it." Angie raised her bottle and tapped it to Cyn's. "Deal. Bring on the single life!"

Cyn giggled and took a swig. "After this, let's go get a massage."

"Totally game for that." Angie flipped to her stomach on the lounger. "Wait, what if the massage dude is hot?"

"He won't be." Cyn brushed her hair out of her eyes.

Angie glanced at her. "He could be."

"Nope. We'll request a female. That way, we won't have to worry." Cyn shot her a wink.

"Oh, good call. Happy ending massage for me!" Celia got up and dove back into the pool.

"Fabulous. At least she's happy." Cyn giggled.

Angie snorted. "Right?"

Come hell or high water, Cyn was determined to see this through. And now she'd have support from Angie. She could do this…she just had to stay away from Shane the rest of the time he was in town.

How long was he in town exactly? She shook her head. It didn't matter. She hadn't seen him since the wedding and had no plans to. He'd called and left a voicemail. "Just checking in on you," he'd said. He'd texted a few times, too, but she hadn't responded to any of it. She felt kind of bad, but she had to steer clear of him. He was too much of a temptation.

Cyn licked her lips and forced back the thoughts of his body. And his tongue. And his cock—good God, his cock. It'd been four days since she'd had that amazingly perfect *and* large cock inside her, and she'd be a fool to deny she wanted it again. Her whole body clenched, and she groaned. It wasn't going to happen again. Blowing out a harsh breath, she forced herself to relax. She could do this. Totally could do this.

<hr>

"So, you and Cyn, huh?" Joey glanced at Shane as he navigated the jogging stroller with his daughter, Madi, strapped safely inside.

Shane cringed but didn't break stride as he ran next to Joey through the park. "So much for the 'don't ask, don't tell' approach."

They rounded a corner on the paved trail. "Yeah, well. What can I say? I'm curious, so I'm asking."

Shane wasn't shocked Joey asked. He'd figured at some point Joey would give in and want to know what the deal was, but no matter how much Shane had anticipated his best friend asking about his younger sister, Shane wasn't entirely prepared with an answer. "You seriously want details about me and your sister?"

Joey laughed. "Not *deeetails*. Just high-level."

"Honestly, I have no idea where she's at with it, but I dig your sister in a big way." He glanced at Joey. "I didn't expect it."

"What didn't you expect?"

"Her."

Joey let out another chuckle, and Shane shot him a sideways glance. "All right, Romeo. I don't know how you couldn't have expected Cyn. The girl has had a crush on you since grade school."

Shane's eyes went wide. "What?"

"Don't even try and tell me you didn't know that." They rounded another corner, jogging alongside a small pond. "Dude, seriously?"

Shane slowed and finally stopped entirely. "What are you talking about?"

His best friend came to a stop a few feet ahead of him, glancing over his shoulder. "Just what I said. Cyn has had a crush on you since grade school. How did you not know this?"

"I don't know... I guess because we were kids, and she was your baby sister?" Shane walked up to him and wiped the sweat from his brow with the bottom of his T-shirt. "But that was grade school. Even if I knew, I'm not seeing how you think that means I should've expected her."

Joey clapped Shane on the shoulder. "I said, *since* grade school."

"Ohhhkay. And what does that mean?"

"That means all through middle and almost *all* of high school, she crushed on you."

"No shit?"

Madi let out a squeal, and Joey glanced around the front of the stroller. "True story." He reached in and adjusted his daughter in the seat and then got back behind the stroller. "Running now."

How the hell did Shane not know Cyn had crushed on him pretty much their entire adolescence? He ran after Joey. Maybe he didn't notice because, like he'd said, Cyn was his best friend's little sister. "I never knew."

"Don't you remember how she was always wanting to tag along? Or how she was always trying to wrestle with you?"

"Yeah, but I thought...hell, we were kids. I thought she was cute, but only because she was your little sister and also because, duh, she *was* cute. But I guess I missed the fact that behind all her cuteness and requests to hang out with us were due to a crush." He crossed behind Joey, keeping pace with him.

"Okay, so now that we've established that little missed fact, what's next?"

Shane was still trying to wrap his head around the fact that he'd clicked with her sexually in a way he never had with anyone else, and now, added to it was the info about her having a crush. It wasn't a big deal; lots of people hooked up with their childhood crushes. But maybe it was. "I have no clue. But let's just say we have a…connection."

"Connection?"

"Joey, you don't want *deeetails*, remember?"

"Okay, shit. Right. But…okay, is that it, just *that* kind of connection?"

"Yeah." They rounded another corner. "I don't know, but I can say it's the kind I've never had with anyone in my life."

Joey blew out a breath. "Thank God."

"What the hell does that mean?" Shane glanced at him.

"Told you at the bachelor party, don't hurt her, and it sounds to me like the kind of connection you're referring to is the same kind I have with Steph. If it is, then no way you'll hurt her."

"I don't know about that, but regardless, I'm not a dick. I wouldn't hurt her anyway. I'm not in the business of breaking hearts."

"I know you're not a dick, but you're the guy my little sister pined over for pretty much a year after you left for boot camp, and if you're not serious about her, at least be sure you're straight-up about that."

"I hear you, man. Look, I know I swore up and down I wouldn't go there with her, Joey. I'm sorry I didn't honor that."

"Pfft, you think I didn't know you meant it when you said it? But, dude, I also knew that if you had an eye for her, and knowing she was probably still carrying a torch for you, there was no way in hell you weren't going to go there with her. Don't sweat it."

God, his best friend was awesome. Always was and always would be. It meant the world to Shane that Joey wasn't pissed, or worse, disappointed in him. "You know I love you, right?"

"Yes, dear. I love you, too." Joey laughed.

They ran in silence while Shane mulled over what Joey said about the connection between him and his wife. It was too soon to know if the connection between Shane and Cyn was more than just sex.

Right now, the connection was definitely chemical. But in addition, Shane genuinely liked her. How could he not? She was a smart-ass with a bright-as-the-sun smile and a personality so real a person couldn't help but want to be near her. For sure, Shane wanted to be near her, and so he intended to do just that. As soon as they got back to Joey's, he was going to send her a text, see if she wanted to hang out.

Of course, if they ended up having sex again, he sure as hell wasn't going to complain. Taking her to bed a few more times…wouldn't be a problem for him. In truth, even if they never had sex again, which would totally suck, he still wanted to hang with her more.

As much as he could for the rest of the time he was in town even.

CHAPTER FIFTEEN

AFTER CYN READ THE TEXT FROM CARLOS, SHE SLID HER phone in her back pocket. It was the fourth one she'd gotten from him that morning. With a hard shove, she pushed the emotions poking her insides like a pin away and sorted through a stack of catering menus in the client planning room of her small office. She hadn't replied to her ex, didn't intend to, but good grief, he was laying it on thicker than peanut butter.

After picking three menus for her client to choose from, she gathered the various options for table settings. Cyn eyed the clock; her client was running late but would be there any minute. She didn't have time to deal with Carlos and his "I love you's" and "I miss you's". The only person he loved was himself. Selfish bastard. Cyn shook her head right as the bell on the front door jingled, letting her know someone had walked in.

Cyn walked to the reception area to greet her client. "You ready to get—"

"Hi, baby."

Cyn stopped short, somehow managing to school her features. "What do you want, Carlos?"

"Baby, I want to talk."

She crossed her arms. He looked good, as usual. White dress shirt, pale peach tie and slim-fitting gray slacks. His dark hair was groomed to its normal perfection. And his expensive cologne somehow managed to ooze across the small distance separating them and funnel through her airway. *Shit.* She had always loved that particular scent on him. The bastard knew it, too. "Well, I don't want to talk to you."

He took a step closer. "You read my texts?"

"Yep." Cyn moved behind the reception desk, needing some sort of separation between them. He was going to try and convince her, like he always had when he fucked up, to come back to him. There wasn't a chance in hell she'd go back to him again, but Cyn didn't entirely trust herself either. Bad habits could be hard to break, and Carlos had been just that—a bad habit.

He moved to the counter in front of the desk, separating them and rested his forearms on it. "You haven't answered."

Cyn flipped through the pages of the schedule book, wishing her assistant hadn't taken the day off. "Nope."

He sighed and adjusted the cufflink on the end of his sleeve. "How about lunch? Can we talk then?"

Cyn let out a sigh. "What part of 'I don't want to talk' wasn't clear?"

He jerked his head back, and a frown creased his brow. "Come on, baby. You can't be serious." He reached for her arm, but Cyn jerked away.

"Oh, believe me, Carlos, I am *beyond* serious. And quit calling me baby. Last I saw, you'd found someone else you can use that endearment on. Save it for her."

"Come on, Cyn. I'm done with her. You know I love you. And I miss you."

The office door opened, and praise the heavens, her client walked in. She peeked around Carlos. "Hey there, Mr. Bowden. Glad you finally made it."

"So sorry about that, Cynthia. Traffic was horrible." Her client shifted the binder he held from one hand to the other. "Did you need a minute?"

"Nope. All ready to go." A smile pasted on her face, she focused on Carlos. "Thanks for stopping by. So sorry you misunderstood. I won't need any more samples."

Carlos looked back and forth between her and her client before shaking his head. "Let me know if you change your mind." He rapped his knuckles on the counter, turned and left the building.

Cyn swallowed, forcing the lump that'd risen down her throat and turned her attention from the office door to her waiting client. "Ready?"

Mr. Bowden tilted his head to the side. "Why do I feel like I just interrupted something?"

Because you did, but I'm so glad you did. "Not at all. Let's get your final details locked down for your event." She smiled and motioned him toward the client room.

"Sure thing." He nodded with a smile of his own and moved to the room.

Cyn followed, beyond grateful he'd shown when he did. Carlos had come loaded for bear, and although she knew things had changed on her end, she really hadn't been prepared to deal with him.

It wasn't that her feelings for him were gone…but maybe they were. She thought about it as her client sorted through the various options she'd set out for his corporate event. Carlos had done one hell of a number on her heart and mind over the last year, slowly extinguishing the flame of feelings she'd once had for him. Once those were gone, she'd been left with only physical desire, but over the last several months, he'd killed that inside of her, too.

"I think I like this table setting best," her client said.

Cyn cleared her throat. "That one works, Mr. Bowden." She noted it on the order form. "Twenty-five tables, right?"

"Yes. And, please, call me Josh."

"All right." She glanced up. He was smiling at her, and she nodded. "Josh." Cyn eyed the menus. "What about food?"

With his arms crossed on the tabletop, he leaned toward her. "Which do *you* think is best?"

"Well, it depends on which type of finger foods you prefer. The greasy, loaded with cheese kind or the dry, flake off onto your shirt kind." She pulled one of the catering menus from the stack and held it open. "And then, there's this kind."

He peered at the menu. "Wedge salad bites?"

"Yep. Complete with bacon bits."

"And dressing?" Josh laughed.

She giggled. "You bet. Not cheese, but just as messy, plus plenty of bits to mess up your shirt too."

"Maybe we should do some pigs in a blanket and little spinach and cheese quiches? Less mess, but still cheesy."

"Perfect!" She set the menu aside and made a note on his order. "What else? Have you decided if you want to do the photo booth?"

"I hope you don't mind me saying this, but you have a really beautiful smile. And a great laugh, too."

Was he flirting or simply paying her a sincere compliment? Crap, she couldn't tell. Not wanting things to go from business-normal to business-weird between them, Cyn went with the latter. "Thanks. Very nice of you to say." She gathered the table-setting flyers into a neat pile. "The photo booth?"

He raised a brow and tilted his head to the side. "Do you have one here?"

Shit. He might be flirting. "Uh, no. Sorry." She pulled the stack of entertainment brochures from the cabinet behind them. "I can call the vendor and arrange a demo for you if you'd like." She spread the various options out in front of him.

"A demo might be cool. Will you be there too?"

"Sorry, no." Definitely flirting. And things officially just got weird. "Look, Mr. Bowden, I'm not—"

"Josh." He smiled, toying with the edge of one of the flyers. "Look, I don't want things to get awkward. I just figured…" He shrugged.

Cyn drew in a relieved breath. He was likely harmless, but she never mixed business with pleasure, so moratorium or not, she wouldn't take him up on his offer. However, there was nothing wrong in letting herself embrace the lighthearted feelings his flirtation inspired.

"I'm flattered. Truly. But I never mix business with personal."

"What if I fired you?"

"Cute. But we both know you won't." With a smile, she rolled her eyes. "Look, I just got out of a relationship, and I'm not ready to get back out there and date. At all. And although I appreciate the compliment, I appreciate the business more. That, at least, pays my mortgage."

Josh laughed. "Great sense of humor, too. Okay, okay, you win. I won't fire you. But after this party is done, and you're over your ex, keep me on your list."

"Will do." She nodded. "Shall we get back to the details of the event?"

"Gladly." He smiled and picked through the entertainment flyers. "Photo booth would be great. No demo needed."

"Great!" With a smile, Cyn noted it in his paperwork.

That had gone surprisingly easier than she'd thought it would. However, there was a whole year ahead of Cyn where any number of opportunities could come her way. She might not be a beauty queen, but she wasn't unattractive either. Cyn never had a problem meeting men; she just never met the right ones.

Josh was good-looking, young, slender, and definitely dressed well. Plus, he seemed very responsible—her typical type, kind of like Carlos had been. And Will before him. Then Brad, before him. Ugh!

Shane was a whole other story. It'd sucked cutting him off,

but she couldn't risk seeing him again and getting attached—even more so because he didn't even live in L.A. anymore and would be going home soon. He'd never hurt her like any of the other guys she'd dated. At least, she assumed he wouldn't. The problem was her. She was the one who apparently had no ability to read people. Cyn no longer trusted her judgment. Coming face-to-face with Carlos, she'd been reminded of just that. And yeah, she'd known Shane just about her whole life, but that didn't mean she really *knew* him.

He was like something out of a fantasy for her, though, and probably too good to be true. After all, she hadn't been right about any of the men she'd picked to be with in her past, so trusting herself with Shane would be stupid.

Cyn stared at her hands. Damn, broken picker. Josh could well and truly be all he appeared to be, too, but Cyn had no intention of knowing for sure. She shook her head. It was going to be a long year.

SHANE TACKED the last piece of molding in place. He'd been working on the guest bedroom, adding new paint and trim. Next on deck was the guest bathroom: A new drop-in sink and faucet, plus some tile repair. He planned to tackle the living room after that. He'd been there every day, working from morning until night, but, more importantly, staying busy enough that his mother wasn't hovering over him. Naturally, Shane followed the list she'd provided him and was sure to check off the corresponding little box when he'd completed each task.

Really, Shane was a tad surprised she wasn't perched on his shoulder the whole time, giving him direction on what he should do differently. This latest boyfriend of hers was keeping her busy, thus out of Shane's hair. Which was perfect as far as he was concerned.

"Have you had any lunch, darling?"

Shane cringed and then glanced up to find his mother in the doorway. He wiped the sweat from his forehead with the back of his hand and stood. "I grabbed something already, thanks."

"Oh, good. Preparing a sandwich was not on my to-do list today." She glanced around the room. "It's shaping up in here."

That was almost a compliment. He followed her gaze. "Not too bad. I'll be able to start in the living room by the weekend."

"Oh no, dear. There won't be any working over the weekend. Derrick will be watching television, and I'd prefer not to interrupt him."

Shane bit his tongue. *The fuck? Interrupt him?* "Okay, sure." He shrugged, then squatted down by the trim and smoothed his hand over the nail holes. "I hope that's enough time to get everything done."

She frowned and pursed her bright pink lipsticked lips. "I'm sure you can stay a little longer if needed."

He bit his tongue again. No point in reminding her that he had a job *and* a life to get back to in Texas. Not like she cared. She'd already decided he'd do what she wanted, when she wanted, and that was that. The woman had always been this way and probably always would. Shane let out a sigh as he stood and disconnected the air hose from the nail gun. As long as he was doing what she wanted, all things stayed copacetic between them. Fighting her would only make this whole trip —and job—unbearable, and he wasn't getting paid enough to deal with unbearable. In fact, he wasn't getting paid at all. "I'll get it done."

His mother smiled her best Texas beauty-queen smile at him and patted the side of her perfect blonde hair. "Wonderful. Can I get you something to drink, darling?"

"No, thank you." He picked up his jug of water. "Got

what I need right here." He tossed an equally practiced grin back. Yeah, no point in bringing on the unbearable. Of course, by the time the week ended, he might not have a tongue left, so arguing with her wouldn't even be possible. He stifled a laugh and coiled up the air hose, trying like hell to ignore the fact that she was still standing there, hovering.

"Always so self-sufficient."

The sneer in her voice made him cringe. "Not a bad thing, Mom. A trait I got from my father, plus the years in service added to it. I'd think you'd be proud of that fact."

Shit. That one had slipped out. Shane blew out a breath and gathered his other tools along with his patience.

"It's just not the life I would've chosen for you, darling."

He turned his back and loaded his tools into the work bucket. "Well, regardless, it's what *I* chose. Besides, I'm sure Dad is proud."

"Yes… I'm sure he is." She cleared her throat. "I'll leave you to it then."

When Shane glanced over his shoulder, she'd already walked away, having no desire to hear anything more said about his father, he was sure. She hated when Shane brought his dad up—always had. Shane had never understood it completely and still didn't.

Whatever her issue was with his father, she'd kept it to herself, at least verbally. But she'd never kept the disdain from coloring her reactions whenever Shane mentioned him. It didn't matter. She could date as many men as she wanted. Hell, she'd even remarried a couple of times, but as far as Shane was concerned, none of them held a candle to his father. They never would.

He glanced at the time on his phone. It was a little after two p.m. Was Cyn busy working? He'd sent a couple of texts and even left a voicemail for her, but she'd yet to reply. In fact, he hadn't talked to her since the wedding. As far as he could tell, he hadn't done anything to piss her off at the reception, so he wasn't sure what the deal was.

This past week had been spent at Joey's house with his wife and daughter, and it'd been great, but Shane hadn't stopped thinking about Cynthia. He wanted to text her again, but he'd be damned if he was going to chase her. If she didn't want to talk to him? Fine, they wouldn't talk. Which sucked on so many levels Shane had lost count.

Maybe she was freaked because she'd said those three little words when they'd been together the night before the wedding. Shane had let it slide, knowing full well she hadn't meant them. Not like he was stupid. They'd just slipped out in the heat of the moment.

After he gathered the rest of the tools from the room and cleaned up, Shane headed to the guest bathroom to start on the sink. He'd be in town till the end of next week and hoped like hell Cyn would come around because Shane couldn't shake the constant craving for her.

Christ, every time he thought about her and let his mind wander, even momentarily, to the memories of sex between them, his dick got rod-hard in his pants. He'd jacked off more in the last four days than he had in the last four years. Which was fucking insane.

She had a magic mouth and pussy, yeah…but more than that, Cyn was just plain magical. Her personality, her goofiness, her smile and her constant, and sometimes unsolicited, opinions—all magic in his eyes. Man, she was bossy as hell, a bit of a control freak, too, and Shane wanted more of her. He sighed. Seven days—plenty of time to get his fill of her. If, by chance, he wasn't topped off after the week, he'd just have to pay a few more visits to Cali in the near future.

But the woman needed to call him back, for fuck's sake.

CHAPTER SIXTEEN

Cyn carried a big pile of wedding gifts up Ryan's walkway to his front door. Maiya had the door open before Cyn reached it, thank God.

Her new sister-in-law grabbed the top two off the pile. "Holy shit, where did these all come from?"

"Mom and Dad's house. I guess some of the family who couldn't make the wedding sent them there instead of your house." Cyn walked through the front door.

"Holy crap!" Ryan rushed down the last few steps on the staircase and grabbed another two boxes from her. "From Mom and Dad's?"

Cyn set the bag she had hanging from her wrist down and shook out her arm. "Give the man a prize." She laughed. "There's more in the Jeep still."

"More?" Maiya set down the two she'd grabbed on the pile Ryan started. "Where the hell are we going to put all this stuff?"

"Hell if I know." Cyn brushed her hair out of her face. "Re-gift?"

Maiya barked a laugh, and Cyn headed back outside for another pile. When she glanced over from behind the Wrangler, Shane was striding across the lawn. *Oh fuck.* In an instant, Cyn's entire body tensed as heat pooled between her thighs. Six days—six long-ass days—since she'd seen or talked to him. Touched, licked, sucked… *Good lord!* And here he was, walking toward her, baseball cap pulled low, no shirt and faded blue jeans hanging even lower on his narrow hips…looking all delicious and edible.

He rounded the back of her vehicle, and Cyn licked her lips and took a step back. Then his delectable, mouthwatering scent hit her like a freight train, and she grabbed the side of the Jeep to steady herself.

Shane regarded her for a moment, his head tilted at a slight angle, lips pursed, as he ran his palm over the back of his neck. His gaze, lit with desire, roamed from her eyes to her mouth and continued down her body, then wandering all slow and deliberate back to her eyes again.

And she felt every damn second of it like a physical touch.

Slipping his hands into his front pockets, his lips arched into a slight, very sexy grin. "How ya been, Cyn?"

"I'm…" *Shit!* Cyn blew out a breath and cleared her throat. Jesus, he looked good. Really good. Like, no man on earth had the right to look that good, good. His tanned skin glowed in the sunlight. His muscled chest whispered to her— she swore it did—begging to be touched. And his abs? Fucking hell, his abs needed her tongue on them too. Or maybe it was the other way around; maybe it was her tongue that needed to touch his abs? Didn't matter. Either way, the need to touch him rose inside her like a tidal wave, drowning all thought and prior rational decisions made.

"That good, huh?"

Cyn shook her head and dragged her eyes away—not an easy task—from his tempting body. "Yeah. Good. You?" Talking to him was apparently a problem at the moment; looking at him was, too. *Focus, Cyn. Unload the Jeep.* Grateful for the distraction, she leaned inside the tailgate and piled up a couple more boxes.

Shane took the pile before she had a chance to lift it. "Just stopped by to say hi to Ryan and his lady. I've been…not so good."

"Oh?" She snapped her gaze back to him. "Why, what's wrong? Are you okay?"

He gave her a sideways glance from below the brim of his hat. "Been trying to reach you. Haven't heard back." Shane walked away, packages held with ease in his big arms.

Guilt hit Cyn like a ton of bricks, and she bit her bottom lip. Moving around the side of her vehicle, she stared at his muscular body and the Semper Fidelis tattoo in black, Old English lettering across his upper back. Too freaking sexy. But more than that, Shane was a nice guy. Had always been a nice guy. In high school, he was the kid everyone wanted to hang with, and every girl wanted to date. Polite, never arrogant and always respectful, too.

With her eyes on the front door, Cyn leaned a hip against the side of her Wrangler and let out a sigh… And the boy of her dreams came back outside, walking straight toward her. She sighed again. God, he was beautiful. Their eyes locked and stayed that way until he reached her, stopping less than a foot away. Cyn tilted her head back to keep her gaze on his. "I'm sorry."

He gave her a brief nod. "I'll let you make it up to me."

Beating back the urge to touch him, Cyn crossed her arms. "How so?"

"Dinner." He traced two fingers down her arm. "Then breakfast."

A blaze of heat seared her skin where he'd touched her, spreading through her body, and Cyn's breath hitched in her throat. "I can't." Her voice was a bare whisper.

"Can't? Why's that?" Shane stepped closer and rubbed his palms up and down her arms.

His scent hit her hard, and she had to suppress a groan from slipping out. Cyn dropped her gaze only to be greeted by the sight of his broad chest. *Shit.* Mouth gone dry, she swallowed. The desire to snake out her tongue and lick his sun-kissed skin was killing her. "I'm having a hard time remembering why."

"Oh yeah? Why's that?" Shane pinched her chin between his finger and thumb, tilting her face up to him.

Their bodies were barely touching, and the temptation to lean forward and press against him rolled through her. Cyn licked her lips. "Fuck…"

"Reading my mind." Shane's lips twitched in a slight grin before he touched his mouth to hers.

As he started to pull away, Cyn curled a hand around the back of his neck and held him close. Just one more taste…just one—snaking out her tongue, she licked his top lip. *Oh fuck yes.* Shane ran his hands down her back to her ass, jerking her body tight against him and slammed his mouth down on hers. Their tongues collided, and Cyn's libido went into overdrive.

Shane moved them backward, and Cyn found herself being lifted into the back of her Wrangler. He broke from her mouth. "Girl, where'n the *hell* you been?" He spun his hat backward, bent his head to the side and bit the tender skin of her neck.

Cyn gasped, arching against him, as she scraped her nails down his chest. Electrified lust bolted through her. "Fuck, that feels good." When her fingers met the waistband of his jeans, she tugged the button open and wedged her hand inside. The heat of his hard cock was like a brand on her palm as she closed her fist around the shaft. "Want this, Shane."

"Coulda been having that all week." He moved back to her lips and dived his tongue in her mouth again.

"Holy shit, *really*?"

Startled, Shane yanked from the kiss but didn't move

away. Cyn buried her face in Shane's heavenly chest and couldn't help but smile. "Sorry, Ryan."

"Maybe you two want to take this elsewhere? I have neighbors, you know."

"What happened? *Awww*…did you two get caught making out like a couple of teenagers in heat?" Maiya laughed and peered over the top of the back tailgate, and her brows went sky-high.

Cyn grinned at her sister-in-law, who, based on her expression, could clearly see Cyn had her hand down Shane's jeans. Cyn shrugged. "Yeah, well. It happens."

"Cyn," Shane whispered, giving her hips a brief squeeze. "Might want to take your hand outta there."

Cyn gazed up at him. She let a lazy smile spread across her mouth as she slid her hand up his length to the head and then let him go. "If you insist."

With a groan, he let out a breath, his big body shuddering against hers. "Killing me." He took a step back while he buttoned his pants. "Apologies, Ry. No disrespect meant."

Ryan barely suppressed a grin. "Hey, don't worry about it, bro. None taken."

"I hope not, considering our history." Maiya snorted, crossed her arms and grinned at her husband.

Ryan curled his arm around Maiya's waist and planted a hard but quick kiss on her lips. "Exactly." He turned to Shane. "Help me get the rest of this stuff inside, then you two can take off to fin— Ya know, I don't want to know any more than that." Shaking his head with a laugh, Ryan raised his hands in surrender.

Cyn hopped down from her tailgate. "Whatever. Deal with it." She handed Ryan a few packages. Shane grabbed what remained, and he and Ryan took them to the house. Cyn glanced at Maiya, who'd lit a cigarette. "All right, g'head, say it."

Maiya blew out a stream of gray smoke. "Say what?"

"That I'm fucking up."

"Who'm I to say you're fucking up?" Her sister-in-law shrugged. "But let me ask you something."

"Anything." Cyn smoothed her hands down her shirt and braced for the question.

"If you'd known Shane was in town, would you still have made that vow?"

"I don't know." It was the truth; she didn't know. The whole point of the moratorium was to figure out what was wrong with her, hopefully fix it, *and then* be able to have a good relationship with a man. That hadn't changed just because Shane Conlon had been, and wanted still to be, in her pants, had it? "Maybe?"

"I guess only you can decide that. Are you going to follow through with the year off?"

Cyn looked down at her Chucks and tucked her hands in her back pockets. "I don't know."

Maiya nudged Cyn with her shoulder. "Whichever you decide to do, keep your vow or give it up, do it because it's what you want. And know that I've got your back either way."

"I love you, Maiya." Cyn smiled.

Maiya stubbed out her cigarette on the bottom of her shoe. "Love you too, chica." She glanced around Cyn. "Looks like he's coming back for you."

Cyn froze, her mind in a tug-of-war with itself. She should tell him no. She should get in her Jeep, back out of the driveway and never see him again. At least not for a year. Or, she should give him a blowjob *immediately*. Maybe screw his brains out after. He had unbelievable recovery time… *Gah!* She should do a lot of things, like take care of some work that needed doing. Or go water her lawn. Plant some flowe—

"Cyn?"

She looked up and blinked a few times. He'd put his T-shirt back on and had added a flannel over the top. Jesus, he'd make burlap look sexy. "Yeah?"

He smiled and crossed his arms. "Ready?"

"For what?"

"Hmm." He chuckled and moved to his rental. "Meet you at your place."

"But—"

Shane slid inside the SUV and shut the door. Cyn pressed her lips together, staring at him as he started the vehicle and backed out of the driveway. She threw her hands in the air. "Well, okay then."

Maiya laughed. "Gotta love when they do that."

Guess he'd made Cyn's mind up for her. Freaking alpha males and their tendency to take control, ordering women around. If she didn't find it so fucking sexy, she might actually be pissed off. "Yeah, that was pretty hot." Cyn swung the tailgate of the Wrangler closed and moved to the driver's door. "He's here for another week. Looks like I'm postponing my moratorium till he goes."

"Sounds like a plan." Maiya ran her fingers through her long hair. "Call me later. Or…when you come up for air and sustenance." She chuckled.

"Later, Maiya." Cyn slid behind the wheel. Who needed food when she could feast on a body like Shane's? Air, well, hell, she'd be getting plenty of that each time she cried out his name or moaned in sheer pleasure. She threw the Jeep in gear and backed out of the driveway. With a final wave to Maiya, Cyn headed to her house.

CHAPTER SEVENTEEN

Shane pulled into Cyn's driveway. He'd stopped at the grocery store on his way, picking up some fixins for dinner. He planned on making some juicy burgers and enjoying a few beers with Cyn, then taking her upstairs and having her for dessert. After gathering the bags, he closed the hatch and made his way to the front door.

Cyn opened it before he made it up the first step and rushed to him. "Let me help you."

"Got it already." He bent, kissed her cheek and then moved inside the house. She followed, closed the door and scooted around him to the kitchen. Fine by him, he got a perfect view of her full ass. "You always wear jeans like that?"

"Like what?" She took one of the bags and set it on the counter.

"Ones that mold to your already incredible ass."

"Don't know about incredible, but yeah, I wear jeans that fit me. Why?"

He hooked her around the waist and pulled her close. "Don't stop. Makes me hard every time I see you in them."

Cyn smiled and gazed up at him. "Good to know." She

pressed against him, and her eyes widened. "Your dick is hard, Shane! Damn. And now all I want to do is suck you off."

He groaned, wanting that too. But not yet. First, he needed to feed her. "You can suck my cock after we eat."

She frowned. "No fair."

"The way I see it, we're even." He swatted her ass.

"How do you figure that?" She rose on her toes and circled his neck with her arms.

Shane kissed the tip of her nose. "I'll be tortured by your fine ass the whole night. By the time we get done eating, I'll be aching for your hot mouth as much as you're aching to put it on me. That's how."

"I see your point." She kissed him, and Shane groaned into her mouth, loving the taste and feel of her.

Man, he was so freaking glad she'd shown up at Ryan and Maiya's house. He was beginning to think she'd dodge him the rest of his trip. But nope, Lady Luck smiled down on him and now here he was at Cyn's house, with her in his arms, kissing his brains out. Shane planned on taking all she was willing to give him tonight and, if he had his way, the remainder of the week, too.

Cyn's phone chimed on the counter, and she broke the kiss. "Sorry, let me check that."

She stepped away, and Shane set to unloading the groceries. "Did you start the grill?" She stared at her phone, reading the message. Maybe she didn't hear him. "Cyn?"

"Hmm?" She glanced up.

"Did you already start the grill?"

"Umm." She returned her focus back to her phone, and her brow creased into a frown. "Yeah. I did."

"Hey, you okay?" Shane moved to her.

She tossed the phone onto the counter. "Yeah. Fine. I'll go check the grill." She glanced at him as she walked away.

Shane had no idea what'd just happened, but whatever it was, it wasn't good. One minute, she was all happy and pressed against his body, tongue down his throat, and the next, she looked like someone just kicked her dog. Her phone beeped again, another text coming in, and Shane eyed the device on the counter. He wasn't about to check the message. It wasn't his business, but whoever it was had already upset her, and Shane wasn't about to tolerate that.

Cyn came back inside and appeared a bit less distressed than when she'd left. She moved to the sink and washed her hands. "What can I do to help?"

Shane leaned his back against the counter, crossing his feet at the ankle. "It went off again."

"What did? My phone?" She eyed the cell, then reached for it. "Shit."

"Maybe you shouldn't read it."

She glanced at him before looking back to the screen. "Too late."

Shane studied her features and watched as, once again, her brow creased, and this time, her mouth pressed into a thin line. Something was definitely up. "Something wrong, Cyn?"

She let out a sigh and rubbed her forehead. "I don't want to talk about it."

He moved to her. "All right, but whatever it is, it's now sharing the room with us. I'll cook. You have a beer. If by the time we're ready to eat, it's not gone, you start talking."

"Shane—"

"Cyn, I respect your privacy. So you deal with it, then let it go. But hear me when I say, if you can't let it go, clearly, we need to talk about it. Got me?"

She blew out a harsh breath. "Fine."

"Good." He pressed a kiss to her forehead and began prepping burgers.

Cyn moved to the six-pack of beers. "Angry Orchard?"

"Good stuff. You ever had it?" He formed a pile of ground beef into a patty.

"Yeah, I just didn't figure you for anything other than a Bud guy." She popped the caps off of two bottles.

"Stick around. There's lots of things you'll learn about me." He smiled at her and prepared another patty.

She slid a bottle his way and then tipped hers back in a long swallow. "We'll see."

Just as he was about to reply, Cyn burped—a very unladylike burp.

Shane threw his head back and laughed. Loud and hard. Cyn's eyes went wide, and she covered her mouth, her cheeks going bright red. Shane laughed harder. When he finally got himself slightly composed, he leaned toward her, let out another chuckle and kissed her cheek. "Girl, *that* was awesome."

Cyn was mortified, and her face burned hot with embarrassment. She hadn't meant to let that burp fly; it just sort of erupted from her. Shane thought it was hilarious, obviously…the man was still chuckling as he finished preparing the burgers and then took them outside to the grill.

She took another swig of her beer and read through Carlos's texts again. He'd started with the usual, "Baby, I miss you and love you," crap, but when she hadn't replied, he'd started being a dick, calling her out on reading and not replying. Cyn navigated to the "settings" screen on her iPhone and turned off the "read receipt" notice. Now, he wouldn't know if she'd read his messages or not.

Just then, another message rolled in from him. Cyn swiped the screen to read it.

Carlos: Why are you doing this?

She stared at the text for a long time, debating whether or

not to answer him. If she didn't, he might just keep texting all night. If she did, he might see it as some sort of invitation or open door. Cyn blew out an exasperated breath. "Fuck it." She typed out a message to him.

> Cyn: Understand this, please...beyond this reply, I have nothing to say to you, and I want you to leave me alone. Please. Just let me move on, and you move on too. Take care, Carlos.

> Carlos: There's a ton of things to discuss, baby. Please just meet me for coffee, hear me out. If you're still not interested once I'm done talking, then you can walk away and never look back.

> Cyn dragged her teeth over her bottom lip. Maybe if she went and met him, heard him out, he'd leave her alone. But it wasn't like Carlos ever respected her needs before, so why the hell would he now?

> Carlos: Cyn, please, baby?

She sighed and rolled her eyes.

> Cyn: I'll think about it.

The hair on the back of her neck stood on end with annoyance—annoyance with herself and with Carlos. She set the phone to vibrate and tossed it in her purse. If he texted again, she wouldn't hear it, which was for the best. Shane had already picked up on her change in mood when the first texts rolled in. She wasn't about to taint the evening further with having a discussion about it.

Brushing off her agitation, she drew in a cleansing breath and peeked her head out of the back door. "Can I get anything started in here?"

Shane closed the lid on the grill and came toward her. "Nope."

"I'm feeling a little helpless." She smiled.

"Or, you could choose to feel at ease while someone else takes a little care of you." He smoothed his palms up her arms, bent his head and kissed her.

Cyn cupped his face in her palms and stroked her tongue over his. Shane's scent and taste permeated every inch of her mind and body, washing away any remaining frustration and lighting a fire within her core in its wake. She moaned into his mouth as Shane wrapped his arms around her waist, pulling her tight against his hard body.

What exactly it was about him that got her motor running, she wasn't sure. Cyn just knew that when he kissed her, her body erupted into a flaming ball of desire. And she couldn't get enough.

Shane hooked his hands under her arms and lifted her in the air. Christ, he was strong. Cyn whimpered as a thrill zipped down her spine. Wrapping her legs around him, she deepened the kiss. A frantic clash of tongue, teeth and lips sent lust racing through her veins, and all she could think about was getting naked with him—like immediately.

With a tight grip on her ass, he hiked her higher. And then they were moving. Shane broke from her lips. "Goddamn, Cyn."

Cyn rolled her pelvis, rubbing against his erection. "Fuck me on the kitchen table." She licked his neck.

"I should make you wait a little longer, but since you're little miss impatient tonight, and my dick is rock hard, I think I'll do just that."

Her ass met the hardwood of her kitchen table, and Shane yanked her tank top over her head. Her bra went with it, and before she could untangle the fabric from her arms, he bent his head and sucked one tight nipple into his hot mouth as he gripped the other in his free hand. Shane bit the tight bud, then sucked it between his lips again. Cyn gasped, her head fell back, and with her arms still caught in her shirt, she clasped her hands together behind her back. His mouth on her tits was the best thing ever—*the* best!

"Love your tits." He moved to the other, sucking and biting the erect flesh.

"Shane! God, yes, just like that."

He pulled away and moved his hands to her jeans. "Need to get these off you."

"Need to get my top and bra untangled too." She giggled.

Shane tilted his head to the side, and a slow smile arched his mouth. "Nah, I think I'll keep you tangled."

"Oh! Ha. All right then." She licked her lips, and Shane let out a growl. For fuck's sake, she loved when he did that too.

He slid her off the table, popped the button on her jeans and drew the zipper down. With one swift motion, he pulled her jeans to her ankles and off her feet. In the next breath, he turned her and pressed her chest down to the tabletop. The cool wood was an intoxicating contrast on her heated breasts and stomach, and Cyn let out a gasp. She felt a tug on her tangled top and bra, and then, the fabric was pulled tighter. She grinned. "Oh shit."

She couldn't see him, but definitely heard his movements as he slid on a condom behind her. And then, like he'd done before, his hand landed on her ass cheek with a loud *CRACK!* Cyn gasped and went up on tiptoe. "Shane!"

"Fucking love your ass too." He smoothed his palm over the stinging spot before gripping both buttocks, spreading her ass cheeks apart. "Girl, I'm gonna have this ass. Not tonight, but soon."

She groaned, arching her back further. Every time he called her girl, Cyn's insides turned to molten lava. It was like the word had been dipped in undiluted lust. She'd been called babe, baby, honey—any number of endearments over the years, but never girl. When Shane called her girl, he said it with the slight Southern twang he'd acquired, and it just plain and simply did it for her. In a big fucking way. "Want that." Her voice was breathless as tingles spread from her ass to her clit.

"I know you do." He slid the shaft between her legs, parting the lips of her pussy with the blunt head. Back and forth, he teased the mouth of her cunt, dipping the tip barely inside but sliding past it to drag over her clit again. Cyn arched with each pass, desperate for him to bury himself inside her, riding the wave of need he built within her. Shane bent over her, cupped her chin in his big palm and slid his thumb into her mouth. "Make it nice and slick for me."

She moaned around his thumb, rolling her tongue and sucking. He pulled it from her mouth as he moved off her, and she felt the blunt head of his cock part her folds again. In one thrust, he drove inside her channel and slipped his thumb into her asshole at the same time.

The thickness of his prick and thumb stretched both of her openings, and a harsh gasp burst from her lungs. Cyn clasped her hands together tightly, straining against the fabric binding her arms. "Oh fuck! Yes!"

"Ah, fuck yeah! I feel you clenching around me."

She was overcome, stuffed full of him and wanting nothing more than for him to fuck her hard, fast and without mercy. "Shane…" Her voice came out on a whimper, but Cyn didn't care. She was desperate for him—desperate for the place she knew he'd take her. "Please?"

With one ass cheek still gripped tight in his hand, Shane drew out, then slammed back into her. Cyn gritted her teeth, pressed her forehead to the cool wood of the tabletop and gave herself over to him.

SHANE LET GO of Cyn's delectable ass cheek and grabbed hold of the tank top he'd secured around her arms, using it for leverage to yank her back onto his cock. Every inch of his skin tingled in hyper-awareness of her. Her hairless tight cunt, her even tighter asshole, her full ass as it jiggled each time he banged his hips against her...fucking hell—those things on their own were enough to drive a sane man crazy. But all of her combined was almost more than he could bear.

Cyn was a fantasy and wet dream come to life.

Shane gritted his teeth, stroked his thumb in and out of her tight ass, and shuttled in and out of her tight pussy. Hard and deep, exactly how he knew she needed it. Taking his thumb from her ass, he bent over her and nipped her ear. "That sweet clit need some attention?"

"Yes, please."

"Mmm. So sweet." Shane raised one of her knees onto the table. The shift in angle forced his cock deeper, and she let out a guttural moan. He reached around her hip and pressed his fingers to her clit. "Can't get enough of you."

She tilted her hips back. "Oh God, yes. Fuck, just like that."

"Gonna come for me?" He rubbed little circles on her clit.

"Yes! Fuck, yes!" She scratched at the skin of his stomach.

With a growl, Shane thrust his hips, keeping himself buried deep inside her. His balls tightened, and his orgasm tingled at the base of his spine. Her scent swirled in his nose, drowning him. Her little moans and pleas shot straight to the head of his prick, making it swell further. "Come for me, girl. Come on my dick." Cyn rocked her hips, and her tight channel clenched around his shaft. "Fuck yes, that's what I want to feel." Shane kept pressure on her clit with his fingers and continued stroking deep in her channel.

"Yes! Shane!" Raising her head off the table, Cyn screamed, and her cunt clamped down on his dick in rapid little spasms.

Shane's orgasm hit like a freight train. With a growl, he gritted his teeth and buried his forehead in the center of her back. Deep in her core, he froze as his dick jerked, spurting his climax inside the condom.

His orgasm felt endless, his cock twitching in release as her cunt spasmed around his thickness. Christ Almighty, Shane thought he'd come hard with her the last time they'd had sex, but this time he'd come even harder. It was amazing. She was amazing. Shane was so blown away he was sure he'd never get his fill of her.

Still trying to catch his breath, he gave her shoulder a soft kiss before rising off of her. He made quick work of untangling her arms and then helped her to her feet. She was still breathing heavy as he turned her and held her to his chest. "You okay?"

"Mm-hmm." She circled her arms around his waist. "Perfect."

Shane kissed the top of her head. Yeah, perfect was the best word for it. "Me too."

"I think you probably burned the burgers." She giggled.

"Shit!" He laughed. "Better go check on those, huh? Some cook I turned out to be."

She glanced up at him, her smile brighter than the sun. Shane melted. Screw the burgers, he could always make more. He bent his head and covered her mouth with his. Desire swirled in his belly, and he knew he'd want her again. A.S.A.P.

After all, who cared about food when she was all the meal he needed.

CHAPTER EIGHTEEN

Cyn eyed the clock, then slid from beneath the cradle of Shane's arms and out of bed. It was after four a.m., and she couldn't sleep. Well, she was asleep or passed out, rather, after a marathon round of sex. Incredible sex. Mind-blowing, life-altering, unable-to-walk-properly-for-days sex. But now, sleep was playing hide-and-seek with her and considering Cyn was doing the seeking, she was losing.

She yawned, stretching her arms over her head. In the dimness of the room, she glanced over her shoulder at the sleeping man in her bed. Shane Conlon—Shane-motherfuck-ing-Conlon was asleep in her bed. Again. She had a feeling he'd be occupying the left side of her king-sized mattress the remainder of the week.

There was a time in her life she would've paid every penny she had to have him in her bed. Of course, as a teenager, that amounted to a couple hundred bucks in her savings account, but still. She'd have paid it for the chance to have him next to her in bed just once. Though at that age, she'd only fantasized about making out with him until her lips fell off. And maybe letting him get to second, possibly third base. But really, the heavy crush she'd had on him, she might've let him go all the way.

After throwing on Shane's T-shirt, she migrated to the kitchen and fished her phone from her purse. Her eyes went wide when she looked at the notifications. Fifteen text messages. *Fifteen?* All of them from Carlos. *Holy shit.* "For fuck's sake, really?" Unlocking the phone, she pulled up the message inbox. Cyn rubbed her forehead, took a seat at the table, and glanced over them.

They'd started out normal or nice enough anyway. But as each message went unanswered by her, they'd gotten progressively worse. Maybe he'd been drinking because why else would he be acting this nuts? Regardless, Carlos was starting to get a little crazy and maybe even a little scary. The last message had been sent barely an hour ago. Cyn read it over, her eyes getting even wider than they already were.

> Carlos: YOU FUCKING WHORE!!! I drove by your house. Whose SUV is that in your driveway? Fucking bitch… I can't believe you're doing this to me. You're going to be sorry you ever met me, Cyn!

There was no maybe about it. Carlos had officially gone crazy *and* scary. Cyn swallowed and debated what to do. She moved to the fridge and grabbed a bottle of water. And that's when anger spiked through her like a wildfire. Who in the hell did he think he was talking to? Fuck that. And fuck him. Cyn leaned against the counter and tapped out a message.

> Cyn: I don't know who in the hell you think you're talking to like that, but you can take your filthy insults and save them for the bitch you were fucking around with behind my back. I'm done with you, Carlos. Fuck off!

She hit the Send button and stared at the screen a

moment before setting the phone on the counter. Fury boiled in her stomach and burned the back of her throat. Cyn was a Donnelly woman—that meant she was independent and took care of herself.

It also meant she took no shit.

From anyone.

It was how she was raised, never mind the fact that she'd done her fair share of arguing and battling with her siblings. She was a damn seasoned veteran. Carlos better step the fuck back because there was no way in *hell* she was going to tolerate any more of his shit.

Tipping the bottle of water back, Cyn took a long swallow.

"Hey, you okay?"

Startled, she jumped—pretty much out of her skin—and spilled water down the front of Shane's shirt she was wearing. She swiped her hand down her chest. "Jesus, you scared the hell out of me!"

"Sorry." Shane moved to her. "Easy, it's just water." He took the bottle from her, grabbed the dishtowel by the sink and handed it to her. "Why are you up?"

She wiped the towel down her arms and thigh. "I couldn't sleep." She glanced at Shane just as he crossed his arms over his very bare, not to mention sexy-as-hell chest. In that position, his biceps bulged, and his abs got tight, and Cyn's mouth watered. *Good Lord.* She licked her lips.

"Why couldn't you sleep?" He circled her wrist with his hand and pulled her to him.

Cyn laid her palms out on his warm chest and smiled up at him. "Just couldn't. No biggie."

His brow furrowed, and he sighed through his nose. "Ya know, let me explain something to you. In case you forgot, I've known you damn near your whole life. Because of that—"

"Shane, I know you—"

"Shhh." He placed a finger to her mouth. Cyn pursed her

lips and rolled her eyes. He cocked one brow and continued. "Because of that, I was lucky enough to see you in action during your rebellious teen phase."

He pulled his finger away, and Cyn took this to mean it was her turn to talk. "So? I saw plenty of your rebellious phase, too. Your point?"

Shane pulled her a little closer and smoothed one hand down her back to her ass. "My point is, I witnessed you spin tales. Total lies to your parents about where you were and what you'd been up to. So, realize this: you have tells. And I know all of them."

Cyn bit her bottom lip. Shit, did he really know her tells? Did she even really have tells? She frowned. "I don't have tells."

He kissed the tip of her nose. "Girl, quit arguing and just admit I'm right."

Shit. Fuck. Hell. Sonofabitch. She sighed. "Okay, whatever. So I have tells. Still don't know what your point is." She looked away, trying to ignore how awesomely good his body felt. And also trying to ignore the fact that his protective alpha male demeanor was a total turn-on. She was more than ready to show him how much she liked it…by getting on her knees and sucking his cock until he shot down her throat. *What the hell is wrong with me?*

"What's up, Cyn?" He glanced at her phone on the counter. "More texts?"

Cyn bit her tongue. She didn't want to talk about it with him, or anyone really. But she had a feeling he wasn't going to let it go. "Yes. More texts. But it's fine now. I handled it."

"You want to tell me who's upsetting you?"

"What makes you think I'm upset?" The man cocked his head to the side with an expression on his face that screamed, "Seriously?" *Good Christ.* Cyn drew in a deep breath and blew it out. "Okay, fine. It was Carlos. My ex-boyfriend."

He smoothed his hands up her back. "And?"

"He wants to talk. I don't want to talk, and so he's being a dick about it."

Shane's brows drew together. "Define being a dick."

Cyn shrugged as she trailed her fingertips over his collarbone. "You know, like people can sometimes be when they don't get their way. But I handled it." Desire swirled low in her tummy, and she rose and kissed his neck. "Let's go back to bed."

A soft groan came out of him, and he slid his hands back down to her ass. "How did you handle it?"

She took his reaction as an opportunity to navigate away from the topic of Carlos and smoothed one hand over his shoulder to the back of his neck. "I told him to fuck off." She smiled and licked just below his ear.

"Don't think I don't know you're trying to distract me with your hot tongue." He squeezed her ass cheeks tight in his palms.

Cyn giggled and nipped his earlobe. "Is it working?"

"No."

Like hell, it wasn't working. Cyn trailed her tongue down the side of his neck, nibbling the sensitive skin along the way. His big body shuddered against her, and she smiled. "Liar."

<hr>

SHANE DELIVERED a stinging slap to one of Cyn's butt cheeks, and she yelped and then went back to sucking at his neck. She was right, he'd lied about being distracted, but she didn't need to know that. His dick thickened in his boxer briefs, and he pulled her tighter against him. "Temptress."

"Mmm. Look who's talking." Cyn kissed down his chest to his stomach as she went to her knees. "You do your fair share of tempting, too." She gazed up at him and licked her lips.

Shane's stomach dropped at the sight of her kneeling in

front of him, and he swallowed his groan. "You looking for something down there?"

Hooking one finger in the waistband of his boxer briefs, she slid the material over the head of his erection. "Yep."

Gazing down at Cyn, he cupped her cheek and swiped his thumb over her bottom lip. "This conversation isn't over. Just on hold."

She raised a single brow. "If you insist."

"Take what's yours, then."

Her eyes flared, and without hesitation, she sucked him to the back of her throat, moaning around his thickness. Tingles danced up his cock to his balls, spreading through his body. Goddamn, her mouth was like heaven.

Shane slid his fingers through her hair and gripped the soft strands at the back of her head. She moaned again, drawing him in and out of her warm mouth as she cradled his sac in her palm.

Shane's knees buckled, and he grabbed the counter with his free hand to hold himself steady. "Fucking love the way you work your mouth on me."

She glanced up at him, her brown eyes alive with fire, as she pulled him from her mouth and licked down his length to his balls. In the darkness of her kitchen, Shane was a goner. Totally spun on Cyn. He knew, without a doubt, he'd never want anyone else.

Ever again. Because he was hers.

CHAPTER NINETEEN

Impatience had brought Cyn to Shane's mother's house in search of him. She knocked on the front door and waited. After sending a few texts and getting no answer and also hitting his voicemail, she'd decided to pop on by. There was a question she wanted to ask him. His rental SUV was in the driveway, so she figured he had to be there. She knocked again and crossed her arms, rocking her hips from side to side.

The door swung open, and Cyn's head spun at the sight of what greeted her. A bare chest leading to faded blue jeans hanging low on his lean hips made Cyn's stomach clench. All that muscle, glistening with a light coating of sweat—Mother of all the saints, he looked good—had desire pulsing through her, arrowing straight to her clit.

"Hi." He crossed his arms, and Cyn groaned.

"For the love of God, you're killing me. You look so fucking good, I can't stand it." She brushed past him into the house. "It's not even fair." She turned to look at him after he closed the door. "In fact, it should be illegal."

"What?" His lips curved into a devious smile, and Cyn knew her panties were now wet.

Yeah, he knew exactly the effect he had on women. He

must. But then again, he wasn't an arrogant asshole, so maybe he didn't. Maybe he just knew the effect he had on her. "I want to suck your cock so bad right now, I can't even see straight."

He frowned. "Girl, you're crazy. I'm all sweaty and funky. No way I'd let you."

Like she cared. Scary thing was normally she would care because, eww, gross. But the truth was, she didn't care. It was Shane's sweat and funk, and his scent was like heaven on earth to her. Desire thrummed through her limbs, and the need to taste him invaded her mind. It was all she could do not to lick every drop of sweat from his skin right that moment. "Wanna bet?"

"Cyn." He ran his palm over his hair. "What'm I gonna do with you?"

She took a step closer. "Kiss me."

"Come on, now. I'm all sweaty." He chuckled.

Oh fuck this. Cyn pulled his arms away from his muscled chest, leaned in and licked a line up the center of his pecs. His salty flavor hit her tongue, and her pussy clenched. "Fucking hell, you taste good."

Shane cupped the back of her head. "Holy…damn."

"Are we alone?" She swirled her tongue around one areola.

"Yeah. But…"

She moved to the other, sucked the peak into her mouth and smoothed her hands down his abs. She could not get enough of him. "But what?"

Shane grabbed her by the shoulders and straightened her. "Cyn, look, I can appreciate all that you're doing right now. Honestly, the idea of fucking you in my mother's house is a damn good one. But we need to finish our conversation from last night."

"Ugh, I don't want to talk about Carlos." Cyn cringed, hating how whiny she sounded. The texts had started up again that morning, about five minutes after she'd gotten to her office. They hadn't gotten any worse, but they hadn't gotten any better either.

Shane led her into the kitchen and ordered her to sit. "Have you heard from him again?"

Cyn blew out a breath. Obviously, he wasn't going to let the topic rest. This was the downside of a through-and-through alpha male. They were protectors by nature. And Shane was definitely a strong, dominant man, determined to protect her. "Yes. But it's no big deal."

He moved to the refrigerator, took out a bottle of water and handed it to her. "Why do I get the feeling it's becoming a big deal?"

"Because you're being paranoid?" Cyn cracked open the bottle and took a sip of the cold liquid.

"No, actually, I'm being smart and trusting my instincts." He leaned his ass against the counter and crossed his arms and then his feet at the ankle.

Dammit, he was being annoying. But at least he looked hot doing it. Honestly, Cyn understood his concern—didn't agree, but understood. At the heart of it, he was looking out for her. Something he'd been doing, along with her older siblings, since they were kids. And she couldn't help but appreciate him for it. "Don't you want to know why I came over here?"

"You're changing the subject."

"Duh, of course, I am. I said I didn't want to talk about Carlos." She laughed. "Anyway, a friend of mine, Tarra Layne, is singing tonight, and I want to go see her show. I want to know if you'd like to come with me."

He stared at her from across the kitchen for what felt like forever. She couldn't read his expression, and nerves started to raise the hair on the back of her neck. What if he didn't want to hang out with her outside of the bedroom? But this wasn't supposed to be anything more than the bedroom anyway.

Crap. Maybe she shouldn't have asked. *What am I doing?* She should tell him never mind. "You kno—"

"A date, Cyn?"

Cyn frowned as surprise took the place of her nerves. "I don't know if I'd call it that." Getting to her feet, she moved to him. She hadn't thought about it as a date until he said something. Dating was not something she wanted to be doing. Fucking him, yes. Dating? Not in the cards. "How about just a couple of old friends going out to hear some kick-ass live music?"

"Old friends, huh? Who you calling old anyway?" He shook his head and ran his warm palm down her arm. "What time?"

Cyn shivered. Good grief, her body was beyond hypersensitive to his touch. "She goes on stage at nine. We can grab some food close by where she's playing."

"Dinner and a show? Dunno, it kinda sounds like a date to me." His lips curled into a grin.

She swatted his arm. This was so *not* a date. It couldn't be…could it? *Shit.* Maybe it was. "Knock it off, Sergeant."

Shane laughed and pulled her to him for a kiss. When he let her go, she was breathless, and her body had turned into one big ball of arousal. She gazed up at him, lust swirling hot in her belly.

"I want you," he whispered.

"Take me." She trailed her fingers down his sides, enjoying the play of muscles beneath her touch. "Any way and anywhere you want to."

Shane's eyes flared, and he grabbed her hand and walked her toward the stairs. "Gonna be a quickie."

"Yee-haw! Don't hear me complaining." She grinned as she climbed the steps behind him.

When they got into his childhood bedroom, Shane slammed the door. "Pants off now."

"Fuck yes." Cyn barely had the button undone on her

jeans before he was at her lips, sucking and nipping at her tongue. He shoved his pants down, and his erection rose hot and hard between them. Cyn gripped it in both hands, stroking. He groaned into her mouth and yanked her shirt up, then shoved her pants down.

She got one leg free of the denim, and Shane fell onto his back on the bed, taking her with him. Cyn straddled his hips, positioned the thick head at her opening—Shane groaned and grabbed her, halting her movement. "Condom, Cyn."

"Shit. Fuck." She looked over at his jeans on the floor. "You got one in your wallet?"

"Yep."

Hopping off, she yanked his wallet from his jeans, flipped it open, found the condom and tossed it to him. "On. Now. Jesus Christ, I'm dripping down my thighs. I'm so wet for you."

"I know. The head of my dick just got a taste of your honey." He grinned and slid the latex down his shaft.

Cyn got herself back into position. "Fast and hard, Shane."

"Girl—"

Cyn slid down his prick, taking every inch of him as deep as he'd go. She threw her head back and fucked him. Rode him fast and hard like they both needed. Shane sucked her nipples and held tight to her hips as she rocked back and forth. It was so fucking good that when she came, barely three minutes later, she saw stars, and her limbs tingled.

There was something to be said for quickies. They were so worth it. So very fucking worth every hot second they lasted.

SHANE SAT NEXT to Cyn in a dim bar in downtown Pasadena, listening to a gorgeous, longhaired redhead belt out song after song. Cyn was right, the singer was talented. Shane leaned over and placed a kiss on Cyn's cheek. She smiled and touched her face where his lips had been.

She always looked so surprised whenever he showed her any sort of affection. Shane liked that he inspired such a genuine reaction from her, but he also wondered if there was something else behind it.

A woman shouldn't look shocked when being paid attention to. They should expect it. He was an affectionate man, always had been, and with Cyn, he found himself touching her constantly. He held her hand. Stroked his fingers over her cheek. Played with her hair. Caressed her leg. All without thought because touching her felt natural. "Why do you always look so shocked when I touch you?"

She leaned close. "What?"

He laughed and bent to her ear. Clearly, now was not the time to ask. "Nothing. You want another drink?"

"Sure." She returned her attention to the stage as the beat of a slow song began. "Oh God! I love this song." She glanced at Shane. "It's called 'Difference'. She just made a video for it, too. Amazing."

Shane signaled the waitress and ordered them another round. Leaning back in his seat, he put his arm around Cyn as she sang along with the love song about broken hearts and people failing at relationships. It was a sad and truthful ballad, and the depth of feeling that Cyn's friend, Tarra, sang the lyrics with wrapped around him, making his heart ache.

Shane hoped like hell he'd never have to experience sprouting feelings for someone and not having them returned.

He glanced at Cyn. Her expression was solemn as she watched her friend sing. He'd already sprouted feelings for her. Somewhere between all the sex and talking, in less than two weeks, his heart had opened up and leapt right into Cyn's hands. He doubted she knew she was holding it.

By the time the song was over, Shane had fallen deep into his thoughts—and now fears—that maybe Cyn wouldn't return the feelings he had for her. But it was crazy to expect anything from her. After all, he was leaving at the end of the week and considering he lived more than a few states away, the distance would make things difficult. He'd visit for sure, and maybe she'd visit him too, but it would still be less than ideal.

The singer stepped off the stage and headed straight for their table. Cyn stood and hugged her friend before turning to him. "Tarra, this is Shane Conlon. I've known him pretty much my whole life."

"How awesome! It's so good to meet you. Thanks for coming out," Tarra said.

Shane shook her hand. "It was a pleasure. You're extremely talented."

"Ah, thanks." Tarra motioned to her band with a smile. "We're giving it hell for sure. So, Angie couldn't make it?"

"Not tonight. Not sure where she's at, actually. She missed a great show, though. You want a drink?" Cyn motioned to the bar.

"Water, please." She fanned herself. "Is it hot in here, or is it just me?" Tarra took a seat at their table. "She's supposed to do a write-up on 'Difference' this month."

"God, I love that song! It's so perfect." Cyn took her seat. "And yeah, it's pretty freaking hot in here, but then again, so are you up on that stage." Cyn winked, and right on queue, her friend rolled her eyes.

"I'll grab your water, Tarra." Shane bent and kissed Cyn on the top of her head. "You need anything besides water, babe?"

She smiled up at him. "Nope. I'm good."

Shane stepped away and grabbed three waters. When he returned, he resumed his spot next to Cyn. Their un-date night had been a good one. Dinner and some incredible live music, ending with Cyn alight with her usual bubbly personality. Shane leaned back and soaked up the moments like a sponge. Every so often, as she chatted with her friend, Cyn reached over and smoothed her hand down his thigh. He soaked that up, too. Shane had a feeling he wouldn't have many opportunities to be like this with her, and he didn't want to miss a second of it.

CHAPTER TWENTY

Shane checked his cell after cleaning up the painting
equipment in his mother's formal living room. With a smile,
he read the text from Cyn. She was having dinner at the
Donnelly house, and he was expected to join.

> Shane: I'll be there. Need me to bring anything?

Cyn: You know better than that.

> Shane: True. Gonna stop by your place and clean up first.

Cyn: Cool. Grab my blue sweat jacket from the hall closet, please?

> Shane: So much for not needing to bring anything. Lol

Cyn: Yeah, yeah. I'll make it up to you later.

> Shane: Holding you to that.

Cyn: Hope so. See you soon.

Shane slid his phone into his back pocket and finished gathering the tools. Tomorrow, after laying down the trim, the room would be done. In less than a week, he'd be on a plane back to Texas. He didn't want to go, but other than not wanting to leave the woman he'd spent every spare moment with over the last week, he had no reason to stay.

There was a business and a life to get back to in Texas. Though thanks to Cyn, Shane feared the life part of that package would now be lacking. Damn, if that didn't just suck to high heaven.

Once he was done at his mother's, he drove to Cyn's house. He'd moved his things from Joey's place after their un-date on Monday night and had stayed with Cyn the rest of the week. The time with her had been out-of-this-world amazing. They'd had sex in pretty much every corner of her house and always in her bed in the morning.

The sex has been mind-blowing. But falling asleep with her cradled tight in his arms and waking up with her warm, soft body pressed against him had been the best parts of each day.

How in the fuck he was going to give her up, Shane had no idea. He just knew he had to go. They hadn't talked about it at all, plus she hadn't mentioned anything about wanting him to stay—hadn't even hinted around it. Which kind of sucked, but he wasn't going to read into it.

Not wanting to spoil what little time they had together, Shane hadn't mentioned his impending departure either. It was just this unspoken thing that hovered over everything. And that definitely sucked too.

Shane grabbed Cyn's blue hoodie and headed out the door to her parents' house. An evening at the Donnellys would be awesome, too. Jimmy and his girl, Sonja, and her daughter, Casey, were still in town. Ryan and Maiya weren't leaving for their honeymoon in Paris until Saturday, so they'd be at dinner, too.

The Donnelly clan had grown by leaps and bounds with all the marriages and kids being brought into the world. He was beyond grateful to still be considered part of the family. But tonight, he'd be by Cyn's side, and Shane had no clue if the rest of the clan knew they'd been together pretty much since he'd gotten back into town. Joey knew, of course, and Ryan did, too. If Ryan knew, then Jimmy definitely knew. Angie and Celia for sure knew. As far as everyone else, Shane had no idea. It wasn't something he should be worried about, but he couldn't help but feel a tad nervous at what their reaction would be.

Brushing off his unease, Shane stepped up to the front door and raised his hand to knock.

Angie swung the door wide before his knuckle connected with the wood. "You know better than to knock." She stepped aside and ushered him in.

"It's been a long time, so I wasn't going to assume, Angie. Good to see you." He bent and placed a kiss on her cheek.

She closed the door and linked her arm inside his. "Don't matter how long it's been. Family is family, Shane."

"Thanks, Angela." He smiled at her as they walked down the main hallway to the kitchen. Mrs. Donnelly was at the counter mixing up her famous potato salad. Shane moved straight to her and held his arms open. "Can I get a hug from my favorite Mom?"

"Of course you can!" A warm smile graced her elegant face as she wiped her hands on the towel. Rising on tiptoe, she wrapped her arms around his shoulders. "So good to have you home, Shane."

He kissed her cheek. "It's been really good to be home. Can I help you with anything?"

"Yes!" She pursed her lips and raised one brow. "You can take your handsome self out of my way and to the backyard."

Angie laughed. "You know better than to ask something like that. Boy, you *are* slipping."

Shane shook his head and sighed. "Just being polite."

"You always were a polite boy. By the way, Cyn's been waiting for you and driving everyone crazy in the meantime." Mrs. Donnelly winked at him. "I've had to kick her out of the kitchen three times already. So, hurry and let her know you're here before Mary tries to rein her in, and the hair pulling begins."

Apparently, Mrs. Donnelly was aware he and Cyn had been spending time together. That woman always knew more than any of the Donnelly kids gave her credit for, which, of course, always got them into more trouble. Some things never changed. "You got it, Mrs. D."

"See? Always polite." She nodded at Angie. "You and your siblings could take a few lessons from Shane." She patted his shoulder. "But, Shane, you can call me Roseanne now."

Shane frowned. He wasn't sure if he could. "I… But, Mrs…" She put her hands on her hips and tilted her head to the side. Shit. Yeah, okay. Polite or not, she wasn't going to take no for an answer. "Yes, ma'am."

She rolled her eyes and moved back to the potato salad. "It's a start. Now shoo. I need to finish cooking for an army." She stirred the spoon in the bowl. "Not you, Angie. You stay. But go find Celia first. I need her, too."

Angie pouted. "Aw, Mom. I want to go see if Mary and Cyn are gonna duke it out."

"There won't be any of that." Shane walked toward the back door. "You have my word on it, Mrs. D—Roseanne."

"That's better." Roseanne smiled. "Thank you, Shane."

Shane stepped just out of earshot as Cyn's mother started giving Angie instructions on what she needed done. No doubt Angie would be along soon enough, though. Shane stepped out to the back patio and found Cyn in the middle of the yard. She was running in circles with a gaggle of kids chasing her, a red dodgeball tucked tight in her arms.

She glanced over and stopped short as soon as she caught his gaze…and a big, bright smile spread across her lips.

All the air left Shane's body like he'd been sucker punched in the stomach. Fucking hell, she was beautiful. Six more days was all he had left with her, including the rest of today, as well as the day he was flying out.

He better make the most of it because leaving her was going to suck more than he could imagine.

Cyn spotted Shane as soon as he stepped foot onto her parent's back patio. As always, she lost herself in his beauty and bulk. He was utterly perfect physically. Damn near perfect in every other way, too.

"Auntie Cyn, throw the ball!" Mary's son, Cam Jr., yelled as he ran past her.

Cyn shook herself, focusing back on the kids just as Tori, Katie's daughter, tackled Cam, taking him to the grass. "Man down!" Tori rolled over, laughing.

"That's not how dodgeball works, Tori!" Cam got to his feet and ran after her.

"Hey, hey. Break it up." The kids ignored Cyn, and then Jacob came running over to join in the fray. "Come on, you guys." Ah, the hell with it. She loved the kids, but she had other things on her mind now. Cyn tossed the ball into the growing pile of children and walked toward the tall drink of water, watching her with his arms crossed and a smirk on his face, she couldn't wait to kiss off.

As she got closer, her heart raced in anticipation of touching him. She'd spent a lot of time touching all that hard-muscled yumminess in the last week. And she hadn't yet had her fill. He was leaving soon, and Cyn didn't want to think about it, had refused to even allow the thoughts to surface. The one time she'd given his too-soon departure any light, her heart had sunk in her chest…and that meant feelings had shown up.

Feelings were not supposed to bloom in her heart for Shane Conlon. Hell, they weren't supposed to bloom for anyone. Cyn was supposed to be single right now, figuring her shit out. That'd been her plan until Shane showed up with all his fineness, flipping some unknown switch in her body with his magic tongue and cock.

The new plan was to have a lot of really incredible sex with Shane until he left, and then get down to business. So far, she'd been on course, or so she thought. Until now. *Dammit.* A severe case of the feels hadn't been factored into the budget. If she let the feels out to play, she'd never get back to her goal.

Plus… Shane was leaving…going home to Texas. Sure, she'd get back on track, but what worried her was that she'd now be doing it with a longing heart. And there was definitely no freaking budget for that, either.

When she reached him, Shane dropped his arms to his sides and gazed down at her. His blue eyes sparkled in the fading sunlight, and Cyn wanted to drown in them. "Been wondering when you were gonna get here." She pulled him down, circling her arms around his neck.

Shane smiled, and his hands went right to her waist, sliding around to her lower back. "I'm here, girl."

"Yeah, you are." Cyn licked her lips, and Shane's eyes darted to her mouth. She loved that he paid attention to the little mindless habit she had, turning it into something she tried to always do in front of him now. Almost every time, it earned her a kiss. "Come here, baby."

"Told you, I'm here." His features, along with his tone, softened, and he stroked a hair away from her eyes.

"Yeah, but I need you here." Cyn pressed her lips to his. Shane moaned, slid one hand up her back and into her hair as he pulled her closer with the other. God, he tasted good, like mint and a flavor that was all Shane. Careful to keep the kiss

G-rated in front of the kids, she broke from his lips and pressed her forehead to his chin. "That's where I needed you."

He pressed a kiss to the top of her head. "You got me. Anytime you want me."

A shiver ran through her. He'd been saying things like that to her the last day or so. She wasn't sure if he meant them, considering he was leaving. But he was wrong because soon enough, she wouldn't be able to have him anytime she wanted.

He'd go, and she'd have nothing… *Fuck!*

The goddamn feels had for sure taken hold, dragging her into the deep end of the pool.

Cyn let out a sigh and ran her hands down Shane's arms. She glanced over just as Angie stepped outside, and Maiya and Celia walked out right behind her. All three stopped and looked at Cyn like they could see it, too.

What the fuck was she going to do now?

* * *

Cyn sat on the bed, legs curled under her, in the bedroom she and Mary had shared as kids. After everyone had finished dinner and dessert, Maiya, Angie and Celia had dragged her away from Shane's side and brought her upstairs.

"What are you going to do?" Angie rolled to her side on the bed and propped her head in her hand.

"Fuck if I know. I didn't plan this." Cyn tucked a lock of hair behind her ear.

Maiya laughed and stretched out on her stomach. "Chica, the good stuff is never planned. You should know that."

"Yeah, but Maiya, he's leaving. Talk about piss-poor timing." Celia sat on the edge of the mattress and stroked Cyn's hair.

Cyn groaned. "Exactly."

"I know it's complicated, but maybe you should just go

with the flow and see what happens?" Maiya rubbed Cyn's thigh.

"Maybe it's a good thing that he goes. I mean, it might make the being single plan easier. I'm still game to do it with you." Angie picked at her eyelashes.

"Right, because I'll be all sad and pathetic, so I won't even bother looking at other guys." Cyn dropped her face into her palms and then drove her fingers into her hair. "Ugghh! What a fucking disaster."

"When does he go?" Angie laid her head down on the mattress.

Cyn stretched out, resting her head on Angie's hip. "Six days. Well, technically, five if I don't count the day he actually goes back to his life in Texas."

Celia stroked her fingers through Cyn's hair again. "Better make the most of it."

"Tell me what to do. I mean, isn't that what you're all supposed to be doing right now?" She looked between the three of them, all too aware of the desperation threading her tone.

"Chica, you gotta do what's right for you." Maiya clasped Cyn's hand.

"Maybe the long-distance thing might work. Or—" Angie groaned.

Cyn looked up at her. "Or what?"

Angie pursed her lips. "Can't believe I'm going to say this, but have you thought maybe you could move to Texas?"

"Are you insane, Angie? I can't—" Cyn pushed herself up to a sitting position. "I have a business to run, plus family and all my friends here. No way am I moving to Texas."

"Okay, breathe, firecracker." Angie laughed. "You know I don't want you to go. You're like my best friend, next to my best friend, of course, but you know what I mean. I love you, Cyn. I'd be heartbroken if you left."

Maiya frowned. "Angie, jeez. What if the only way for

them to be together is if she has to move there? You'd support her, and you know it."

Good Christ, they practically had her packed up and living in Texas already. Cyn just wanted to figure out how to brush off the feelings she was having for him, not jump into dreamland talking about moving in with him. For fuck's sake, she didn't even know if he had feelings for her. "Okay, time out, you two. I'm not moving anywhere. So, let's just drop that little debate. I don't even know if he's interested in anything more than sex."

The three exchanged a look before Angie rolled her eyes. "Oh, he totally is."

"Yeah, he is." Maiya laughed, and Celia nodded, laughing too.

Cyn glared at her sisters and sister-in-law. "All right, psychic trio. What makes you say that?" All three laughed again, which only annoyed Cyn more. What were they seeing that Cyn wasn't? "I'm serious."

Angie sat up and pulled her long hair over one shoulder. "Cyn, the man stares at you like he's over the moon in love with you."

"At the very least, he's in some serious like with you. But yeah, Angie's right, definitely over the moon." Maiya nodded.

"Totally over the moon and back. His freaking eyes follow you no matter where you are in the room, Cyn. And not in a creepy way, but in a more swoony kind of way. It's sickeningly sweet," Celia said.

Cyn couldn't help the smile that came. Did he really stare at her like that? The idea birthed a flurry of romantic feelings in her belly. "Damn." Unable to wrap her head around the idea, Cyn blew out a breath as she leaned back on her hands. "I think what you're all seeing is a man who's in love with fucking me."

Maiya snorted. "No shit, right? I know a little about that."

"Gross, do not want to hear about you and my brother!"

Angie held her hand in the air, laughing. "Kidding, kidding. I'm just jealous."

"I've never had a woman look at me like that, even though I eat pussy like a champ." Celia grinned.

"Oh my God, Celia." Maiya laughed. "Get down wit' yo bad self!" Maiya high-fived Celia.

"Gah, go easy, little sister!" Jesus, she loved Celia and fully accepted that she was gay, but Celia was still her little sister and hearing about her sex life, no matter what her sexual orientation was, was sometimes…not easy. Cyn blew out a breath and rolled her eyes. "But since we're now sharing so openly, the man rocks my world. I'm serious. The other day, I went to visit him at his mom's house. Fuck, he was all sweaty and funky, and I wanted to suck his cock so bad my mouth was watering."

"And you wanted *me* to go easy? Fucking hell, Cynthia!" Celia fell back on the bed, laughing.

Angie scrunched up her face. "Okay, that's really gross. No, thank you to the ball sweat."

"I know! God, I know." Cyn groaned. "That's precisely my point, Angie. I would never, I mean fucking, *never* give a guy head who's been sweating in his jeans all day. But with him? Yeah. Want it. Crave it. It's a sickness."

Maiya bent forward laughing, too. "That is so awesome! It's gross, but it's awesome." She straightened, fanning herself. "That's some serious pheromone kind of stuff you're talking about."

"Exactly! So, what the fuck'm I gonna do? I feel like I'm like ruined for all men now. What if I never find that with anyone else? Or worse, what if—" Cyn held her hand up, "—hypothetically speaking, of course, what if he turns out to be an asshole like every other guy prior to him because, hello?" Cyn raised her pointer finger and wiggled it. "Broken picker."

Angie tilted her head to the side and frowned with a "don't be stupid" expression on her face. "Yeah, right. We're talking about Shane Conlon here. High school football star turned U.S. Marine, who served his country for eight years, plus his contract work afterward. That man is loyal from the top of his head to the bottom of his feet."

"Gotta say, I kinda agree with your sister." Maiya brushed her hair out of her eyes.

Everything Angie said was true, except really, just because he was loyal to his friends and his country did not mean he would be loyal to her. It's what happened to Cyn. Always.

Shane was a good guy, but still, shit happened and hearts got broken. The fact that Cyn was attracted to him was all the proof she needed. Shane would end up turning into king dickhead in the long run. There was just no way around it. "Doesn't matter."

Maiya jerked her chin. "How does it *not* matter?"

"Because it doesn't." Cyn climbed off the bed and straightened her shirt. "I'm not going to let my heart get any further involved." She checked her lip gloss in the mirror. "Aside from that, Carlos keeps blowing up my phone like a freak from hell. And let's just say he's beyond ancient history in my book now."

Celia sat up. "What's he been saying?"

"Yeah. Spill." Maiya moved beside Cyn.

Cyn glanced at her. "At first, he wanted to talk. But now, he just sends all these angry messages. He's always had a temper." Cyn waved her hand. "Whatever. I had to block him because it was getting excessive."

Maiya leaned her hip against the dresser. "Define excessive?"

"Just a bunch of texts. I'm not worried about it." Cyn shrugged one shoulder.

Another frown furrowed Maiya's brow. "Let me get this straight. He's got a temper and is actively harassing you."

"I wouldn't go that far. Lots of guys have tempers. And technically, because I blocked him, he's not harassing shit.

Like I said, I'm not worried about it." Cyn glanced at Maiya.

"I could totally kick his ass. I've been taking kickboxing in Arizona." Celia got off the bed and crouched in a defensive stance, fists raised in front of her. With a grin, she straightened and moved to Cyn.

Cyn grinned at Celia. "You're so cute."

"Maybe you should be worried. And now my gut is in a knot. What if something goes down? What if he shows up at your house like some freak, Cyn?" Maiya touched Cyn's arm.

"He won't. Seriously. So don't worry. I don't want you worrying while on your honeymoon." Cyn clasped Maiya's hand. "Everything will be fine."

"Carlos might be an asshole, but he's a harmless one. Sounds like a classic temper tantrum to me. You won't need to kick his ass, Celia." With a chuckle, Angie got to her feet too. "Nothing's gonna go down. At least not anything more than Cyn eating a gallon of ice cream on my couch after Shane leaves."

"Ugh, you three. Killing me. No help. No help at all." Cyn laughed and left the room.

Angie followed. "I'll supply the ice cream and tissues. I think that's a huge help."

"Fine. I'll try not to worry. Angie'll hold down the fort, and when I get back, I'll take the second shift." Maiya followed them down the stairs.

"I leave in two days, but I'm only an hour flight away, so there's that." Celia hopped down the last steps.

"See? We're helpful." Angie grinned at Cyn.

"I'm not gonna need the ice cream." When Cyn reached the entryway to the family room, she immediately caught Shane's gaze and had to swallow past the lump that'd instantly formed in her throat. Cyn stopped short and turned to her sisters and Maiya. "Fuck. Make sure it's Boom Chocolatta, okay?" she said to Angie.

"You got it." Angie kissed Cyn's cheek as she slid past her into the room with Maiya and Celia in tow.

Shane got to his feet and moved to Cyn, a smile on his face. "You about ready to head out?"

Not taking her eyes from his, Cyn ran her palm down his thick arm to his hand and clasped it. "Definitely."

Shane bent and kissed her forehead before pulling her into the room. They made the rounds, saying their goodbyes to the large group. Ryan and Maiya were heading out in the morning to Paris, and she pulled Maiya into an extra-special embrace. Cyn adored her sister-in-law and was beyond happy to have her as part of the family. "Take lots of pictures, okay? And please don't worry."

Maiya pulled away with a smile gracing her pretty face. "Will do on the pics. No promises on the worrying. Email me if you need to talk, okay?"

"Sure." Cyn rolled her eyes with a small grin and stepped away.

There was no way in hell she'd email Maiya while she was on her honeymoon. Whatever happened, if anything, after Shane left, she'd deal.

CHAPTER TWENTY-ONE

Cyn passed Carlos's car as she slowed in front of her home and pulled into the driveway. *What the hell is he doing here?* She threw the Jeep in Park and stepped out. Carlos was already out of his car, on his way up the drive, approaching her. Cyn stopped at the back of the Wrangler and crossed her arms. "What do you want, Carlos?"

"Can we talk, please? I just want to talk to you, Cyn." Sincerity blanketed his features, and guilt started to rise, but Cyn pushed it away.

She blew out a breath and brushed her hair out of her eyes. "I think you said everything that needed saying in your text messages."

As Cyn turned to walk away, Carlos clasped her upper arm, halting her movement. "Baby, wait…"

She glared down at his hand and then his face. "Let me go."

He did as she asked, raising his hands in surrender. "I know I've been a jerk—"

"*That* is an understatement."

"You're right and…look, I'm sorry."

Cyn crossed her arms again. There was no point in talking. There was nothing to debate…maybe if things were different—maybe if Shane weren't in the picture, and maybe if Carlos hadn't turned out to be a cheating bastard, she would've considered it.

Prior to Cyn catching Carlos cheating, she'd always taken him back, so it wasn't exactly a surprise that he wasn't taking no for an answer. "Sorry isn't good enough anymore."

"Baby, please." His voice cracked. "I know I fucked up big-time, but just please, give me five minutes. I'm begging you."

Before she could control it, guilt rose hard and fast, lodging a lump in her throat. *Oh Christ!* Cyn let out a sigh and looked away from the tears welling in his eyes. She'd loved Carlos a whole lot. And even though he'd killed every shred of feeling she'd had for him, it broke her heart seeing someone hurting that she once cared about so deeply. "Fine." Cyn pivoted and headed for the house. "You want coffee?"

"Coffee'd be great."

Cyn stepped inside her entryway and headed straight for the kitchen. Carlos took a seat at her kitchen table, and Cyn set the coffee pot up to brew. "I'll be right back."

He nodded, and she left the room, heading for her bedroom. The hair on the back of Cyn's neck prickled in some odd awareness of what she didn't know. The whole situation just felt off to her somehow.

Cyn knew without a doubt that anything Carlos had to say would contain nothing but contradictions and bullshit, but she'd hear him out this one last time. In the past, whenever she tried to end things with him, he'd eventually show up, tail between his legs, begging her to come back to him. Each time, she'd grab hold of whatever bait he cast.

Cyn changed from her work clothes into a pair of faded jeans and plain white T-shirt. She took a moment to freshen up in the bathroom and then made her way back to the kitchen. Each time he pitched his game, she believed—though she knew deep in her gut it was all a ruse—that he wanted her.

And true to his promises, things would smooth out between them again, but never for very long. The truth was, Carlos never wanted her. At least not in the way she wanted him. Their relationship was always simply a game to him.

She pulled two mugs from the cabinet and fixed them both a fresh coffee. Cyn brought them to the table, handed one to Carlos and took a seat across from him. "Okay, talk."

He leaned forward, resting his elbows on the table, cradling his mug in his palms. "I miss you."

Cyn took a sip of the fresh coffee. She wasn't going to tell him she missed him back—the truth was, she didn't.

When she didn't answer, he continued. "I know I fucked up, baby."

She cringed, her skin crawling at his use of the endearment. "You said that already."

"Guess I did." He sipped his coffee. "Look, Cyn. That woman at my house…nothing happened. Now, I'm not saying it wouldn't have, but bottom line is, nothing happened."

"Doesn't matter."

He sat back. "Of course, it matters." He ran his fingers through his hair. "I'm lost without you. I can't sleep. I can't eat. God, I can't think straight, Cyn." He traced the rim of his cup. "You have to come back. I love you, Cyn."

Oh, for fuck's sake! Cyn had waited forever to hear him say those words to her. Had longed for them, especially while she cried herself to sleep at night in a mad state of confusion, trying to figure out why he didn't feel the way she did. Or why, if he didn't feel the same, he wouldn't let her go. "I waited to hear you tell me you loved me for what seems like forever." She rested her fingers on his forearm. "And I appreciate you finally saying it."

He looked at her fingers before placing his hand over hers. "Why do I feel like there's a but coming?"

"Because there is." She pulled her hand away. "It's too late."

"Is there someone else?"

"No." She picked up her coffee mug. It wasn't a lie, not technically anyway. In less than a week, Shane would be gone. Besides, it was none of Carlos's business whether or not there was someone new in Cyn's life or not.

Carlos sat back in his seat. "Whose blue SUV is that?"

What the flying fuck! "Spying on me, Carlos?"

"No. Not spying. I just came by a few times because I wanted to talk, but when I saw another car in the driveway, I figured you had company. So, who is it?"

Cyn debated what to say to him as she sipped her coffee. The remorse that'd been present in his expression a moment ago was now gone, and in its place was a look of smug satisfaction. The bastard thought he'd caught her. Cyn nodded. "Not that it's any of your business, but it's a very old friend of my family."

"He or she?"

"Okay—" Cyn set the cup on the table, "—I think we're done talking."

"Wait!" He blew out a breath. "Dammit, fine. I just don't understand how you can just walk away. Please don't walk away, baby."

Ugh! Cyn's skin crawled with disgust. How in the hell did she ever love this man? "You cheated on me. Just because I got there before you fucked that chick does not mean it doesn't count. You had every intention of sticking your dick in that woman. And I'm sure you sealed the deal after I left your place that night." She stood. "I'm done. This is done, Carlos."

He got to his feet. "I can't believe you're doing this. How can you do this?"

"Well, believe it." Cyn took her mug to the sink and then faced him again. "I think we're done talking."

"You ruined my life, Cyn. Fucking ruined it!" Carlos

swiped the mug off the table, and it crashed onto the floor, smashing into pieces.

"You asshole!" Cyn ran toward him and pointed in his face. "Get the hell out of my house!"

"You're right, we're done fucking talking. For now." He stalked out of the room.

Cyn followed after him and slammed, then locked the door after he left. In a huff, she moved back to the kitchen, grabbed the trash can and knelt in front of the broken mug. Careful not to cut herself, she picked up the bigger pieces and tossed them in the trash, and then grabbed the dustpan and swept up the rest.

Grateful Carlos had just about finished his coffee, she wiped up what little liquid was on the floor. As Cyn got to her feet, she looked up to find Shane standing in the kitchen. A chill zipped down her spine, and she jumped— "God dammit, you scared me!"

"Whoa, sorry. Guessing you didn't hear me come in." Shane moved to her and pulled her into his arms. "You okay?"

She gazed up into his soft blue eyes. "Much better now."

"You have an accident?"

"Broke a coffee mug. One of my favorites, too." She pouted. There was no way she was going to tell him about Carlos—especially that he'd been the one to break the mug in one of his little fits. Shane would kick into alpha-male-overdrive mode and probably go after Carlos, and that was the last thing any of them needed.

"Aw, that sucks." He stroked her pouty lips with the pad of his thumb. "We'll just have to go get you a new one."

Cyn smiled and tipped her head back. "How about you just kiss me until I forget all about the mug?"

"Whatever you need, Cyn." Shane bent his head and covered her mouth with his.

His sweet taste washed through her, and all thoughts of

Carlos and broken mugs vanished into thin air. Shane was by far the best medicine she'd ever had. And he was leaving.

Cyn closed her eyes tighter, willing the sad thought away. She didn't want to think about him leaving, so she deepened the kiss and pressed her body tight against his big, strong one. Right now, he was in her arms, and that was just going to have to be good enough.

CHAPTER TWENTY-TWO

Cyn got ready in the master. They were going on a date—a real one. Not to say that the ones they'd gone on weren't real. They were. It was just that Cyn had called them everything *but* dates. "Dinner with friends." Or "karaoke with her sister and friends." Then, "happy hour." And "the movies."

It was rather cute, and Shane started referring to the time they spent together outside of the house as their "un-dates". Every time he did, Cyn would roll her eyes and shoot him a grin that made him want to kiss her lips until she panted for breath. So, he usually did.

He stepped out into the hall and stuck his head into her bedroom. "You 'bout ready?"

"I'll be out in a minute. Go wait in the living room, like a good date should," she said from behind her bathroom door.

"All right then. Don't make me wait too long, now." He chuckled and made his way to the living room. Settling on the sofa, Shane stretched out his long legs, crossing his cowboy-booted feet at the ankle. His skin tingled with excitement; he couldn't help it. He was taking her country dancing and was beyond eager to get her out on the floor again. Shane recalled

"

the first dance he'd ever had with her—the night of Ryan and Maiya's bachelor and bachelorette party. They'd ended up in the corner making out. A smile spread across Shane's lips. He wouldn't trade that night for the world.

"Okay, ready."

Shane scrambled to his feet, his eyes glued to her the whole time. She wore a fitted mini-dress, a gorgeous shade of coral. The color of the fabric enhanced her already sun-kissed skin. It had short sleeves and a rounded neckline that scooped low enough to taunt him with a fair amount of visible cleavage. The edge of the dress, which landed mid-thigh, had a delicate ruffle. To top off her outfit, at the end of her fit legs was a pair of worn brown leather cowgirl boots.

"Oh God. Why do you look like that? Is this okay?" She twisted from side to side, the ruffle fanning out from her tempting thighs. "Say something, Shane."

"Girl…" He blew out a breath. "Dayyumm."

She dipped her chin and raised her brows. "Is that a good dayyumm or a bad one?"

Shane shook his head and chuckled. "Come on now. You look unfuckingbelievable!"

"Yeah?"

He stepped to her and pulled her against him. "Oh yeah."

"You sure?" She licked her lips, gazing up at him.

Shane growled and bent close, keeping his lips a bare breath away from hers. "I'm so sure that if we don't go right this instant, I may end up bending you over the arm of the couch."

"Well…" She cleared her throat. "I guess I better call us an Uber car then."

"Guess you better." Closing the distance, he took her mouth in a hard kiss. Shane drew in a breath through his nose as he tangled his tongue with hers in a frantic dance. Cyn moaned and wrapped her arms around his neck. Lust sparked hot between them in the same way it had the first time he'd ever kissed her. Shane lifted her off her feet, holding her tighter against him. Lord, have mercy, this woman was everything he ever wanted.

Cyn broke from his lips and gasped. "Fuck, you kill me."

"Why's that?" He ran his lips down her throat.

"Because now my freaking panties are soaked, and I *need* you to bend me over the couch."

He chuckled and set her back on her feet. "Well, we're even. My dick is hard as steel, and I want inside you more than I want to breathe, but I'm gonna make us both wait." He kissed the tip of her nose.

She frowned. "And why are you making us wait?"

"Because I wanna take my girl dancing." He smiled.

Her eyes went wide before she narrowed them and shook her head with another tempting smirk on her lips. "Fine."

Shane swatted her ass and stepped past her. "Call that car."

Shane resumed his spot on the couch as Cyn requested the car via the app on her cell phone. He called her his girl. He'd meant the words—she *was* his girl. In every way, but he hadn't intended to just let it slide out so casually. No taking it back now, and he couldn't say he was unhappy about that.

Once again, Shane had no idea how he would manage leaving her in less than a week. He chewed his thumbnail and stared down at the area rug. Cyn had filled all the cracks inside him that Shane hadn't even realized were there. He had to be insane to give her up.

"Car'll be here in four minutes." She opened her small purse. "I need to fix my lipstick."

"Did you smudge it?" He looked up at her and grinned.

"You smudged it!" She laughed and moved to the mirror near the front door. "You gotta let it dry before you go kissing it off me, you know."

"Not my fault your lips are always begging for me to kiss

them." Shane got to his feet again. "Just doing my duty, ma'am." He stepped behind her and kissed her neck.

"Ohhhh, I get it. Like a public service, right?"

"Zzzaactly." He ran his palms over her hips to her stomach, then up to her breasts.

"Are those begging for attention, too?"

"Always. They're just so needy!"

She chuckled. "You're right. They are. I think I need you to come all over them later. You know, after you fuck between them."

"Like I keep telling you, whatever you need, you get." Shane bent his knees and rolled his hips, grinding his erection against her full ass. He watched her in the mirror as a gasp escaped her lips. Cyn arched, rubbing against him, and Shane gritted his teeth. Jesus, he couldn't get enough of her.

An alert sounded on her phone, and Cyn looked down at the screen. "Damn. The car is here. Fucking hell, Shane. I'm all worked up now."

"Good. I like knowing your pussy's all wet for me." Satisfaction flowed through him as he stepped back from her. Damn right, she was wet for him. She was always wet for him, just like he was always hard for her. Their chemistry was off the charts and kept growing.

"And I like knowing your dick is throbbing hard right now." She laughed and grabbed her purse.

He was tempted to make the car wait—it'd be worth it for the chance to sink into her heaven before they went. Determined to hold off, he blew out a breath and tamped down his arousal as best he could. This was their first official date, and he wanted this night with her more than anything. Waiting a few hours for the heaven he always found in her would be worth it. He took her hand. "Let's get gone."

Cyn stepped inside the country bar, hand in hand with Shane. The rhythmic sound of Christina Aguilera belting out "The Real Thing" echoed around them.

Shane bent to her ear. "Let's grab a beer."

She nodded, and he led her to the main bar. This was the same place they'd met up after Maiya's bachelorette party. Cyn glanced over to the far corner of the club where she'd first kissed Shane. It'd been almost three weeks since that night.

Which meant after avoiding him for a week after the wedding, she'd had two weeks of non-stop cataclysmic sex. Two weeks of consistent orgasms. Two weeks of a man paying attention to her without her having to wait, ask, beg or yell for that attention.

So far, Shane had given her everything she'd ever imagined wanting or needing in a relationship, with one very big exception. She couldn't allow herself to think of them as a couple. Cyn still didn't trust him or herself. It wasn't fair to him, she knew, but it couldn't be helped. And he was leaving.

Shane turned from the bar and handed her a shot glass. She looked down at the amber liquid. "Jameson?"

"Of course." He held his glass up. "Toast?"

"You make it."

"Hmm." He smiled, his bright blue eyes calling her name. "New beginnings."

Shit. Cyn drew in a breath and nodded. *Or another ending.* They tapped the edge of their glasses on the bar top and then tossed them back. The whiskey burned on its way down her throat, but warmed her insides. Shane handed her the bottle of beer, then bent and kissed her. The warmth from the shot spread through her to her limbs, ignited further by his kiss.

"Come on, girl." Shane pulled her toward the edge of the dance floor.

The Chicks "Baby Hold On" played, and several couples danced, some two-stepping, others doing a waltz. Cyn took a sip of her beer and watched. She couldn't do half the dances she'd seen at this bar, but regardless, Shane would be dragging her around the floor soon enough. Good thing she was a fast learner, and Shane was a strong lead. He'd support her until she caught on.

She took another swig of her beer, her eyes glued to the many couples circling the floor. Shane had chosen this activity as their official first date night, and Cyn realized whether she wanted to admit they were a couple or not, tonight, the dancing would force them to be exactly that. Of course, it was definitely possible to dance with someone and not be a couple, but when a woman danced with a man they were intimately involved with, there was no way around it.

Cyn glanced up at him. He'd called her his girl earlier. She'd let it slide, choosing not to comment or set him straight. She didn't have the heart to. But in truth, even if she'd never admit it to him, when he'd made the statement, her heart swelled in her chest, and she knew, deep inside, she wanted exactly that—to be his and only his.

The song changed, and Shane nudged her with his hip. "Love this song. Come on. Dancing to this one."

"You're leading, right?" She laughed as he escorted her onto the floor.

Shane pulled her to the edge of the floor and cradled her waist in one arm. "We'll do a two-step again."

"Okay." She smiled. And then they were moving.

He rounded the first corner of the floor, steady and smooth in his footwork. "This song's a good one for you."

Cyn glanced over her shoulder and back to him. "Why's that?"

"It's called 'Smoke' by A Thousand Horses." He grinned, looking over her head. "You're like smoke, Cyn."

Damn, that dimple of his! And when he smiled like that, he looked so beautiful, Cyn went weak in the knees. She didn't know what to say about the song. Instead, she stayed quiet, listening to the lyrics—in awe of his moves, admiring his beautiful face—while he led her around the floor.

It was going to hurt like hell when he left, but she'd deal. She'd find a way to get over it because there was no choice in the matter. But for now, Cyn was in his arms. And for now, she'd let herself pretend she was his and he was the man who'd never make her feel lonely while he shared her bed.

For now…

SHANE SET the darts down on the side rail. "How about a game of pool?"

"You're on." Cyn grinned and took a swig of her beer.

Shane took her hand and walked her to one of the empty bar tables. "Care to set a wager down?"

"Hell, yes!" She looked over from the rack of pool sticks.

He bent over the table, racking the balls in the wooden triangle. "Name it."

"Winner gets to tie the other up tonight in bed." She rolled one of the cue sticks on the green felt pool table top. "This one's not too bad."

He chuckled. "Only one game then? Or you want to go two out of three?"

"Definitely two out of three. You could be some kind of pool shark. I might need to get my feet under me first." She moved to the end of the table where he'd rolled the cue ball. "I need at least one game to assess my opponent."

Shane propped his hands on his hips. "I suggest we play four games then. First one's practice."

She bent over, lining up her shot on the twelve balls on the other end. "Going soft on me, Sergeant?"

"I wouldn't drea—" Shane watched as the cue ball sped down the table, crashing into the clustered solids and stripes, and then as the two ball sank into the corner pocket. "Well,

God damn. Guess maybe I'm the one that should be sizing up my opponent." He laughed.

"You might be right." She grinned, aimed and sank the five ball.

Shane rested his ass on one of the bar stools along the wall as Cyn sank all of her balls one by one. She was amazing—just incredible. But not because she was kicking his ass at pool but because there was just no end to the things she could do. Everything about her was appealing. Her body, yes, but more than that…her heart and soul. Her vivacity was downright contagious.

Finally missing a ball, she grinned at him. "Your turn."

"Ha." He took the stick from her. "You do realize you just made room for me to do my work." Shane aimed and sank a ball. "Thanks for that."

As he lined up his next shot, Cyn moved to the end of the table and tugged the neckline of her dress down…just enough to get an unbelievably distracting view of her breasts. Shane missed *and* scratched. "Wow!"

Cyn jumped up and down, giggling as she pointed at him with both arms extended out in front of her. "Oldest trick in the book! And you totally fell for it!"

Shane laughed and brought her the stick. "Bad girl. Gonna have to punish you for that when we're home."

"How so? You'll be the one tied up." With the stick in hand and a grin plastered across her kissable lips, she sank her last ball. "I'm about to take this first round." She lined up on the eight ball.

"Yes, ma'am, I believe you are. Good news for me is, it doesn't count." Shane took a gulp of his beer and watched as she won the game. "Nice. Let the wagered games begin!"

"Think you can handle it?" Cyn chalked the tip of the stick and glanced at him with a raised brow as she blew off the excess blue powder. "Lotta pressure, Sergeant."

Shane chuckled and racked the balls. "You'd be surprised how well I work under pressure."

"We'll see." She bent over the table and nailed the cue ball. "You ever ride bulls down in Texas?"

"A bull?" He took the stick from her. "No. Harley, yes." Taking aim, he sank a solid-colored ball. "You're stripes this time."

"You have a Harley? What color is it?" She tilted her beer back.

He bent, sizing up his next shot. "She's silver with royal-blue flames."

She moved to the side of the table, watching as he sank another ball. "Ooh! Nice bank shot. I bet the blue comple-ments your eyes."

"Seriously?" He trailed his palm along her lower back as he passed behind her. "I'll let you be the judge of that." Shane missed the next shot and handed her the stick. "Tell you what. You come visit, and I'll take you for a ride, and you can tell me if she matches my eyes."

Cyn grinned and moved to the other side of the table. "It's possible."

Not the answer he was hoping for, but it was better than nothing. Shane took a swallow of his beer. The thought of having Cyn in his home and also on the back of his bike made his insides go a tad soft. The chance to have her in his bed made his dick stir in his jeans. "I think you'd love Texas. Have you ever been?"

"Nope." She sank a ball. "You're in the country, right?"

"Not quite. It's a suburb of Dallas."

"Oh. I hadn't realized. Definitely no bulls then." She pursed her lips and took another shot, but missed.

He took the stick from her. "I think we can find you some if needed."

"I'll hold you to that." She kissed his cheek before moving to her beer.

Shane took out the eight ball. "What else will you hold against me?"

Cyn moved back to him and wrapped her arms around his neck. "How about me? Can I hold me against you?"

"Always." He gazed into her eyes. "Give me those pretty lips."

"Mmm. Come get them."

Shane bent his head and kissed her. Smoothing his tongue over hers, he slid a hand down to her ass. She moaned and pressed closer. She tasted of beer mixed with the sweetness he knew as his girl. *His girl.* Christ…he loved the way that statement rolled through his mind and fitted around his heart. Breaking from her lips, he caught her gaze again. "I do believe I'm winning."

She frowned and gave him an eye roll. "Two more games to go. Hold your horses; you haven't won anything yet."

"Trust me. I'll win." With a grin firmly in place, he swatted her ass. "Rack 'em."

CHAPTER TWENTY-THREE

Shane slid into the backseat of the Uber car beside Cyn. As the driver confirmed their destination and pulled away from the curb, Shane slid his palm over her bare thigh. He'd had a blast with her. They'd danced…a lot. Drank a lot, too. Cyn smiled, laughed and joked with him, and Shane couldn't keep his hands off her. She'd teased him pretty much all night, rubbing her full ass on his groin any chance she got. The whole date was awesome, and he *could not* wait to get her home. And naked. Immediately.

Cyn leaned against him and brushed her soft lips over his ear. "I want you."

A shiver ran down Shane's spine, and his dick thickened behind his zipper. He trailed his fingers over the bare flesh of Cyn's inner thigh, then higher. She was wet for him, he was sure.

Shane didn't need to touch her pussy to prove it. But damn him if he didn't want to anyway—because she was his, and because she felt like satin beneath his fingertips, and also because making her come anytime he wanted was fucking hot. However, considering the close proximity of the driver, he'd wait.

Cyn parted her thighs ever so slightly and slid an arm behind his shoulders. Shane moved his fingers higher, itching to hit his target, barely able to hold himself back. Cyn gripped the back of his shirt and bit her bottom lip.

Shane stifled a groan. His dick was so hard he could pound nails straight through two-by-fours, and as soon as he got her in the door, he was fucking her. Right there in the living room, plus everywhere else in the house he could. As he traced tiny circles on the skin of her inner thigh with his fingertips, he bent to her ear. "Hot and wet for me?"

She nodded. "Touch me. Please?"

Shane nipped at her earlobe and inched his fingers higher, grazing the edge of her panties. "You want my cock, don't you? Need me to stuff that tight cunt full so you can come all over me?" Cyn gripped the back of his neck and moaned as she bit his shoulder.

Fucking hell, they needed to get home now.

CYN PULLED AWAY from Shane's neck and stared at him in the dimness of the backseat of the car. He had a look in his eyes like he wanted to eat her alive. And then maybe go back for seconds. Cyn smiled and licked her lips, beyond willing to feed him. She'd almost come from his words alone and knew once he buried that absolutely gorgeous and thick shaft of his inside her, he'd make her come hard enough to register a ten on the Richter scale.

Shane moved his hand from her inner thigh and raised his fingers to her mouth. Without hesitation, she opened, and he pressed them inside. Cyn moaned, sucking and curling her tongue around the edges. He bent close to her ear. "Gonna fuck this hot mouth tonight."

She nodded, his fingers still between her lips and rubbed her hand over the hardness trapped behind his zipper.

Shane grabbed her wrist. "Then I'm gonna fuck your tight pussy until you beg me to stop."

Good God, the dominant tone of his whispered words had her clit throbbing and every inch of her body clenching in need. The driver needed to hurry up and get to the house before she lost her ever-loving mind. Shane ran his fingers from her mouth, down her chin and neck, to the swell of her cleavage.

She bent close to his ear, sliding her palm up his length. "What if I don't beg you to stop?"

Shane speared his fingers into her hair, tugged her head back and stared into her eyes. "Girl…" His gaze wandered over her face to her lips before he jerked her forward and planted a kiss on her so consuming that chills skipped over Cyn's skin and her head buzzed with the intensity of it.

Shane didn't need to finish whatever statement he was going to make. The kiss conveyed it all. Cyn felt it in her bones and with every fiber of her being. Shane Conlon wanted her so much more than in just a sexual way.

As he stole her breath with his lips and tongue, Cyn wrapped her arms around his neck and held on tight. The connection between them was electric and wild…and definitive. And Cyn had no choice but to let herself be swept away in all of it.

The car slowed, and he broke the kiss, leaving Cyn breathless, dizzy and completely absorbed in everything Shane.

"Thanks a lot, man." Shane opened the door and angled out of the backseat, pulling her behind him.

He moved toward her front door, and Cyn trailed behind him in silence, still in a daze from her little realization in the car while hormones bounced around her insides. She couldn't think about it—all that she'd felt in that kiss.

She couldn't give him what he wanted…at least not for a year. After that, she'd be able to tell if he was the real deal, genuine perfection he appeared to be. She hoped. Just not now, not yet.

Shane let go of her hand and unlocked the front door. He had a key to her house because he'd been there for a couple of weeks now. It was no big deal. Not like they were living with each other…except it almost sort of was. They acted like a couple, cohabitated like they were one. Fucked like they were one too.

Everything Cyn ever wanted, she had with Shane. Every idea of what a relationship should be, and could be, he'd given her, and more, because she'd never expected sex to be like it was with him.

He pulled her into the house, closing the door behind them. She needed to tell him…to maybe try and explain why things were moving too fast. And why she couldn't be his girl.

But she didn't get the chance because his lips were on hers again, and she was lost in his tongue and taste. His scent and strong body enveloped her, and Cyn let it all slip away. The fears. The doubts. And whatever she thought shouldn't be happening between them.

At that moment, whether it should be or not was irrelevant. It was happening, and Cyn felt powerless to stop it.

She broke the kiss and dropped to her knees. No words were spoken as she unbuttoned his jeans and slid the zipper down. Shane cupped her cheek in his palm, and Cyn rested against it as she pulled his thick shaft free of his boxer briefs.

With her eyes on his, Cyn parted her lips and slid the flushed, swollen crown into her mouth. The bead of pre-ejaculate that'd gathered at the tip hit her tongue, and she moaned as she swallowed.

Could she really be powerless to stop something she kept volunteering for? She didn't want to stop, but continuing wasn't an option either.

Shane stroked her cheek. "Girl…"

Tonight…she had him tonight and a handful of others.

Cyn closed her eyes and took him to the back of her throat. She didn't need to stop; it was going to happen regardless.

He was leaving.

SHANE STARED down in awe at the woman who'd stolen his heart. Something had changed in her expression once they'd gotten inside the house. Maybe it was the kiss he'd given her in the car. He'd been so overwhelmed by all the emotions racing through his mind, kissing her was the only way to best express everything he was feeling.

Cyn slowed her movements, gazing up at him. Shane's heart clenched in his chest for a million reasons, but the biggest being that he did not want to leave this woman. With a moan, she swirled her tongue around the head and then took him deep into the hot depths of her mouth, and Shane's head spun.

He smoothed his palm over her hair and threaded his fingers through the soft strands. He wanted her…all of her. Forever and always.

But he wouldn't tell her yet. Couldn't risk spooking her and lose what little time he had left in L.A. Less than a week until he had to go, and he intended to make the most of it. But somehow, some way, he'd figure out how things could work between them long distance. There was just no way around it.

"Cyn…" She looked up at him, and he urged her to her feet. "I want you."

"You have me." She kissed him.

God, how he hoped she meant those words in the literal sense. Shane picked her up and carried her down the hall to her bedroom. Cyn wrapped her legs around his waist and nipped at his neck.

A desperate need to absorb and memorize every touch,

kiss and moment this night would bring, as though it might be his last rose inside him, tempering his typical urgent need to fuck her senseless. Sex between them had always been explosive, and he loved it that way, but tonight, he wanted to take his time.

He set her on the bed and smoothed his palms down her chest. "Take your dress off for me." She did as he asked, removing her bra too. Shane's mouth went dry as he took in her body, from her full breasts to her lace panties. "So goddamn beautiful." He went to his knees in front of her and cupped both mounds in his palms before leaning forward and licking over one nipple.

He bit the tight point, and Cyn jerked against him, gripping the back of his neck. "Love when you play with my tits."

"Mmm." Shane stood, urging her to lie back on the bed, and then bent over her as he moved to the other nipple. Still gripping both globes, he lapped at the taut nub, then nibbled it too.

The heavenly scent of her bare skin flowed into his lungs, racing through his bloodstream, fueling his desire. He moved down her soft tummy, licking and nipping along the way, stopping to kiss around her belly button as he slid her panties down her legs.

"Shane…" She tugged at his shirt.

"Shh. I got you." After removing his shirt and jeans, Shane moved onto the bed beside her. He propped himself on an elbow and trailed his fingertip around her belly button, and continued lower to her clit.

He loved that she had no pubic hair, loved how smooth the skin of her pussy felt. She gazed at him and moaned as he pressed against her clit, massaging the bundle of nerves with tight circles. "Love how you feel and how wet your cunt gets for me when I touch you."

"Mmm, babe." She rolled her hips and cupped her full

tits, squeezing them together. Raising one, she dipped her chin and licked over one nipple.

Shane let out a groan, and the head of his prick throbbed. "Going to be *the* fucking death of me. Spread your legs nice and wide for me. And keep playing with your tits."

She did as he asked, and he drove two fingers inside her. Cyn rolled her hips and whimpered as she licked her lips. His balls tightened, and Shane drew out his fingers and delivered a quick slap to her pussy.

Her hips shot off the bed, and she screamed his name.

Oh yeah, that's what he'd wanted to hear. She moaned, and he gave her a quick kiss. "You like that?"

"Yes!" she breathed. "Fuck, yes."

Shane circled the mouth of her cunt with his fingertips and drew her wetness up over her clit. "Dripping for me now."

"Need…"

"What do you need, Cyn?" He teased her clit.

She rolled her hips. "Need you…oh fuck!"

"Need what?" He slid his fingers inside, curling them to stroke over her G-spot.

"Everything, Shane. You. Your cock. Your mouth. Everythi—"

Shane delivered another swift slap to her cunt, and as she arched on the bed, he cupped her mound in his palm. His dick throbbed, growing impossibly harder. Her reactions were enough to make him lose his damn mind. Everything he did to her, she liked and wanted more of. "Made for me, Cyn. Goddamn made for me."

So caught up in the moment, Shane didn't bother to try and hold back. There was no point in censuring himself anymore. The words weren't bullshit. Every one of them was true. She *was* made for him.

Rising from the bed, he grabbed a condom from the

nightstand drawer, tore it open and slid the latex over his shaft. "How do you want me to take you tonight?"

Cyn looked up at him and licked her lips. "All ways."

"Girl…" Shane stood against the side of the bed, gripped her thighs and slid her to the edge. He placed the head at her entrance. "Watch as I slide inside you."

Cyn rose up on her elbows and stared between them as Shane slid just the tip in. She let out a moan. "Fuck, that's so hot. Fill me all the way. Please, baby?"

"So polite. Such a good girl." Shane's lips quirked into a grin as he gripped her thighs and drove balls deep inside her.

"Oh God! Yes!"

Heaven help him, this woman was Shane's every fantasy come to life. Before the night was done, he'd make sure she knew without a doubt that he was made for her, too.

CHAPTER TWENTY-FOUR

Cyn sat at her desk in her office well past business hours. She hadn't been able to focus all day—too wrapped up in thoughts about the prior night with Shane. The sex had been beyond intense, more so than it'd already been between them. Something had shifted in him—between them, and she didn't know what the hell she was going to do about it.

Leaning back in her seat, she rubbed her hands over her face and let out a breath. Along with the rising emotions over his behavior, her body kept springing to life with arousal each time she replayed the night in her mind. The whole situation was unexpected and crazy, as well as mind-blowing. And no matter how many times Cyn had told herself over the last couple of weeks that she would not—absolutely could not develop feelings for Shane, they'd grown anyway.

Without her permission, yet with her full participation.

Agitation with herself and the situation pulsed through her as Cyn finally shut down her computer and gathered a pile of customer files and invoices. Shane would be leaving. And she needed to let him go. But fucking hell, she didn't want to.

With a sigh, Cyn put the papers back down and propped an

elbow on the desk, resting her forehead in her palm. What in the hell was she going to do? Burying her feelings wasn't working for shit, but there was no way she was going to run home and confess all the hearts and butterflies bouncing around her heart.

Cyn slumped back in her chair and toyed with a loose thread on the seam of her jeans. Shane didn't need to know how she felt. No one did. Things were just too complicated between them, except not really—just that he lived three states away, and she was supposed to be single, working on herself and fixing her broken picker.

Bottom line, trusting her judgment was no longer possible. Cyn hadn't picked a good man...well, ever. Shane was no different, though she *really* wanted to believe he was. She just couldn't be sure. And since he was leaving, the opportunity to be sure wasn't possible.

Chasing after what her heart thought she wanted was just stupid, and what she'd always done in the past. Instead, she needed to listen to her head; however, that was a mess, too. "Ugh! This is crazy. I'm crazy!"

Cyn scooped up the pile of documents again, engaged the alarm system and left the office. The sun had set well over an hour ago, and she glanced around the empty lot as she walked across the pavement to where she'd parked. She unlocked the Jeep with the key fob and then, carefully balancing the stack of paperwork in one arm, she reached for the door hand—

Cyn was slammed forward against the still-closed driver's door. Paperwork slid from her grip as her breath gushed from her lungs with the hard impact.

"*Now* we're going to talk." The threatening growl in Carlos's whispered words sent an eerie chill down her spine. He grabbed one of her arms, wrenching it behind her back. "Whether you like it or not, bitch."

What the fuck did he think he was doing? Cyn would've been scared if she wasn't so stunned and pissed off. How dare he manhandle her in such a way! Finally regaining her breath, she turned her head to the side and glared at him over her shoulder. "Like hell!"

"We'll just see about that." Carlos yanked her away from the Wrangler, opened the door and pushed her inside. He followed after her, shoving her over the center console to the passenger seat.

Cyn reached for the passenger door handle, but Carlos was faster than she expected, and he grabbed both of her wrists. Wrapping a thin scarf around them, he bound them together. How in the fuck was this even happening? Cyn got a good look at his face, the overhead dome light illuminating his features. She cringed. The expression in his eyes was like some sort of crazed mental patient who'd snapped. "Carlos, please? What the hell are you doing?"

"Shut your bitch mouth." He reached behind his back, and in the next moment, he pointed a gun at her face. "It's not your turn to talk."

Cyn lost her breath, and her eyes went wide. "Carlos."

"You never did know when to shut up." Setting the gun in his lap, he produced another scarf from his pocket and shoved it between her lips as a gag, tying it behind her head. Righting himself behind the wheel, Carlos slammed the driver's door closed and started her Jeep. After backing out of the parking space, he squealed out of the small lot.

Cold dread filled her veins. Holy shit, things had just gone from zero to twelve thousand in a matter of two seconds. Trying not to panic, Cyn stared out the windshield and passenger window, her head spinning as they sped down residential side streets. He'd pointed a gun at her. A fucking gun. Jesus. The tint on her windows was so dark no one would be able to see her. Cyn glanced over at Carlos. His face had hardened into a determined expression, his lips pressed tight together in a harsh frown. The gun lay in between his legs.

What the hell was she going to do? What the hell was *he* going to do?

Cyn glanced at the floor. Her purse was tipped over, its contents strewn around her feet. Her cell phone was down there, exactly where she couldn't see. But she had to do something. Anything…there was no way she could let him just take her somewhere, but how the hell was she going to stop him? Cyn drew a breath in through her nose, trying to calm her frazzled nerves. Carlos wouldn't hurt her, not truly hurt her—at least, she hoped.

He rounded a corner, and Cyn realized they were nearing her neighborhood. He was taking her to her house? Jesus, this was insane. Sure enough, after a few more turns, he pulled into her driveway, opened the garage door and parked inside. Turning off the Wrangler, he got out, rounded the front end and opened her door. "In the house, we go."

She had a brief moment to wonder what he'd done with the gun as he gripped her bound wrists and yanked her out. Cyn stumbled into him with a grunt as she tried to gain her footing. Carlos tugged her into the house, shutting the door behind them.

She blinked, adjusting to the darkness as he led her through the kitchen. Once in the living room, he sat her down in the corner chair and started pacing in front of her. The room was dark, save for the glow of the streetlights spilling through her front window.

When Carlos turned away from her, she caught the brushed metallic reflection of the butt of the gun sticking out from the back of his jeans. *God, please help me?* Foolishly, she'd hoped he had left it on the front seat. Fear rose in her chest, and bile burned the back of her throat. Holy fucking shit, this was bad. This was beyond bad.

"How could you do this to me? How the fuck do you think you're just going to walk away from me?" He stopped his pacing and turned to her. "I will not be ignored, Cyn!" Carlos rushed forward and got in her face, his nose almost touching hers. Cyn jerked back from him, blinking. He grabbed her by her hair, yanking her head back before shaking her hard. "Do you fucking hear me!"

Cyn squeezed her eyes closed as tears trickled down the side of her face, dripping into her ears. *Oh God!* Terror pulsed through her bloodstream, and her heart pounded in her ears. She sucked in a harsh breath around the gag, trying to calm down so she could think. There had to be a way to get away from him. Cyn tried to recall every television show or movie she'd ever watched where someone had been held captive and got away. So stupid, but it was the only thing that came to her.

With his hold still tight in her hair, Carlos gripped her face hard in his free hand. "Not much to say now, huh? Not with that gag in your mouth, anyway. Works for me." He let go of her and stalked away. "Tell me to fuck off? That you're done? I don't fucking think so. I'll show you done, you fucking slut."

This was it; she might not get another chance. She pushed all her burning fear down. With Carlos's back still turned, Cyn rose from the seat, raised her bound hands and plowed into the back of him. Screw the gun, it didn't matter. The room was dark, and Cyn was banking on him not being a good shot and also her running faster than he could track.

Unable to control her body, she let the momentum carry them both to the ground. They landed with a hard thud, and Cyn rolled to her side, scrambling to get to her feet.

Carlos was on her before she got even one foot planted on the floor. He grabbed her by the back of her hair and yanked her to the ground. Cyn landed on her back, her head slamming into the hardwood floor. Pain erupted in her chest and sides as her breath punched out of her with a deep, rattled groan.

Carlos straddled her stomach, his teeth bared, with his lips peeled back in a crazed sneer. The gag had come loose, and she opened her mouth to scream. But couldn't. Still struggling to catch her breath, Cyn tried to draw in some air, and as she did, Carlos slapped her across the cheek—the blow so hard stars exploded behind her eyes. *Oh my God!* Taking her by the hair, he raised her head and slammed it down on the floor. Pain resonated loudly through her mind, and then he slapped her again. Cyn's head jerked in the other direction, and her mouth filled with the coppery taste of blood.

"What the fuck?"

"Sha-*aane!*" The last of his name came out on a wheeze. Cyn bucked her hips, trying to get her ex off her. At once, Carlos's weight was gone, and not because of her efforts. Cyn rolled to her side and worked to get her feet under her. When she turned around, Shane and Carlos were locked in a struggle. They slammed into the end table, and the lamp crashed to the floor.

"Cyn, run! Now!" Shane's voice echoed around the room. He turned with Carlos and shoved him away. Carlos came back at Shane, and Shane raised a fist and punched him in the jaw. Cyn's ex flew to the side, hitting the wall, but again came back at Shane.

"Shane, he has a gun tucked in the back of his pants!" Cyn looked around, frantic for something to hit Carlos with.

"Cynthia, fucking run now. And call the cops!" Shane punched Carlos in the stomach, and her ex doubled over.

"I'm not leaving you." With her wrists still bound, she grabbed the vase from the entryway table and held it over her head. "Goddammit, Carlos, stop!"

With Carlos still bent over, holding his stomach, Shane hit him with an uppercut to the jaw, then spun Carlos, pressing him face-first against the wall, his arm wrenched behind his back. Yanking the gun from the back of Carlos's jeans, Shane tossed it away from them. "Big man with a gun, huh? Big man assaulting a woman?" Shane pulled him away from the wall and slammed him against it again. "Not so big now, are you, you fucker!"

Carlos let out a disturbed laugh. "You the one she's fucking now?"

"Shut your mouth." Shane glanced over at Cyn. "This is Carlos?"

"Yes." Cyn set the vase down and swiped her tears away, cringing as her hand passed over her cheeks where Carlos had hit her.

"Call the cops, Cyn. Now."

She licked her lips, the sting from the cut making her wince. "I don't have my phone."

"Back pocket." He yanked Carlos's bent arm higher. "Don't you fucking move, or I swear I'll rip your arm right the hell out of the socket and beat you bloody with it." Shane glanced at her again, his breath sawing in and out of him. "Grab my phone, Cyn."

Carlos groaned in what she assumed was pain, but didn't say anything. She knew how that felt, having an arm wrenched behind your back. Carlos had done it to her in the parking lot. *Asshole.* Cyn stood there, her limbs vibrating with adrenaline, blood rushing loud in her ears.

"Cynthia, babe? Did you hear me?" He paused, his gaze intent on her. "Ah, fuck."

She blinked, caught in a total daze, unable to respond to him. She frowned, her ears ringing as she tried to focus on breathing.

Shane managed to pull his phone from his back pocket and hit a few keys with his thumb. "Yes. This is Shane Conlon, I need an officer and an ambulance at four-oh-sixty-six, Billings Avenue… Yes, ma'am. I have an intruder in custody. The ambulance is for the resident, Cynthia Donnelly… No, she's conscious but appears to have been assaulted." He shook his head. "No, ma'am… Yes, ma'am. There's a gun at the scene. I need to secure it… No. No." He glanced at her and then back to Carlos.

Cyn cringed, nerves still bouncing through her like a Ping

Pong ball. She still couldn't believe Carlos had a gun. A shiver raced down her spine and spread over her skin. He could've killed her. Glancing around the room, she spotted it in the far corner.

"Fuck this shit. Let me go!" Carlos yelled.

Shane grunted. "Ma'am, I'm holding him against a wall at the moment, so I won't be able to stay on the line… Thank you." Cyn looked back to see Shane pull the phone from his ear and toss it to the couch. "Cyn, do you have any zip ties in the garage?"

Raising her bound hands, she looked at them. They were shaking. Curling them into fists, she squeezed and flexed them again.

"Cynthia! Babe, look at me."

Cyn snapped her gaze to Shane's.

"Yeah, you're the one she's fucking now." Carlos spat blood onto the floor.

Shane pushed him harder against the wall. "Last warning, Carlos. Shut your mouth, or I'll be forced to help you shut it."

"She's got a hot mouth, don't she? You like that ass too, I bet." Carlos laughed.

Shane grabbed Carlos by the back of the hair, yanked his head back and slammed it hard against the wall. Carlos went limp, and Shane let him slide to the ground. "Had about enough of that shit." Shane crouched down and rolled Carlos to his stomach. "Cyn, I need you to get me something to secure his hands with. Sweetheart, do you have any zip ties in the garage?"

"He had a gun," she heard herself say. "Shane, he had a gun."

The room spun and then went black.

SHANE RAN TO CYN, catching her before she hit the ground. He laid her down on the couch and smoothed her hair away from her face. Goddamn-motherfucking-sonofabitch. Her lip was split and bloody. One cheek red, the other swollen—a bruise already appearing on her flesh.

Anger spread through him like hot lava. He wanted to tear Carlos limb from limb. If he hadn't already knocked him out, he'd do it again. As it was, it was taking every ounce of self-control Shane had not to get up and kick the fucker in the face.

He'd put his hands on Shane's woman. He'd hurt her. God knows what would've happened if Shane hadn't gotten there when he did. A shiver raced down his spine, and he cringed as he gently stroked her cheek. He glanced around the room in search of the gun. Spotting it in the far corner, far enough away from Carlos, he turned his focus back to Cyn and untied her wrists. "Wake up, honey."

She roused a bit, letting out a groan. Her eyelids fluttered, and then she finally opened them. "Hi."

Relief washed through him, but concern replaced it. "You okay?"

As if she suddenly realized what was going on, she knifed up and looked around the room, a frantic look in her eyes. "Where is he? Oh God, Shane, there's a gun!"

"Shhh. Babe, it's okay." He gripped her arms and gently shook her, and she focused back on him. "Cyn, just breathe. You're safe. Cops are on their way."

"Oh God! I was so scared." She threw her arms around his neck and started crying.

"Me too." Shane cradled the back of her head, holding her tight to his chest. "I'm here now. I got you." He glanced over at Carlos, who was still passed out, and white-hot rage spiked in his gut. Two tours in Iraq, plus contract work in Afghanistan, and never had he been as scared as he was when he walked into Cyn's house and found her on the ground, some crazed motherfucker on top of her, slapping her around like she was some sort of punching bag.

Sirens rang in his ears, and Cyn sucked in a harsh breath. "It's okay. Just stay here. I'll let them in."

She tightened her hold. "Please, don't go. Please?"

Shane closed his eyes tight, drawing in a hard breath. "Okay, come on." He stood with her and then walked to the gun. Picking it up, he removed the clip and checked the chamber. It was empty. Taking her by the hand, he moved to the front door. "Babe, I need to hold the weapon above my head. When we open the door, the officers are probably going to have their guns drawn. Just stay behind me, okay? And don't panic." He stared into her eyes, hoping like hell she wasn't going to lose it. "Sweetheart, do you understand?"

She looked down at the gun as she raised her hand to her throat. "Yes."

"It's going to be fine. Just stay behind me." He kissed her forehead before shifting her behind him. Holding the gun over his head, he twisted the knob and opened the door.

Three officers had their weapons drawn. "Freeze," one said.

Shane raised his other hand. "I'm Shane Conlon. This is Cynthia Donnelly, the victim behind me. The intruder is inside, unconscious, on the living room floor. Gun has been unloaded."

"Step forward slowly, both of you."

Shane did as instructed, hoping like hell Cyn followed direction.

"Ma'am, step to your left. Sir, slowly put the weapon on the ground."

Shane, again, did as they instructed, keeping his arms in the air. Cyn did as they directed, too, thank God.

One officer holstered his weapon and stepped to Shane. "Turn around and drop to your knees."

While the others kept him at gunpoint, Shane did exactly

as he was told, placing his hands on the back of his head and interlacing his fingers. The officer grabbed Shane's hands and began searching him for additional weapons. His wallet was also pulled from his back pocket. When he was done searching him, Shane felt the added pressure of the officer's knee in his back, and then the cold steel of a cuff was around his wrist. In one motion, both arms were lowered, and the other wrist cuffed.

"Why are you cuffing him? It's not him. It's my ex, Carlos Ortiz...he's inside." Her breath hitched, and a tear trickled down her cheek.

Shane's heart clenched, and he gritted his teeth. Fuck, he wanted to kill that bastard for hurting her.

"He's clear."

Shane was uncuffed, and another officer who'd joined the one searching him handed Shane his wallet. Cyn ran over and pressed herself to his side. Shane wrapped an arm around her.

Two new officers approached. "We're going to need to get a statement from the two of you separately," one said.

The other motioned to Cyn. "Ma'am, let's move to the ambulance, and we can talk there."

"No. I'm not going anywhere until Shane can come with me!"

There was his girl, trying to control the situation. So typical of her. Shane smiled. "Cyn, babe. It's okay. Go with them so they can attend to you. I'm going to be talking with the officers for a minute."

"I'm not going anywhere!" She crossed her arms.

Letting out a sigh and knowing she was not going to budge, Shane looked to the officers. "Mind if we talk by the ambulance?"

"That'd be best." The officer extended his arm toward the ambulance.

"Fuck you and fuck this! She's a cunt!" Carlos's voice boomed from inside the house. Shane looked back at the door to see him being escorted out of Cyn's house by an officer. His hands cuffed behind his back.

"No reason to see this." Shane turned with her and started toward the ambulance.

"This isn't over, Cynthia! Not by a long shot," Carlos yelled as he was walked to a waiting patrol car.

"Ignore him," Shane said and kept them moving.

As the EMTs got her lip cleaned up and an ice pack on her cheek and the back of her head, Shane sat in silence, blood boiling over inside his veins. When the medic was done, Cyn gave her statement to the police. Shane had to step away because the officers wanted them separated while they got the story about what happened.

Once again, he thanked God that he'd gotten there when he did, but he wished he'd gotten to her sooner. Like…before the fucker even got her in the house. Never mind the fact that Shane should've been listening to the warning bells that'd been going off in his gut ever since Monday night.

He'd known that night something wasn't right, but he'd let it go. He never should have. He had one full day left in town, but there was no fucking way in hell he was leaving her now. He'd just have to extend his trip a little longer—for how long, he didn't know, didn't care either.

He just knew he wasn't leaving.

CHAPTER TWENTY-FIVE

CYN ROLLED TO HER SIDE IN BED, HER WHOLE BODY SHOUTING in protest. Holy hell, she was sore. Every-damn-where. She hadn't gotten very good sleep either. Every time she thought she heard a noise, she jerked her head in the direction she swore it was coming from, only to find nothing there.

"You okay?" Shane laid his hand on her hip.

"Mm. Just sore." Cyn felt his warm body curl against her back, and she closed her eyes.

He kissed her shoulder. "Warm bath would help."

"Yeah, I guess it would. I'm just so tired. Want to sleep more."

"Then sleep, babe. I'm here."

"'Kay." She adjusted the pillow and winced as the throb in her head doubled. The EMT didn't think she had a concussion but had instructed both Shane and her on what to look for, just in case. Cyn blew out a breath. "Head hurts, Shane."

"Let me grab you some Tylenol. Sit tight." He kissed her shoulder again, and then she felt his absence as he got out of the bed. He was back before she even realized, standing next to her side of the bed. "Here, babe. Let me help you up."

She gazed up at him. His chest was bare, and he wore only

his boxer briefs. Her head might be killing her, but she wasn't blind. The man never failed to take her breath away. "No, it's okay." Raising on her elbow, she took the two pills from him and swallowed them down with the water bottle he'd brought. Lying back down, she closed her eyes. "Thank you."

"Worried you might actually have a concussion. Look up at me, Cyn."

With effort, she opened her eyes and gazed up at him. He had her cell phone in his hand, the flashlight feature turned on. She squinted at the bright light.

"Sorry. Need to see how sensitive you are to the light. Too much?"

"Duh! It's bright!" She chuckled.

"Too bright?"

She smiled. "Nah, not more than normal. Did I pass?"

When he was done with that, he cupped her chin in his hand and stared into her eyes. "Do you feel dizzy?"

"Only when you stare at me like you want to eat me for dinner." She licked her lips. "Not really. Just tired and achy. How'd I do? Did I pass?

"Come on now, I'm being serious, and you're being frisky." He chuckled. "Yeah, you passed, but I'm still worried." He pressed a kiss to the top of her head and stepped away.

Cyn felt the bed dip, and then his warm body was pressed against her back again. Shane rested one hand on her hip, and she closed her eyes. "You're being paranoid."

"And that's what you told me on Monday about Carlos, and look how that turned out."

"Touché. But I already know it was my fault." She yawned.

"I did not even say that, so do not put words in my mouth because I will definitely paddle your ass if you continue down that path. It was not your fault. Not mine either. It was that crazy bastard's fault." His voice was a low rumble and beyond serious.

"Fine."

"Good. Now, sleep more. You need it." He pressed another kiss to her shoulder.

Cyn edged closer to him. She'd given in and agreed with Shane to appease him, but couldn't help but wonder if there was truth to the idea that if she'd listened to him, or to Maiya even, this wouldn't have happened. She didn't have a chance to consider it more because sleep took her. Finally.

SHANE WOKE early with Cyn's body curled against him. Most of the night, she'd been having dreams, likely nightmares about the attack. She'd woken a bunch of times, disoriented and crying. The times she hadn't woken up, she'd cried out in her sleep or yelled Carlos's name. Shane had hated hearing the pain and fear in her cries and her words. All he could do was hold her—it wasn't like he could fight Carlos in her dreams.

Hoping not to wake her, he rose from the bed, threw on his jeans and headed to the kitchen. First thing he did was put in a call to her parents, letting them know what happened. The second thing was cancel his flight home. He'd let Cyn know later that he was staying, or maybe he'd wait to tell her tomorrow. It wasn't important.

The only thing that mattered to him was that he was staying and planned on being there until he was sure she was okay. No matter how long it took.

Swallowing the rest of his coffee, Shane set the cup in the sink and made his way to her bathroom. He stepped under the spray, hoping to gain some of his own relief. His body wasn't really sore from the altercation, more that his head was all fucked up over what'd happened. His mind vacillated back and forth between fear of losing her and rage at what happened. Guilt was in there, too. He should've been there, but no matter what, he was there now.

After finishing in the bathroom, Shane made his way back to her bed. He hadn't gotten much sleep either. He could've stayed awake, but in truth, he was so freaked about what happened, he just needed to be as close to Cyn as he could get.

CYN CAME AWAKE in her bed alone, but could hear the sounds of voices somewhere in her house. Her family must be there. She sat up, slow and easy, and groaned. Her body was beyond unhappy with her. Christ, she felt eighty. She eyed the clock. One p.m. At least she'd gotten a few more hours in, though she could probably go back to sleep without much effort whatsoever.

The need to pee forced her from the bed, and she padded to her bathroom, closing herself in. After taking care of business, she ran her fingers through her hair and got a good look at the damage Carlos's handywork had done to her face.

A purple bruise decorated one cheek, and her bottom lip was still swollen, the split in it incredibly sore. She brushed her teeth carefully. When there was a knock at the door, Cyn bent over the sink, rinsed, and then wiped her mouth gently on a towel before opening the door.

A gentle smile curved Shane's lips as he looked her up and down. "Like you in my shirt. How you feeling?"

Cyn smoothed her palms down the front of his XXL T-shirt. "Sore. Hungry, too."

"Your parents are here, and a few of the clan."

Cyn looked up at him and frowned. "I figured. Define a few?"

He laughed. "That's my girl. Still full of spunk." He bent

forward and kissed her cheek. "Jimmy and his woman. Angie, Mary, and Joey and Steph."

She rolled her eyes but then smiled. "Is Madi here too?"

"Yeah. Sonja's daughter, Casey, is playing with her in the living room. None of the other kids are here, though."

"Ugh, Shane!" Frustration bubbled up, zipping through her, and she blew past him into her bedroom. "I don't want the baby in that tainted room. We need to sanitize it." She yanked a pair of sweats from her drawer. "Jesus! I feel like I need to sanitize the whole freaking house."

Shane crossed his arms. "I already took care of it."

She stopped, one leg half in her sweats. "What do you mean, 'you took care of it'?"

"Just what I said. I took care of it."

Cyn pulled her pants the rest of the way on, grabbed a pair of socks and threw them on, too. Blowing out a breath, she smoothed her hair away from her face. "Fine. I'll just go check it out."

"Fine."

Shane followed as she walked to the living room. Anxiety rode her hard, sending chills up and down her spine. She just…needed to see for herself. Cyn glanced around. The broken lamp had been cleaned up. The end table put back in place. Everything appeared to be where it was supposed to be. Little Madi let out a squeal from where she sat on Sonja's daughter's lap, and Casey looked up at Cyn from the couch.

Cyn forced a smile and as even a tone as she could. "Hi, pretty girls!" She rushed past them to where Carlos had spit blood on her floor. That'd been cleaned, too. She turned back to Shane, who was leaning against the wall, his arms once again crossed in front of his big chest. "Did you use the bleach wipes under the kitchen sink?"

"Nope."

"Why not?" She stomped back to him.

Shane circled her arm in his palm. "Because I used a bleach and water solution instead."

"Oh." His way was probably better. Jesus, she was being a bitch. Embarrassment settled heavy like a brick in her gut, and she looked up at him. "Thank you."

"You're welcome." He kissed her forehead. "Your mom is cooking in the kitchen. Still hungry?"

Cyn rubbed the spot he'd kissed her and yawned. "Yeah. I think." She shrugged. "Maybe I should just go lay back down."

Shane pulled her into an embrace. "Whatever you want, sweetheart."

She rested her cheek on his chest. "Okay."

"Okay, let's go." Turning them, Shane walked her back to her bedroom and helped her into bed.

After he closed the door, leaving her in silence, Cyn turned over and stared blankly at the thin Roman shades covering her windows. Her head felt like it was filled with cotton, but she wasn't sure if that was from the physical assault or the emotional one. She just knew her head was all sorts of fucked up.

Cyn adjusted the pillow beneath her head. How could she be so wrong about Carlos? A broken picker was one thing, but picking someone like Carlos went way past broken and landed dead center in the realm of shattered. He'd always had a bit of a temper—who didn't when provoked? God knew she'd seen him throw his fair share of fits, but nothing like last night. Last night had been a mind fuck. Last night had been a nightmare. And she still couldn't wrap her brain around it.

"SHE WENT BACK TO BED." Shane settled at Cyn's kitchen table across from Angie and Mary and glanced over at Sonja and Jimmy, sitting side by side on the window seat along the back wall of the kitchen. Roseanne—*Jesus, it's strange calling her that*—was at the stove stirring a pot of chicken noodle soup.

It was just like the Donnellys to come together to support and care for one of their own. Cyn might be okay, thank God, but there was no way the family wouldn't be right there to make sure of it. They took care of each other, even if sometimes they bickered or fought like any other family. It was one of the main reasons why Shane cared so much about them. After his father died, his perceived family died with him. The Donnellys were where he found what he needed. They stood in the gap for him and made sure, in their own way, that Shane was loved. They weren't perfect, but in Shane's eyes, they were amazing.

"She okay?" Jimmy asked.

"Yeah, I think so." Shane rubbed the back of his neck. "Did you hear her in the living room, though?"

Angie leaned forward. "No. What happened?"

"She got a little upset, is all." Shane blew out a breath. "She was worried about Madi playing in the living room. Said she needed to make sure it was disinfected."

Mary raised her coffee cup. "Ah, Cyn's dreaded control monster rears its head."

"Shut up, Mary. She went through hell last night." Angie stood, the chair screeching across the tile floor.

"What? I'm just saying." Mary waved her hand at Angie, dismissing her. "Stop being so protective. I'm not attacking Cyn. Everyone knows she's got a penchant for controlling situations."

Shane sat back with wide eyes as the two bickered.

"You *are* attacking her. You're always criticizing her, too. You go through what Cyn did last night and see how well you handle it. You think you know everything. I'd say that's your way of controlling things. So what-the-hell-ever. Back off of her." Angie stormed from the room.

Jimmy stood. "Well, isn't this fun?" He held out his palm

to Sonja. "Care to join me in the living room with my niece and your daughter?"

Sonja smiled, taking his hand. As they walked out of the room, Joey and Steph came inside from the back patio. "So, I take it Angie and Mary are going at it again?"

"Keep your comments to yourself, Joey." Mary's tone was impassive. "Angie's just being sensitive as usual."

"All right, I've had about enough of this."

Everyone froze, and Shane looked over to find that Roseanne had stepped away from the stove and into the center of the room—her hands on her hips, a dishtowel thrown over her shoulder. She had a look on her face that Shane remembered seeing when they were all kids. And he was grateful she didn't have a wooden spoon in her hand.

Roseanne glanced between them all. "Mary, make yourself useful and go out back and find your father."

Mary rolled her eyes and stood. "Yes, Mom."

"Shane, have you checked on Cyn lately?" Steph asked.

"Yes, but I have a feeling Angie headed that way a few minutes ago." Shane rubbed the back of his neck. The tension in the room had his shoulders aching, or maybe that was just residuals from the prior night. Either way, he was uncomfortable.

Roseanne came to his side then smoothed her palm over his shoulder. "What time do you fly out tomorrow?"

He looked up at her. "I'm not."

She tilted her head to the side. "Oh?"

"You're not what?" Everyone turned around as Mr. Donnelly entered the kitchen, Mary close behind him. He walked straight to Roseanne and kissed her cheek. "You needed something?"

"Yes. I needed to get Mary out of the room before her siblings took a piece out of her. And then I would've had to take a piece out of all of them." She smiled.

Her husband swung his head around to Mary. "Stirring

the pot again, Mary Claire? Keep it up, and one of these days, you're going to end up licking the spoon."

"Daddy!" Mary frowned and resumed her seat at the table.

Shane stifled a laugh, but Joey wasn't as successful. Their father cast his fatherly glare—the one they all had a healthy fear of as kids—his oldest son's way, and Joey coughed, getting himself under control. Then, Mr. D. focused back on Shane. "Son, you're not what?"

Shane smiled at the endearment, one he'd always used with him since his own father died. "I'm not leaving tomorrow, Mr. Donnelly."

"Good. Very good."

"Shane, please call him Joe. For goodness sake, you're an adult now. Joe, tell him it's okay." Roseanne shook her head.

Mr. Donnelly smoothed his hands over his small pot belly. "Absolutely." He sniffed and, with a few long strides, moved to the stove.

Roseanne rushed after him. "Stay out of that soup, Joe! It's not done yet." He grinned at her, the spoon she was stirring the soup with halfway to his lips. "Don't make me beat you." She laughed.

Steph took a seat at the table. "How long are you staying?"

Shane ran his hand over his short hair. "For as long as I need to."

"Does Cyn know you're staying?" Mary moved to the coffee pot.

"For Christ's sake, Mary. Really?" Joey glared at her. "I'm sure Cyn knows."

"What? It was just a question. God."

"Joey, watch your mouth. Mary, find something to put in *your* mouth because you're beginning to agitate *me* now. Joe... give me that spoon!"

Joe Sr. laughed and kissed his wife on the forehead. "Mary, come with me. I have an errand to run."

"Why does everyone always get mad at me? Sheesh! No, Daddy, I need to go pick Julia up from dance class anyway. Plus, Cam is at home with both boys." Mary moved to her mother and kissed her cheek. "Tell Cyn I was here?"

"Mmhmm." Roseanne patted Mary's arm. "Kiss the kids for me."

"Regardless, I'm glad you're staying, Shane." Mary came over and kissed his cheek, and called out her goodbyes as she walked out.

"She doesn't know I'm staying yet." Shane looked among all of them.

Steph leaned forward, resting on her elbows. "I'm sure she'll be grateful. I know I'm grateful."

Jimmy wandered back in. "What'd I miss besides Mother Mary laying down her opinion on everyone?"

Joey blurted a laugh, and Steph started giggling. Roseanne rolled her eyes. "James, don't you start too. Your sister means well. It's not her fault she was born second in the birth order, and as a result, she and Katie mothered all of you, plus babysat all of you until they nearly ripped their hair out."

"Okay, Mom, but can I just say, I'm real glad Katie isn't here. She'd be rearranging the furniture and reorganizing Cyn's cabinets." Jimmy laughed and grabbed a beer from the fridge.

"Afraid he's right, Roseanne." Joe Sr. was back at the pot on the stove, spoon in hand.

Roseanne threw her hands up in the air. "I give up. I swear, sometimes I think you're all harder to handle as adults than you were as kids." She shook her head with a laugh and left the room.

Joey cleared his throat. "I'm glad you're staying too. And I'm just going to thank you again for being here last night."

"A-fucking-men." Jimmy raised the bottle in salute. "Otherwise, Sonja might be representing me and Joey in a murder trial because we may've killed that bastard had he done the unthinkable to Cyn."

"If I didn't agree with everything you just said—" Joe Sr. clapped Jimmy on the back, "—I'd be correcting your language."

"Yeah, well. Let's just say I'm glad I was here, too, so no thanks are needed. How I didn't manage to commit murder last night is beyond me." Shane shook his head, trying to clear the vision of Carlos on top of Cyn.

The images had stayed up close and personal since last night and were showing no signs of letting up. He planned on letting her know sometime later that day that he was staying. But there hadn't been an opportunity yet. Shane assumed she'd be good with it, but he had to admit, the tone in which Mary asked him if Cyn knew made him wonder if maybe she wouldn't.

How could she not be, though? They'd had an amazing couple of weeks, and then the shit last night slammed into both of them. He just couldn't imagine going back to Texas and leaving her now. Especially after her little display in the living room.

He was glad no one, least of all Mary, had witnessed her anxiety-ridden need to ensure the room had been cleaned up. Plus, her reaction to him cleaning the blood had convinced Shane that she *needed* him to be there.

Whether she knew or not, she'd just have to be okay with him staying because he wasn't giving her much of a choice.

CHAPTER TWENTY-SIX

Cyn woke, curled over Shane's chest. The steady beat of his heart, combined with the warmth of his arms around her, was soothing, and she cuddled a little closer. If she wasn't mistaken, Shane was flying home to Texas today. Cyn had no idea what time it was, but figured he'd probably set an alarm to ensure he'd get up on time.

She turned her head and pressed her nose into his chest, breathing him in. His familiar scent mixed with the fresh scent of outdoors wove its way into her. She was going to miss him. She wasn't necessarily shoving him out the door, but she was ready for him to go. It was time.

Smoothing a hand up his side, a thrill skipped down Cyn's spine. She would definitely miss this… His skin felt warm and silky smooth under her palm. Amazing because he was for sure a typical guy, rough and rugged, yet not his skin. Blame the beauty queen genes inherited from his mother.

Cyn moved her palm in the opposite direction to his hip. Curving around, she grazed his cock through his boxers and felt him stir beneath her. She smiled and pressed her lips to his chest and felt his arms tighten around her. Cyn kissed along his pecs to one areola, licking over the flat disk as the nipple rose to a peak in response.

Shane moaned, trailing his fingertips down her back to her backside and sliding them through the seam of her ass cheeks. Cyn let out a whimper, grazed his nipple with her teeth as she slipped her hand down his boxer briefs and grabbed his cock. "Oh God, yes."

He was rock hard—*rock fucking hard*—in a matter of seconds. All for her. Cyn's channel clenched, her clit pulsed, and she knew she was already soaking wet for him.

"Need inside you." Shane thrust his hips forward, his shaft sliding hot and smooth through her palm.

Cyn rolled, pushed her panties off, and, without preamble, straddled Shane's hips. He'd already slid his boxers down, and she gripped his shaft in her palm again, positioning the head at her entrance.

"Cyn!" He sat up.

She shifted, allowing just the head inside the mouth of her pussy. "Oh fuck, yes. Yes!"

"Cynthia, wait! *Fuuuuckkk!*" Shane grabbed her hips, stopping her from sliding any lower. "Let me get a condom. Jesus, you feel…"

"I don't want anything between us, Shane." Gazing into his eyes, she ran her nails down his shoulders. "Let me fuck you this way. Please, babe? I need to feel you." She sucked in a breath and pressed her lips to his neck.

Shane groaned. "Oh, goddamn." He spread her ass cheeks apart, giving her that nice sting she'd become accustomed to feeling with him, as he eased her the rest of the way down his prick.

The heat of his cock rippled through her core. She was on the pill, so pregnancy wasn't a concern, and she was sure he was clean. Thing was, he was leaving, and she needed this last time with him to have no barriers, nothing separating them. Shane going home was for the best, but she'd have this to hold on to. She'd commit every moment to memory.

And selfishly, she wanted to send him off with something he'd have a hard time forgetting. God knew she wasn't going to forget anytime soon.

"Anything you want. Take what you need—what's yours." Shane ran his palms up her back, and Cyn arched, riding his thick shaft. With her head tilted back, she felt his lips touch her sternum and then a hand cup one full breast, raising it to his mouth. His warm lips closed around her nipple, and she let out a whimper, grinding her clit against his pelvis.

"Shane…" Cyn undulated above him, her hips rolling forward, taking him deep inside her core before easing him out again. Each breath she took was followed by a moan.

Shane slid a hand up her spine, tangling his fingers in her hair. "Need your tongue." He urged her head up and covered her mouth with his. With their gazes locked, he tangled his tongue with hers. A low rumble from deep in his chest vibrated between them, sizzling over Cyn's skin.

Slow and easy, she rode him, kissed him and got lost in everything that was Shane. He smoothed a hand over her ass cheek, sliding his fingers to where they were joined, stroking the lips of her pussy spread tight around his shaft. The orgasm that'd been building rushed forward when he moved his fingers back and spread her arousal over her tight asshole. She broke the kiss with a gasp and pressed her forehead to his. "Shane…want you there. Want you to take me there."

"Gonna be the death of me," he whispered and pressed a fingertip inside her hole. "Your cunt is so tight, I can't even imagine how good it'd be in your ass. You feel like a dream wrapped around my dick."

With a whimper, Cyn increased her pace, his words taking her even higher. "Need to co—"

Shane moved his other hand down her ass, curled it between them, gathered more of her wetness and lubed her asshole with it. Then he pressed two fingers inside. "Ride it, girl. Give it to me."

With his cock filling her pussy, along with his fingers stretching her ass, Cyn's climax surfaced, hovering just at the edge. Angling her hips back, she gripped his shoulders for leverage as Shane rocketed into her, and she ground down against his pelvis.

Cyn's climax whipped through her like a tornado—her pussy clenching around his thickness while her clit pulsed with each powerful wave. Shane grabbed her ass, pumping into her harder, and a guttural moan tore from her throat.

Cyn's body went limp, her climax still rolling through her as Shane tightened the grip on her ass cheeks so hard her cunt spasmed again. "*Ohhmyyygahhhd!*"

In the next moment, Cyn found herself flipped over, and her back hit the bed. Still buried inside her core, he pressed her knees to her chest and rocketed into her, his hips slapping against her backside as he drilled her channel with hard, deep thrusts. "Already loved fucking you. Love it even more now."

Cyn gazed at him in the dim morning light of the room. His muscles were hard and tight, the veins in his neck and arms standing out in sharp relief against his smooth skin as sweat dripped down his chest to his abs.

Fucking hell, he was amazing. She wanted to lick that trickle of wetness. She wanted to taste every inch of him. And she had. She just wanted to do it again.

"Grab those tits for me." He thrust into her. "Need to come...for you. Fuck, Cyn. Tell me where." He gritted his teeth.

"Inside me, Shane. Wanna feel you fill me." Cyn cupped her breasts and pressed them together. Craning her neck forward, she pulled one breast up and licked over the nipple.

"Fuck yes. Take it, girl, 'cause, yeah, that just did it..." Shane inched back onto his haunches and gripped his balls and shaft at the base. The head of his cock was still buried inside her channel. With a loud groan, his climax hit. "*Fuuuuckkk!*"

Cyn lost her breath when she felt his heated release spurting inside her. With a harsh moan, her head fell back on the pillows, and she closed her eyes, savoring each throbbing pulse of his cock inside her—filling her in more ways than one.

Branding her was more like it.

After a few moments, Shane's sweat-slick body blanketed hers. Wrapping her shaky limbs around him, Cyn held him close. "Wow… That was…" She stroked his back as they both tried to catch their breath. "Guess this'll be one hell of a memory to go back to Texas with, huh?"

Shane chuckled as he pressed soft kisses to her neck. "Definitely. But I'm not going back just yet."

What? Did he just—her head snapped up. "What?"

———

SHANE FROZE, his nose pressed against the soft skin of her neck. The tone behind her "what" didn't sound like a welcome one. He raised his head and stared down at her. "I said I'm not going just yet."

She frowned. "But your flight is today."

He shifted, rolling them to their sides, then brushed her hair away from her eyes. "My flight *was* today."

"I don't understand."

He pressed a kiss to her nose. "Hold that thought." Reluctant to do so, Shane slipped from her channel and rolled off the bed. He grabbed a towel from the bathroom, wiped up and before walking out, grabbed another for her and brought it to the bed. After handing it to her, he slid under the sheets. "I canceled my flight."

Finished with the towel, she sat up and chucked it, overhanded, across the room. "Why on earth would you do that?"

Yeah, there was definitely nothing positive about her tone *or* the words she was using. Shane wasn't sure how he expected her to react, but it definitely wasn't in this way. "Considering what happened, I don't think I should go yet. Why do you sound pissed instead of happy?"

"I'm not pissed." She flopped back onto her back in a huff. "I'm just…shocked. I mean, I guess it's fine, but…you know, no. You should've talked to me about it before you made this decision, Shane!"

Pissed might've been an understatement. He frowned. "Sorry. I guess I thought you'd be okay with it."

She blew out a breath and rubbed her hands over her face. "Ugh. Okay. Fine. It's fine. I'm just freaking out for no reason. So you're staying a little longer. When do you fly out?"

"I haven't decided yet." Shane watched her, waiting for a response. Instead, Cyn looked over at him—an expression in her eyes he was a little afraid to decipher—and said nothing.

Talk about a cold bucket of water and a punch in the gut. Fuck's sake, this was definitely not how he envisioned this conversation going. "Wow. Okay then." Shane rolled away from her and stood. "I'm going to grab a shower."

"Fine… Great."

After getting the water going, Shane moved under the spray. Cyn's rejection burned like a hot poker in his heart. Apparently, she wasn't feeling any of the feelings he was. Obviously, things between them meant more to him than they did to her.

Great time to find out the joke was on him. *Fuuuuckkk!* Shane's head fell forward, and the hot water beat on the back of his neck.

He had no idea what to do now.

Maybe he should just go home, get back to his life. He cringed and smoothed his palms over his skull. The thought of leaving her so quickly after the attack made his stomach fold in on itself.

He couldn't *just* get back to his life now. Not without being completely distracted the whole time. He wouldn't be worth shit on the job, all consumed with thoughts of how she was doing every minute of the day.

For fuck's sake, Carlos could've killed her, and Shane would've lost her—everyone would have. Cyn was not a woman to be lost.

Thanks to God and good timing, she was alive and well, but considering her behavior in the living room the night before and her harsh reaction just now, he had to wonder how bad the fallout was going to be from the attack. Even a bit of Post Traumatic Stress Disorder was possible and would definitely explain both emotional reactions.

Shane turned off the water, grabbed the towel hanging over the shower door and stepped out. No, he couldn't *just* leave now. If he was right and she was experiencing PTSD, the ride was about to get real rough. He'd just have to deal with whatever roller coaster of emotions she was going to experience and direct his way.

When he finished in the bathroom, Shane made his way to the kitchen and found her sitting on the window seat. She had her knees pulled up to her chest, coffee mug in hand, as she stared out the window. After pouring himself a mugful, he turned and faced her, resting his hips against the counter. Silence stretched between them as Shane sipped the warm coffee. The urge to say something rode him hard, but he tamped it down.

"I'm okay. And I know you think I'm not, but I am."

"It's not that I don't think you're okay. It's just…" Shane needed to choose his words wisely to avoid pissing her off further. He imagined he'd be doing a lot of that—choosing his words wisely *and* pissing her off—in the coming days or weeks. "I think you're still in a bit of shock. I also think…well, actually, based on my own experiences with trauma, what happened to you is gonna require a lot of talking and some time in order to truly be okay. Am I making sense?"

"You're making plenty of sense, but I don't really want to talk about it." With a shrug, Cyn blew out a harsh breath and then sipped her coffee.

"What about talking to a professional?"

She cut him a side-eye glance and then returned her focus to the window. "Don't be ridiculous. I don't need that."

Shit, yeah, treading lightly was going to be the tune for the next who knew how long. Shane moved to her and took a seat on the bench. "All right, but hear me out?"

She rolled her eyes. "I don't need professional help, Shane. But whatever, say what you need to."

Coffee mug held tight in his hands, Shane braced his elbows on his knees and drew in a deep breath. "When I got out of the Marines and even while still in, I had to talk to someone. A few times. It's normal, Cyn. After a trauma—"

"Shane, you can hardly compare your being in Iraq and Afghanistan—basically a flipping war zone with death all around you, and God, I can only imagine how horrible that was—to my little incident with Carlos. That's just absurd."

He sighed through his nose and took in her profile. "Cyn, trauma is still trauma. And everyone copes differently."

"Right, and I'm telling you, I'll cope just fine. Jesus, it's only been what? Barely forty-eight hours? Cut me a little slack."

She had a point. He straightened in the seat and took a sip of his coffee. Regardless, Shane couldn't shake the feeling that it wasn't going to be so easy. "All right, Cyn."

"Thank you." She stood. "I'm going to go shower. After that, I don't know. I guess we figure it out from there."

With concern pumping hot and fast through his veins, Shane watched her as she left the room. Nope, he would not be leaving. Anytime soon.

CHAPTER TWENTY-SEVEN

After locking the glass and metal front door, Cyn looked around her quiet office and tried to calm the nerves playing hockey in her stomach. She'd been handling business from home, meeting clients at coffee shops, and hadn't been on premises since the attack over a week ago.

The thought of being in the office, or worse, *leaving* the office after work, was more than she could stomach. Every time she thought about it, heat would crawl up the back of her neck, making the hairs stand on end, and she'd start sweating like she was sitting on top of a hot stove. And then her heart would race. She'd excuse herself from the room if she wasn't alone, but since Shane had decided to stay in town, being alone was a rare thing.

That morning—which she couldn't recall the reason now—she'd decided it was time to get back to normal. Cyn wiped the sweat from her brow. She was seriously rethinking that decision now. Carlos was out on bail, thanks to the attorney his family was paying for. There was a "no contact order" in place as part of his bail, but a lot of good that'd do her if he chose to ignore it.

Pulling herself back from the tunnel of fear, Cyn walked

down the hall from the reception area to her small office. After setting her things on the desk, she took a seat, pulled her laptop from her bag and started it up.

The shrill ring from her cell phone echoed from her purse, and Cyn jumped clean out of her skin. "Jesus Christ!" She pressed her hand to her chest. Fishing the device from the bottom of her purse, she swiped the screen and put it to her ear. "Hello?"

"Hey. How's it going? You all right?"

Cyn blew out a harsh breath. "I'm fine, Shane! Jesus Christ, I *just* got here. I haven't even finished booting up my laptop yet."

"Come on now. Go easy. I just wanted to check on you."

She paused, knowing and hating that she sounded like a complete raving bitch. Yet, she couldn't seem to stop ripping Shane's head off and tap dancing on his kidneys every time he opened his mouth to ask if she was okay—but for the millionth time, she was fucking fine!

And she really wanted him to just stop asking. Plus, whenever she asked him when he was going home, he wouldn't give her a straight answer, and it was seriously beginning to piss her off. It wasn't that Cyn wanted him to leave exactly. She didn't mind Shane being there. She just… She'd had a plan and wanted to get back to that plan. "I thought you were going for a hike with Joey today?"

"I am. But who knows if I'll have cell service once we get out there, so I figured I'd check in before we took off."

Annnnd now she really felt like a bitch. Cyn frowned and rubbed her forehead. Her whiplash emotions were enough to give *her* a headache. Never mind what they were doing to Shane. Poor guy was just being attentive—in all the ways Carlos never was. Or any other guy in her past, for that matter —and here she was again, acting like he was doing something wrong. "Oh."

He was quiet for a moment, his breath the only sound in

her ear. "What time do you think you're going to get out of there?"

Cyn glanced at the clock on her computer screen. "I don't know. I have a couple of clients coming in. Before three, I hope."

"Sounds good. I'll be back by two thirty and meet you there."

"Shane, you don't have to do that. It's not necessary."

"I know what I don't have to do. I also know what I want to do. Necessary or not, I'm meeting you there. So deal with it."

The authority in his tone brooked no argument, damn alpha that he was. It sucked because she had liked this side of him. A lot. But now, it only served to annoy her. Cyn sighed loud enough so he could hear her. "Fine."

"Fine. Have a good day."

With that, he disconnected. Cyn pulled the phone from her ear and tossed it on her desk. "*Fiiiine.* Ugh. I'll show you fine, mister-alpha-male-who-thinks-he-knows-what's-best for—"

"Hey, boss? Who're you talking to?"

Once again, Cyn jumped from her skin, but this time with an added scream.

"Oh my God, I'm soooo sorry." Her assistant came rushing over to her. "Shit, I'm really sorry, Cyn. I didn't mean to startle you."

When Cyn finally caught her breath, she started laughing. "It's okay." She shook her head and got to her feet. "Not your fault, Lisa. I didn't hear you come in."

"Might've been that little rant you were caught up in." Lisa raised her brows and smiled.

Heat flooded Cyn's cheeks. She had been ranting, hadn't she? Like some sort of lunatic. Cyn rolled her eyes. "Yeah. Might've been."

"Well, I'm here. You're here. How about a cup of coffee,

and then we get some work done?" Lisa rubbed Cyn's shoulder.

Work was the farthest thing from her mind, but that was the whole reason for being there, wasn't it? That, and she wanted to see if she could actually do it and not be a total basket case the whole time. So far, she was failing. Cyn forced a smile. "Sounds like a plan."

"Cool. I'll be right back." Lisa exited Cyn's office. Cyn resumed her seat and finished logging into the planning database. A few minutes later, her assistant returned, mug of coffee in hand for Cyn. She set it on the desk. "I'll check the schedule and see who's on deck next."

Cyn glanced up from the laptop screen. "Thanks. Pretty sure it's the Andersons' event. They're scheduled to be in at ten. But let me know if there's anything I missed."

"Will do."

Lisa left Cyn's office, and once again, she was alone. Not technically alone since her assistant was in the office, too, but she still felt a little isolated. She tried to shake off the feeling and focus on work, but it wasn't easy. She could do this. She had to.

Shane had mentioned a therapist a few times since last Saturday, and Cyn was still reluctant. Not running her business properly was not an option. Moreover, as far as she was concerned, seeing a counselor wasn't an option either. Not in her book, anyway.

Also, there was the little issue of Shane. He'd been set to leave—Cyn had been ready for him to leave until the little run-in with Carlos. Anger pulsed through her. She was supposed to be single right now—technically, she still considered herself single…sort of.

Yes, she and Shane were having sex nightly—the most incredible, mind-blowing sex of her life—and he was staying at her house. But that didn't mean they were a couple. Not officially. Again, not in her book anyway. Good sex…did not a relationship make. Plus, all of his helpful, considerate behavior was bugging the ever-loving shit out of her.

Annoyance spilled through her, and she dropped her head into her palm. What the fuck was wrong with her? Annoyed because he was *considerate*? Really? God, wasn't that the one thing she'd always wanted? Well, one thing on a long list of things, but still. And truly, if she examined her little mental list of what she wanted in a man, Shane had damn near checked off every box for her. And awesome sex was pretty freaking high on the requirement list. He'd fulfilled that dream item the very first night they were together. So, what exactly was her malfunction, anyway? Cyn pulled her hand away from her face and stared down at her fingers. "Fucking broken picker."

How in the hell would she ever trust her own judgment again? Especially after the last "pick" she'd made. That'd turned from bad relationship to nightmare break-up. Her choosing Carlos gave new meaning to the broken picker issue.

Shane kept telling her that the attack wasn't her fault, and yes, she understood. Carlos had lost his damn mind, but hadn't she contributed by simply staying with him for as long as she had? Hadn't she brought it on herself because she'd allowed him to treat her like crap as well as allowing him to breeze in and out of her life like it was a revolving door?

She had. No matter what Shane said, as far as Cyn was concerned, a good chunk of the blame fell on her shoulders.

To make matters worse, Shane was still in town, showing no sign of leaving. Plus, acting like they were a couple and— Cyn just couldn't get past her doubts. He was a nice guy. But weren't they all "nice guys" at one point? They sure as hell were, and because she couldn't tell the difference, there was no fucking way she was going to just trust Shane because he was who he was.

He was still a guy, and since he was interested in her, he was likely a broken one.

"Cyn, the Andersons are here."

Cyn jumped at the sound of Lisa's voice, but thank God, didn't scream this time.

"Sorry, honey."

"No, it's fine. I'm fine." Cyn eyed the clock on her laptop and cringed. An hour had passed, and she'd just been sitting there, staring into space, trying to sort out the tangled web of thoughts in her mind. *Shit.* So much for not failing at doing her job.

ARRIVING ABOUT THIRTY MINUTES EARLY, Shane rested his ass end on the front bumper of his rental SUV and waited for Cyn to come out of her office. He'd had a great morning and afternoon with Joey. The hike they'd taken in the hills just outside of Glendale had been much-needed fuel for his soul. The lunchtime shooting-the-shit banter with his best friend had definitely topped off Shane's tank.

Wanting to avoid bugging her further, Shane hadn't reached out to Cyn since their phone call in the morning. The fact that he'd bugged her to begin with had not been lost on him. It'd been the theme of each and every day since the attack. That was until they were having sex. When they were fucking, Cyn wasn't bugged at all. Then again, kinda hard to be annoyed with him when he was giving her multiples.

Sad thing was, it was the only time Shane felt like she let him close to her anymore. She kept asking him how long he was staying, and each time, he deflected the question. Reason being, he wasn't sure himself how long he planned to stay, so he couldn't really give her an answer.

She didn't like it, but he didn't like it much either. In the meantime, he kept an eye on his checking and savings account balances and banked on things working out exactly how they were supposed to.

He shifted and stared down at his boots. The rental was

costing him a decent amount each day, and his small mort-gage payment would be due the beginning of the next month. Plus, all the utilities. But the good news was Shane had a pretty hefty savings, as well as some investments, due to all the hazard pay and per diem he'd made while deployed. In addition, he had the trust money from his father's life insurance invested still. He wasn't wealthy by any stretch, not by society's standards anyway. He just preferred to live a low-profile life, but because he did, he could float for a long time or as long as he needed to while he was in L.A. with Cyn.

Maybe he'd pick up a few side handyman jobs in order to keep himself from getting bored. He could also do some work on Cyn's house while she was at work—though that might agitate her, too. Shane blew out a breath, checked the time and glanced over at the entrance door to her office. Just as he thought he might go inside to check on her, she emerged.

She glanced at him, adjusted the strap of her laptop bag on her shoulder and walked his way. "Hi."

"Hi there." He placed a hand on her hip and bent to kiss her, but only landed a quick peck because she pulled away too quickly. Though it stung, Shane ignored her reaction and straightened. "How'd it go?"

"Fine." She shrugged and moved toward her Wrangler.

He stuffed his hands in his front pockets and followed. "I think that's becoming your favorite word."

Cyn tossed her bag and purse from the driver's side over to the passenger seat. "If you say so." She turned back to him. "How was your hike with Joey?"

He smiled. "Fine."

She rolled her eyes, but a small smile tilted her lips. "Whatever."

"Oh wow! Shit!" Shane widened his eyes.

Cyn's brow furrowed. "What?"

"False alarm."

"Shane! What?"

"Well, you almost smiled for a second there. I got scared hell might've frozen over." He smirked. "But all is still on fire down there. Poor damned souls. You're back to frowning."

"Ugh, whatever." She rolled her eyes and slapped his arm. "Can we get out of here, please?"

"Careful now, you almost smiled again. You're gonna knock the earth off its axis." He hooked an arm around her waist.

"Shut it." She smirked, then licked her lips.

Surprise rolled through him, and in its wake, his dick thickened. Cyn knew exactly what licking her lips did to him. His girl was in need, and Shane was happy to be her supplier. "Licking them lips? You need something between them?"

Pressed against him, Cyn's eyes sparkled with lust as she stared up at him. "Only if it's your cock that's sliding between them."

Shane bent his head and trailed his lips over her ear. "You want me to fuck that pretty mouth of yours?"

She let out a little gasp and gripped his T-shirt in her fingers. "How about you feed me, then fuck me?"

With a growl, he nipped her earlobe. "Done. Get your fine ass in your Jeep and meet me at your house."

He swatted her bottom before letting her go. She yelped and rubbed her butt cheek as she stepped back. "Fine."

"You know what 'fine' means, don't you?" He slid into his rental.

"Nope. But I'm betting you're gonna tell me." She slid behind the wheel. "Just do it after…" She winked and shut the door.

Shane chuckled, closing himself in the SUV. The moments of fun banter with her were few and far between anymore, and he hoped it'd carry over through dinner. Plus, his prick was rock hard as the anticipation of her sweet mouth pulsed hot in his veins. No matter how difficult and tense things had been, at least the chemistry between them remained strong. He was grateful for that. It was all they had. The sex might be the only stable good thing between them right at that moment, but Shane was sure once Cyn got through the healing process, there'd be more. There had to be.

CHAPTER TWENTY-EIGHT

Cyn slid into the passenger seat of Shane's rental and glanced around. He'd had the SUV since he'd gotten into town, which, if she remembered right, had been about a month ago. Give or take a day. "How much is this costing you?"

Shane glanced over at her as he turned the key in the ignition. "Why?"

"Because you've had it the whole time you've been here. That's gotta be adding up to a pretty penny."

He backed out of her driveway. "It's fine, Cyn. Don't worry about it."

There it was again, the standard "don't worry about it" answer she seemed to be getting from everyone lately. She shifted and glared at him. "Don't tell me what to worry about, Shane! I asked you a simple question. Have the courtesy of answering it. At the very least, tell me to mind my own business, but for fuck's sake, don't tell me not to worry about it. I'm getting real fucking sick of that answer."

He glanced at her, then focused back on the road. "All right. Mind your own business."

"Ugh, really? Fucking wow!" She crossed her arms and faced forward. "Fine."

"You already know what 'fine' means." His tone was low and calm as he pulled onto the main road, a completely impassive expression on his face. Which just pissed Cyn off more.

"Yes, smart-ass. I know what it means." She cringed at her cutting tone of voice and also that she'd called him a name. Jesus, it was like she'd lost all boundaries where he was concerned and saying anything had become an acceptable norm. But Cyn was well aware that this behavior was not acceptable or the norm for her.

He spared her another glance. "Tell me."

God, he was annoying. Didn't he understand that pushing her only pissed her off more? Cyn groaned and stared out the side window. "It doesn't matter."

"Oh, it does, but I'll give you a pass. For now."

"What the hell is *that* supposed to mean?"

"It means—" he leaned closer to her, "—that maybe I'll make you tell me later by putting you over my knee."

Lust-infused heat flooded Cyn's body and rushed straight between her legs. A soft gasp left her, and she licked her lips. "Dammit, Shane."

He rubbed his hand up her thigh. "You're wet now, aren't you?"

"Not fair." She was—totally was. The thought of him bending her over his knee and swatting her ass until she begged him to either stop or keep going, she wasn't sure which, made her libido stand up and flail.

They had sex every day, sometimes more than once. She may not have been sure of what they were doing exactly or even sure about him at all, but Cyn was more than sure his dick was made of crack. His tongue, too.

On a daily basis, in between work or being annoyed and anything else that cropped up, she thought about giving him head. All things considered, it served as a pretty decent distraction. In fact, all in all, she'd sucked Shane's cock more times than she'd sucked dick in her entire sexually active life. Blowjobs weren't her thing, never had been her thing, but with him, it was totally her thing.

In addition, on a scale of one to ten, the sex between them was an easy twenty. Even when she was annoyed or pissed with him, kinda like she was right then, she still wanted to fuck him. If she didn't know better, she'd say she was losing her mind because she wanted sex all the time now, but not with just anyone. She only wanted it with Shane. Cyn bit her bottom lip and frowned. Maybe she'd already lost her mind…

"You're thinking about sucking my dick right now, aren't you?"

Cyn crossed her arms. "Yup. But you're thinking about me sucking your dick, too, so I guess that makes us even."

Shane blurted a laugh. "Now that's a game I don't mind being tied in."

What if the sex had become a distraction for her? Some subconscious-mind kind of bullshit she was unaware she was pulling to avoid dealing with the Carlos issue?

Maybe she was in trouble. Maybe Shane and everyone else were right, and she needed to deal with what had happened with a professional. Anxiety crawled up the back of her throat, and Cyn swallowed it down. She could barely consider the idea without wanting to vomit.

Screw this. If the sex was serving as a distraction, she'd take it. She leaned across the center console, licked a line up his neck to his ear and cupped his balls through his jeans. Shane tangled his fingers in her hair, groaning as she pressed her palm against the bulge she felt growing behind his zipper. "I want you in my mouth right now."

"Gonna be the death of me, girl."

Cyn tugged open the button on his pants and slid her

hand inside. "Always so hard for me." She nipped his earlobe and fisted his shaft in her palm.

He groaned and thrust his hips up, and his length slid through her grip. "Fuck…as much as I want you to keep doing that, you need to stop because, hello, California drivers, and we're almost to Ryan and Maiya's."

"Boo hiss." Cyn pouted but stroked him once more for good measure. "Guess I'll just have to wait." She pulled away, sliding her hand free but stroking him slowly as she did.

"Come on now. I'm fine with you being the death of me, but not literally." He smiled, tugged her close again, and kissed her.

"Killjoy." She giggled.

"Yeah, that's me."

And just like that, the tension between them evaporated…at least until he annoyed her again. It didn't escape Cyn's notice that it was because of the sex. But whatever, lost mind or not, it was what it was. Not like she was running around screwing anything with a pulse. Cyn had no interest in that. She was only like this with Shane. They had good sex. They had incredible chemistry. Outside of that, she wasn't sure what they had…because they weren't supposed to have anything! Because he wasn't supposed to still be in L.A.!

Ugh! And hello, whiplash, Cyn was annoyed. Again.

SHANE SAT in a chaise lounge on Ryan and Maiya's back deck. Cyn was positioned between his legs, her back resting against his chest. He had his arms around her waist, enjoying the feel of her petite body snugged up close to him.

Maiya was on the other chaise smoking, and Ryan sat on the edge, her feet in his lap while he rubbed them. Angie was across from them in one of the regular deck chairs. They were having great conversation—all talking about anything and everything, and sometimes over the top of one another.

But not his girl. Cyn was quiet, her head on Shane's chest as he held her.

"I dare you, Ryan. I dare you to do that shit at Mom and Dad's and see what happens." Angie laughed.

"No way. I am no fool. Mary'll come after me with a frying pan! You do it."

Maiya laughed. "I dare you both to do it. Tell you what, though, that's something I'd pay money to see. However, I'll be hiding around the corner and watching from a safe distance."

"That's because you're a smart woman." Angie raised her beer to Maiya. "Ryan, how did you land such a smart woman?"

"Pfft, easy. My good looks and charming personality."

Shane laughed, and Maiya blew out a cloud of smoke with a cough. "No, baby. It was the khakis. They did me in."

"Was that it? Just the khakis?" He tickled her foot.

"*Hayhayhayyyy!*" Maiya jerked her foot away. "None of that!" She laughed. "'Bout to get yourself kicked, Mr. Donnelly."

Angie clapped her hands. "Get him, Maiya!"

"She's all talk." Ryan pulled his giggling wife close and kissed her. "You're not gonna kick me, Mrs. Donnelly."

Maiya wrapped her arms around her husband's neck and rubbed her nose over his.

"Ugh, you two are beyond cute." Cyn smoothed her hands down Shane's thighs.

Shane kissed her cheek. "Agreed."

"It's almost gross." Angie tipped her beer back.

Maiya peeked around Ryan to Angie. "Do you need a bucket, Miss Thang?"

Angie let out a loud burp and then laughed. "Nah, I'm good."

"Well, that was pretty! Thank God you didn't bring a date tonight." Ryan straightened and went back to rubbing Maiya's feet.

"Thanks!" Angie crossed one leg over the other. "Off the market at present moment."

Cyn shifted and sat up. "You met someone?"

"Hell no, I didn't meet someone. I'm still doing your 'stay single for a year' thing." Angie shrugged. "You're not, like we agreed to, obviously, but I figure what the hell. I may as well see how it goes."

"What 'stay single for a year' thing is that?" Shane asked.

Cyn stiffened and glanced over her shoulder at him. "Don't worry about it. It's nothing."

Angie visibly cringed. "Ignore me, Shane. It's just the beer talking."

Maiya had gone silent, staring straight ahead. Shane looked over at Ryan, but he looked just as confused as Shane was. Shane looked back to Angie, and she shrugged. He shook his head. "Wait…what'd I miss? Did we just enter the *Twilight Zone* or something?"

Cyn sighed. "And that would be the cue that it's time for me to leave." She got to her feet. "You ready?"

What the hell? That was all far too strange. Clearly, she was keeping something from him, and he intended to find out what it was. He stared at her and realized Cyn didn't give a shit one way or the other if he was ready to go. Nor did she give a shit if he knew what the hell she was talking about.

Agitation flared hot in his bloodstream. He'd been damn patient with her, dealt with her mood swings and her mouthy temper tantrums *and* verbal abuse pretty fucking well over the last two weeks. But there was no fucking way he was going to deal with her keeping secrets from him. Just wasn't going to happen.

Shane got to his feet. "If you're ready to go, then we can go. But this conversation isn't over." Shane stepped away from her to Ryan and Maiya. "Thank you both for the awesome dinner. I had a great time."

"You're welcome. Happy to have you both over," Maiya said.

Ryan stood and shook his hand and pulled him into an embrace. "Anytime, man. You know you're always welcome here." When Ryan let Shane go, he clapped him on the shoulder and nodded. "Any time."

"Appreciate it." He moved to Angie and bent to kiss her cheek. "As always, good to see you, Angie."

"You too, Shane." She frowned and mouthed an "I'm sorry" to him. He shook his head and gave her a "no big deal" expression. Whatever Angie had let slide, she sure hadn't done it with malicious intent. He turned to see Cyn making her way into the house. "Okay, then. Guess we're going." He shrugged and followed after her.

And once again, he buckled up to continue on the roller coaster named Cyn Donnelly. Yes, he'd always loved the excitement of the twists and turns, and the big drops down the hills, and even the loops, but he was starting to feel pretty beat up and beyond worn out.

Cyn needed to go to therapy and face the bubbling sea of shit she was carrying around. If she didn't, Shane would have no choice but to walk away from her.

It broke his heart even thinking about it, but he was starting to wonder if that particular fate—the loss of what he'd found with her—was unavoidable.

***

Cyn sat in silence on the drive back to her house. The dead air continued once they'd gotten into her house and even after she'd taken a shower and dressed in her pajamas. Only once she was settled on a lounger on the back patio, mug of hot tea in her hands, did it come to an end.

Shane took a seat in the lounger beside her. "I want to talk about what happened at your brother's."

"Well, I don't. How about we talk about when you're going home instead?"

Shane jerked back in the chair as though she'd slapped him. "You really want me to go home?"

Cyn shrugged and stared out to the pool and the darkness of the backyard. If he stayed, she'd deal. If he didn't, she'd deal. Either way, she was good. "It doesn't matter."

"Cyn, it fucking matters."

She really did not want to do this with him. Any of it. She was too tired, too emotional and too…fine. "Then I guess it matters to you."

"Damn right, it matters to me. I care about you. I'm worried about you. Christ, you won't even sit in your own living room, for fuck's sake."

"Why do you care if I sit in my living room or not? Big fucking deal!"

"You are *not* fine, Cyn." He leaned forward, bracing his elbows on his knees. "You refuse to talk about the attack. With anyone."

"So what? Why can't you leave me alone about it? Why do you have to keep bugging me, harping on me constantly? I'm fucking fin—" Cyn groaned and pressed her lips together, knowing exactly what he'd say next.

He let out a sigh and ran his hand over his head. "Exactly."

"Yeah, sure. 'Fucked-Up, Insecure, Neurotic and Emotional', right? Fuck you, Shane."

"Fuck me? Sure. Anytime, Cyn." He stood. "But while you're fucking me, you need to see a counselor. You need to talk about it until it's not so big in your head. You need to work this shit out until it's straight again, Cyn. If you don't, it's gonna eat you from the inside out. It already is."

White-hot rage seared through her veins. Fuck him, she

did not *need* a counselor. Cyn got to her feet, and with her hands propped on her hips, she stepped up to him. Cursing how short she was, Cyn craned her neck back and glared up at him. "What I need is for you to leave me the fuck alone about it. Which, obviously, you can't seem to understand, leading me back to my first question: *When. Are. You. Going. Home!*"

He glared right back, and the muscle in his jawline twitched. He had damn near a foot of height on her, but it didn't matter. She was pissed with no intention of backing down. He needed to get this through his big meathead skull of his. Cyn was well aware of the fact that she'd been on edge a lot. But truly, it was because no one would leave her alone about the attack or her mood or if she was okay...*blah blah blah*. If they'd back the hell off, she'd be just fucking fi— *Ugh!*

Shane sighed through his nose and then cleared his throat. "I'll go home after you have your first session."

"*Are you fucking nuts!*"

"Maybe, but that's not really the concern right now." His voice had gone low, sounding deep and gravelly.

Cyn tried to ignore how the sound rippled over her. She did not need to be getting all horned up right then. What she needed was to stand her ground. She licked her lips, and his eyes followed the movement of her tongue. A bolt of lust hit her straight between her legs. *Goddammit!* Standing so close, his scent rolled through her, and Cyn barely suppressed a moan. "Well, I guess you're not leaving because I already told you, I'm *not* seeing a counselor."

Shane tilted his head to the side. "Guess not, then."

He took a breath, and her breasts grazed his lower chest. *Fuck!* "You have to go, Shane."

"Why, Cyn? Tell me why I have to go." He stepped closer, and Cyn's breasts pressed into him.

She didn't want to tell him about the moratorium *or* the reasons behind it. She didn't want to tell him anything. The idea of letting him into the dark corners of her heart and mind—the places only she visited as of late—and sharing her fears and insecurities made Cyn want to run as fast as she could in the opposite direction.

He'd know her weaknesses and flaws, and he'd use them against her. Cyn couldn't be that vulnerable with him…or anyone, for that matter. She breathed deep, her chest rising, forcing her breasts tighter against him. Her nipples peaked into hard points beneath her shirt. *Jesus, this is insane.* "Because I just need you to."

"Need, huh?" Shane placed his hands on her upper arms and bent to her ear. "When you're taking my prick deep inside your pussy, you don't need me to go. What you need *then* is for me to fuck you harder."

Cyn shivered, and a gasp escaped before she had a chance to stop it. Anger, mixed with hot lust, swamped her senses—a crazy, dangerous combination. Curse her body for betraying her in this way. It was as if she was a prisoner to her vagina. And only his dick was the key.

A sweaty round of hate sex was exactly where this little argument between them was heading—but considering her little bone of awareness in the car earlier that night, maybe sex wasn't the best idea. "I'm not discussing this."

His hands flexed on her arms, but he didn't let her go. "Tell me what happened at your brother's, Cyn. If it affects us, I need to know. If it's the reason you're so eager for me to leave, I need to know that, too."

"Why? God, why can't you just leave it be? Why do you have to push? Always!" She pressed her hands against his chest, trying to shove him away, but of course, all six-foot-three, two hundred and thirty pounds of him wouldn't budge. *"Fucking hell, Shane!"*

"I've had about enough of you yelling at me."

Before Cyn realized what was happening, Shane picked her up and tossed her over his shoulder. She wiggled, swatting at his ass as he walked them into the house. "Put me down! Goddammit, Shane! I will not be manhandled by you!"

CRACK! His palm landed on her ass cheek, and Cyn squealed. She craned her neck to the side and bit into the side of his back.

"*Yee-ouch!* Dammit, Cyn, that hurt!"

He slapped her ass again, and she lost her breath on a yell as arousal pumped through her. *Shit.* "Put me down, Shane!"

He bent forward, and Cyn fell back onto her mattress. "As you wish."

"Sonofabitch!" She went to sit up, and he shoved her back down. "Goddammit, Shane!"

Shane came over her, his chest heaving with his breaths. He poised above her, resting his weight on both of his arms on either side of her. "I *do not* want to fight with you, Cynthia!"

"For someone who doesn't want to fight, you do a stellar job of pissing me off on a regular basis."

He gazed down at her, his expression hard and determined. He smoothed her hair away from her eyes. "Don't you get it?"

"Don't you?" she whispered as she focused on his mouth. Goddammit, this was too much. Her heart raced, pounding in her ears as lust spread through her like warm honey. A moment stretched between them in the silence, and he bent his head and tried to kiss her. Hating that all she wanted to do was kiss him back, instead, Cyn bit his bottom lip and dragged her nails down his back.

Shane growled and threaded his fingers into her hair, tugging her head back. At the same time, she spread her legs, and he settled between them. Cyn curled her legs around his hips, and he ground the erection behind his jeans against her center. She couldn't fight this anymore, and she didn't want to. If sex with Shane was what was carrying her through, then fuck it, she'd go with it. She already hated herself. She may as well add a little more to the pile. With a whimper,

Cyn sucked his bottom lip, then took his tongue inside her mouth.

As the kiss grew frantic, so did Cyn. She needed his skin against hers. She needed his pants off. She just fucking needed him. Now. Shane broke from her lips and moved his mouth down to her neck. Cyn tugged at his shirt. "Shane! Please…I need you."

"Told you." He smoothed his hand down her side to her hip and onto her ass.

"Fucker! Ugh!" Cyn bit his shoulder hard. When he growled and gripped her ass, she pulled away. "Just shut up and fuck me, please."

He rose off of her. "Like it better when you ask nice."

She sat up and pulled open the top button of his jeans. "Tough. I'm still pissed at you." And herself. After getting his pants undone, Cyn yanked them down his hips and gripped his length in her palm. In the next second, she had the swollen head sucked between her lips. A moan laced with pure satisfaction vibrated in her throat when his taste hit her, and Cyn's head spun.

Shane drew in a harsh breath. "Watch those teeth, girl! Fucking hell, your mouth is…"

Cyn moaned and took him deeper, twirling her tongue around the bulbous head as more pre-ejaculate coated her tongue. Shane pulled away and yanked her shirt over her head. She glared up at him. "I wasn't done!"

"Oh yeah, you're done." He flipped her over and yanked her sweats down. "Fuck me, your ass is still bright red from my palm." He smoothed his hand over her bottom. "Thinking I need to make it glow brighter."

"Shane…" She wiggled. "Either fuck me or let me keep sucking your dick. Just shut the fuck up and do something." As if in a state of madness, fury pulsed through her, racing in time with her arousal. Her clit pulsed, and her channel ached to be filled. She was tired of playing around. She needed to be filled by him, one way or another. And she was tired of wait-ing. He grabbed both of her arms and yanked them behind her back. "Shane, dammit! I'm serious!"

And then she felt him grip both of her wrists in one hand and—

CRACK! CRACK! "Tell me to shut up again!"

Cyn's head shot up. "Fuck you!"

CRACK! CRACK! CRACK! "That mouth of yours. Gonna gag you if you don't learn how to use it nicely." *CRACK! CRACK!*

Oh God! With each blow, Shane landed, her clit pulsed harder, and she felt her arousal run down her thighs. Cyn gasped and then let out a deep moan. *CRACK! CRACK! CRACK!* Her ass stung to the point of mindless pleasure. Over-come and lost in the haze of her arousal, Cyn's eyes glazed over, and she pressed her forehead to the pillow.

Shane ran his fingers through her folds and growled. "Sopping, sloppy, wet for me." He bent over her. "You like that full ass of yours spanked, don't you? It's all nice and bright red now. You want more?"

"Yes," she breathed.

"Swear you're gonna be the death of me—" Shane kissed down her back and smoothed his hands over her heated bottom, "—the *goddamn* death of me." He slapped her ass again.

Cyn had become nothing but a deep well of need. The need to be left alone and the need to be held close. And a need to be free of the anger and anxiety that plagued her almost constantly.

She'd been fighting tooth and nail to keep herself from drowning in the insanity of it all. But right then, under Shane's masterful touch, she'd lost any fight left within her. He was filling her emptiness in a way she'd never expected or even thought possible.

She knew it was wrong. It was wrong to use him in this

way, and it wouldn't last—could only be temporary, but for the moment, it was working.

For the moment, it was all Cyn had.

SHANE FELT her body still beneath his palm as he smoothed it over the bright red haze covering her ass cheeks. She'd finally stopped fighting him and succumbed to what her body was seeking.

He was well aware that Cyn needed so much more than just sex in order to sort through the tangled web of shit she was carrying around, but because she refused to seek help, right now, this was his solution. Not the best, but at least it gave her some peace from what he was sure was a screaming mind.

He'd been down the same road she was on, and it was an angry, lonely place. She was lashing out at a lot of people, but because he'd been the closest to her in the last few weeks, he'd taken the brunt of it. Tonight, he'd hit his own breaking point with the situation. Shane was human, after all, but still, he wasn't happy with himself that he'd allowed his own insecurities to get the better of him.

Cyn whimpered as he slid two fingers through her folds once again. She was dripping wet with arousal. With each slap he landed, her body had softened, and her pussy had gotten wetter. It was all he could do not to bury himself inside her moist heat and fuck them both into oblivion. But not yet.

Shane spread her ass cheeks apart, loving the sight of her tight, puckered asshole. Fuck, he wanted in there. Instead, he got to his knees. "One knee on the bed." He helped her do as he instructed. "Don't move." Shane spread her swollen pussy lips with his thumbs and licked through her folds.

With a deep groan, he swallowed her taste and went back for more. She whimpered, arching her ass higher. Cyn was heaven on his tongue, and he couldn't get enough. The head of his dick throbbed, thickening further. He was beyond ready to pound into her tight channel, but he needed this from her first. Shane dived his tongue into the mouth of her cunt and pressed his thumb to her clit. Rubbing tight little circles in the swollen bud, he thrust his tongue in and out of her, fucking her with his mouth.

With her hips rocking, she let out a high-pitched moan, and Shane knew she was about to go over the edge. He slapped her ass with his free hand before gripping the full mound of flesh hard as he kept up the pressure on her clit with his thumb, thrusting his tongue into her sweet channel.

Cyn went off like a rocket, crying out his name and shaking as her orgasm ripped through her. Shane sucked up every drop, and when she finally began to settle, he let her go and stood behind her. Once again, he gripped her full ass in his hands and spread her cheeks. "Taking you here tonight."

She nodded but said nothing.

Shane bent over her and pulled her hair away from her face. "Cyn, you want me in your ass tonight?"

She nodded again.

He trailed his thumb over her bottom lip. "Need you to ask me for it."

"Want you there. Fuck me in my ass, Shane. Need you, babe. Please?" She sucked his thumb into her mouth, and her eyes rolled back in her head.

"I'll always give you what you need." Shane grabbed a bottle of lube from the night table drawer. He poured a generous amount into his hands and then smoothed it over her still-red ass cheeks. Cyn moaned and raised her other leg onto the bed. Poised on her knees, bent forward, head on the mattress with her legs spread wide, she made an incredible display for him. Her full ass was raised in perfect height to his cock. Her tight little puckered hole right there waiting for him to fuck. "God Almighty, you have the most incredible ass."

"Take it," she whispered.

Shane held the bottle above her, trickling the oil down between her ass cheeks. "Need to get you ready first." He smoothed two fingers over her hole, massaging it before he pressed them inside. Adding more lube, he worked it inside her. "Need you nice and slick for me. Fuck, you're so tight. Gonna love being inside you. Promise you're gonna love it too." Shane continued to work her, sliding his fingers in and out, then added a third, stretching her farther.

Cyn moaned and whimpered, rocking her hips in time with his strokes. The sight of her bent over in submission to him in this way had Shane's head spinning. Lust and anticipation ping-ponged through him as he fucked into her tight ass with his fingers. She was almost ready, and so was he.

Pulling his fingers free, Shane poured another generous amount of lube into his palm and took himself in hand. He stroked the oil along his shaft, groaning, and then tapped her asshole with the edge of the head. "This what you want, girl?"

"*Yessss…*" Cyn rolled her hips.

"Take it, Cyn." He positioned the head against her tight hole, and Cyn exhaled a low moan as she pressed back against him. Shane took hold of her ass cheeks, gripping the full mounds and spreading them apart. Slow and easy, he worked the head in, little by little, stretching the outer ring of muscles. He worried even with all the lube, it might be too much for her, and hurting her was not what he wanted. "You okay?"

"God, yes, it stings. But don't stop."

Deep moans came out of Cyn each time he pushed, and she pressed back, taking him deeper until he was finally past the tight muscle and the head was buried in her ass.

"Fuck! Oh fuck! Please…don't stop." She gripped the blankets.

He placed his hand on her lower back. "Easy now. Give your body a moment to adjust."

She moaned and shifted. "More, Shane."

"Okay." Shane took a full breath and pushed deeper. Her tight channel squeezed his dick as he buried himself all the way inside her, and his hips met the back of her thighs. "Jesus Christ, Cyn. You got all of me."

"Yes…Oh God, yes." Cyn rocked forward and pressed back again.

Shane growled, drew out and back in, keeping a steady pace. She was taking him—all of him. The feeling so intense it was all he could do not to lose his ever-loving mind. His balls drew up tight, and his orgasms tingled at the base of his spine.

He wouldn't last long. The sight of her was just too erotic, her body open like this too sexy, and the grip of her channel too good. "Rub your clit. Gonna come for you soon. Want you to come too."

Cyn slid her hand beneath her body and rocked back against him. "Harder, Shane…please?"

"Jesus—" God help him, he was lost to her. Gritting his teeth, Shane slapped his hips against her, drilling into her, unable to stop the sounds coming out of his mouth as he fucked her sweet ass hard and fast.

Shane's name belted from Cyn's mouth on a scream as she came, and he followed right after.

"*Fuuuuckkk!*" His orgasm hit with a force hard enough to take him to his knees. Shane held tight to her hips and buried himself deep as his cock spurted in release over and over again inside her.

Out of breath, he fell over her, and they both collapsed onto the mattress. He rolled them to their side and wrapped his arms around her. Cyn's body shook against him as she breathed heavy, still trying to catch her breath, too. Shane pressed his nose to her hair and held her tighter. "You okay?"

"Mmhmm." She shifted, and Shane slipped from her channel— "Ohh! Mmm… You?"

"I'm perfect. But I think I need to grab you a towel." He went to sit up, and she held his arms to her chest.

"Don't want you to move yet."

"Whatever you need, girl." Shane pressed a kiss to her shoulder and laid his head back down. Cyn rolled over and faced him, then pressed her face to his neck.

Happy to have her in his arms, he stroked through her hair and trailed his fingers down her back. Her skin had cooled from the sweat dampening it and felt like silk beneath his fingertips.

Cyn had pushed him hard tonight, but he'd pushed right back. Like usual, their argument ended in sex, but tonight's round had been the most intense out of all their encounters yet, and there had been so many to date he'd lost count.

Shane listened to her breaths even out, feeling them tickle the skin of his neck as she fell asleep in his arms. He didn't want to leave, and tonight, she'd pretty much made it clear she didn't want him to stay.

In no way did he want to be where he wasn't wanted, but he couldn't shake the thought that things would be different if it hadn't been for the attack. It'd been an unexpected inter-ruption in what he felt was the beginning of a relationship between them. If he just held on, stood by her, they'd get through it together.

Regardless of the timing, Cyn already had his heart, and he had no intention of taking it back. Their start together might've been a rocky one because of what she was going through, but in Shane's eyes, when this was done, their foun-dation would be rock solid and stronger than anyone else's he knew.

Coming through a war and emerging with your life intact meant a person had won. Cyn would come through this with him by her side, and they'd win. They'd have each other. Shane just hoped she'd see it his way…eventually.

CHAPTER TWENTY-NINE

Shane stood in front of the paint sample rack at Home Depot, debating on the perfect color. Sage? Coffee? He couldn't decide. He'd gotten up that morning with a mission on his mind. That mission being Cyn's living room—the room was getting a makeover.

As soon as Cyn had left the house for work, Shane was up and out the door. Maybe if he did a little face-lift, nothing too crazy, she'd feel comfortable going back in there. He had time to kill while she was at work anyway, so why not?

Hopefully, Cyn would be happy about it and not pissed. Things had been a little calmer since dinner at Ryan and Maiya's last week…resulting in a big fight followed by their rather energetic make-up plus anal sex, so he was hopeful.

Chances were she'd be pissed, but he was willing to take the risk because making her happy, even if it took a while, was worth it.

He glanced between the greenish shade and the tanish one and went with the sage—or Willow Leaf, the label said. Three gallons of satin would do the trick, plus some tinted primer, and he was ready to go. On his way to the registers, he took a peek at the area rugs and found a perfect one with shades of red, tan and a darker green in the pattern. Wasting no time, he grabbed it.

Crown molding would be beautiful, too, but there was no way he could fit that in before she got home from work. He'd called Joey to see if he was game to give him a hand, but like most people were doing, his best friend was working. He'd left him a message, but for now, Shane was flying solo. Considering he only had eight hours, at best, to pull off a makeover miracle on his own, he needed to move his ass.

On the drive back to her house, he stopped by a small, locally owned furniture store and made another snap decision on a new coffee table, end tables and a set of lamps. He eyed a new sofa but figured he better not push it. When he got back to Cyn's house, he unloaded the back of the SUV—thank fuck the backseats folded flat—and set everything in the garage.

Once in the house, Shane turned on the iPod dock and got to work. Kenny Wayne Shepherd's "Slow Ride" came through the speakers, and Shane muscled the sofa and chair into the center of the room and draped them in plastic. The existing coffee table and end tables, he moved to the garage, along with the one remaining lamp that hadn't been broken in the struggle between him and Carlos.

Shane grunted at the memory as he came back into the house. Painter's tape in hand, he taped off all the necessary areas and then laid plastic drop cloths down to cover the entire floor. Shane stretched and eyed the clock. Just past eleven a.m. Time to rock and roll.

Edwin McCain's "I'll Be" started playing as Shane opened a can of primer and got the tray ready. Roller coated with paint, he started on the biggest wall, singing along with the lyrics. Then continued on to the other two. By one p.m., the room was primed, and at the rate he was moving, he was so not going to make it. He worked fast, but prepping for paint took a long-ass time, plus that whole rolling thing. What he wouldn't give for a sprayer. He probably should've rented one.

Shane grabbed a beer from the fridge while the primer dried. He leaned against the counter, legs crossed at the ankle, and wondered if he'd lost his damn mind. The doorbell rang, yanking him off the train to Crazyville. Shane set the beer on the counter and turned the music down on his way to the front door, just in time for a knock to sound. "Hold your horses, I'm coming."

Shane swung the door wide to find Joey standing there, clad in jeans and an old T-shirt, sunglasses pushed up to his forehead, and a grin on his face. "I heard you need a little painting done."

"Dude, seriously? I fucking love you right now."

"And you're gonna love me more when you see your present."

"What'ja bring me, Daddy?" With a chuckle, Shane stepped out onto the front stoop.

"Only because you've been such a good boy. Follow me, my son."

Shane walked with Joey to the back of his pick-up truck. His best friend dropped the tailgate to reveal an absolutely gorgeous paint sprayer. Shane looked over at Joey. "Marry me. For reals."

"Sorry, already taken." Joey cleared his throat and nodded.

"How about a kiss? Just a little one."

Joey laughed. "Maybe later. Come on, help me grab this shit. I brought more drop cloths and a shield. You know how sprayers are, but I'm betting you're more skilled with one than I am."

Shane grabbed the sprayer. "Dude, seriously? Thank you."

"No worries, man. That's what family does. You just been away too long."

Shane couldn't peel the smile off his face, and he swore he

felt his heart actually swell behind his ribs. He rolled the sprayer into the house and went back out and grabbed the couple of buckets Joey brought, too, while his best friend brought the remaining supplies inside.

Joey was awesome, but then again, he was a Donnelly. That's how they were. Salt of the earth, truly. He set the sprayer up and glanced over at Joey. "Primer's drying, but we're close to ready to lay paint. You mind helping cut in?"

Joey looked around, hands propped on his hips. "I'm dressed for the occasion. Just show me to the brushes, cowboy." Right then, the first beats of Big & Rich's "Save a Horse (Ride a Cowboy)" played through the iPod. Shane threw his head back and laughed. Joey shook his head, laughing too. "Yeah, that was too perfect. In a very fucking scary way."

"No shit." Shane tossed a brush Joey's way. "No, you cannot ride me."

"Don't— Oh man, you went there."

"Had to." Shane filled two small containers with paint and handed one to Joey. "Pick a wall."

Joey moved to the front wall with the picture window, and Shane turned the music back up and started on the wider back wall. It took them another hour and a half, nearly two, to cut in around each wall and the front window. When they finished, Shane stood back and eyed their work. "Beer?"

"Uh, let me think about that for a second… Hell, yes?" Joey set the container and brush down.

"Thought so." Shane strode past him to the kitchen and grabbed two beers. Back in the living room, he handed one to Joey and eyed the sprayer. "You rent that?"

Joey tilted his bottle back, swallowed a generous amount, and then burped. "Yup."

"Nice." Shane chuckled and took a swig of his. He burped, too, but managed to contain the enthusiasm of it. "Better get this going. Meter's running."

"That was so ladylike." Joey grabbed an empty bucket and filled it with the remaining three gallons of paint.

"Thank your mother for that."

"Ha. Right?" Joey looked down into the bucket. "Damn, that doesn't look like a lot of paint. You sure it's enough?"

Shane ran his palm over the crown of his head. "Shit, I hope so. Tell you what, you want to go run and grab two more gallons, just in case?"

"I can do that. I'll grab a pizza on the way back, too."

"I'll get you back on all that." Shane set the bucket up with the sprayer and started priming the line. "Cool?"

"All good, brother. Be back in a bit."

"Thanks." Shane eyed the clock. It was just after three thirty. Jesus, this was going to be close. Hopefully, she'd work late. Just as he got ready to pull the trigger on the sprayer, his phone beeped with a message. Shane grabbed it out of his pocket.

It was a text from Stephanie, Joey's wife.

Stephanie Donnelly: Shane, it's Steph. Operation delay Cyn is in effect. I'm heading to the office at 4:30 to distract her into taking Madi for ice cream with me. 😅

Shane: Have I told you that you're an angel?

Stephanie Donnelly: Yes, but please be sure to remind Joey, okay? LOL

Shane: Done! Thanks, Steph.

Stephanie Donnelly: No thanks needed. It's what we do for family.

Shane smiled down at the screen of his phone. Joey was a lucky man. But Shane was lucky too, if only...he shook his head. "If only" was a deathtrap. A lot like an I.E.D: improvised explosive device...an unidentifiable object on the side of the road in Iraq that could have a bomb in it or just someone's clothes—basically something he should stay the hell away from or approach with extreme caution because the risk was far too extreme.

His girl might be extreme, but she *was* worth it, and because he knew that, he couldn't stay away.

Shane raised the sprayer and laid the first coat of paint over the wall. With even sweeps, he had the largest wall coated in a matter of fifteen minutes. He stood back, checked to see he hadn't missed anything. Pleased, he moved to the next.

By the time he'd finished all three walls, Joey sauntered in, pizza box in hand. "Delivery! Oh, hey, that looks fucking awesome!"

Shane wiped the sweat from his brow. "Thanks! You get the paint or just the pizza?"

"Pfft, bitch, please." Joey walked to the kitchen but returned empty-handed. "No, no, I see you got your hands full, deary. I'll grab the paint." He winked and disappeared outside.

Shane grinned and set the spray gun down. His stomach rumbled, and he moved to the kitchen. After washing his hands, he grabbed a couple paper plates and two slices.

"Aw, you can't even wait for me? I'm so hurt." Joey grabbed a couple slices for himself and bit into one.

Shane laughed around a mouthful and then swallowed. "Baby. Do you need a new diaper?"

"Yes!" Joey pouted, took another bite and pulled two fresh beers from the fridge. "Steph text you?"

Shane took the offered beer. "Yeah. She's cool. Thanks for this. The beer and the help."

"No thanks needed." Joey clinked his beer to Shane's. "Can't promise Steph won't call in a favor when she wants the master bath redone, though."

"Anything you need." Shane bit into his pizza and eyed the clock. Shit, it was almost five. "Gonna be super close."

"Better move your ass. Is it ready for another coat?"

Shane tilted his bottle back, washing down the last bite of pizza. "Need to give it another fifteen minutes. Let's go unwrap the new rug and get the tables out of their boxes."

"Meet you out there." Joey grinned and lifted another slice from the box. "Swear to God, two minutes."

"Uh-huh. All right." Shane moved to the garage and got things in order out there. Once done, he came back in and laid another coat on the walls, then touched up any drips. The extra gallons Joey had grabbed got used with a little leftover for future touch-ups. Perfect.

Shane stepped back and turned in a circle. "What d'ya think?"

"Looks fantastic. Really. I can't say I'm impressed because I wouldn't expect anything less from you, but dude, seriously, solid work." Joey clapped him on his shoulder. "And it's almost six, and Steph just texted. So you better move your ass. Thinking you got forty-five minutes max until Cyn gets home."

"Fuck. Shit. Hell." Shane grabbed the sprayer and brought it outside. Joey came out after him, empty paint cans in his hands. "Joey, can you flush this thing while I start tearing down plastic?"

"On it."

"Thanks." Shane ran back in and carefully started pulling blue tape from the trim and then the plastic drop clothes. When done, he slid the couch and chair back in place, careful to not touch the walls with them. He'd already removed the old area rug, so he ran out and grabbed the new one and laid it down on the hardwood floor.

After that, he brought in the tables. He hadn't removed any nails, so the pictures and other wall decorations, including the flat screen, went back into place, as well as the large Roman shade on the picture window. Shane spun in a circle again, making sure he hadn't missed anything. "Lamps!"

"Got 'em." Joey ran out, returning with both lamps in hand.

Shane grabbed one and set it on the end table near the chair while Joey set the other up next to the couch. After arranging a few more decorations in their places, the room was put back together. Shane glanced at the time—six forty-five. Any minute, she'd be pulling up. Shane palmed his phone and shot Cyn a text.

> Shane: Hey girl, you coming home anytime soon?

> Cyn: On my way. In traffic on the 5. Need anything from the store?

> Shane: Milk. Wine. Creamer.

> Cyn: Will do.

> Shane: Thanks. See you soon. Careful driving. Stop texting.

> Cyn: Stop messaging me, you freak. Lol

Shane laughed and blew out a breath. "I just gave her a grocery list. It'll give me time to shower."

"Good call. And that's my cue to go. Hope she likes it. Good luck."

Shane gave his best friend a hug. "Me too, man. Me fucking too."

After seeing Joey off, Shane made sure the kitchen was cleaned up. The final touch was a vase full of white roses he'd given her the other day that were still in perfect bloom. She'd kept them in the kitchen. Shane set them in the center of the coffee table, lit a few candles and headed for the shower.

While under the spray, he prayed she'd be happy with the update. Shane wanted so badly to see that smile of hers.

CYN PULLED into the driveway and attempted to pull in the garage but couldn't because—*what the fuck*—her coffee table, end tables, lamp and area rug were where her Wrangler was supposed to go. Agitation reared up like a tsunami, and Cyn threw the Jeep in Park and turned off the engine.

Stepping out of the vehicle, she opened the back and pulled out the two small sacks of groceries. "Don't know what the hell he thinks he's doing." She closed the tailgate and walked into the garage. "But he better have a goddamn good reason why my shit is in my garage and not in my living room where it belongs."

Cyn stormed into the kitchen. "Shane?" No answer. The lights were off, and only the fading sunlight lit the room. Cyn continued on, heading for her bedroom, but stopped short in front of the living room. The blinds were closed, as she'd been keeping them, so the room was more than dim but for the flickering light coming from a few candles in the space. "Shane?"

A light came on, and Cyn focused in that direction. Shane was sitting in her overstuffed chair, leg bent with an ankle resting on one knee and a single white rose in his hand. "Glad you're home." He smiled.

Cyn frowned. "Why is my stuff in the garage?" She rubbed her forehead. "And why are you sitting in here?" Shane's smile faded, and Cyn had a sinking feeling she was missing something. Shoving the feeling aside, she crossed her arms and waited for an answer to both questions. He just stared at her, an expression on his face she swore looked a lot like confusion and maybe sadness. *What the fuck!* "Shane?"

He got to his feet and approached her. "Do you not see?"

"I see that my stuff is in my garage, and I don't know why." Craning her neck back, she stared up at him.

"Yeah—" he glanced away and then back to her, "—I get that you see that. But don't you see why?"

"Shane, what the hell're you talking about? Can you not answer my question?"

"Wow, really?" Shane moved to the window and opened the shade. The room filled with the fading daylight. Then he moved to the other end table and turned on the lam—

Wait! Cyn's eyes went wide as the room came into focus around her. She looked at the end table, the one that wasn't hers, to the lamp that also was not hers. She shifted her focus to the different rug in the center of the room to the coffee table, then let her gaze travel over the—*oh my fucking God*—walls. "What did you do?"

"I gave it a facelift. I gave it a change so you could—"

"Why would you do this? I didn't ask you to do this?" Rage boiled within her, lying in wait to explode like a volcano. "What the hell, Shane? So I could what?"

"So that maybe you'd feel better about the room and be comfortable coming in here again." His voice was low, his tone filled with...disappointment?

She pushed that down, too, fuck his disappointment. "I didn't ask you to do this. Did it occur to you that maybe you should've asked me first? This is my home, Shane. Not yours. Fucking hell! And so you know, I am *not* paying you for this." She pointed her finger at him, and he flinched. She pushed that down, too. It didn't matter. "Take it back if you want because I don't want it." Cyn turned and stormed down the hall toward her bedroom.

"Hey, Cyn?" She stopped short at the harsh tone in his voice and looked back at him. "Receipts are on the table. You fucking take it back if you don't want it." Shane dropped the rose in his hand on the floor and disappeared into the kitchen.

Again, his voice was low, but this time, his tone was laced with anger. Cyn stared into the space he no longer occupied, fury bursting through her at a fevered rate. The door to the garage slammed, and she flinched. Well, fuck him and his tone, plus his grand gestures. He shouldn't have done this.

Cyn moved to her bedroom, closed the door and locked it. Sliding off her pants, she climbed into bed. He could sleep on the couch when he came back—*if* he came back. As her anger cooled, Cyn's last thought was one filled with guilt before sleep finally took hold.

CHAPTER THIRTY

Cyn felt the bed dip and then the familiar feel of Shane's body spoon up behind her. He wrapped an arm around her waist, snugged her closer to his body and pressed his nose to her hair. She had woken up a little while ago, a bad dream, she guessed, but then wandered out of her bedroom to see if Shane had come back. He hadn't.

She did, however, really look at all the things he'd done to what'd become her least-favorite space in her home, and although Cyn still didn't want to go into the room, she realized what he was trying to do for her. And her heart broke.

She'd run back to her bed, tears streaming down her cheeks, guilt coating her insides like thick molasses, feeling like the biggest raving bitch this side of the Mississippi.

Shane moved his hand down her stomach to her hip and let out a sigh. Unsure if she wanted him to know she was awake, Cyn hadn't moved or responded to his touch. But the guilt was growing. And shame was weaving its way through her veins, too. This kind and loving man was only trying to take care of her, and no matter what she did, Cyn couldn't seem to let him.

It was as if she'd lost all control of her moods or temper or even the ability to see the concern people had for her.

Shane, along with everyone else close to her, kept saying she needed to see a therapist, but Cyn just…she just didn't want to give in. And maybe it was stupid, but she really felt as if giving in and seeking professional help meant Carlos had won. There was no way she could let him win, and that meant dealing with it herself.

But no matter how hard Cyn tried, she failed and ended up blowing her top like some lunatic on steroids.

"I'm sorry I lost my cool and walked out," he whispered to the back of her head.

Cyn closed her eyes as a tear ran over her nose onto the pillow. He was sorry? For fuck's sake, he had no reason to be sorry.

Shane moved his hand around her stomach again. "Babe, I know you're not asleep."

Dammit. It didn't matter. Cyn remained quiet and tried like hell not to wipe her nose that was now running. She felt him pull away and return, and then a tissue was dangled in front of her face. *Ah, Christ.* Cyn tugged it from his hand. "Fine."

He lay back down and resumed his hold on her body. "Told you."

"Whatever. You didn't know. You just got lucky." She blew her nose.

Shane chuckled against the back of her hair. "Gonna be the death of me."

Cyn's heart cracked a little more, and she knew there was no way that'd happen. This man had already put up with so much shit from her, she couldn't imagine him actually breaking or dying from it. Never mind the fact that any other dude on the planet would've cut and run five minutes after he'd walked in on her ex-boyfriend in the middle of a psychotic break and attacking her.

Shane Conlon was a goddamn rock. In fact, he was her

rock…even though she swore to everyone, including God and herself, that she didn't need him. With her tears back in the game—running like a faucet—Cyn rotated within his embrace and faced him. The thought of needing him terrified her. In the pale light of the room, she took in his strong features. Cyn smoothed her fingertips over his cheeks and then touched the dimple centered on his chin. She loved that gorgeous dimple. "I'm the one who should be sorry."

"Cyn—"

She pressed a finger to his lips. "No. Shh…listen. *I* am sorry. I don't know what else to say. I can't make any excuses. I can't blame anyone. I can't even—" she sucked in a shuddering breath, "—I can't even figure out what my issue *is* exactly. I do know that I'm fucked up, but I know that I *will* be okay once whatever this is passes. I know I'll get through this."

He stared at her a moment before he bent his head and kissed her forehead. "Apology accepted." Shane smoothed his palm over the back of her hair. "Can I ask you something?"

She sniffled. "Sure."

"Why won't you even consider seeing a therapist?"

Cyn flinched. She couldn't answer his question. He'd just argue her points of why, and she was too tired to argue anymore that night. "Shane, please? I don't want to fight again."

He sighed through his nose. "I don't want to fight either. Trust me on that. Just promise me one thing?"

Christ, he was relentless. "Maybe."

"Ha. Fair enough. Promise that you'll at least think about it, Cyn? Just…think about it."

"How could I not think about it? Everyone brings it up so much we could choke a horse with it." She wrapped an arm around his waist and snuggled closer.

It was true that no one let her alone about the therapist topic, but she knew that's not what Shane meant. He wanted her to think about it, as in consider it—as in decide to go because she thought it was a good idea. Cyn didn't want to think or do any of those things. She just wanted to feel normal again. She just wanted to rewind the clock and have none of it happen at all.

"Not the same, but I'll take it. For now." He slid his hand down to her lower back. "Can I ask you something else?"

"Oh God, really?" She let out a mock snore. "G'head."

"Did you at least like the paint color?"

"Maybe."

"You did. You totally loved it. It's okay, you can admit it."

Cyn giggled and then shrugged. "Not gonna admit anything, Sergeant."

Shane moved his hand down to her ass, cupping one butt cheek in his palm. "What about the rug? Did you like the rug?"

"Can't say, I didn't really get a good look at it." She pressed her lips to his throat.

He slid his palm to the back of her thigh and raised her knee over his hip. "The tables?"

Cyn kissed along his neck and smoothed a hand down his side. "Didn't really notice."

Shane rolled his hips, and the blunt head of his erection grazed her clit. "Liar."

"I am not," she breathed. Damn, if she wasn't already wet for him. How did this man do this to her? Obviously, he was sexy and gorgeous, with an incredible body, and also great in bed…but that wasn't it. There'd been plenty of men over the years in her life that had those very same qualities. With Shane, it was different. Everything was different…but how could she be sure?

"Mmhmm." Shane framed her chin between his thumb and fingers and took her lips in a soft kiss.

Cyn lost all focus and let his mouth take over. Tender, sweet and filled with intensity…her heart cracked more. A feeling she'd felt too many times—for too many of the wrong people—welled in her chest.

Love whispered, like a warm breeze, through her mind, and she hushed it, but it whispered again. *Dammit.* Cyn wouldn't allow herself to feel it.

But she felt it coming from him. Shane hadn't said the words, and she prayed he wouldn't, but Cyn felt it in the heat of his kiss and the brand of his touch.

With a shift of her hips, the swollen head of his cock teased the mouth of her pussy. Cyn moaned against his lips, tangling her tongue with his. Shane rolled them, and she raised her other leg as he slid his length fully inside her.

He broke the kiss and propped himself up on his forearms. Staring down at her, he thrust his hips forward. Cyn gasped as he ground against her clit, moving back and forth with his cock buried deep in her core. She matched his movement, digging her heels into the mattress as her body arched with each roll of her pelvis.

Shane stroked her cheek with his thumb but stayed quiet, save for the breaths coming from him as their bodies moved together. He was making love to her...he was saying, "I love you" with his body and with his soul, and she felt it through every part of her being. She closed her eyes, and Shane kissed her again.

And Cyn's world was knocked from its axis.

Wrapping her arms around his sides, she held on to him with all her strength as their bodies slid together and her orgasm built. Again, he broke from her lips, groaning as his pace increased, but only just a little. There was nothing rough or rushed about what they were doing. This wasn't fucking... that was very clear. But it was no less passionate than every-thing she'd already experienced with him. In fact, it was prob-ably more so.

Shane reached back, gripped her thigh and raised her leg higher, changing the angle. Cyn gasped as he raised his pelvis from hers and slid back in, this time grazing her G-spot. Cyn arched her head back. "Oh God."

"Cyn…" He kissed down her neck and took a breast in his hand.

She rocked her hips. Shane flicked the pad of his thumb over her nipple, then dipped his head and sucked it into his mouth. She arched on the bed, and he rolled his pelvis forward. Her orgasm surfaced, hot tingles spreading over her skin. "Shane!"

He released her nipple. "Come for me."

Shane didn't have to ask because her orgasm had already broken free. Warmth spread through her as wave after wave rocked her body, her pussy spasming and clenching around his thickness. "Yes!"

Shifting again, Shane slid his hands beneath her ass, tilted her pelvis up and continued thrusting inside her. "God, yes. That's my girl."

The change in angle was another assault on her clit. Cyn gasped and gripped his ass. "So deep, baby."

Shane groaned and buried his face in her neck, grinding into her. "So good. Love your cunt."

"Come for me, Shane. Let me feel your thick cock come inside me."

He growled and bit her neck, driving into her harder, faster—

His orgasm hit, and Cyn nearly came again from the feel of his prick jerking inside her, spurting all his hot seed deep within her pussy. He shuddered above her. "Yes! Fuck, yes!"

She dug her nails into his ass and wrapped her legs around him. She didn't want him to move away. She wanted him there for as long as he'd stay. Shane buried his fingers in her hair and settled between her thighs, all of his weight on her. And Cyn held him even closer.

For the love of all things holy, she didn't know what she was going to do when he finally did leave.

CHAPTER THIRTY-ONE

Two days later, Shane followed the hostess through the restaurant at a golf club in Pasadena where his mother was waiting. She'd texted him that morning, asking him if he'd meet her for lunch. He'd been so shocked at the invitation, he just stared at the message for a long while and finally replied that he'd come. With everything going on between him and Cyn, the last thing Shane wanted to deal with was his mother, but curiosity won out, so there he was, heading to her table.

The hostess motioned to the table, and Shane thanked her before bending and giving his mother a kiss on the cheek. "Mom."

"Shane, darling. So good to see you again. Please, have a seat."

"Sure." He took the chair across from her. "Good to see you too." The waiter placed a menu in front of him and then filled his water glass. "Nice place."

She smiled and sipped from her water glass. "Thank you for coming."

"Sure." He placed his napkin on his lap and hoped like crazy that the conversation between them might become an *actual* conversation instead of their standard light and polite chit-chat because, at the rate they were going, Shane wouldn't make it past ordering his food. "To be honest, I was kind of shocked by your invite."

His mother tilted her head to the side. "Oh? Why's that, darling?"

Shane cringed. She rarely called him by his name, always using the obnoxious endearment instead. In the rare cases she used his name, it was in combination with the expression. Unless he'd pissed her off, then she used his name. Usually in a very clipped tone. "Because it's not something we do."

"I'm not sure I'm following."

Jesus, she was going to make him say it outright. Talk about starting off with a bang. "We don't usually spend time together, Mom."

"Well." She looked down, probably adjusting her napkin on her lap. "I suppose that's true."

"Mom, listen—" he leaned forward and lowered his voice, "—why don't you just cut to the chase and save us both the pain of an entire lunch together."

She narrowed her gaze on him and pressed her lips together.

Shane looked up to see the waiter beside the table. Perfect…time to order food. Shane sat back and glanced over the menu while his mother placed her order. When she finished, Shane gave his selection, and once again, they were alone. He studied her across the table. As usual, she looked beautiful, definitely younger than her fifty-six years.

"I would really like it if we were closer, but honestly, I am simply not sure how to connect with you, darling." She straightened her salad and dinner forks. "I thought this might be a nice way to start." Her lips curved into a meek smile.

If he didn't know better, he might actually think she was sincere. Except his mother was *never* sincere. Shane cringed at his cynical attitude. Was he really that jaded? He hated to think so. Maybe she actually did want to be closer. He drew in a deep breath and took another drink of his water. "All right, Mom. I'm willing to try. Let's start over." He stretched his hand across the table, palm up.

She smiled, leaned forward and laid her hand in his. "That pleases me so much, darling." The glass of Chardonnay she ordered arrived, and she let go of Shane's hand and settled back in her seat. "So, tell me about Texas?"

"Well, not much to tell, really. I live just outside of Dallas, in Garland."

"Near where my father's family is?"

"Yes, actually. Uncle Bob and Aunt Cerine are still there. They're doing well, by the way. You should call sometime."

She nodded and sipped her wine. "It's been years since I've spoken to either of them. Not since my daddy died, really."

"That's a long time, Mom."

"I suppose it is." She set her glass down. "What else?"

He wasn't used to her wanting to know things about him, and because of that, Shane wasn't used to sharing things with her—not personal things anyway. Nervous energy bounced through him, but he tamped down his trepidation. He said he'd try, and that's exactly what he intended to do.

***

SHANE SAT in Joey's kitchen, beer bottle in hand, cursing himself for being so stupid.

"Dude, it's not your fault."

He shook his head. "Joey, I should've known better."

"Come on. She's your mother. It's only normal to trust your own mother."

"Not my mother." Shane tipped the bottle back and took a long swig. "Christ, you should've seen her. All sincere-like.

Asking about my life in Texas, about my home and job. All so she could figure out if she'd get the house from me."

"Yeah, it's fucked up. I'm sorry, bro. I never knew your dad left the house to both of you."

"Honestly? I knew, but never really thought about it. I mean, why the hell would she leave our house? Dad's insurance paid it off free and clear. But, of course, she took out a second mortgage on it. Which was fine, I guess." He shrugged. "But she can't sell it without me signing over my part of the deed."

"What do you think you're going to do?"

"I don't know. Part of me says fuck it, let her have it. Not like I'm moving back here." He tipped his bottle back again.

"You sure about that?"

Shane lowered the bottle and leveled his gaze on his best friend. "Why do you ask like that?"

"I'm just saying, you've been here a lot longer than the ten days you originally planned to be here. And from what I can see, you aren't showing any signs of getting out of town any time soon."

"Only because I'm worried about your sister. Which is a whole other topic I'm not ready to get into right now, but yeah. I don't want to go until I know she's okay, Joey. I'd think you'd appreciate me looking out for her."

"Go easy, I do appreciate it. Believe me, selfish bastard that I am, I'd love nothing more than for you to stay here permanently. But you gotta do what makes you happy, too."

"Your sister makes me happy. Or she did—" Shane blew out an agitated breath, "—before that asshole Carlos attacked her, she made me beyond happy. Now, in between the happy, she gives me a hard time. About *everything*. It's fine, I'm not complaining, but yeah…not easy."

"I can only imagine. We've all had a little taste of Cyn and her constant agitated mood."

"It sucks, and now this shit with my mother. I can't imagine selling that house, Joey." Shane shifted his gaze to the windows. "Been a lot of years since he passed, but to me, that's still his house. Our house, you know?"

"I couldn't imagine my parents selling their house. I can't even begin to imagine what it's like holding onto yours because it's tied to the memory of your father. He was a good man, Shane. I don't blame you for wanting to preserve it. But at the same time, it's just a house. Your father's memory is with you always, regardless of whether or not you own that property."

Shane ran his palm over his head. "Yeah, I know. I know."

"What did you tell her?"

"Not much…when she finally spit out her point, and I realized the play she was making, I got furious and walked out."

"Damn, Shane."

"Dude, if I didn't walk out right then, I would've started yelling. I don't think the rest of the country club would've appreciated my choice of vocabulary." He swirled his bottle of beer. "Though it would've been fun to see her go ten different shades of red had I laid into her."

"No shit."

Shane stared out the kitchen windows to the backyard and sighed through his nose. His mother was a real piece of work. Luring him in the way she did had stung layers that ran so deep inside him, Shane was still feeling the burn. Based on what she'd laid out for him, her new man had proposed to her, and they were going to tie the knot sometime in the next few months and, shortly after, move to Arizona, where his family was. Basically, Derrick had persuaded her to sell the house so they could buy a great big one in the Phoenix area and pay cash for it.

The idea that money from his father's house would end up

buying her *and* her new husband a nice new showplace house, free and clear, made Shane want to puke. Bile burned the back of his throat, and he smoothed his palm over his skull. What kind of man used his woman's dead husband's house for seed money to get her a new one? Shane shook his head and swallowed the last of his beer. Not any kind of man he ever wanted to know or needed in his life.

"I'm going to go check on Madi. You good, or you need another beer?" Joey stood.

"Yeah, I guess I'll take another. Thanks."

Joey stepped out of the room, and Shane picked up his cell from the table. He hadn't heard from Cyn, which had turned into the norm with her. She never texted or called during the day, though on occasion, he'd hear from her when she was leaving the office. She'd make up some excuse why she called, but Shane knew deep down it was because she was freaked out walking from the door to her Jeep. Even if it was still daylight.

Sadness bloomed in his chest. Shane really needed to hear her voice. But more, he wanted to tell her all about what had happened with his mother and know that he was safe to share how hurt he was over the whole thing. He just didn't think he could bear her rejecting him.

Bad enough, his own mother didn't give a fuck about him. Shane didn't need to be cast off by Cyn, too. Although it wasn't like he was feeling a whole lot of want from her side to begin with. She wanted his dick, though. And what he could give her…she took all of that, but aside from the sex, she didn't give a whole lot back.

God, he wished she'd seek some help. But no matter what he said or how many times he'd tried to convince her, she wasn't budging. Now, with this level of rejection from his mother and her wanting to take away a part of his childhood, he felt pushed past his limits and worn down to the bone. Shane wasn't sure how much longer he could hang on, waiting for Cyn to figure her end of things out.

He knew there was a future for them. There wasn't a doubt in his mind, even with the big mess in the middle of their start, they were meant to be together.

CHAPTER THIRTY-TWO

Cyn sat across from Angie in a booth at their favorite pizza place. Right when Cyn was ready to leave the office, Angie had strolled in, long legs wrapped in new skinny jeans and a new pair of black patent leather Doc Martens on her feet. Her sister had inherited their father's darker features, where Cyn was a mix of both of their parents. Tonight, Angie's long, almost black hair had been straightened to perfection and skimmed her lower back. Her sister loved to alternate between long waves from hot rollers or a curling iron or pulling it straight with a flat iron. Either way, it always looked beautiful.

Angie bit into her slice of Hawaiian pizza. "So, tell me how things are with Shane?" she mumbled around her mouthful of food.

"Fine, I guess. He redid my living room. It's beautiful, of course." Cyn picked a piece of pineapple off her slice and tossed it into her mouth.

"I heard. Can't wait to see it. Very sweet of him, Cyn."

"Yeah. I know. Handy around the house, *and* the sex is mind-blowing."

"Oooh, juicy, juicy. Tell me more."

Cyn laughed. "No."

"Brat. You know I'm not getting any right now."

"Anyway…" Cyn sipped her soda. "Thanks for bringing that shit up last week."

"It was an accident. You act like I did it on purpose." Angie took another bite of her pizza.

"If I didn't know better, I'd say you did."

Her sister frowned. "Don't be like that, Cyn."

"Fine." Silence stretched between them, and Cyn busied herself by eating as her ever-present agitation vibrated her limbs. Her temper was getting the better of her more and more—like all of the freaking time now. With everyone. Except not so much with Angie, at least not until right then. *Shit!* Cyn flopped her pizza onto the plate and blew out a breath.

Why the hell couldn't she get herself straight? Cyn could barely make it five minutes without something or someone pissing her off. Dealing with clients had turned into a nightmare, too. By the time each day had finished, tension had built so high within her she thought she might explode. And then she usually would. Most times at Shane.

At first, she'd chalked up her moodiness to what had happened with Carlos. But for fuck's sake, it'd been almost three weeks since "the night," and nothing had gotten better. *Fuck!* Cyn looked at her sister. "Well, as a result, we had a big fight."

"You and Shane?" Angie grabbed another slice.

"No, me and Santa Claus. Who do you think, Angie? God!"

"What? God, nothing, Cyn. It was *just* a question. You should try answering instead of jumping down my throat and trampling my lungs."

Cyn brushed her hair out of her eyes. "Fine. Yes. Shane and I had a big fight. Better?"

"Getting there." Angie rolled her eyes and lifted her pizza.

"Maybe that's why he redid the living room for you. So, what happened?"

Cyn rolled her eyes. "He wanted to know what you were talking about. He wouldn't drop it." She shrugged. "So I changed the subject."

Angie bit into her pizza and again spoke with her mouth full. "To what?"

Cyn crossed her arms and sneered. "You have heinous table manners." She handed her sister a napkin from the dispenser.

"Whatever."

"I asked him when he was leaving."

"No shit. That's harsh, Cyn. What'd he say?"

"I don't think it was harsh at all." Cyn chuckled, wondering what Angie's response would be next. "He said he'd leave after I'd had a session with a counselor."

"Interesting." Angie set her pizza down and wiped her mouth and hands with the napkin before taking a sip of soda.

Irritation flowed through Cyn's veins like ice water. She expected Angie to say something, anything. Ask questions, or whatever. She'd deal. But she didn't know how to perceive the whole bunch of nothing coming her way. Why the hell was her sister stalling? "*What?* Just say it!"

Angie leveled her gaze on Cyn, pulled her hair over one shoulder and leaned forward. "What I'll say is, why don't you lower your voice, hmm? We don't really need the whole restaurant to hear your fit." Angie sat back in a huff.

Cyn glanced around the small parlor. Her sister was right; the whole place didn't need to be unwilling participants. "Fine. Sorry. But explain your 'interesting' comment."

"I guess I'm wondering…why haven't you sought out some counseling?"

Cyn hadn't expected that to come out of her sister's mouth, and she jerked back as if Angie had tossed a cold drink in her face. "What do you mean, 'why haven't I sought out a counselor'?"

Angie pushed her plate away and folded her arms on the table. "Just what I said. I didn't stutter, Cyn."

"Fuck you, Angie."

"Cynthia, what the hell? I'm not going to sit here and just put up with you talking to me like this. And Shane, well, if this is even a taste of what you're serving up to him daily? That poor dude needs a fucking medal. And after how you treated him, he freaking went out and redid your living room for you? Yeah, maybe two medals plus sainthood."

"Don't talk about what you don't know!" Cyn bolted to her feet, the chair legs screeching over the linoleum floor. "You can sit here all you want. I'm leaving."

"Wait. This is crazy. Cyn, come on. Seriously?"

Cyn ignored her sister's plea and stalked from the restaurant. She didn't need this shit and wasn't about to deal with it. She'd had about enough of dealing with everyone else, too. Why didn't the people in her life understand she was stressed? And tired. And really, just fucking done taking anyone's bullshit. If they wouldn't leave her alone, she'd be the one to walk away. As far as a counselor or therapist, or any of the above, was concerned, her decision was final.

She was not and never would go see a goddamn therapist. She didn't need therapy. What she needed was to be left alone.

Fatigue hit Cyn like a ton of bricks as she pulled into her garage. After getting into the house, she tossed her keys on the kitchen counter and made her way to her bedroom. The smell of fresh paint still lingered, and she paused and glanced at the living room. Even with the new decor, a chill ran down her spine. She hated that room now, didn't want anything to do with it. It didn't matter that Shane had tried to make it pretty for her again. She hadn't stepped foot into it since that night. And she didn't intend to.

Cyn crossed her arms and continued to her bedroom. She

kicked off her shoes, slid off her jeans and climbed under the comforter. She was so tired—beyond exhausted—and she just wanted to sleep. Really fucking sleep for as long as she could. And preferably without any nightmares plaguing her.

Cyn curled around one of the pillows, the one Shane used, and closed her eyes.

CHAPTER THIRTY-THREE

Shane opened Cyn's garage and made his way into the house. Angie had called him and filled him in on the disastrous dinner date she'd had with Cyn. Things were getting worse, and Shane was running out of ideas and time. "Cyn?" he called out as he moved from the kitchen toward the living room.

She wasn't in there, but Shane hadn't expected her to be. The girl was still avoiding the room like the walls were smeared with the Bubonic plague, regardless of the fact that they were now coated with new paint. With a shake of his head, he made his way down the hall. "Cyn, where are ya?"

"*No! Nooooo!*"

"Cyn!" Shane ran down the short hall and barreled into her bedroom, but then skidded to a halt. *What the…* Cyn was beneath the covers, laying on her side, sleeping—her brow furrowed and face contorted with a stressed expression.

"*Get off me! No! Stop!*" She swung one arm out and screamed.

Dammit, she was having another nightmare. She'd had them nightly for the past three weeks. Most nights, she didn't wake up, but others, she'd wake, crying and holding on to him for dear life. In the mornings, when he'd tried to talk to her about them, she refused to discuss it, claiming she didn't remember having any bad dreams. It was more evidence that she really needed to get some help.

Shane climbed onto the bed and took one of her hands in his. "Cyn? Honey, wake up." She frowned and rolled to her back, and Shane smoothed his palm up her arm, shaking her a bit. "Cyn?"

"Hmm?" She threw her free arm over her face.

"Sweetheart, wake up. You're having a bad dream."

"What?" She peered at him from beneath her arm.

Shane lay down next to her and pulled her arm away from her face. "You were dreaming."

Cyn rolled toward him and yawned. "Was I talking in my sleep?"

"Mhmm." He smoothed her hair back from her face. "Do you remember any of it?"

She shook her head. "No." She scooted closer. "What time is it?"

"Almost nine-thirty." He rubbed her back. "How was dinner with Angie?"

"Ugh, don't ask." She rolled away.

Shane frowned. He wasn't going to tell Cyn that Angie had called him. Instead, he hoped Cyn might tell him what happened so maybe he could broach the subject of a therapist again…but he knew with that would come an argument between them. He didn't want that either. "Too late."

She rose from the bed and pulled on her jeans. "Angie is a pain in my ass. And frankly, I'm tired of dealing with her shit."

"Wow." He sat up. "That sounds pretty harsh, babe."

"Whatever. I don't even care anymore." She walked out of the room.

Shane got to his feet and followed. With each step he took, he braced himself for the fight that he desperately wanted to avoid. The best way to do that was to just drop the subject, but for fuck's sake, he couldn't. When he reached the kitchen, he leaned against the doorframe and crossed his arms. "You should care, Cyn. She's your sister. She loves you."

"Yeah, well." She pulled a mug from the cabinet. "I'm making tea. Do you want some?"

"Sure." He moved to her and wrapped his arms around her waist from behind. "Can I say something to you, and maybe you just listen and not get mad?"

She let out a sigh and rested her head back against his shoulder. "I'll listen, but I can't promise I won't get mad."

Shane closed his eyes and pressed his nose to the side of her hair. Should he push the subject again? God, this was beyond hard and scary and fucking nerve-wracking. Screw it. In the span of two seconds, Shane decided to drop the subject of counseling…for now, in favor of talking with her about her sister and maybe about staying—as in moving back to L.A. and also about the situation with his mother.

"Well, spit it out?" Cyn stepped out of his embrace and went back to preparing their tea.

A lump rose in his throat, and Shane forced himself to swallow past it. "Yeah. All right." Unsure of where to start, he stepped beside her and leaned a hip against the counter and just went with the only thing that came to mind. "Do you fight with Angie a lot?"

"No. I fight with Mary. But lately, Angie has been on my nerves."

"Okay, so maybe you should call her and talk about it?"

She filled the kettle with water. "I don't want to talk about it."

"But…"

"But what, Shane? Jesus, will you get to your point already?" She dropped the kettle, with a bit too much force, on the burner, then lit the flame.

Shane ran his palm over his jaw and did his damnedest to

not take her agitated tone personally. "I guess I just hate to see you and Angie not getting along."

"How about you not worry about it, okay?"

"You said you'd listen and not get mad."

"No—" she stepped around him to the refrigerator, "—I said I would listen, but that I couldn't promise to not get mad. Regardless, I'm not mad."

"You sound mad." He frowned. "You look mad, too."

She set the carton of half and half on the counter, again with a bit too much force, especially for his liking. Shane cringed and braced himself for another lashing via her words. Cyn glared at him. "I am *not* fucking mad, but if you don't get to your point, I'm definitely going to be."

"Cyn, look. I hate to see you fighting with your sister, and I hate coming home to find you having yet another nightmare. I'm just worried about you, that's all. Why is that such a bad thing?"

"Home?" She let out a cold-sounding laugh and brushed her hair away from her eyes. "This isn't your home, Shane."

Ouch! That was a direct hit and definitely stung. Shane closed his eyes and blew out a breath. "Yeah, about that."

"Yeah, about that, is right. How about we discuss that, hmm?" The teakettle started to whistle. Cyn shut off the burner and poured the water into the waiting mugs. "You decide you're finally heading back to Texas?"

Shane cupped her elbow in his palm. "Come on now. I don't want to fight with you."

"Who's fighting? We're just discussing." She jerked her arm away and slid his mug toward him.

Shane picked up the tea she'd prepared for him and watched her as she made her way to the table and took a seat. Again, he drew in a deep breath in preparation for whatever might come out of Cyn's mouth, then let his words fly. "I've been thinking about moving back here."

CYN JERKED her eyes back to Shane as she set her mug down on the table, hard, the hot tea sloshing over the sides. Some of it hit her fingertips, but she ignored the burn from the liquid. "Why in the hell would you do that?"

"Because…" He furrowed his brow, and he tilted his head to the side. "Because I want to be with you, Cyn."

"Be with me, huh?" She grabbed a napkin from the holder and wiped up the spill. This was not happening. He'd lost his mind. That was the only acceptable explanation she could come up with. "What the hell makes you think I want that?"

Shane stared at her, a hurt and confused expression in his eyes, and Cyn blocked it out—and blocked the slight sting of guilt that crept up the back of her neck. It didn't matter. She was not doing this with him.

What the fuck did he think, he was going to just move back to Los Angeles and what? Move in with her?

No. No way. This was so not happening. He had to go. Like now.

"I know you want it, Cyn. Don't shovel any bullshit my way." He shook his head. "I know you have feelings for me. Same as I have for you."

Cyn gritted her teeth and glared at him. Yup, he'd lost his ever-loving-motherfucking mind. She moved from the table and dumped out her tea in the sink. "Whatever feelings you *think* I have for you make no difference. Whether I actually have feelings for you or not makes no difference, either. You can't stay."

"Why's that?" He set his mug on the counter as if nothing was wrong, and that just fueled her anger more. How the hell was he so calm?

Cyn braced her hands on the counter. "I don't want you to stay."

"Bullshit."

"To hell with your bullshit. I don't want this. I never said I wanted this." She crossed her arms. "I don't want a relationship. And if you recall, I've been trying to get you to leave for the past two damn weeks. But you don't seem to listen to me, do you? Tell me, Shane, how does that make you any different from Carlos? He never listened to me either."

"Okay now, *that* was fucked up, Cyn. *Really* fucked up." He straightened from his lean against the counter and pointed his finger at her. "Don't you *ever* compare me to that fucking piece of shit again." His tone was stone-hard, and so were his eyes.

Apparently, she'd hit a nerve, and although she hesitated a moment, knowing she was way out of line, Cyn blew right on past the warning in his eyes and pressed on. "What the fuck ever. Doesn't matter, not like you're gonna listen anyway."

"I know you want this, Cyn. You can lie to yourself, but you can't lie to me."

"I like fucking you. That's it. There isn't any more," she lied, and bile burned the back of her throat. Once again, Cyn pushed it down, blocking out the regret she knew in her gut she'd feel later. "Pretty much done with that, too. In fact, the only thing I want from you now is for you to get your shit and get gone."

Shane reeled back as if she'd stabbed him. And Cyn guessed maybe she had. Flaying open his heart with her words was just as damaging as if she'd literally used a knife on him.

He stared at her, and the mere few feet separating them felt more like a million miles. He blinked a couple of times before shaking his head. "All right, Cyn. You want me gone? I'm gone."

An ache bloomed in Cyn's chest, and her stomach folded in on itself. She swallowed past the lump in her throat and leveled her gaze on him. "Yes. I want you gone."

"Think about what you're saying to me. If I walk out that door, there's no coming back."

Cyn folded her arms over her middle in an effort to hold

herself together. At that moment, her insides felt like they were on her outsides, and she was literally raw and coming undone. Her heart screamed for her to stop, to tell him she was wrong and that she wanted him to stay, but her mind… her mind screamed louder. "I want you gone, Shane."

Shane nodded once, turned away and walked out of her kitchen.

Oh God! Cyn doubled over, squeezed her eyes closed and let out a silent scream. *What am I doing? Oh Jesus, fuck fuck fuck!* She fell to her knees and covered her mouth with her palm as sobs wracked her body. She couldn't stop. Why couldn't she stop—the anger, the verbal tirades, all of it—she was losing her mind. Tears streaked down her cheeks as she sucked back the sound of each cry, keeping herself quiet.

Her body shook, and she rocked back and forth, cradling herself on the floor of her kitchen, begging God to make it all go away.

To make her go away.

CHAPTER THIRTY-FOUR

Shane gathered his things, stuffing them into his large duffel bag as fast as he could and walked out of Cyn's house in a matter of minutes, slamming the door closed behind him. He *had* to get out of there before he lost his shit.

Shane had never run from anything in his life, but he'd just run from Cyn. She'd cut into him so deeply, he couldn't see anything but the bright shade of red coating everything in his line of sight. His heart ached—a physical pain like no other he'd ever felt in his life. Not even the injuries he'd sustained in battle had compared to what he was experiencing right then.

He'd caught a glimpse of her on her knees, her face buried in her hands, in the kitchen as he passed by. The physical pull to go to her, pick her up and somehow figure out how to make this right between them had been an additional lancing he felt over every inch of his skin.

But he couldn't stop.

He couldn't pick her up.

Shane couldn't do anything but leave.

Tossing his bag across the seats, he slid behind the wheel of his rental and started the engine. She didn't want him—or so she said. It didn't matter that he knew deep in her heart she did. The woman had made her choice and done so loud and clear. One thing was for sure: Shane would not stay where he wasn't wanted.

This wasn't much different from his mother…and that right there was something he had not seen coming. Cyn was nothing like his mother, or so he thought. Yet she'd rejected his love, just like his mother always had. It was a severe slap in the face. "What a fucking mess."

After shooting a quick text to Joey, letting him know shit had just blown sky-high between him and Cyn, Shane backed out of her driveway and drove away from the house. Thinking about his mother, he hadn't even gotten to tell Cyn about the house and the shit his mother was pulling on him. Shane slammed the butt of his hand on the steering wheel. "So stupid!" He'd thought to maybe keep the house, and hoped eventually, Cyn would move in with him. He'd thought, quite stupidly, that maybe she'd want to build a life with him. Build a home together. Maybe even a family. Goddammit, what a fool he was.

He parked the SUV in front of Joey's house and gripped the steering wheel tight in his palms. How was this happening? Shane couldn't wrap his mind around it, but no matter what, he knew all roads led back to Carlos. *That* motherfucker was out on bail, awaiting his court appearance for the attack on Cyn. The desire to seek his ass out so Shane could extract a piece of it rumbled through him like a heartbeat.

Shane looked up to see Joey standing on the front stoop. With a nod, he got out of the truck. Stepping up the walk, Joey met him halfway and took his bag from him. "Thanks for letting me stay."

"Don't even mention it. I called Angie. She's on her way." Joey opened the front door.

"Cyn won't be happy about this."

"Tough shit. She either doesn't need to know, or she can get over it."

Shane blew out a breath and took his bag from his best friend. "Okay then. Guest room again?"

"Down the hall to your left." Joey clapped him on the shoulder. "It's gonna be okay, Shane."

Shane nodded as he moved past Joey to the guest room and swallowed down the boulder-sized lump that'd risen in his throat. He loved his best friend and his family. And he loved his best friend's sister.

Fuck… *Fuuuuckkk!*

He dropped his bag and lay down on the bed, staring at the ceiling. Shane needed to book a flight home. He needed to get back to his life and try and figure out a way to let go of Cyn. He also needed to make a decision about his parents' house. Letting his mother sell it felt like a huge betrayal of his father. Leaving Cyn felt like an equal one, but of his heart as well as hers. Shane laid there for a long while, running scenarios through his mind until a soft knock on the door drew his attention. "Come in?"

Angie poked her head in the door. "Hey."

He sat up. "Hey, Angie. You okay?"

She shrugged. "Worried is all. Steph's got a pot of coffee brewing. You want to come out to the kitchen with us?"

"Yeah, I'm worried too." Shane ran his hand over his head. "I'll meet you out there."

"Okay. See you in a few." Angie closed the door, and Shane moved into the attached guest bath.

After taking care of business, he splashed some cool water on his face. Fatigue weighed heavy on Shane's body making every movement feel like he was trudging through quicksand. Jesus, he was tired, but he was pretty sure it wasn't from lack of sleep, though there'd been plenty of that. With a sigh, Shane made his way to the kitchen. Joey and Angie were at the dining table, and Steph was in the pantry.

Joey looked up. "You get a flight booked?"

"Trying to run me off?" Shane moved to the coffee pot. "Way to make a dude feel welcome."

"Damn straight, brother. You eat me out of house and home." Joey let out a chuckle. "Smart-ass."

Shane poured himself a cup of coffee. "Takes one to know one."

Angie let out a giggle and crossed her arms. "I love watching you two together. I was too young to witness your tirades when you were in high school, so this is all gold to me."

"Happy to be your entertainment tonight, Ang." Shane joined them at the table and took a sip of the hot brew. "Especially considering how fun your dinner date was."

Steph emerged from the pantry. "I knew I had these. Cheesy creasy, you'd think I was hiding the vault combination to the Federal Reserve." She set a bakery box of donuts in the center of the table.

Joey's eyes got big as saucers. "When did you buy these?" He flipped the lid open and pulled out a chocolate-glazed donut.

"Yesterday." She looked to Angie. "And now you see why I hide them."

Angie retrieved a frosted sprinkled one and bit in. "Why?" she said around her mouthful.

Steph rolled her eyes and laughed. "Oh lord, you're no better."

Shane laughed and shook his head and then looked away. His chest ached with an overwhelming feeling of loss. He didn't want to be away from the only people who, since his father passed, felt like family to him. He hadn't realized how much he had been missing them until he'd come back to town almost a month ago. He hadn't realized how much he needed them either.

Going home suddenly felt like a death sentence.

Cʏɴ ᴛᴏssᴇᴅ and turned beneath the covers, unable to find a comfortable position. Obviously, she'd grown used to having Shane in bed beside her, and now…he wasn't.

And it was all her fault.

She'd thought about calling him several times since she'd basically thrown him out of her house, but decided against it. Him leaving was for the best. Shane needed to go back to Texas, and she needed to get on with her life. Mainly, Cyn needed to get on with the fixing of whatever it was about her that consistently attracted emotionally stunted men. And also, last but not least, Cyn needed to fix her fancy new inability to control her random bursts of temper.

She reached for the abandoned pillow beside her and pulled it to her chest. Shane wasn't emotionally stunted. On the contrary, he'd been attentive, affectionate, in-fucking-cred-ible in bed and sweet. Never mind fun, funny and easy to talk to. Cyn bent her head to the cotton pillowcase and drew in a deep breath. The scent of his shampoo and cologne flowed through her senses, and Cyn squeezed her eyes closed, willing the tears away.

The bastard even knew how to dance. And not just shake his ass on the floor in a really cool way like some guys knew how to do. No, he knew how to waltz, swing and two-step, which was the only one she was pretty good at.

He seemed perfect. But no one was perfect.

It wasn't the first time Cyn had thought somebody was exactly as they appeared to be. And with Carlos, hell, she'd been so fucking off base with him it wasn't even funny. So not funny that as a result, now she completely doubted her judg-ment and ability to read people.

Cyn flopped onto her back and tossed the pillow aside. It didn't matter that she'd known Shane her whole life. It didn't matter that Joey was his best friend, and it also didn't matter that everyone in her family loved him. He needed to go, and Cyn needed to let him go. And then she needed to get her shit straight.

With a harsh jerk, she yanked the blankets higher and folded over the edge. Why the hell had he thought he could just move back here? It was a free country, but seriously, what the fuck was up with his thinking. And why did he think she'd want that, too? Cyn frowned and stared into the darkness of her bedroom.

Maybe because even though she'd fought with him plenty over the last three weeks, she'd also sucked his dick and fucked his brains out any chance she had. Sometimes more than once a day. Her body tensed and clenched as the familiar desire for him sparked to life. Plus, prior to the explosion in her living room, thanks to Carlos, Cyn and Shane had gone on some dates and did boyfriend/girlfriend-type things together. Even spent time with her family. And maybe also because he was sort-of-kind-of living with her... *Fuck!*

Cyn let out a groan and raised her knees on the bed. "*Dammit! Fucking hell! Sonofabitch!*" She reached for her phone and swiped across the screen. She should call him—tell him she was sorry. But if she did, their merry-go-round would never end.

Fuck's sake, how the hell was she supposed to deal with this mess herself? Anger beat through her in time with her pulse. She was furious with him. She was furious with herself. *And* fucking Angie...what the hell was up with Angie earlier in the night?

Shane had wanted to discuss Cyn's dinner date with her sister, and there was simply nothing to discuss. Big deal, they'd had a fight. Sisters did that—even though Cyn rarely, if ever, fought with Angie.

Restless agitation raced through her. She needed to sleep. She needed to forget any of this happened. What she wouldn't give to wish it all away—wish herself right back to the night of the bachelor and bachelorette party. Cyn never would've gone near Shane Conlon.

Knowing what she knew now, she wouldn't have touched him with a ten-foot pole—which was a total lie.

A wave of sorrow crashed over her, joining in with the party of every other emotion that'd set up camp inside her, except for the anger. The sadness had extinguished that one, and Cyn did everything she could to call it back. The anger was easier to handle and had become a constant companion as of late.

As if right on cue, her tears made their appearance…and quickly escalated into full-blown sobbing. Cyn cried so hard her body shook from head to toe. She missed him—so fucking much that her chest felt hollow.

Is this what real love, followed by a broken heart, felt like?

This was so much worse than anything she'd ever experienced…and maybe that was because Shane hadn't broken her heart. No, she'd done that to herself.

With tears still streaming, Cyn tossed off the covers and went to the bathroom. She grabbed the Benadryl from the medicine cabinet and popped two small pills. She needed to sleep. And she needed to forget. And she needed to not dream.

SHANE SETTLED in the family room at Joey's house across from Angie. She was on the couch, her long legs curled beneath her as she ran her fingers through the lengths of her dark hair. He'd asked her at the kitchen table, over donuts and coffee, about the topic of being single that'd come up at Ryan and Maiya's house the other night. Angie had said she'd fill him in later—well, later had come, and now he was waiting.

Normally, Shane was a patient man, but at that moment,

his reserve tanks were bone dry. He propped his ankle on his knee and took another sip of coffee.

"She's going to be pissed if I tell you."

For fuck's sake, finally! "Then I guess we won't tell her that I know."

"Yeah, I guess." Angie fiddled with a thread on her jeans. "I just feel bad, I mean…I didn't know it was a secret, you know?"

"Look, Ang, I get it. I do, but it's not like I'm going to use whatever it is you're about to tell me against her in a bad way. I care about your sister. A lot." He blew out a breath. "I get that she didn't want me to know. We even had a fight about it. Please understand, if shit wasn't so crazy with her right now, I'd respect the hell out of her privacy and mind my own business. But seriously, because shit is so crazy right now, I feel like I need to know. Maybe it'll help me make sense of this mess. Does it have anything to do with Carlos?"

Angie let out a sigh. "Yes, but not the attack." She shifted and stretched her legs out in front of her, resting them on the coffee table. "I'm only going to tell you because I know you love her. And because I don't think it's any big deal and that, truthfully, her reaction to me slipping up the other night probably has everything to do with how screwed up her head is right now *because* of the attack instead of the no-dating thing being some sort of secret."

Shane decided to let Angie's comment about him loving Cyn go—no reason to deny or admit what was already true. Obviously, Angie could see it, so there was no point in trying to pretend otherwise. Outside of that, Shane couldn't imagine what the big deal was, especially if it really had no tie-in to the attack. "Why would not dating be a secret? Honestly, I'm really confused, Ang."

"Just before the wedding, Cyn and Carlos broke up. She caught him with another woman. Like, his hand was in the cookie jar, for real."

"She didn't give me all the details, but I imagine that must've been pretty ugly for her." Shane dropped his booted foot to the floor and leaned forward. "Go on."

"So, Cyn was on a quest of sorts. You know, to figure out why she kept picking all these fucked-up guys. Carlos's shit pretty much broke the camel's back, I guess." Angie sipped her coffee. "Anyway, she decided she was going to stay single for a year and figure out why her picker was broken."

Shane frowned. "Come again?"

"She was going to stay single for a ye—"

"No, not that part. Broken picker? What the hell does that mean?"

"Oh!" Angie giggled. "It's a term Maiya came up with, I guess. Cyn has a broken picker. You know—" she held up her pointer finger and wiggled it at him, "—her picker is broken. She always picks assholes."

How funny. Maiya was an interesting lady, for sure, and absolutely perfect for Ryan. "Okay, so…" Shane ran his palm over his stubbled jaw. "So she thinks her picker is broken, and she decided to stay single for a year. Huh."

"Until you."

"I guess maybe I threw a wrench in her plan, right?"

"A big, huge wrench. Big. Enormous!" She laughed. "I was supposed to do it with her. We'd made a pact."

"But then I showed up."

She flipped her hair off one shoulder. "Well, you showed up before we made the pact, but it didn't matter."

"Why didn't it matter?"

"Because I guess it was…" she paused. "I guess after you two hooked up the night of the bachelorette party and again at the wedding." She winked, and Shane felt his face get hot, and he cleared his throat. "Yeah, she told me all about it. That's what we do." She grinned. "Anyway, she'd said she wasn't going to touch you again and start her moratorium.

That's when she asked me to be her wingman…or woman, rather."

"But she did—" he cleared his throat again. Screw it. Again, no point in pretending things hadn't happened, just like Angie laid out. Shane might be a private guy, but this was Cyn's sister, so… "She did touch me again. Hasn't stopped touching me, so I guess that plan didn't work."

"Right. So she went to plan B." Angie sipped her coffee.

"Plan B?"

"Cyn figured she'd spend the time with you while you were here, you know, because you were just too yummy to resist, and *then* when you went home, she'd do her year."

Shane had to laugh. Yeah, he'd blown her plan to bits. "Okay, yeah. I get it. But, Angie, this doesn't seem like something to keep from me. Why wouldn't she just tell me?"

Angie shrugged one shoulder. "Hell, if I know. Why does Cyn do anything these days? I mean, come on, she practically ate my face for dinner tonight. That's not normal for her. With Mary, hell, yes. Totally normal. But with me? It doesn't happen."

Shane didn't get it. He leaned back in the seat and glanced around the room. It wasn't a big deal that Cyn had wanted to remain single for a year. He actually thought it was a really good idea she had—of course, now that he was in her life, it wasn't necessary, not considering the chemistry between them and how well they got along, at least until the attack. Jesus, things had gotten really fucked up. "She needs therapy, Angie."

"Ya think?" She dropped her feet to the floor. "Tell me something I don't know, Shane. But she won't go."

"Honestly, I think she has PTSD. She's displaying all the symptoms. Anger and lashing out at people in a completely irrational way. She refuses to talk about the attack." He got to his feet and stood in front of the picture window. "Hell, she won't even go into the living room at her house."

"Shit. What are we going to do? I mean, she's not *crazy* crazy. She's just a little fucked up right now—which anyone would be."

"Of course." Shane faced Angie. "Here's the thing. Cyn, when in her right mind, wouldn't have cared if I knew about her self-imposed year of being single."

"Celibacy, too." Angie got to her feet.

He glanced at her. "Even more props to her for that. That's a damn tall order, I imagine." Shane cringed at the thought of her being with anyone else. Bile rose in his throat, and he pushed it back down. "Yeah, ya know, not gonna even think about that, but here's the deal: It's only the stress of the attack and her inability to cope with what happened that made her freak out about something that was no big deal. It's also what's making her fight with everyone."

"Even me." Angie frowned.

"Even you, sweetheart." Shane gave her arm a squeeze.

"Right, so what do we do now? I mean, she won't even discuss it with Mom."

Shane tucked his hands in his back pockets and stared out of the window into the darkness of the backyard. He was out of ideas. And he was out of energy, too. He'd tried, and he'd lost. "I don't know, Angie. But I do know it's time for me to go home."

"Shane, you can't just leave."

"I have to. Cyn can't hear me, and I've run out of creative ways to say it. I can't help her. She doesn't want my help. I have to accept that. You probably should, too."

"Soooo, what, then? We just let her keep on this path of madness until she has some sort of mental breakdown?"

"I hope not. You were right, what you said before about me loving Cyn." Shane let his head fall forward, and he rubbed his hands over his face. After blowing out a harsh breath, he shook his head and turned back to Angie. "I love her more than she knows, and I can't stand that she's going through this, but I can't help her, Ang."

"Shane, you can't leave. She needs you." Tears streamed down Angie's cheeks, and Shane's heart broke for the second time in one night.

Shane pulled her into an embrace. "Maybe she needs me to go. Maybe if I go, she'll get some help."

"What if that doesn't work?"

Shane's gut twisted with fear. Truth was, he wasn't leaving because he thought it might cause Cyn to get some help. He was leaving because she'd sent him away. In addition, he'd grown weary of the fight.

Hope had lost its spark within him. He didn't know if Cyn would get the help she needed once he was gone. He didn't know anything except the sharp ache of his broken heart and that the woman he knew he was meant to be with didn't want him.

He stroked the back of Angie's long hair and tried to figure out what to say to her. In the end…it wasn't much, but it was all he had. "It's going to be okay, Angela."

CHAPTER THIRTY-FIVE

Cyn stepped from the shower and toweled off. That day marked the third since she'd sent Shane away. Two nights without him beside her in bed, and the coming night would be the third. Two days without his scent, his lips, his touch and his body buried inside hers. Cyn braced her hands on the counter and stared into the sink. She'd heard through the old reliable family grapevine that he was still in town, but he had to be leaving soon, right?

Her gut clenched, and her heart ached at the thought of him leaving. She blinked, trying to stave off the tears that seemed to be on ready standby and supply since he'd left—or rather since she'd thrown him out. She probably needed to keep that statement accurate. Shane wouldn't have left her… maybe. But Cyn sure made certain that would never happen.

Because she'd left him first.

A few tears escaped, and Cyn grabbed a tissue, blotted her cheeks and blew her nose. She cared about Shane, there was no denying that, and she didn't want to leave things as they were—all ugly and unsorted. She would rather make peace and say goodbye to him in the right way.

Regardless of the fact that Cyn didn't trust herself, therefore couldn't trust Shane, the guy was still a nice one. And she'd known him her entire freaking life. He didn't deserve what she'd dished out to him.

Though she looked like hell, thanks to her random crying jags, Cyn did her best to make herself presentable for public viewing. A dab of Preparation-H under the eyes and a generous amount of waterproof mascara was totally going to save her ass and her eyes.

After finishing in the bathroom, she tugged on a pair of Capri yoga pants and a T-shirt—nothing too flattering. The last thing Cyn wanted was for Shane to think she was there to lure him back.

Because she wasn't.

That would be stupid and selfish.

Really fucking selfish.

With one last look in the mirror, she adjusted a stray hair and then made her way out the door.

The drive to Joey's was quick enough, maybe quicker than she wanted. Cyn pulled into the driveway and turned off the engine. Nervous energy bounced through her, and as gross as it was, boob sweat was making its presence known. She pulled a tissue from her purse and shoved it between her breasts. The typical curse of having a large chest. "Jesus, it's not even hot out!"

Cyn cringed, knowing full well her sweating had nothing to do with the heat and everything to do with being nervous to see Shane. What if he didn't want to speak to her? Like ever again? Christ, she'd made a huge mess.

A knock on her door window had Cyn jumping out of her skin. She screamed, clutched her chest, and looked over. Joey was standing there, hands raised in surrender. Cyn rolled her eyes and opened the door. "Jesus Christ, Joey! Are you trying to give me a fucking heart attack?"

Joey lowered his hands as he tilted his head to the side. "No, honey. Not really on my agenda today."

Cyn stepped out of the Wrangler and slammed the door. "Well, you could've fooled me. You don't just sneak up on a person like that. Christ."

Joey crossed his arms. "Ya know, not for anything, but you're sitting in my driveway, Cyn. I saw you pull in over five minutes ago, and when you didn't come to the door, I came out to see if you were okay. I even opened the garage, came out that way, which, since it's right in front of you, I'm kinda surprised you didn't notice. But I'm guessing you were what? Daydreaming?"

Cyn glanced over at the open garage door. *Holy shit.* How the hell had she not seen the garage door open? And five minutes? How had she been sitting in his driveway for five minutes? She was losing her freaking mind.

Or he was, which was entirely possible, considering the baby and sleep deprivation, though Cyn had a feeling she was reaching pretty far on that one. "Doesn't matter. You just startled me. Forget it." She opened her driver's door, reached in, grabbed her purse and slammed it again. "I came over to talk to Shane."

"Not possible."

"What do you mean, *not possible?*" she imitated his voice, adding a layer of sarcasm. "He and I have some stuff we need to settle, Joey. What? You his bodyguard now?" She moved past him.

He caught her arm. "Go easy, little sister."

Cyn jerked away from him. "Don't tell me to go easy. I'm plenty easy. And if you comment on that in any freaking perverse way, so help me, I will slap you in the back of the head."

Joey laughed. "Good one." But then his expression turned serious. "Here's the thing, you can't talk to Shane because he left over two hours ago to catch his flight back to Texas. He's probably about to take off, if not already in the air." His face softened, the expression in his eyes one Cyn didn't want to identify because it looked far too close to pity. "Sorry, honey."

He couldn't have said what she just heard him say. No way. "What?"

"Shane's gone, honey."

Cyn let her purse go, and it fell to the ground with a thud. "But he can't be gone. I need to talk to him, Joey."

"You can call him in a couple of hours."

Wetness coated Cyn's cheeks, and her stomach twisted into a knot. "You don't understand. We have stuff we need to settle."

Joey grabbed her arm and pulled her to him. The side of Cyn's face hit his chest, and his arms came around her. Joey squeezed her tight against him, patting her back. "Aw, sweetheart. It's okay. Cyn, it's gonna be okay, honey."

"But we have stuff we need to settle, Joey. He can't be gone."

"Baby girl, I'm sorry." Joey smoothed his big palm over the back of her head.

Cyn let him hold her while she collected herself, or attempted to anyway, and tried to wrap her brain around the fact that Shane was gone. He was really gone, and it was her fault. The fucked-up thing was, she hadn't gone there to cast bait, but she guessed a small part of her wouldn't have turned him down if he'd tried to take a bite. Truth was, Cyn missed him. A lot—a whole fucking lot more than she'd even admitted to herself. And now he was gone.

She stepped back from Joey and wiped her face. "It's fine. Yeah, I'll just call him." She nodded as she picked up her purse and fished for another tissue. "I'm fine."

"Why don't you come in, have some coffee."

"No." She sniffled. "I'm fine." Cyn glanced up at Joey and laughed, but then started crying again. She was fine, just like she'd been saying for weeks to everyone, especially Shane: Completely fucked up, insecure, neurotic and emotional.

Shane drilled that shit into her head until she wanted to vomit. And she had, verbally, anyway. The more Cyn thought about it, the harder she laughed. But the tears kept flowing, too.

Joey stepped close again and placed his hands on her arms. "Cyn?"

"What?" She pressed the tissue to her nose and giggled.

"Honey, are you okay?"

"I'm fine." Another laugh blurted out of her, and she stepped back and doubled over, cradling her stomach and laughing like some sort of crazy person. Cyn shook her head, suspecting maybe that assessment wasn't too far off from the truth, which was exactly the sobering thought she needed.

She straightened and drew in a breath. "Totally fine." She laughed again before regaining full composure. Cyn wiped under each eye and glanced at the tissue. Black streaks coated it. "Sonofabitch. So much for waterproof mascara, huh?" With a shrug, she balled up the used tissue, tossed it in her purse and retrieved another.

"Honey, you're kind of freaking me out."

"Yeah, well. Get in line…it starts behind me. I'm freaking myself out."

Joey frowned, but Cyn ignored it and moved to her Jeep. "Tell Steph hi and kiss Madi for me, okay?"

"You sure you don't want to come in? I don't think you should be driving just yet."

"Nah, I'm good. All good. I'm fin— Fantastic. I'm fantastic." She grinned and slid inside the front seat. If she never said the word fine again, it would be too soon. Who the hell knew a word could hold such emotional memory, for fuck's sake. Cyn tossed Joey a forced grin as she backed out of the driveway.

Yeah, totally good. She was great. Just fucking outstanding. Not!

Cyn drove, pretty much blindly, back home. And somewhere along the short trip, her heavy sadness morphed into anger. How could he go and not even tell her he was leaving? Cyn pulled into her garage.

Hot agitation pulsed through her in time with her heartbeat. How in the *hell* does a person spend the last almost fucking month in someone's bed—fucking and sleeping beside them—and just up and fucking *leave* without saying goodbye? "An asshole! That's what an asshole does."

Cyn got out, closed the garage door and moved into the kitchen. She slammed her keys down on the counter and picked up a pile of mail. "Yep, total fucking dickhead." With her mind a befuddled mess of everything—frustration, hurt, anger—*including* the kitchen sink, she tossed the mail aside and headed for her bedroom, but stopped short when the living room came into view.

Cyn looked around the space. Once more, she took in the new paint, rug and tables Shane had bought in an attempt to get her to feel comfortable in the room again. The guilt train screeched into the station, wheels ablaze. Assholes and dickheads didn't do things like this for people. Not even people they cared about. Cyn dropped to her knees, and one more time, tears fell, sobs wracking her body to the core. Fuck! Shane was gone. Really gone, and she'd done it. She'd sent him away.

Cyn had lost the best thing she'd ever had, all because of what? Stubborn pride? Ego?

Or was it fear…yes, fear for sure. Fear of losing a fight that was nothing more than a fantasy in her mind. Carlos had clearly lost. The asshole was facing jail time—she hoped. But Cyn had lost, too, because losing Shane wasn't worth a fictional victory over Carlos.

Nothing was worth losing the best thing that'd ever happened to her.

SHANE STEPPED inside his small three-bedroom ranch house in Garland, Texas, and dropped his large duffel bag on the kitchen floor. Everything was just as he'd left it. Spotless, though a good dusting was in order. One skill all grunts possessed was how to clean. As a result, keeping a clean house was second nature to Shane.

There was a pile of mail on the counter, thanks to his neighbor, and the few plants he had were amazingly still alive. They actually looked better than before he'd left. He'd definitely be picking up a couple cases of beer for Jesse and Iris in thanks. Maybe even have them over for a cookout.

Shane grabbed his bag and headed to his bedroom. After unloading, he put everything back where it belonged and then wandered to the living room. Fucking hell, the house was quiet—too quiet. He'd never noticed that before. Or at least it'd never bothered him before.

Shane stretched out in his father's old La-Z-Boy recliner, remote control in hand, debating whether or not to turn the television on. It would solve the quiet problem, but what he really wanted to hear instead was Cyn's voice. Even if it was her bitching at him about nothing at all—because it wasn't like he ever left the toilet seat up or socks on the floor. Or dirty dishes in the sink, either. Of course, hearing her tell him how bad she wanted his body inside hers would be better. Toss in one of her bigger-than-life, bright smiles, and he'd be in heaven.

The dull emptiness that hadn't left his chest since he left Cyn's house grew deeper. Cyn was missing from him. He missed her—so fucking much his heart ached with it. She was the other half of him, and although Shane had been doing just goddamn fine before her, he didn't quite know how to move forward without her.

Shane placed the remote on the end table and picked up his cell. He hadn't heard from her. But he hadn't reached out either. Regret burned the back of his throat. He should've gone to say goodbye. Or, at the very least, called…sent a text, even. But he couldn't bring himself to do it.

It wasn't pride; he knew how to admit when he was wrong. It was more that he'd had enough. He couldn't take how she was treating him, and somehow, reaching out one last time felt like it might make things harder.

He loved her…that much he knew. He also knew she didn't love him back, not the way he needed her to.

Shane scrolled through some of the pics he had of them together and ones of her alone. God, she was so beautiful. In his eyes, she was everything he never knew he wanted…and more. But she'd given up trying, though, really, she hadn't ever tried at all.

It was over, and Shane had to accept that. He had to get on with his life. He had to take care of his business. Moreover, he had to get over Cyn. How he was going to do that was a fucking mystery.

She'd torn his heart into a million pieces, and there wasn't enough thread in the world to stitch it back together. He'd survived a lot in his service to his country, taken his fair share of injuries too, and Shane knew he'd survive this too, but for the life of him, he didn't know how because this felt so much worse. This felt impossible.

"Fuck love. And fuck this." Shane tossed the phone aside and retrieved the remote. Turning on the TV, he kicked open the old recliner and flipped to whatever sports event he could find.

Never again would he go down the love path.

CHAPTER THIRTY-SIX

CYN CRAWLED, IN A STATE OF ABSOLUTE HYSTERICS, TO THE
center of the living room. She collapsed on her side to the rug
Shane had bought for her. Tears, set on perma-flow, blinded
her vision and streamed down her cheeks, wetting her face.
She wept and wept, and when she thought there was nothing
left, Cyn cried some more.

Absolutely convinced she was losing her mind, she fought
to catch her breath. A heavy weight had settled on her chest,
and her mind reeled and tangled, twisting her thoughts into a
mess of emotion…and through it all, the tears kept on.

Thoughts of the night with Carlos played through her
mind. The gun. And the moment she decided to take her
chance, rushing him, and him hitting her so hard she saw
stars.

But then Shane was there…he'd come home. Thank Go
— *Home.* Cyn covered her face, and a cry erupted from the
depths of her gut, so raw her whole body arched off the floor.
He'd come *home* to *her* and saved her. God help her, what had
she done?

"Shaaaaaaane! Oh God!"

Agony filled every part of Cyn—body and soul. She rolled

to her side, curling into a ball. She couldn't breathe, couldn't think…all she could do was weep. Everything was pouring out of her. The anger, fear, agitation, regret and guilt…and she was powerless to stop it.

"Cynthia? Oh my God, honey! What are you doing?"

Cyn felt Angie's hand on her shoulder, and she jerked away from the touch.

"Oh fuck," Maiya said. "Chica, we're here."

She felt another hand smooth over her hair, and again, she tried to jerk away from the tenderness, but one of them was at her back and the other in front of her. She didn't deserve their care. She didn't deserve anything, not after what she'd done and how she'd treated everyone these past weeks.

"Let's get her up and to her bed," Maiya said.

"Got it." Angie placed her hand on Cyn's back.

"*N…nooo*—" Cyn sucked in a breath, "—*j…j…juss le…eave m…mee.*"

Maiya smoothed Cyn's hair back from her face. "No can do, chica. We're getting you in bed, and we're not leaving you until you come through this."

"On three?" Angie said.

"Yep."

Cyn felt an arm slide beneath her from the front and one from the back, and then she was righted, both her sister and Maiya forcing her to sit up. She opened her eyes to find Maiya squatted down in front of her. "Getting you to your feet, Cyn. It'd be great if you help a little, chica."

Cyn nodded and swallowed.

"Good. Put your arms around me." Maiya slid her hands around Cyn's waist, and Cyn felt Angie at her back.

Cyn did what her sister-in-law asked as they both counted to three and then lifted. Cyn tried to help, but her legs felt like jelly, right along with her insides. With a grunt, she was pulled to her feet, and Cyn leaned against Maiya.

Maiya held her tight for a long moment. "I've got you, Cyn. We both got you, honey."

"*W…whyy ar…rre yo…uu he…eere?*"

"Joey called us." Angie stroked Cyn's back. "He was worried. Guess he was right to be."

"*Bbb…igg j…jjerkk.*"

"Yeah, well, be glad he's not here. Come on, sweetheart, let's get you into bed." Maiya pulled away and moved to Cyn's side.

Angie was at her other side, and together, they walked her to her bedroom. All the while, Cyn sobbed and sniffled. She'd sent him away. She loved him, and she'd sent him away. Her body broke into chills, and she shook all over, more than she already was. "I ff…fuckked uppp sssoo baddd."

"It happens." Maiya steered them into Cyn's bedroom. "It's fixable, chica."

Angie stepped away and pulled the blankets back on Cyn's bed as Maiya turned, and helped Cyn to sit. Maiya raised Cyn's legs onto the bed, and Cyn lay down and curled around herself again.

Chills wracked her body, and her teeth chattered. She didn't try to talk anymore; she could barely understand her own words. The situation wasn't fixable. The expression on Shane's face when she told him to leave flashed in her mind, and Cyn squeezed her eyes closed and started crying again. The man had no reason to ever speak to her again, let alone forgive her for anything.

"Angie, go get a rocks glass of Jameson." Maiya climbed onto the bed.

"Just what I was thinking. I'll bring the bottle."

Cyn glanced up as Maiya stretched out next to her. "Cyn, I know what you're thinking. I know you think it's hopeless, but, honey, nothing is ever hopeless. If I learned anything, I learned that."

Cyn shook her head and wiped her cheek. She'd fucked this up so bad there was no way Maiya was right.

"Aw, darlin', you'll see." She handed Cyn a tissue. "Blow your nose, sweetheart."

Cyn took the tissue and did her best, but her nose was so packed not much came out. Angie returned, glass in one hand —half full with the amber liquid—and the bottle of Jameson in the other. She handed the glass to Maiya before moving to the other side of the bed. Cyn felt the mattress dip, and then Angie stretched out behind her.

Maiya sat up and held the glass in front of Cyn. "Cyn, drink some of this, honey. We gotta get your nerves settled a bit."

Cyn rose on one arm and took the small glass from her sister-in-law, who'd become a best friend and as much of a sister to her as Angie and the rest of her blood sisters were. Cyn put the glass to her lips and sipped.

"Yeah, how about a little more. Like maybe all of it." Maiya raised a single brow.

"We have a whole bottle, so drink that down, sis." Angie rubbed Cyn's back.

Cyn looked at Maiya through her blurry, tear-filled eyes, nodded and drank down the remaining booze. The warmth of the whiskey coated her throat and tummy. Maiya took the glass and handed it to Angie. "Fill 'er up, Ang."

"At your service."

After a moment, Maiya had the glass in her hand again. "Another, but just a sip of this one."

Cyn was so desperate for a reprieve from her emotional hurricane, she took the glass and, instead of sipping as Maiya had suggested, she tossed the whole thing back. The burn wasn't as intense, but it was still effective. She handed the glass to Maiya, lay down on the pillow and closed her eyes.

"That wasn't a sip, but all righty then." Maiya lay down, too.

Cyn felt her two sisters curl around her, both with an arm around her waist. The booze spread through her veins, smooth and steady, as Cyn focused on her breathing. Her head pounded, and her heart raced, but as the booze did its job, her body and mind began to settle.

A haze wrapped around her, and combined with the warmth of Maiya and Angie against her, Cyn's body grew heavy, and sleep took hold.

CHAPTER THIRTY-SEVEN

Cyn woke alone in her bed, head and chest aching, along with a very heavy heart. Sitting up slowly, she grabbed a tissue from the box on her nightstand and blew her nose—And oww, that didn't help the ache in the head thing. Her bedroom door was open, and she could hear voices off in the distance. Assuming Angie and Maiya were still there and having no idea what time it was, Cyn wiped her eyes and headed for the bathroom.

After she'd washed her face, she made a point to not look in the mirror—she knew she looked like death warmed over, but worse, she couldn't stand the sight of her own face. Cyn was disgusted with herself for all that she'd done to everyone.

Especially for what she'd done to Shane. He didn't deserve it. And she didn't deserve him.

With weariness weighing heavy on her shoulders like a wet wool blanket, Cyn made her way to the kitchen. And stopped dead in her tracks. Holy shit—her mother was at the table, along with Angie, Mary, and Katie. Maiya and Stephanie were perched on the window seat.

What the hell! Cyn's kitchen wasn't small by any stretch, but Jesus, the amount of estrogen filling the room had to be pushing maximum overload and breaking some obscure laws of physics. The thought made Cyn smirk before she pressed her fingers to her forehead and attempted to put a leash on the demon that always seemed to jump out of her mouth.

Feeling like she'd gotten herself somewhat under control, she looked back up at the gaggle of women in her life. "Did someone die, or is this when you sit me down and have some sort of an intervention?"

Maiya let out a snort, and Angie blurted a laugh. Cyn's mother shot them both a look and then turned her gaze to Cyn. "No one has died. Thank God. Now, how are you feeling?"

"Intervention it is, then." Cyn nodded and moved to the counter. Steph was there, so she knew there was already a pot of coffee ready.

"What makes you think we're staging some sort of intervention?" Mary asked.

"Because you brought out the big guns. Katie's here." Cyn pulled a mug from the cabinet.

Katie chuckled, and Cyn glanced at her oldest sister and gave her a small smile before pouring herself a coffee. After taking a sip of the hot brew, she turned and faced her family. "Honestly, Mom? I feel like I've been rode hard and put away wet."

"That's quite the visual." Katie winked at her. "But I do know what that feels like."

Cyn took a seat at her countertop bar and faced the most important women in her life. She supposed an intervention made sense…to *them*, but what they didn't know was they were wasting their time and hers. Cyn's mother rose, moved to the coffee pot and refilled her mug. Cyn glanced over at her. Her mother caught her gaze, and Cyn felt the first, then second, tear roll down her cheeks.

Mom put her mug down and immediately moved to Cyn and pulled her into an embrace. "Ah, my sweet girl." She stroked the back of Cyn's hair. "It's going to be okay. I know it doesn't feel like it right now, but it will be. I promise you."

Wrapping her arms around her mother's waist, Cyn absorbed the comfort that—no matter how old a person got—they sometimes needed from their mom. Her mother stroked her back, and Cyn let the tears flow, not that she had much of a choice because it seemed that the anger she'd been marinating in and spewing everywhere, was all fizzled out. In its place was raw hurt. She cried over what Carlos had done to her, and she cried for what she'd done to Shane…she knew she'd hurt him.

Cyn wanted to fix it—all of it. Herself and the situation with Shane. But fixing herself was the first step. Cyn sniffled, and her mother handed her a tissue. Pulling away, she blew her nose as she glanced around at her sisters. They were all crying too.

"So…" She glanced down at her fingernails. Her normally perfect manicured nails looked like shit, which was because she'd been neglecting them. She'd been neglecting a lot of things. "I've decided I'll go to therapy."

"Oh, chica, that's awesome!" Maiya hopped up and came running to Cyn. "That's the best thing I've heard all day!"

Angie was next, moving beside her. She gave Cyn a kiss on the cheek. "Do you want me to go with you? You know, for the first time or something?"

Cyn let a small smile arch her lips. She loved Angie, all of her sisters really, even Mary. But Angie…Ang had always been hers. Even with their age difference, she and Angie got along. She played with Barbie dolls with Angie long after Cyn had lost interest in them, all because Angie wanted to play. "I think this is something I should do myself, honey. But you can meet me afterward with some Boom Chocolatta and a spoon."

Angie laughed. "I'm so down with that."

Cyn leaned her head on her mother's shoulder. "So the intervention wasn't necessary. Last night's—" She glanced between Maiya and Angie. "That was last night, right? I didn't lose days to some weird emotional coma, right?"

Angie giggled. "No, it was last night. But, for real, wouldn't it be cool if you could actually do that?"

"Do what?" Mary asked.

"Jeez, Mary, keep up. What she means, little sister, is that if your heart is broken or you're deeply sad about something, it'd be cool to just go into a little coma and get a short break from the heartache." Katie rolled her eyes.

"Oh. Weird." Mary frowned.

Cyn laughed. "And that's why we call Katie the big guns. Plus, she's the only one Mary listens to and doesn't boss around."

"That's not true!" Mary got to her feet and rested her hands on her hips. "Stop picking on me."

"Sit down, Mary. You need a Valium or an orgasm… something. I don't know which, maybe both. But just cool your jets." With one brow raised and arms crossed on the table, Katie stared up at Mary.

Mary sat almost as fast as she'd stood, right on command, and Cyn had to suppress a "Told you so." Somehow, she managed to not say it. It wasn't worth it, not right then, anyway.

Their mother smoothed Cyn's hair back from her face. "One of the servers at the restaurant has mentioned someone they go to. They sound like they might be pretty good. I'll ask her the name."

"Okay." Cyn nodded and smothered a yawn with the back of her hand. She was tired. But more so, she was weary…and she was defeated, hopeless even. At least those were the feelings that kept rising and receding, only to rise again inside her.

"Good. I think we'll get out of your hair unless you want us to stay?"

"No. I'm okay." Cyn looked at Maiya and Angie. "Unless you two want to stay again?"

Maiya ran her fingers through her hair. "Wish I could, honey. I need to get home to Jacob. He's missing me something fierce…and Ryan is too. Personally, I think it's really just Ryan doing the missing." Maiya let out a small chuckle. "Little man loves his auntie Cyn, so he knows that I needed to be here. But I'll stop by tomorrow right after work."

"I'll stay, Cyn. No worries, honey." Angie rubbed Cyn's back.

Relief washed through Cyn. She didn't want to be alone again for fear there'd be a repeat of last night's drama. "Thanks, Ang."

Once everyone was gone, she and Angie crawled into Cyn's bed. Angie had her laptop propped on her lap and was browsing through Netflix to find something for them to watch. Cyn didn't much care what her sister picked, as long as it wasn't a chick flick. The last thing she felt like watching was a happy-ever-after love story. Happy was a stupid pipe dream— one Cyn didn't want to be reminded of.

She cradled Shane's pillow against her chest. "I miss him, Ang."

"Aw, baby doll." Angie smoothed her palm over Cyn's hair. "I know you do. Why don't you call him?"

Cyn sniffled and wiped the tear that'd emerged and trickled over her nose. "No."

"Why not? I bet he misses you, too."

"I don't know how he could. After the way I treated him? I wouldn't blame him if he hated me."

"Hey, if he hates you, it means he loves you." Angie focused back on the computer.

Cyn frowned. "What? Angie, you're crazy. That makes no sense."

"Oh, it makes perfect sense. Trust me on that. Hate is a strong emotion, just as strong as love, and when a man loves you like Shane does? There's no doubt he might hate you a little, too. Ask Mom, betcha she'll agree with me. Love and hate? They go together, Cyn."

Cyn let out a sigh. It made sense, sort of. She'd definitely felt hate for the men in her past relationships, but it was only after they'd pushed her past the point of no return, and it was just too painful to love them anymore.

Hate was easier to feel. But hate also paved the road to her getting over those guys, so if Shane hated her, eventually he'd get over her. The thought made Cyn's stomach cramp, folding in on itself. She didn't want Shane to hate her. And she definitely didn't want him to get over her. But Cyn didn't know how to stop either from happening.

She'd done the damage and made her bed. The only thing for her to do now was lay in it.

A FEW DAYS LATER, Cyn emerged from the counselor's office feeling…not so relieved but more like she'd just gone through the spin cycle in an industrial-sized washing machine. Her insides felt scrubbed raw. And her mind was filled with the memories of the night with Carlos. Having to tell that story in detail sucked more than the night she'd experienced it. Bile had burned the back of her throat the whole time she talked.

The therapist had assessed her issues, based on some questions that she'd asked, and determined that Cyn was only one symptom away from actually having PTSD. Instead, the woman felt she had ASD: Acute Stress Disorder.

It made sense enough to Cyn, but really, all Cyn cared about was the fact that she was sick of feeling like a total nut job in her head and also real fucking tired of being pissed off all the time and biting everyone's head off.

As she crossed the parking lot to her car, her cell phone beeped with a text alert, and she pulled it from her purse. Swiping her thumb across the screen, she read the message.

Angie: Are you out yet?

Cyn: Just barely. Walking to the car now.

Angie: Cool beans. Meet at my place. Maiya is here, and we have ice cream and whiskey.

Cyn: Oh shit. LOL Okay, be there in 40 or so.

With a smile on her face—which was a totally unexpected thing and quite rare as of late—Cyn tucked her phone away and slid behind the wheel of her Jeep. Her sister was a freaking angel, and Maiya was too. Ice cream and whiskey seemed like the oddest combo on the planet, yet the absolute perfect one.

After the heavy, heart-wrenching session with the counselor, Cyn needed a bit of a reprieve from her emotions. And, of course, Angie and Maiya knew exactly how best to give her that. Pulling out into traffic, Cyn drew in a few cleansing breaths and queued up her iPod. The familiar beat of her friend Tarra Layne's song "Beautiful Day" flowed through the interior of the vehicle, and Cyn smiled again.

It was a beautiful day, and things were looking better than they had in a long time, but she had a feeling the next several sessions were going to be just as difficult as this first one had been. The counselor assured her that it would get easier, and Cyn really hoped the woman was right.

Traffic was lighter than she'd expected, and she got to Angie's in less than the forty minutes she'd figured on. After parking, Cyn made her way to her sister's front door.

Mid-knock, Angie swung the door wide. "Why are you knocking? Did you lose your key?"

"No, I think I left it at home in my other purse." Cyn stepped past Angie.

"All good. Maiya's in the back."

Cyn followed Angie through the kitchen to the back door.

Maiya was stretched out on the outdoor loveseat, whiskey in one hand, cigarette in the other. She glanced up as soon as Cyn stepped outside. "What's up, chickadee?"

Cyn took the spot next to her. "Oh, you know, just been through a rinse and spin cycle, AKA therapy. You?"

"I cooked my boys dinner. Kissed them both on the top of their heads, grabbed a bottle of Jameson from the cabinet and high-tailed my ass over here." Maiya grinned and took a drag of her smoke.

"When are you going to quit smoking?" Angie approached with three bowls of ice cream, precariously balanced in her hands.

Cyn jumped up and grabbed one of the bowls. "Oh my God, you could have dropped the Boom Chocolatta. What is wrong with you? Never ever risk the Chocolatta!" Cyn giggled and shoved a spoonful in her mouth.

Maiya grinned and took the bowl Angie offered her. "Never mind about my smoking. It's been a topic as of late with Ryan. And, yeah, no shit about the risk to the ice cream. Don't you have a tray? You're a Donnelly, for fuck's sake. You all have serving crap galore."

"Who needs a tray when you have hands and skills?" Angie laughed. "But yeah, I do have a shit ton of trays. Don't tell my mother." Her sister lit the gas fire ring centered in the square, slate-tiled table centered between the loveseat and two chairs. "So, why are you and Ryan discussing your smoking?" Angie took a seat in one of the cushioned chairs and spooned up a mouthful of ice cream.

"Now, this is a topic I *do* want to talk about." Cyn smiled again. Wow, she actually felt the twinge of a cramp in her cheeks. Jesus, had it really been *that* long since she'd smiled regularly that her cheeks were cramping? The realization only made her smile more. She wasn't cured by any stretch, but apparently, simply talking about the attack with Carlos in detail had already started to lift a burden Cyn hadn't realized she was carrying.

"You two, I tell you what. Never mind that now. Cyn, tell us about the session. Did you like the therapist?" Maiya propped her feet on the table and wiggled her toes in front of the flame.

"Okay, fine, but first—" Cyn swallowed a spoonful of chocolate bliss and then continued, "—where's the whiskey?"

Maiya laughed. "I got mine before I came outside."

"Damn, I need another arm." Angie hopped up, ran in the house and was back before Cyn got two more mouthfuls of ice cream in—two glasses and the bottle in hand. She placed them on the table, filled each one two fingers full and resumed her seat. "Okay, go!"

Maiya burst into a fit of giggles. "You are so fucking cute, Angie. We gotta find you a man. For real."

"Ugh, no way. I don't do blind dates." She sipped her whiskey, then tilted her head to the side. "What a strange flavor."

"Ang, you know you don't have to do the moratorium anymore, right? I mean, that's kind of the farthest thing from my mind right now. Not really fair for you to continue."

"I have decided that being single for a little while is working for me. Doubt I'll do a year, but for now, I'm okay with it." Angie shrugged. "Okay, so? Therapist?"

Knowing her sisters weren't going to let it go, Cyn took a deep breath, along with another mouthful of ice cream, and shored up her emotions. "She's this interesting-looking older lady. Glasses that are too big for her face. Gray hair that sorely needs a style and she had on a horrid beige cardigan sweater. She probably owns only orthopedic shoes."

"I guess it's a good thing you're not going to her for fashion advice then, hmm?" Maiya nodded with a grin and lit a cigarette.

Cyn leaned forward. "True. It's kind of like talking to a

really nice older aunt. Or godmother, you know? I like her, though." She swirled her spoon in her ice cream.

Maiya blew out a stream of smoke. "Comfortable. Safe." She smiled. "I feel that way about your mom."

Genuine happiness flowed through her heart, hearing Maiya talk about the admiration and love she felt for their mother. Once again, Cyn knew her brother had struck gold when he found Maiya. "I'm glad you feel that way, Maiya." She squeezed her sister-in-law's hand and smiled.

"Me too." Maiya nodded as a small smile arched her lips.

Cyn blew out a breath. "So, anyway, she made me talk about what happened with Carlos, in full detail, of course. It was rough. Not gonna lie about that. But the crazy thing is, I feel better already." Cyn sat back. "Then she asked me some questions, and when I expressed that I didn't want to be on pills, she said that was entirely my decision. I'm pretty relieved about that. I mean, I have nothing against medication, but I'm relieved no one's forcing it on me."

Angie curled her legs beneath her. "That all sounds so wonderful, Cyn! Are you going to see her again?"

"Yeah, I guess I'm going to do twice a week for the next few weeks. We're just going to talk about it until it's just…I dunno, I guess, till it's gone."

"You are so fucking brave, and I am so fucking proud of you." Maiya leaned over and wrapped her arms around Cyn.

Angie came over and slid on the other side of Cyn, wrapping her arms around her, too. "Ditto."

Tears sprung and dripped down Cyn's cheeks. "I love you guys."

"We love you too!" Maiya pulled away and swiped away a tear dripping down Cyn's cheek. "Here for you always, chica. Always."

"Thank fuck for that. I don't think I could go through this without either of you. And I'm so sorry for how horrible I've been to both of you."

Angie stroked Cyn's back. "There is no need for apologies. None of that matters."

Cyn shifted and rested her head on Angie's shoulder. "Think I'm ready for more whiskey. It's been a really emotional day."

"Bring on the whiskey!" Maiya patted Cyn's leg and then picked up her glass for her.

Cyn took it and held it up as Maiya and Angie raised theirs.

"Sláinte," Angie said.

"Sláinte," Cyn repeated with a nod. All three of them tapped the bottom of their glasses on the table and drank the booze down.

The whiskey burned as it coated her throat, and as the warmth spread through her, Cyn knew she was blessed. Blessed with a family that always had her back. That would love her without hesitation, even when she was unlovable, and also glue her back together when she'd been shattered.

It filled her heart with joy, but the feeling was bittersweet since Shane wasn't there. And to add insult to injury, Shane didn't have the kind of unconditional love that Cyn got from her family. In fact, the only place he received that kind of love was from *her* family…and she'd gone and sent him away. Ugh, she was such a shit.

Jesus, she'd made a colossal mess of things with him. And she could only hope the therapist would be willing to help her sort that issue out, too.

CHAPTER THIRTY-EIGHT

Cyn sat across from Jean, her therapist, in one of the overstuffed leather chairs. Today was her sixth session. She'd been going twice a week for the past three weeks, and although it'd been one hell of an emotional journey, it was actually getting a whole lot easier. And Cyn was feeling a whole lot better, too.

"Did you have any dreams over the weekend?" Jean shifted in her seat and crossed her legs. Today, the woman wore a red cardigan over a white blouse, a pair of sensible tan khakis and equally sensible brown shoes. Her overgrown bangs were pulled to the side in a barrette while the rest of the gray locks fell messily, skimming the top of her shoulders. Cyn was no fashion or beauty expert, but it was clear Jean was in need of a complete makeover.

Cyn tilted her head to the side and thought for a moment. "I actually don't think I had any bad dreams. I mean, I suppose I could've and just not remembered, but I definitely feel like I'm getting more rest. I'm nowhere near as exhausted as I was."

"That's a good sign. What about the living room? Did you

spend some time in there as we discussed you would last week?"

"Ah, yes, my homework assignment." Cyn chuckled.

Jean smiled, her laugh lines crinkling around her eyes. "Yes, homework indeed."

"Angie and Maiya came over and we watched a movie in there."

"Wonderful! How did you feel during? Any flashbacks?"

Cyn shrugged one shoulder. "Some, but nothing that sent me reeling. Mostly, of Shane struggling with Carlos and how scared I was he was going to get hurt."

"Did you share the memories with Angie and Maiya when they came up?"

"Yes." Cyn brushed her hair out of her eyes. Two weeks ago, Cyn never would've been able to share what was going on in her mind. But worse, a little over three weeks ago, she would've shoved the thoughts away faster than they'd surfaced, effectively convincing herself they'd not surfaced at all. It was a very dark, emotional place she'd held herself in, and Cyn was beyond grateful she was no longer there.

"And they were supportive, I assume?"

"Always. And after, we talked about it, which I actually managed to do without crying. Amazing, right?" Jean nodded, and Cyn continued. "After we talked, in true Angie form, she steered the convo to the redecorating Shane had done to try and make me feel better in the room. Of course, then I broke down and cried."

Jean leaned forward. "Tell me about that."

Cyn blew out a breath. "Well, you already know how he redid the room for me and how I was just the biggest bitch in the world to him about it."

"But you also apologized."

"Yeah, but still. It was still shitty."

"Cynthia, it's very important that you not beat yourself up. Backsliding isn't helpful in this process. It's okay to feel remorse for your actions, and I'll remind you again, you apologized to him that night, if I remember correctly."

Cyn looked down at her hands. "I guess I just feel bad. About everything with him."

"Have you thought about contacting him?"

"Are you kidding? I think about it every day. But you said I shouldn't yet. Are you saying now I should?"

Jean took a sip of her water. "I think you've made excellent progress and that we've worked through much of the trauma you'd been suppressing. Your anger appears to have subsided, and you've faced the ultimate issue, which was the hurt that Carlos caused emotionally, more than physically."

"Jean, that was about as clear as black paint."

That got a laugh out of the woman. "In the beginning, when we first started meeting, I felt it was necessary to put the Shane situation on the back burner in order to address the more critical issues. At this point, what is it that *you* feel is best to do? This is not a decision I can or will make for you."

"Okay then." Cyn licked her lips. "What would you do?"

"Nice try." Jean smiled again, her pale blue eyes sparkling with amusement. "How about you tell me what's stopping you from contacting him?"

Cyn frowned. "You always ask the hard questions."

"Yes, well. That's what you pay me for."

"And your dry humor cracks me up." With a grin in place, Cyn rolled her eyes. "I guess I'm afraid he won't speak to me. I mean, he probably hates me. I know I'd hate me."

"What makes you say that?"

"Because I treated him like shit. Hell, I treated him the way all my exes treated me, Jean. And that's just gross. The fact that I could be that way? Ugh, yeah, gross." Cyn scrunched up her face and then frowned.

"There were mitigating circumstances."

Cyn shook her head and looked away. "Doesn't matter. I don't get a free pass because I couldn't handle my shit. I should've been able to handle my shit. And I didn't. I totally failed. And I just spread that shit all over everyone, Shane especially."

"I see." Jean pursed her lips. "Sounds like you have some forgiving to do."

"Forgiving? I'm barely grasping the concept of forgiving Carlos—not quite there yet—but Shane didn't do anything that needs forgiving."

"You forgot someone on that list, Cyn."

What the hell was she talking about? Cyn was completely confused. Shane didn't need forgiving. Neither did anyone else she was close to. Cyn had been the one doing all the damage. She'd been lashing out at everyone. Jean wasn't making any sense, and frustration churned in Cyn's belly—not the hot anger she'd felt constantly before therapy, thank God, just normal frustration. "Who on earth do you feel needs forgiving?"

"You need to forgive yourself, Cynthia."

What on earth? "How can I…" Cyn licked her lips and shifted in her seat. "Why would I…" She crossed her arms. *Forgive myself? How the hell…* Shock bounced around Cyn's brain like a Ping Pong ball, triggering a mind-blowing bomb.

Jean took a sip of her water and then continued. "Tell me what you're feeling."

"Shock. Confusion. And a whole lot of what the fuck… If that's even a feeling. Sure feels like one, though."

"It qualifies." Jean shifted and uncrossed and re-crossed her legs. "I take it self-forgiveness is a new concept for you."

Cyn clenched her hands as her stomach twisted into a knot. "I guess I've never thought about it."

"I think it applies to the trauma with Carlos, too. We've talked in depth about the fact that you blamed yourself for what happened. Forgiving yourself is necessary where that matter is concerned, too."

Cyn stared in silence across the room at the gray-haired,

frumpy woman who she'd been vomiting her guts up to for the last three weeks. Jean was smart and made sense, even though sometimes that was really annoying, but so far, the woman had been right about everything she'd suggested. Maybe she was right about this, too.

Jean glanced at her watch. "It seems time's up for today. How about you give it some thought, and we'll talk more about it on Thursday when we meet again."

Grateful they were done for the day, relief washed through Cyn, and she blew out a breath. "Okay, see you Thursday."

Cyn pondered the thought as she made her way out of the building to her Wrangler. She wasn't sure if she could forgive herself for what happened with Carlos, and as far as Shane was concerned? There just was no way she could ever forgive herself for hurting him like she did. Dammit, she was making such good progress too.

With a heavy heart and deep in thought, Cyn headed for home. Would Angie and Maiya agree with Jean? She just couldn't see it. Maybe talking to her mother about it was a better option. *Dammit.* Cyn wanted to get better. She was definitely feeling better, or at least *had been*, until today's session. Now she felt like shit all over again. As far as she was concerned, she didn't deserve forgiveness. And anyone who thought she did might just be as nuts as she was.

CYN BIT into the strawberry pastry her mother had made and then sipped her coffee. "She says I need to forgive myself, Mom."

"Well, you do." Her mother took the seat to Cyn's right. "How's the pastry? Moist enough?"

"It's freaking delish. You're not supposed to agree with her. You're supposed to tell me she's nuts."

Her mother looked at her with one raised brow as she lifted her coffee cup to her lips and took a sip.

Cyn cringed. "I don't like that look."

"If I told you that I didn't agree with her or that she was nuts, I'd be lying. And that's something I don't do to my kids." Her mother set her cup down. "Let me ask you something."

Cyn sighed and rested her arms on the table. "Sure."

"Don't you think you've punished yourself enough?"

Cyn shot straight in her seat. "What?" That was not the question she expected, yet Cyn should've known because it was exactly the kind of direct-hit question her mother *would* ask. Damn. Shit. Fuck. *Fucking hell!* Tears stung Cyn's eyes, and she blinked, trying to force them back. She hadn't looked at her actions as punishing herself. Like, in any way. And frankly, she wasn't sure how many more realizations she could handle in one day. A tear escaped, slipping down her cheek, and Cyn wiped it away. "Mom, I don't think I realized I was punishing myself."

Her mom leaned over and pulled Cyn into an embrace. "Oh, my sweet girl, I'm so sorry that you've had to go through all of this. I absolutely cannot stand watching any one of my kids struggle or hurt. If I could take this away from you right now, I would." Her mother pulled back and cupped Cyn's face in her palms. "But I also know that, as hard as all of this has been, it's your journey, and when you get to the end of it, you're going to be stronger than you ever imagined."

Cyn closed her eyes as tears streamed down her cheeks. "This sucks. Forgiving myself feels like some kind of cop-out or get-out-of-jail-free card."

"Yes, it sucks. And no, it's not a cop-out or free ride—farthest thing from it, actually. Cyn, everything happens for a reason, and you may not know what that reason is now, but eventually, you will."

"What if I can't do it?" Cyn sniffled.

Her mother sat back. "What if you can?"

"What if Shane never forgives me?"

"What if he does?"

"Ugh, Mom, that's not helping."

Her mother laughed. "I'm totally helping. You just can't see that yet, either. I love you, Cynthia, and I know you're going to figure this out."

"'Kay." Cyn's voice was clogged with tears. She leaned forward, and her mother pulled her into another hug. She cried a little longer until the tears finally ebbed. After blowing her nose, she finished the delicious strawberry pastry her mother had made and drank her coffee.

They made small talk for the remainder of Cyn's visit until finally, Cyn felt a little more settled in her mind. After she left and arrived home, her mother's words stayed with her throughout the remainder of the night and into the next morning.

The things she'd said made sense, in a "trust in things bigger than you" kind of way. They'd been raised Catholic, but as they'd gotten older, or rather, as her mother had aged, her views had turned in more of a spiritual direction rather than a religious one. Her parents still went to church every weekend, but their outlook on God and religion had changed a lot since when Cyn and her siblings were kids. It was cool and a whole lot more focused on love and comfort rather than sin and salvation…

Cyn supposed forgiveness was born from love. Love of others and love of self. Forgiving others didn't have much to do with the person who did the harming, but more so with the person who'd been harmed, setting them free.

Maybe it was possible if Cyn forgave herself, she'd be set free, too. And maybe, just maybe, Shane could forgive her, too.

CHAPTER THIRTY-NINE

C‌YN STRETCHED OUT ON THE COUCH IN HER LIVING ROOM, television turned to the news. She wasn't watching. She was thinking about Shane and wondering how he was doing. Was he okay? Was he hurting? Was he thinking of her too, or did he just hate her guts...then again, like Angie said, hate and love—similar beasts.

She'd had eight sessions with the therapist, and Cyn was beyond glad she'd done it. Shane had been right the whole time. Cyn had needed the help, needed to talk through what had happened to her with a professional. She just wished it hadn't taken her so long to finally get there and accept the help she'd so desperately needed. But there wasn't anything she could do about that now. She'd been a little—or maybe a lot—nuts and caught in a web threaded by anger, fear and denial.

Cyn glanced around the room. Shane had done such a wonderfully sweet thing for her, and, to be honest, she loved the paint and the new rug and tables. And Cyn realized she didn't hate the room anymore. She loved it. But for two very specific reasons: Cyn finally felt the stranglehold that the attack by Carlos had on her had released. And also because Shane had made the room beautiful for her.

Up until then, Cyn had not allowed herself to contact Shane. But she'd spent the last two sessions with the therapist talking about how she'd pushed him away. And more importantly, why. All of it led back to the attack and beyond to Cyn's already fragile self-esteem.

She'd already been questioning her judgment regarding men, and when Carlos did what he did, what little faith she had in herself was just blown to bits. Every time she'd fought with Shane, it was like a demon had risen inside her, but also, each time she'd tried to push him away, it wasn't because she didn't trust him but because she didn't trust herself.

Shane didn't deserve any of that shit. And when Angie said Shane deserved a medal as well as be considered for sainthood, she was right. More than right. Shane deserved so much better than Cyn had given him. He deserved to be loved and cherished and cared for. Daily.

Cyn may not have the best judgment when it came to men, but her judgment regarding Shane had always been solid and true. Now, she just had to figure out if he'd ever be willing to forgive her. But even if he did, would he ever want her back? God, she hoped so.

Cyn eyed her cell on the coffee table. Should she call him directly, or should she call Joey and try to get a feel of the situation? *Shit...* Cyn picked up the phone and scrolled through her contacts. Finding the one she wanted, she hit the Call button.

"Hey there, chica! How's it going?"

"Maiya? Can I come over? I need to talk."

"Yep. See you in twenty."

"Thanks." Cyn pulled the phone from her ear and went in search of her shoes. She needed a plan, and Maiya would know exactly how to help her.

Cyn sat in one of the large leather chairs in Maiya and Ryan's formal living room. Not much had changed with the decor in the room, but Cyn could definitely see the little touches of Maiya around the space now. Ryan had gotten rid of all the furniture in the family room in favor of Maiya's set, claiming hers was nicer. In Cyn's opinion, both sets of furniture were nice, but she knew it was Ryan's way of making his home his and Maiya's now.

Her brother was such a good man, like Shane.

The ache that'd taken up residence in Cyn's chest doubled, and she rubbed her sternum. God almighty, she missed him—more than she'd ever missed anyone in her life.

Maiya came rushing in from the kitchen with her hair all wild and flowing around her face and a bottle of beer in each hand. "So, I called Angie."

Cyn took the offered bottle. "She's coming?" She sipped the beer. "You think that's necessary?"

"Yep. Why not, right? Between the three of us, we should be able to figure out your next move." Maiya took a seat on the sofa, curling her legs beneath her.

"This is stupid. I should just call him. But I'm fucking terrified that he's going to hang up on me."

The front door opened, and in came Angie. She set her purse on the floor next to one of the tables. "Okay, got here as fast as I could. I was in the middle of a hair appointment."

"You are so high maintenance." Maiya tilted her bottle back.

"Back at ya!" Angie pulled her laptop from her purse and set it on the couch.

"Your hair does look cute." Maiya smiled. "New color?"

Angie opened the laptop. "Thanks, just darkened it a bit. Added some purple highlights, too."

"Wild child." Cyn rolled her eyes and glanced at Maiya.

Angie stuck out her tongue at Cyn before she ran out, returning with a beer for herself. She set the bottle down on the end table, took a seat on the couch next to Maiya and propped her computer on her lap.

"Holy crap, put that thing on a coaster!" Maiya jumped up and grabbed a coaster from the table drawer and placed it under the beer. "We don't need Ryan having a nervous breakdown."

Angie broke into a fit of giggles. "But it's just so much fun seeing him lose his shit over stuff like that."

Maiya chuckled. "Are you kidding? I caught him lint-rolling the comforter the other day. He said there were fuzzies all over it from the extra blanket."

"You're shitting me, right?" Cyn brushed the hair out of her eyes.

Maiya shook her head. "Not one bit. And you know that earned him a blowjob in the closet."

Angie scowled and raised her hand. "TMI! I do not want to hear about you sucking my brother's dick."

Cyn laughed again and then cleared her throat. "Okay, blowjobs aside, can we get back on topic?" Cyn leaned forward, resting her elbows on her knees. "Angie, please tell me you're not working."

"Hell no, I'm looking up flights to Texas for you." Angie glanced up from the computer screen.

Cyn sat up straight. "You're what?"

"Good thinking, Ang." Maiya nudged Angie's shoulder with her fingertip. "I think you going to Texas is a great idea, Cyn. Just show up at his door."

"Thanks!" Angie took a sip of her beer. "There's a direct flight tomorrow morning at five."

Nervous energy propelled Cyn to her feet, and she started pacing. "I can't just show up at his door, you guys!"

"Why not? I showed up at this very door, and look how good that turned out." With a shrug, Maiya raised her bottle to her lips. "Ryan was a little shocked, of course, but then we ended up having sex on the couch."

Angie let out an exasperated sigh. "Do you ever stop? I mean, seriously. You two are like rabbits. And I'm really horny. It's not fair."

Maiya grinned. "I know, it's fucking great!"

Frustration pounded through Cyn's mind in time with her heart, and she stopped, turned to her sisters and pressed her hands to her chest. "Me? Can we get back to me, please? And in case you're all wondering, I miss this man like my life depended on it. That also means I miss his cock. His cock is like crack." She moaned and glanced at her sister. "Sorry, Angie."

"No problem." Angie smothered her grin with her hand.

"Thank you. So can we *pleeeeease* get back to me and what I should do?" Cyn ran her fingers through her hair and tugged on the ends.

Ryan came in the room. "What are you three squawking about?"

"Hi, baby." Maiya smiled. "Don't worry, we're using coasters."

Ryan rolled his eyes but then moved to his wife and gave her a soft kiss. Fucking hell, this wasn't going anywhere. Cyn was no closer to knowing what to do than she was an hour ago.

"Thanks for using the coasters." He smiled at Maiya and smoothed his fingers through her hair. Then he moved and gave Cyn and Angie a peck on the cheek. "Nice to see both of you. So, what's going on? The three of you together usually means some kind of scheme is in the works."

Angie glanced up from her computer. "We're going to send Cyn to Texas."

"Oh, Christ." Cyn placed her hand on her forehead.

"Yep, we are." Maiya beamed.

Ryan looked between the three of them. "What's in Te—Ohhh!"

"Exactly!" Cyn giggled.

"Ambush, huh? That the plan?"

Maiya smiled. "It worked on you."

"Yeah, but…"

"I don't think it's a good idea either, Ry. I mean, it's been like a month. What if he slams the door in my face? Or worse—Oh God! What if he's dating someone else?" Cyn wrapped her arms around her middle. "I think I'm gonna be sick."

Ryan moved to her and rubbed her back. "He's not dating someone else, Cyn. Relax."

She glanced up at her brother. "How do you know?"

"Because I do. Haven't you talked to Joey?" Ryan pulled her over to the sofa and urged her to sit. "You should talk to Joey."

"You are totally holding out, Mr. Donnelly. Spill." Maiya frowned up at her husband.

"Not spilling anything, Mrs. Donnelly. Not holding out anything either." He glanced back to Cyn. "Call Joey. Then decide what you want to do from there."

"All right." Angie closed the laptop lid. "I guess flight plans are on hold."

Cyn frowned. "Okay. I'll call Joey."

Cyn said her goodbyes to her brother and sisters and headed for home. She wasn't feeling any better about the situation. Actually, she felt worse now. Something was going on, and Ryan sure wasn't sharing. She was almost afraid to call Joey and find out what the info was. Ryan refused to share. Even though Ryan said there wasn't someone else in Shane's life, Cyn couldn't help but think there might be.

Shane was a great guy. He was responsible. He was considerate. He was smart. Good-looking. Good in bed—Cyn's stomach rolled over, and she cringed. The thought of Shane in bed with anyone but her made Cyn want to hurl everywhere.

Instead of going over to Joey's house, Cyn went home. She needed to think. Needed to decide what was best for her. She'd come through and dealt with some really harsh shit, thanks to the therapist, but she wasn't so sure she could emotionally handle any additional pain.

For the moment, she was in limbo with Shane. Staying in that position another day or so wouldn't make a difference, but it would give Cyn a little more time to sort her head and be one hundred percent positive she was ready to deal with whatever the outcome might be with him.

At that moment, if he rejected her, she wasn't sure she could survive it.

CHAPTER FORTY

Shane sat at his kitchen table reading through the proposal his mother's real estate agent had faxed over. It'd been just over a month since he'd left L.A., and he'd held his mother off as long as he could. It was time to make a decision. After reading the same line over four times, he pushed the papers aside and glanced out the kitchen window. He couldn't focus…and that was for one very petite reason: Cyn.

Unlike his mother, who wouldn't leave him the hell alone, he'd heard nothing from Cyn. Not one damn text even. Restless energy fueled by agitation pumped in time with his pulse, and Shane rose and moved to the window. Apparently, she was real fucking good at just letting shit go and moving on with her self-imposed single life.

It was a beautiful day, not a cloud in the bright blue sky, but fuck if he cared…his shitty mood made everything appear dull. Maybe a ride on his motorcycle would do him some good. With that thought being the best one he'd had all day, Shane grabbed his baseball cap and headed to his garage.

After blowing the dust off the surface of the Harley, Shane mounted the Softtail and fired it up. His silver and royal-blue-flamed baby started on the first try, the pipes rumbling nice and loud in the garage. Shane walked the bike backward out to the driveway and let the engine warm up a little longer. After a few minutes, he turned his baseball cap around backward, tossed on his shades, and gave the throttle a little twist, rapping the pipes once before pulling away from the house.

Just outside of his rural neighborhood, Shane rounded the first corner and then hit the first long stretch of pavement, opening the throttle wide. The wind stung his face but helped clear his mind. At least a little. His chest ached with guilt. Shane didn't want to lose his father's house, but there wasn't any reason to keep it.

Cyn was gone…he'd lost her.

If she wanted him, she would've contacted him by now. Shane had talked to Joey a few times, but the topic of Cyn hadn't come up. He had a feeling Joey was steering clear of it on purpose, and that was probably for the best. Things had gone sour between him and the guy's sister—shit like that could ruin a friendship, and that was the last thing Shane wanted.

Although Shane lived near his mother's family, he wasn't overly close with them. In fact, the Donnellys felt more like his family than his birth family ever did. It was a very sad but true fact. If Shane signed over his part of the house, letting his mother buy him out, there'd be no reason to ever go back to Los Angeles again.

He could go visit Joey and the rest of the Donnelly family, but he'd risk running into Cyn, and the way Shane felt now, there was no way he could just *run* into Cyn and *not* have his heart break over and over again.

He loved her—was in love with her. And she didn't love him back. Another very sad but true fact. Shane had never been in love. Lust, and maybe very strong like, but never love. Which meant he'd never had his heart broken—the damn thing was shredded.

Shattered and stomped into so many pieces, he was sure it'd take an eternity or more for it to heal.

Shane sped through an S curve and then over a bridge covering a creek, letting the feel of the wind caressing his skin carry him away. Some of the tension in his limbs eased, but it wasn't enough. Nothing would be.

No amount of riding was going to remove the ache in his chest. Fuck it…selling out to his mother was for the best. Staying away from Los Angeles was his only hope of getting past the breakup with Cyn.

He had a list of things he wanted to be sure his mother packed up and sent to him. It would have to be handled outside of the normal real estate transaction, but he didn't care. It was going to be part of the deal. If she didn't agree, then no deal at all.

The items he wanted had belonged to his father. Pictures, tools in the garage, some knick-knacks from his side of the family—nothing of real value, yet priceless to Shane. Over the years, his mother had slowly gotten rid of every trace of Shane's father that she could, but not all of it was gone. What was left, Shane wanted, and he was hell-bent on getting it. Unwilling to go back to L.A., he just hoped everything could be handled by mail or electronically.

At a slower pace, Shane made his way back home. Tomorrow, he'd go through the papers again and be sure everything was in order. He'd be getting a healthy check for his share, but he didn't care about the money. The only thing he cared about was the loss of his last tie to his father and the loss of Cyn. Losing his father at such a young age was something he had no control over. Losing Cyn wasn't much different.

Letting them both go was the only thing he could control.

THREE DAYS HAD GONE BY, and Shane still hadn't gone through the papers. He eyed the stack on the kitchen counter as he fixed himself a late breakfast. Talk about not wanting to deal with a problem. All his bitching at Cyn to deal with her issues, and here he was avoiding his just the same. He sighed and swallowed past the lump that'd taken up residence in his throat since leaving her.

Every time Shane read through the paperwork, intending to also sign the documents, he couldn't get past the second page. It was just a house—a huge part of his past that held precious memories, but still…just a house. However, he was starting to think that maybe his unwillingness to just get the deal done and over with had more to do with Cyn than his father.

It'd been foolish of him to entertain the idea of living in that house with her. She had her own life, her own home, never mind a boatload of shit to work through and overcome. God, he really hoped she was doing okay. So many times he'd wanted to reach out to her over the past month…even if he just got her voicemail. At least he'd hear her voice.

But he hadn't.

Shane stood at the counter, eating the eggs and bacon he'd cooked, cursing himself a coward with each forkful. He took a swig of his milk. Fact was, if she wanted to talk to him, she could've reached out.

But she hadn't.

"What a fucking mess." He took another swallow of his milk before slamming the glass down a little too hard, sloshing a generous wave of the white fluid over the side onto the counter as well as the paperwork. "*Fuuuuckkk!* Good job, dumbass." With an exasperated growl, Shane picked up the now-dripping papers. He reached for a towel and tossed it over the spill…and then the doorbell rang. Jesus fucking Christ, when it rained, it poured—or spilled milk, to be more specific.

After doing his best to separate the papers and clean up the biggest part of the spill, the doorbell rang again, and Shane tossed the soiled towel in the sink, washed his hands and headed for the front door. Whoever was there rang the bell once more by the time he reached it. "Yeah, hold on to your ass. I'm coming!" Shane swung the door wide and—

"I kinda like it much better when you hold on to my ass instead." Cyn pulled off her sunglasses.

Shane's mouth dropped open, and convinced he was seeing things, he blinked a couple of times. Closing his eyes tight, he swallowed before opening them again. Nope, he was seeing just fine. She was still there, just on the other side of his screen door.

"Shane?"

A thick coat of rubber cement had somehow plastered itself all over his tongue, and with no small amount of effort plus a hard mental kick, he managed to get his mouth moving. "What're you doing here?"

"I was hoping we could talk."

Shane frowned. A chaotic jumble of emotional thoughts skittered through him, bouncing around his brain like a damn rubber ball. She wanted to talk? What the fuck did she want to talk about? Why the hell hadn't she just called him? Jesus fucking hell, she looked good. Shane shoved his hands in his pockets to keep from tearing right through the mesh screening to touch her. "Talk?"

"Yeah, talk." She shrugged. "I know I came without being invited, but you think I can come in?"

Shit. Fuck. Hell. Shane pulled his hands free of his pockets and opened the screen door. "Sorry. Come in."

"Thanks." She slid past him, pulling her small suitcase behind her...and her familiar scent hit him in the gut like a sledgehammer. Shane let go of the screen door, and it slammed closed. Cyn jumped and turned around, her hand pressed to her chest. "Holy shit!"

"Shit!" Without thinking twice about it, Shane closed the small distance between them and clasped her upper arms. "Sorry. It's okay, Cyn. Didn't mean to startle you." Again, without a thought, he pressed his lips to her forehead as he ran his palms up and down her arms.

She froze in his embrace but, after a moment, placed her hands on his sides. They stood there for an hour, or maybe just a few minutes, in silence. Shane's lips pressed to her forehead, her hands on his sides, his fingers curled around her upper arms. Until finally, Cyn broke the silence, her words a bare whisper. "I missed you so fucking much."

Shane's heart cracked wide open as he released the breath he hadn't realized he was holding. All the feelings he'd been trying and failing to drown for her came rushing to the surface. It was almost like finally getting air after being submerged under water for too long. "Gonna be the death of me, girl."

Cyn let out a little giggle, and the sweet sound of her laugh rolled through him like a warm summer breeze. Shane wrapped his arms around her and pulled her tight to him. At the same time, Cyn circled his waist and gripped the back of his shirt.

She was trembling, and Shane held her tighter. "I'm so sorry," she said against his chest. "There's so much I'm sorry for. I don't even know where to start."

"Shh." He pressed a kiss to the top of her head. "Not yet, please? Just...just let me hold you for a minute or maybe several."

She nodded and held him tighter. Shane didn't know specifically what she was there to talk about, but when a woman said she wanted to talk, it didn't usually mean good things.

If she'd come to clear the air and formally end things between them in a decent, amicable manner—clearing the air, so to speak, Shane knew he wasn't ready to face that yet.

There was no way she'd come down to Texas to get back together with him, he was sure. They lived in two different states, after all, and she had her whole "be single for a year" mission, plus the healing he'd been praying was finally happening for her.

Bottom line, Shane had her in his arms at that moment, and he wasn't ready to let go.

Hell, he wasn't sure he ever would be.

CYN PRESSED her face against Shane's broad chest and held on to him with every ounce of strength she possessed. The comforting scent of him—cologne and the clean aroma of the sun penetrated her senses, and Cyn drew in breath after deep breath like a starving woman.

She never thought she'd be in his arms again. And by the way, he was holding her, she could pretty much guess that maybe he didn't hate her after all. But she still had to be sure; still needed to make things right between them, and hopefully, with any luck, he'd take her back.

They stood in each other's embrace for a long while before Shane finally rubbed his hands up and down her back, then let her go. Instead of pulling away, he cupped her face in his palms, and she gazed up at him.

His beautiful blue eyes shined with what looked like unshed tears. Cyn's heart clenched like it was locked in a vise, and she smoothed her hand over his cheek. She knew she'd hurt him more than he'd ever reveal, but based on the expression in his eyes, Cyn was getting a pretty good idea of how much damage she'd actually done. "Shane, I—"

"I don't want to talk yet." His gaze roamed over her face. "I can't yet."

"Okay. But I…"

"It can wait. Whatever it is, it can wait."

Cyn let out a sigh. She wasn't going to argue with him, but she had to admit the fact that he didn't want to talk freaked her out. Maybe he'd figured out why she was there, and instead, he wanted to break things off between them, but wasn't ready to do the deed yet.

She knew he cared about her and maybe even loved her, but sometimes love wasn't enough when the damage done was too great. Reluctantly, she agreed, though she knew it'd be easier if he just ripped the bandage off to be done with it instead of making her wait and wonder. "Okay, Shane."

"Okay." He sighed, bent his head and covered her mouth in a kiss.

Oh, sweet heaven, she missed this... Cyn wrapped her arms around his neck and welcomed his tongue with her own. His taste flowed through her, making her blood boil with instant lust. She pressed her body against him, and the kiss grew hotter, wetter and deeper. And Cyn wanted more.

She wasn't shocked. After all, that's how it'd always been with Shane. Cyn couldn't get enough of him. The passion exploded between them, as it always did, thanks to a chemistry she'd never had with any other man but him. Cyn knew without a doubt she'd never find that with anyone else.

He pulled from her mouth and moved to her neck. When his hot tongue stroked over her neck, Cyn let her head fall back with a gasp. She gripped the back of his neck. "I need you."

Shane pulled away from her neck, threaded his fingers in her hair, tugging her head back. "Whatever you need, you get from me." Again, he took her mouth and dived his tongue inside, tangling it with hers, and gripped one breast in his large palm.

He found her nipple through the fabric of her shirt and bra, and Cyn moaned, arching to him. The feel of his erection through his pants against her tummy drew another moan from her, and she moved her hands down his body to his lip of his jeans. She made quick work of the button and zipper and slid her hand down his boxers, taking his length in hand. The warm satin feel of his cock in her palm sent another bolt of arousal through her body.

His prick jerked in her palm, and he yanked from her mouth. "Fuck, girl."

"Want this, Shane."

"Where do you want it?"

"Want you to fuck my mouth. Want you to fuck my tits."

"Goddamn, missed that dirty mouth of yours."

Cyn grinned and stroked her hand up and down his length. "Missed this fine cock."

"Take it. It's yours."

She dropped to her knees, and he shoved his pants down his hips. Though she hoped he meant it, Cyn tried to ignore that he'd said his cock was hers. It was just talk…but she'd take it anyway because whether or not he meant it, she knew it was true. His prick was hers. *He* was hers. And *she* was his.

Shane caressed her cheek, and she glanced up at him as she fisted his length in her palm. His expression softened. "You're so fucking beautiful, Cyn."

Her heart burst with a heavy case of the feels—the only kind that could be described as love. And she almost said the words out loud, almost told him. Instead, without taking her gaze from his, she sucked the swollen crown between her lips.

"*Fuuuuckkk!* That mouth of yours…" He moved his hand from her face and threaded his fingers through her hair, gripping the strands at the back of her head tight in his fist.

Cyn moaned and took him to the back of her throat. The bead of arousal that'd emerged coated her tongue, and her pussy clenched, aching to be filled by him. She'd have him there soon enough. For now, all she wanted was this. His dick in her mouth. His taste flooding her senses. And his body at her mercy—

Without a doubt, Cyn knew the fire between them wasn't

one-sided. It was the same for him as it was for her. There was nothing left to do but go with it, feed it and let it consume her…as it always did.

Shoving aside all thoughts of what might happen next between them—if he'd take her back or not—Cyn sucked her man's cock with earnest. This was heaven. For fuck's sake, Cyn craved him like a starving woman and for the life of her, she had no idea how she'd gone more than a month without him and this. She was fucking ravenous for him.

"Fucking hell. That's it…take it. Goddamn." Shane gripped the back of her hair and fucked into her mouth.

Cyn moaned around his dick, letting him guide her mouth, thrusting to the back of her throat and back to the edge of her lips. And then, before Cyn could stop him, he pulled himself free of her mouth. With her hair still gripped tight in his fist, Shane pulled her to her feet and to his lips. Her body was already on fire for him, her pussy so wet, she knew she'd soaked through her panties. Shane slammed his mouth down on hers and delved his tongue between her lips. Cyn's stomach clenched, and so did her cunt.

With every fiber of her being, and from the depths of her soul to the edges of her healing heart, Cyn knew and accepted the fact that Shane owned her body.

And as he stole her breath, for the first time in a month, Cyn could finally breathe.

***

Shane drowned in everything that was his Cyn. She was in his home and in his arms. He had no idea for how long, and at that moment, he didn't want to know. It didn't matter. All that mattered was his every sense was being assaulted by her in the most delicious ways.

The sight of her on her knees, his cock sliding in and out of her mouth as he fucked between her lips, was one that he'd never tire of seeing. His orgasm had come rushing up on him way too fast, and there was no way in hell he'd allow himself to come yet. His recovery time was always good, thank God, but still…Cyn's pleasure was always his priority. He never wanted to go before her.

Shane stroked his tongue over hers, tasting her, drinking her in and wanting more. Pulling from her mouth, he picked her up and headed for his bedroom.

Cyn let out a giggle and nipped his earlobe. "Ever notice how we never make it more than five feet into the house?"

Shane chuckled. "True story. Not my fault, though."

She tilted her head back and grinned. "You saying it's mine?"

"Damn straight, it is."

"How do you figure?" She nipped his chin.

"You and that fine ass of yours and these delectable tits." He gripped her ass and hiked her higher. "Plus, your voice, your smile, and pretty much your very presence next to me makes my cock hard, so yeah, totally your fault."

"Well, you're one to talk, Sergeant. You and all your hot and hard muscles. Your cock, your voice—ugh and your goddamn dimple! Jesus, it gets me every time." He chuckled again as she touched his chin with a smile so bright his heart full-on melted. "Did I mention your cock?"

"A time or two." As he stepped into his bedroom, Shane slid one hand between her thighs, grazing the seam of her jeans along her pussy. "You've soaked through your jeans. Better get these pants and panties off you now." He bent forward and dropped her onto the mattress.

She squealed as she bounced. "Of course I'm wet. I had your cock in my mouth, and that's like better than my favorite chocolate ice cream— Ooh! How do you feel about me licking chocolate ice cream off your cock?"

"Girl, I swear…" Shane undid her jeans and pulled them and her panties off her legs. Taking hold of her thighs, he slid her to the edge of the mattress and got on his knees. "Gonna be the—"

"The death of you?" She let out another giggle, then a loud moan after Shane bent his head and licked through the bare lips of her cunt.

A rumble slipped from the depths of Shane's chest as her taste hit his tongue. Sweet, hot and heavenly... Cyn absolutely *was* going to be the damn death of him. No way in hell he'd ever find another woman like her. No way he'd survive not having her in his world either.

Shane slid his hands beneath her full ass, raised her hips off his bed and sucked her clit. She rolled her hips, moaning his name as he flicked his tongue against the taut bundle of nerves. Fucking hell, she'd become everything to him, so much more than just the sex. The love he felt for this petite creature filled his chest, shining just as bright as her sweet smile.

I love you... Please stay with me.

"Shane, I'm going to—"

He slid two fingers inside her core and sucked her clit harder.

I love you...I need you.

"Oh God, yes!" She raised her knees higher and dug her nails into his scalp.

Cyn's climax erupted, and as the waves rolled through her, she rocked her hips and squeezed her knees tight around his head. With his gaze locked on her face, Shane curled his fingers inside her, stroking her G-spot, prolonging her orgasm, and felt her channel clench in rapid spasms around his fingers.

Saying she was beautiful, caught in the throes of climax, was an understatement. Pride filled his chest, knowing that he'd been the man to give her that look. The one to take her to heaven...and if he died today, he'd die a happy man, knowing that he satisfied his woman.

Fuck, I love you, Cynthia!

His chest ached with the desire to say the words out loud.

Instead, Shane slid his fingers free of her channel and licked through her slit, tasting her sweet orgasm.

Her trembling legs went limp over his shoulders, and she smoothed her palms over his head. "Oh my God. I think maybe—" She drew in a shaky breath. "Maybe you're going to be the death of me instead."

Shane rose between her thighs and nestled his length between the folds of her cunt. "Not if I have anything to say about it."

"Mmm." She smoothed her hands down to his chest. "Missed this, Shane."

"Can have this any time you want it, Cyn." He looked at her, and she licked her edible lips. Shane's dick twitched, and a tingle spread from the base of his spine to his balls. Her sweet lips were always his undoing. He spread her labia apart with his thumbs and watched as he slid his shaft back and forth over the mouth of her pussy and clit. "God Almighty, look at this. Need a picture of this, I think."

"Picture? Oh my God, *sooo* dirty." Cyn tugged at his shirt. "Need this off you. Need to feel your skin."

"You love it dirty." Shane inched back from her and removed his clothes.

"True story." Cyn sat up, and after tugging off her shirt and bra, she wrapped her arms around his neck and pulled him down to her mouth.

Shane cupped her face in his hands and kissed her slow and deep, taking the opportunity to slow things down a bit. He wanted to drown in everything that was his Cyn and for as long as he could.

She broke the kiss and moved her lips and tongue along his jaw to his neck, kissing and nipping the tender spot. Shane moaned and slid his hands to her full breasts, cradling them in his palms and stroking his thumbs over her peaked nipples.

Cyn whimpered and arched against him, then moved her

hand between them, gripped his cock and positioned him at her opening. "Fuck me, Shane. Pretty please?"

He tilted his head back and gazed into her eyes. "Love it when you ask nice and sweet like that."

Her lips arched in a devious smile, and Shane pressed forward, sliding the head inside her. Cyn's eyes widened. "Yes," she breathed. "Oh fuck, yes, baby."

Shane took her lips again and glided the rest of the way inside her. Her heat enveloped him as her cunt clenched around his shaft. Shane growled against her mouth, grabbed her ass, and pulled her flush against him. Cyn wrapped her legs around him, whimpering against his lips. With a tight grip on her ass, Shane shifted her up and down on his dick, and Cyn rocked her pelvis, grinding her clit against him.

He broke from her lips and pressed his forehead to hers. "Mine."

Cyn nodded, panting as her sweat-slicked breasts rubbed against his chest. Shane moved her faster, gritting his teeth as his balls tightened, his orgasm speeding closer each time her tight heat clenched around him. "Come for me, girl."

Cyn whipped her head back, rocking against him. "Oh God! *Shane! Ohgodohgodohhhgodddd!*"

"Fuck yeah. Gimme all that heat." Shane held her tight against him as his orgasm plowed through him, and her cunt spasmed around his shaft in rapid little bursts. His body seized as his cock jerked over and over, spurting his semen deep inside her channel, filling her.

Shane closed his eyes, completely overcome with her and not wanting the moment to end.

CHAPTER FORTY-ONE

SHANE LAY WITH HER CURLED AGAINST HIM. CYN HAD FALLEN asleep after they'd had sex, or rather after they'd had sex a second time. As was typical for them, after they finished ravaging each other's bodies, they were both equally worn out.

But Shane hadn't been able to fall asleep. Thoughts about their relationship—or lack of one—about where she might be as far as her emotional mess and how she'd wanted to be single for a year kept circling around his brain like a merry-go-round.

She'd come there wanting to talk, and Shane assumed the talking would involve a whole lot of "hey, I'm sorry, and I hope we can still be friends" kind of words. But she'd come to Texas…all the damn way to Texas, and it finally dawned on him that it might be possible she'd come to see if he wanted to try again. Old friends aside, women didn't fly three states away to let a guy down gently. They flew three states, or in some cases across the country or even the world, because they wanted to be with said guy.

He was afraid to even hope for it. Being with her was everything he wanted. But at the same time, he couldn't help but wonder if them being together was really the best thing for her. Cyn had wanted to be single for a reason. She'd been determined to figure out why she kept getting it wrong with all the guys she'd dated prior to him.

Even though Shane knew he wanted her—in fact, there wasn't a doubt in his mind—he needed to know she had no doubts either. As much as it sucked, Cyn needed to come to that same conclusion *after* she'd spent some time alone, and Shane was more than willing to give her the space necessary to get there.

Plus, he had no idea where she was at with her PTSD, either. She seemed to be okay, more like she'd been before the attack, but he couldn't be sure. From his perspective, two things were blocking them from being on the same page, and Shane decided, right then and there, he was going to step aside so she could heal and deal.

His last thought before he finally fell asleep was that he'd wait for her—till the end of time if that's what it took.

———

WITH HER EYES STILL CLOSED, Cyn reached across Shane's king-sized bed, seeking him. Her hand skated across the cool sheets, and she opened her eyes to find him…not there.

Grabbing for his pillow, she pressed it to her face and breathed deep, taking the familiar scent of him into her lungs. Cyn smiled and sat up, glancing around the room. So, this was Shane Conlon's bedroom. A giggle bubbled up and out of her, and she cupped her hands over her mouth as she took in the rustic furnishings in the space.

There was a large dresser across from the bed, with an equally large flat-screen television mounted to the wall above it. Men and their TVs…she swore they'd all have one in every room, and Shane was no different. To the left of the dresser was a wall closet. To the right, and near the door, was a tall chest of drawers. A few pictures sat atop it, along with a couple of books, a few scattered pieces of paper, and what appeared to be a square wooden box. Just past the dresser was a door she assumed led to a bathroom.

Speaking of…Cyn got up and headed for the door. She opened it, and yes, it was the bathroom, thank God, because holy hell, she needed to pee. After taking care of business, she washed her hands and, unable to resist, peeked in his medicine cabinet.

Shaving cream, razor, cologne— *Ooh!* She grabbed the bottle, popped the cap off and inhaled the scent. *Mmm.* God in heaven, she craved his scent. Careful to place the cologne back where she found it, she glanced at the other items. Everything was so organized. She loved that about him. When he'd been with her at her house, he was the same way. Always keeping his things in order. Likely a behavior long conditioned in him, thanks to the Marine Corps.

She peeked in one of the vanity drawers, too, where she found little trays to organize his toothbrush, toothpaste and floss, as well as a few other items. Her exploration continued below to the vanity cabinet, and, bingo, Cyn found the mouthwash. Her suitcase, with her toothbrush, was still out by the front door. Recognizing opportunity when it knocked, she grabbed the bottle and did a quick rinse.

Cyn wiped her face and sighed. Yeah, no matter how his overly organized trait came to be in him, she was grateful for it. It was a thing she found beyond endearing in him.

She thought back to her conversation with Maiya regarding Ryan and his tidy little habits. And how it actually turned Maiya on. Cyn rolled her eyes because, at the time, she couldn't fathom being aroused by someone's obsession with organization or tidiness, but now, she understood it and was ready to seek him out just to get his dick in her mouth…immediately.

With that thought, Cyn exited his bathroom and went in search of Shane. As soon as she left his bedroom, the delicious scent of something cooking hit her nose, and her stomach growled. Shane was cooking. Okay, maybe food first, then a blowjob because, for fuck's sake, he was tidy and domesticated. And so freaking alpha male, it made her head spin.

She wandered down the hallway, thinking about the first night they'd had sex and how she thought she'd hit the jackpot. Truly, at the time, she'd had no idea how big the prize was. Cyn had hit the Publishers Clearing House jackpot. Plus, the Powerball, all in one.

With a little hitch in her step, Cyn made her way through the living room to the kitchen. Shane stood at the stove, no shirt on and a pair of gray sweats slung low on his hips.

Good grief, his bare back was beyond sexy. Broad shoulders, thick lat muscles that stretched down his sides, arrowing into a narrow waistline. The Semper Fidelis tattoo on his upper back a dark contrast to his golden tanned skin.

As if drawn to him like a magnet, Cyn stepped behind him, wrapped her arms around Shane's waist and pressed a kiss to his spine. He jumped, but only slightly, before glancing over his shoulder at her. "Hey there."

Oops. Cyn moved to his side and leaned against the counter. "Sorry, honey. I didn't mean to startle you."

"All good." He bent to her, a sweet smile arching his lips, and pressed a kiss to her forehead. "Hope you're hungry."

"Starving, actually." Cyn rubbed her belly. "I had every intention of sucking your dick once I found you, but then I smelled the food cooking and…yeah, sorry, but you'll have to wait till I've been fed." She quirked a brow and smirked.

He chuckled and gave her a wink. "Roger that. Let's get you fed so we can get to that blowjob."

Lust zipped through her, making her tummy light up with tingles. "Yes, sir!" Cyn couldn't stop the smile that formed on her lips if she tried. "So, whatcha making?"

"Just a little chicken and rice risotto."

"Mmm. It smells delicious. Can I help?"

"Nope." He stirred the contents of the pot. "It'll be ready in about ten minutes. You want water or wine?"

Cyn raised both brows. "You cook, and *now* you're the second coming? Gotta say, Sarg. I'm impressed."

Shane threw his head back as a harsh laugh erupted out of him. Cyn crossed her arms and witnessed the most beautiful thing on the planet: Mouth wide open and clutching his stomach, Shane Conlon laughing harder than she'd ever seen him laugh.

Cyn was in absolute awe…of every single part of this man and all that he was.

And as her mind filled with admiration and respect, her heart filled with love. So much love she thought it might burst. Cyn was undeniably, uncontrollably, and justifiably one hundred percent head over heels *in love* with Shane Conlon.

She smiled, laughing with him, and rubbed her chest as fear settled thick in her throat. If he ended things between them, she wasn't sure she could survive it.

"Gonna be the death of me." Shane hooked her around the waist, pulled her to his chest and kissed the tip of her nose. "The shit you say. Jesus, Cynthia. Too damn funny."

Cyn stared up into his bright blue eyes and then let her gaze roam over his chiseled features. The dimple in his chin called to her as it always did, and she rose up and placed her lips against it. Shane cupped the back of her head before threading his fingers through the short locks. *Say it…just tell him.* "Shane, we need to talk."

He pressed his lips to the top of her head and let out a sigh. "I know."

SHANE STOOD STILL with her held tight against his chest. She was right. They needed to talk. He'd just hoped to have this one last night with her and then deal with the situation tomorrow or the next day. Maybe even the day after that.

He sighed again before pulling away to see her face. "How 'bout we eat, and then we talk? Conversations go easier on a full stomach." She smiled, and he couldn't help but smile back. Shane shrugged. "At least that's what my dad always used to say."

"Sounds like a good way of going about things." Cyn pressed her lips to his neck. "I'll grab the wine. You get the glasses."

"On it." Shane pulled two glasses from the cupboard as she grabbed the bottle of Sauvignon Blanc from the fridge.

She set the wine on the counter. "Bottle opener?"

"Here." He handed her the glasses and then retrieved the corkscrew from the drawer. After drawing out the cork, he poured them each half a glass. "To a successful journey." Shane forced a smile and tapped the edge of his glass to hers.

"Sounds nice." Cyn raised the glass to her mouth, and Shane couldn't peel his eyes away from her lips as they closed over the edge, and she swallowed a small sip.

Desire sped through his veins like a wildfire, and every inch of his skin tingled in awareness of her. Jesus, he didn't think he'd ever not want her.

She smiled as she lowered the glass. "Mmm. This is my favorite kind of white. Aren't you going to have some?"

Shane cleared his throat. "Of course. I just…"

"You just what?" Cyn tilted her head to the side, her soft brown eyes fixed on him.

With the barest shake of his head, Shane sipped the wine. He just wanted to watch her, wanted to brand every detail of this moment and how she looked in his memory—although he knew forgetting any part of her simply wasn't possible. Hell, even the tiniest of features, like the faded freckles on the bridge of her nose and cheeks, were imprinted in his mind. Yet still, considering the decision he'd made earlier—

"Looks like it's about ready." She peered into the pot.

Yanked from his thoughts, Shane forced a smile and shut off the burner. "Looks that way."

Shane pushed his plate aside and swallowed the last of his wine. Setting his glass down, he reached for the bottle. "You have your fill yet?"

Cyn rolled her eyes—her mouth full of the meal he'd cooked for her—and swallowed. "You think? I mean, I had two servings. But it's just so yummy I'm contemplating a third…although my ass is currently winning the argument with my taste buds."

Shane chuckled and filled his glass. "What argument is that?"

"You know, the one where my ass says, 'Hello, mouth? I'm big enough, don't need to be any bigger. Drop the fork, now. Step away from the plate.' And my mouth says, '*Noooooo! Feeeeed meeee mooore!*'" She grinned and sipped her wine.

Shane blurted a laugh and was more than grateful he hadn't been taking a drink because he'd have sprayed it across the table. She'd made him laugh so many times that night he'd lost count. It felt so good to laugh with her again—felt good to just be with her, too. *Damn!* With his heart aching and his laughter under control, he swallowed a gulp of wine, forcing the lump that'd risen back down his throat.

She shoved the plate away. "Okay, yeah. Take this away from me before I eat more."

"Guessing your ass won?"

"Damn right."

"You know, I happen to love your ass, so if it gets bigger, I'm all for that."

"Shane Conlon, I'm quite familiar with how fond of my ass you are. But it's good to know that if it should grow to mammoth proportions, you're all on board with the *bootay*."

"Mmm. Now, all I want to do is make you eat more."

Cyn shook her head and giggled. "You're crazy." She sipped her wine. "God, I love this wine."

"Glad you love it. Glad you loved dinner too." Shane stood and took their plates to the sink. "How about you wander out to my living room and I'll meet you there in a minute or two."

"You're not going to let me help with the dishes, are you?"

He winked. "Nope."

Cyn stood. "Okay, fine, but I'm taking the bottle of wine with me." She stuck her tongue out and disappeared around the corner, her giggle trailing behind her.

After Shane finished in the kitchen, he went to join her. Rounding the corner, he stopped the moment his eyes found her. Cyn had her legs curled beneath her on the couch with the lights off. The blue glow of the television highlighted her profile and made Shane's breath catch in his throat. To him, she was more than beautiful.

She glanced up at him as he approached her, grabbed the remote and muted the sound. "I'm guessing you're ready to have that talk now?"

Shane took a seat on the other end of the sofa. "S'pose so."

"Which one of us gets to go first?" She turned and faced him, raising her knees in front of her and pulling them to her chest.

"Ladies first, always." The urge to touch her, pull her close, rode him like a diesel truck late for a delivery. Instead, he shoved the desire as far away as he could and smoothed his palm over his head.

She blew out a breath. "Well, I've been seeing a counselor. A lot. Twice a week, actually, for the last month."

"That's awesome, Cyn. God, I'm just so damn relieved to hear that." Unable to hold himself back, he ran his hand over her knee.

"I'm sorry it took me so long to do it. I should've listened to you from the beginning. I guess I just thought…" She glanced away.

"Thought you could just deal with it, right? That eventually it'd go away." He gave her knee a squeeze. "Hey, look at me." When she did, he continued. "It's okay. I get it. I went through the same thing myself when I got back to the States."

"Yeah, I guess you probably did." She smiled. "But you're all good now."

"For the most part, yeah." Shane pulled his hand away. "I don't know if it ever goes away completely, you know? But it just…becomes less, I guess."

"Yeah." Cyn scooted closer, crossed her legs between them and rested her elbows on her knees. "I owe you a huge amends, Shane."

Shane had to look away. She was so close, close enough to kiss, and if he gave in to the need pulsing in his veins, they'd end up in bed again. He *had* to be strong and do the right thing. It was for the best that Shane let her have the time she needed, as she'd planned before he rolled into town. Then again, Cyn could tell him she didn't want to be with him. If that were the case, giving her space wouldn't be necessary. She'd have all the space she needed. Shane frowned and looked back at her. "Not necessary, Cyn. You have nothing to apologize for."

"Like hell, I don't. I treated you like absolute shit. I yelled at you, like, all the time. I was a bitch practically twenty-four-seven unless we were naked, of course. Though, I might've been a bitch a few times then too." She frowned.

"Cyn—"

"It's my turn, right?"

"Technically, yeah, but—"

"Then shut it." Her lips pulled into a slow grin.

He let out a groan. "Girl…" Once again, Shane had to

resist the urge to kiss her. Damn her for tugging on a memory, a particularly erotic one, from when they'd first been together.

"It'll be your turn soon enough." She leaned forward and kissed his cheek. "Promise."

Shane cleared his throat as his heart raced, pounding in his ears from her brief contact. "All right. I'm shuttin' it. Continue."

"Thank you." She smiled and ran her fingers through her hair. "I treated you so poorly, and you were beyond patient and kind and…a fucking saint. You were a goddamn saint, Shane. And I want you to know that even though I didn't show it at the time, I appreciated—appreciate it. I haven't stopped appreciating it.

"I haven't stopped thinking about you either. It's also why I'm here. I miss you, and I want you in my life. And I don't know how that'll work, considering we live in different places, but I don't care. I love you and I don't want to be apart from you." She twisted her hands in front of her and blew out a breath. "Okay, I think if you don't say something now, I might cry."

Shane couldn't look away from her as she said all the things she needed to say. In the space of a nanosecond, his heart swelled and then broke into a million pieces. Every single dream he'd had regarding Cyn and having a life with her had just been fulfilled, and none of it mattered because he had to let her go.

Shane rubbed the back of his neck and tried to calm down. *Nothing like breaking my own heart.* Nothing like depriving himself of happiness, too. But this wasn't about him. It was about Cyn and what was best for her, and Shane had every intention of doing right by her. "I miss you, too, Cyn. Thank you for your apology, but it wasn't necessary. I knew what you were going through and why. You don't have to be sorry for that."

She clasped his hand, and he let her. Then she intertwined

her fingers with his, and he let her do that, too. He glanced at her face. Her eyes were wide, and a small smile graced her pretty lips.

"As far as being in each other's lives...I'm not sure that's a good...I just...I don't—" *Fuuuuckkk!* The smile that'd curved her lips fell, and she furrowed her brow and glanced away from him. *Goddammit.* Sometimes doing the right thing sucked —sucked really goddamn hard.

CHAPTER FORTY-TWO

Cyn couldn't look at him. Jesus fucking Christ...he
wasn't in love with her. *Oh my God, he doesn't—* The realization
stung, a hard slap right in the face. Shane missed her, yeah,
and maybe he loved fucking her, but he didn't love *love* her.
Not in the way she loved him.

Cyn jerked her hand away and stood. "Holy shit. I'm so
sorry." She glanced around. "I need to go."

"Cyn, wait. Let me finish."

"No, please don't." With heat rising in her face, she
headed for the bedroom. She needed to gather her things and
get the hell out of there. Christ, she was mortified. That was
the second time Cyn had told him she loved him, except the
first time didn't count. She hadn't really meant it. Saying "I
love you" when someone's giving a person six freaking
orgasms shouldn't count.

This time, she'd meant it. This time, it sure as hell counted
—a whole fuck of a lot. And now, sadly, just like the first time,
she wished she hadn't said it.

By the time she entered the bedroom, steadily blinking
back tears, she stopped in her tracks, realizing her suitcase was

still by the front door. *Damn. Shit. Fuck.* Cyn turned and ran smack into Shane's broad chest.

She let out a startled squeak, and Shane gripped her arms. "Will you stop and listen for a minute? You didn't let me finish."

Cyn tried to step away, but he wouldn't let go. *Great.* Determined to avoid any further embarrassment, she refused to meet his gaze, instead kept her eyes down. "I don't think there's any reason to finish. You said enough that I get the gist of it."

"No. You did not get the gist of it." He edged her backward until she felt the mattress at the back of her legs. "Sit."

Cyn sat and then licked her lips. Frustration pulsed through her, riding on the massive wave of heartache swamping her system. She might have no choice but to listen, but there was no way in hell she was going to look at him while he explained—*in full detail*—why he didn't want to be with her.

"Come on now. Look at me, would you?"

Keeping her eyes trained on the rug, Cyn rubbed the space between her brows. "Say what you need to say, Shane. Then let me go, please."

Shane let out a growl. "I swear to God, you're gonna be the damn death of me. You are so freaking stubborn some-times—" she watched his legs as he paced in front of her, "—I don't even know what to do with you."

"You could just let me leave, and then you won't have to deal with my stubbornness."

"Yeah, that's not happening."

"Fine." She crossed her arms.

"Fine." He stopped pacing and stood in front of her. "You win this round."

Cyn let her gaze travel up his body, but only far enough to see he had his hands propped on his lean hips. In spite of the fact that she was drowning beneath waves of heartbreak, embarrassment, and now frustration, her stomach tightened at the sight of his pelvis. She knew exactly how powerful and gorgeous his body was and how perfectly he fit between her legs. *Fuck me, really?* It truly didn't matter if she was pissed at him or her feelings were hurt.

Cyn still wanted him. The sex was just that good.

Before him, no sex had ever been *that* good, so good that her body craved it even if she was upset with the guy. Yet here it was…that goddamn craving. Cyn licked her lips, and Shane let out another growl. *Dammit.* She'd forgotten how affected he was by her lip-licks, and if she didn't curtail her hydrating activities, they'd end up naked again, and the situation didn't need any more complication. Neither did her heart.

He let out a sigh and resumed his pacing. "Cynthia, what I was trying to say to you is that I think you need to finish your journey."

Her head snapped up. "What journey?"

Shane stopped and pinned her with a hard stare. "You gonna let me get this out?"

Shifting her gaze from his, Cyn swallowed past the lump in her throat and nodded. Jesus, he looked good when he got all stern with her. *Focus!*

"Thank you." He started the pacing again. "As I was saying, your journey. I'm well aware that you'd planned to take a year off from dating." She opened her mouth, ready to question what he was saying… "Girl, so help me, you don't let me get this out, I will flip you over and tan that fine ass of yours."

Cyn clamped her mouth closed and sat on her hands. The last time he'd threatened that, he'd followed through and then some. She crossed her legs and squeezed her thighs together at the memory of the sex they'd had that night. Shane meant his threats, his promises and his declaration. *Fucking hell, focus!*

"Look, here's the thing." He knelt down in front of her, and the softness of his tone hit Cyn right in the feels so hard, she couldn't help but meet his gaze. "I want a life with you. I want it so bad, it's all I can think about. But I think—no, I know, that for now, you need to do what you'd set out to before I came to L.A. I got in the way of your plans; now I need to get out of the way and let my girl work through her stuff. When you're done, we'll figure out how we have a life together."

"How did you—" Cyn frowned. Angie must've told him about the moratorium. Dammit. And now he thought... "Wait, are you telling me that you want me to take the year and that you'll wait for me to do that?"

"I want what's best for you." He cupped her cheek in his palm. "That's what's best for you, Cyn."

Was he fucking crazy? The expression in his eyes was filled with nothing but genuine sentiment. He meant what he was saying to her, that was clear, but... Yeah, this man was beyond sweet and profoundly honorable, but possibly out of his freaking mind too. "And you'll wait for me."

He placed both hands on her legs. "Absolutely."

"And you think this is what's best for me?"

"I know it is."

Yep, it was time to school him. Cyn tilted her head to the side. "Wow. So, has it occurred to you that maybe *I* know what's best for me?"

In an instant, the expression on his face changed from soft and sweet to confusion, and he cocked his head back. "Well, I..."

Cyn stood and stepped around him. "Right, you didn't. What the hell is this, Shane? You just think you're going to make this decision for us and not even give me a say in it?"

"No. I just—"

She faced him as he was getting to his feet. Jesus, he looked good, his face all serious, but she did her best to ignore it. "You just what, exactly? Please, tell me because, frankly, I'm a tad confused."

Shane met her gaze, a steadfast expression in his eyes. "Look, this is important to me. It's important for us. You need to be sure, Cyn."

"I *am* sure, Shane!"

"First off, lower your voice. Second, I know you think you're sure, but has it occurred to you that maybe *I* need to be sure?" He took a step closer.

She raised her hand and pressed it to his chest in an effort to hold him back. If he got any closer, the pheromones he was throwing off were going to knock her to her knees. Literally, fighting with him always served as a spark to ignite their flames, and true to form, their argument was abiding by the rule. "Sure of what?"

Shane glanced down at her hand. "Sure that you really want me. Sure that you're not going to push me away again."

"Jesus Christ!" Cyn took a few steps back. Space was necessary if they were going to solve this with their clothes on. "Did you not hear what I said in the living room? I told you I love you. Do you not get that that means I'm sure?"

Shane blew out a breath and then sat on the bed. "Yeah, Cyn. I heard you. And yeah, that's what it should mean, except with everything that happened with Carlos and you just now getting into therapy, I think giving things some time, giving yourself the time you need, is priority."

"I can't believe you're doing this. Fucking hell, Shane. If you don't love me, then just say that. There's no need to string me along—"

He stood in a rush and was in front of her before she'd even blinked. Jesus, he was fast. "Make no mistake, Cynthia Donnelly. I am *not* stringing you along, and I do love you. Very much. So much I ache for you. *Daily!*" The last was said through gritted teeth.

Cyn's nerve endings popped and tingled along every inch

of her skin. *Ignore it!* "Then why the fuck are you doing this? If you love me, why would you send me away?" She shook her head and raised her arms out from her sides. "You know what? Forget it. I don't want to know."

"I'm not sending you away. Can't you listen? For fuck's sake, you never listen!"

"Now, who's yelling? Like I said, forget it. And PS, I don't need to listen because we're done with this conversation." Cyn spun on her heel and headed for the front door. She was getting the hell out of there. There was nothing she could say to change Shane's mind. He'd dug his heels in, and so had she. Point for point. Tit for tat…and who got the last word was always the question of the day.

Yeah, Cyn might be stubborn, but no more than he was. And this time, she was even willing to let him have the last word if that's what it took to get her ass out the door.

SHANE RACED after Cyn as she headed for his front door. Jesus, she moved quickly when she was pissed. He caught her arm just as she rounded the corner from the hallway. "Slow your ass down."

She jerked her arm from his grasp. "Don't you *eeeeven* try and tell me what to do. I'm so out of here, Shane Conlon!"

"Dammit, Cyn. It's late. Where the hell you gonna go?"

She bent and yanked up the suitcase handle. "None of your business."

He stepped around her and stood in front of the door. "Like hell, it's not my business. Everything you do is my goddamn business."

Cyn fumbled with her purse. "Move, Shane. I'm leaving."

"I'm telling you, girl, you are so gonna be the fucking death of me." He propped his hands on his hips. "You want to go so bad, you can go in the morning. I'll even drive you to the airport. But you are *not* going anywhere tonight!"

With a stone-hard glare, she stepped to him. "Well, I'm not staying here."

Heat spread over every inch of Shane's skin at the sight of her all fired up and in his face. He raised his hand, ready to dive his fingers into the back of her hair, yank her head farther back and kiss her into submission—

Cyn jerked back from him. "Don't you dare! Shane Conlon, don't you fucking dare touch me!"

Shane cocked his head to the side and ran his palm over his jaw. Never had she jerked away from his touch, not in a way that made him believe she actually didn't want him to touch her. "Look, I get that you're pissed at me. I don't like it, but I'll deal with it. But I can't let you leave tonight. Stay in the guest room if you feel more comfortable, but you're not going anywhere until morning."

She glanced away from him and blew out a breath. "Please, just let me go."

"Can't do that." Shane crossed his arms. Still refusing to meet his gaze, Cyn let go of her suitcase, raised her hand and wiped under one eye. Fuck, she was crying. He took a step toward her. "Cyn?"

She raised her hand, warding him off. "Don't."

Shane's heart twisted, and his gut flipped over. This had not gone the way he'd expected. Definitely not the way he'd practiced in his mind all evening. She really believed he didn't love her, which was crazy. Cyn was his everything. "Come on, now. Don't do this."

"I'm not the one who's doing it. You are." She turned away and headed back down the hall, pulling her suitcase behind her.

Shane's head fell forward, and he blew out a breath but flinched when he heard what he assumed was the guestroom door close with a slam. He walked down the hall and stopped in front of the door. Pausing a moment to listen, he heard nothing, then raised his hand to knock but thought better of it and stopped. She wouldn't speak to him the rest of the night. He was sure of it.

Shane rubbed his sternum. His heart felt like a lead weight in his chest, and a dull throb had taken up residence behind his eyes. He hated fighting with her, and he hated how she talked to him when she was pissed. The woman knew how to throw a verbal punch for sure.

Letting out a harsh breath, Shane made his way to his own bedroom and to his shower. He'd give her space tonight, and in the morning, they'd discuss it. After shedding his clothes, Shane stepped under the hot spray. He'd make her see that this was for the best. But that it was only temporary. In a year, they'd be together. Cyn had to see it his way. There was no reason not to.

Once Shane was done in the bathroom, he wandered to the living room and planted his ass on the sofa. With the lights off, he scrolled mindlessly through channels until he found something remotely interesting in hopes it might be enough to distract him from the fact that his girl was likely curled up in the guest bed, probably hating his guts.

The knowledge that Cyn was under his roof and *not* in his bed and arms was not welcome and fueled the bitter taste in his mouth. Every primal male instinct he had was screaming at him to go scoop her up and put her where she belonged, yet his brain was working on overdrive to remind him of his decision.

Shane jerked awake when the sound of a door closing echoed through his mind. He sat up and glanced at the clock. It was just after midnight. At some point, he'd nodded off. Getting to his feet, Shane walked down the hall to the guest room. The door was open, but the light was off. "Cyn?"

He flipped on the light switch and found…a very empty room.

Fuuuuckkk! Wheeling around, Shane headed for the front door. He threw it open just in time to see a taxi pulling away from his house. He ran out to the front yard and into the street. "Cyn!"

Shane watched the taillights as they got smaller and then ran back into the house in search of his phone. Pulling Cyn up in his contacts, he hit the Call button and put the device to his ear. It rang twice before she sent him to voicemail. *Great.* "Cyn, don't do this. Come on back, please? We need to talk it through." Shane disconnected and tossed the cell on the counter.

She was so goddamn stubborn. Blowing out a frustrated breath, he ran his hand over his head. Stubborn *and* insisting he was wrong. Shane's gaze wandered over the countertop until it settled on the paperwork for his parents' house. He gathered the now dry but wrinkled papers and stared down at them.

Was he wrong?

Shane flipped on the light in the kitchen and took a seat at the table. All he wanted was for Cyn to be happy. He turned through the pages. There was no doubt he could make her happy, and even though she'd said she was ready, Shane just needed her to be sure. He leaned back in his chair. She'd come to him, shown up at his door totally unexpected. She'd said she loved him and wanted a life with him…even with the issue of them living in different states.

Shane stared down at the paperwork. The house…his house. What if… *Shit!*

Fucking hell, he *was* wrong. He was so damn wrong it wasn't even funny. Shane's heart might've been in the right place, but he'd been too busy trying to do the right thing by her, he'd missed the obvious.

In less than twenty-four hours since arriving on his

doorstep, Cyn had been the woman he discovered in L.A. *before* everything went haywire due to the attack. Cyn was fully present and ready, *and* she was sure. Shane was just being too pigheaded to listen. Really listen.

Jesus Christ, he needed to fix it, and he needed to fix it now.

CHAPTER FORTY-THREE

Cyn had gotten home the day before and pretty much shut herself up in her home with far more ice cream than any human should be allowed to consume. Having spent the prior day and then all night crying her eyes out, she was beyond exhausted.

After finally migrating to her bed from the couch, she hadn't closed her eyes for more than five minutes, or maybe it was a couple of hours, when she heard a banging at her front door. It was probably Angie. Rolling out of bed, Cyn made her way to her door, peered through the peephole and froze.

"Cyn?" More banging. "Come on. Let me in." Then her cell started ringing. "I know you're in there. I can hear your phone ringing from out here." More banging and then the doorbell. "Cynthia!"

Jesus Christ and all the Disciples, plus the prostitutes! Cyn pressed her forehead against the hard wood and squeezed her eyes closed. Why was he doing this? What the hell did he want? Why couldn't he just leave her alone?

More banging, and then her cell ringing again. "Cynthia Donnelly, you need to open this door rig—"

Cyn jerked the door open. And there he was, fist mid-bang

—looking all scruffy because he hadn't shaved—and fine as hell. *Dammit!* "I'm not doing this with you."

"Doing what?" He grinned and barreled past her, somehow managing to plant a kiss on her cheek as he blew by. "C'mere. Need to show you something."

Cyn let out a resigned sigh and closed the front door. He'd gone into the kitchen, and instead of following him, she took a seat on the couch, pulled the throw blanket that'd been her companion for the last twenty-four hours from the edge, and wrapped it around herself.

Barely a minute passed, and he poked his head around the corner from the kitchen. "Cyn— Oh hey. You're in the living room?"

"Yes, Shane. I'm in my living room." She pulled the blanket tighter and stared down at the edges of it. "Look, I'm really tired, and honestly? I don't have the energy to fight with you, so please, just say what you need to say and then go."

"You have no idea how happy it makes me to see you in the living room. Damn, babe, that's just—"

The endearments were killing her. The pride lacing his words was killing her, too. And only made her love him more. Shane knew what a big deal it was that she was in the living room. The fact that he was praising her for it stung, making her already hurting heart ache more. "Shane, please."

He sat beside her. "Please, what?"

With her eyes focused on her lap, a tear rolled down her cheek, and she swiped it away. She couldn't look at him. Her insides felt like they were on her outsides again, all raw and vulnerable. She hated being this vulnerable. Hated the fact that despite all her efforts and willingness, things hadn't worked out between them. Her picker might be broken, but it wasn't broken when it came to picking Shane. He was a good man. Through and through.

He just didn't want her the way she wanted him. A person

couldn't make themselves feel what they didn't feel. It sucked, but it was just the way it was. "Just…please."

She heard a rustling sound, and then Shane placed a short stack of papers in her lap. "Take a look at these, please?"

Cyn glanced at him before looking back to the paperwork. She picked up the wrinkled pile. "What are they?"

"Just…read them."

"Okay, fine." Blowing out a breath, Cyn wiped the tears from her cheeks and focused on the documents. There were plenty of legal terms among the words, but certain statements like "*Quit Claim Deed*" and "*Monetary settlement*" jumped right off the pages at her. "She isn't even—" Cyn read on. "How can she just do this? Please tell me you're not going to—" Cyn flipped to the last pages and blew out a relieved breath. "You haven't signed them. Thank God. Wait. You're not considering doing this, are you?"

"Figuring that depends on you."

"How so?" She straightened the paperwork and handed it back to him. Shane gave her a small smile, melting her heart straight down to her toes, and of course, Cyn had to stop herself from leaning forward and first touching her lips to that freaking dimple of his, then kissing his sweet mouth.

Shane tucked a piece of her hair behind her ear. "On if you'd consider making it a home again. With me."

Cyn frowned. Had he just said what she thought he did? No, she must've heard him wrong. There was no way Shane Conlon was asking her to make a life with him. No way he'd changed his mind…not after. She shook her head. "I'm sorry, what?"

"You heard me, Cyn." He stood but then knelt down in front of her and took one of her hands in his.

"Shane. What the fuck are you doing? Get up." Cyn's vision blurred, and her cheeks got wet as tears ran in a steady stream from her eyes.

Was he insane…*Oh God! Oh my God!* Shane produced a

small black velvet box from the pocket of his cargo pants, and Cyn's eyes went wide. Wider than she knew they already were. "Shane, oh my God, what are you doing?" Tears still streaming, she raised both hands and covered her mouth.

Shane cracked open the box. "I was wrong yesterday. I should've listened to you, and I didn't. For that, I am so sorry. I love you, Cyn. I want to spend my life with you, and I do not want to waste another second." He removed the ring and took her left hand in his.

"*Shane!*" She let out another sob before swiping at her cheeks.

"Cynthia Rose Donnelly, will you be my wife? Will you make a home, and God willing, a family with me in my father's house?" He held the platinum band with what looked to be a—*holy shit*—multiple-carat princess-cut solitaire at the tip of her ring finger.

"Holy crap, that's gorgeous! Are you crazy?"

Shane shook his head. "Not at all." He smiled. "I promise to love you till the day I die, Cyn, if you'll have me."

How the hell was this happening? She couldn't even process it. Just two nights ago, he'd told her to go off and live her life…be single, and now he was on his knee with a ring— an unbelievably gorgeous ring—proposing marriage? Cyn jumped up and about knocked him over, getting to her feet. "How did you go from sending me away to this? When the hell did you get that ring?" She pushed her hair away from her face and paced. "Please tell me what changed?"

Shane got to his feet, ring still held between his fingertips, and sat on the couch. "Gonna be the death of me, girl. Telling ya." He let out an exasperated sigh and smoothed his free hand over his short hair. "First off, I did not send you away. You snuck out like a thief in the night. Second, I realized after you skipped town that I was wrong."

Cyn stopped short. "Seriously?" She crossed her arms but

then flung them out to her sides. "Can you get any more perfect? I mean, really!" She paced again.

"Wait, what does that mean?"

"It means you cook, you clean. You're endearingly tidy. You smell good all the *goddamn* time. Even when you've been working and should smell like male funk…no, not you. You smell like a bed of fucking roses." Cyn clenched her fists, well aware she was wearing a path in the rug. "Not to mention the sex…but I gotta mention the sex. Fucking hell, it's out of this world. I'm convinced I'm ruined forever. No one will ever live up to you, Shane. Bank on that." She shook her head and ran her fingers through her hair as an all too familiar wave of lust rolled through her, as it always did when she thought about the sex she'd had with him. "And now you show up here and tell me you were wrong?" She stopped and glared at him. "Men don't admit they're wrong, Shane. Trust me on this, I grew up with too many of them. But not you, *noooo*. You're all perfect and right, even when you're wrong. I can't even—and then!" Cyn pointed at him. "Christ Almighty, then with that perfect ring, you get on one knee. I don't even know what to do with you."

"How about you be my wife?" He held the ring up.

Heat raced through Cyn's body, and she dropped her hand as those six little words he just spoke sewed her heart right back together. She swallowed and then licked her lips. He was serious. Totally fucking serious. Cyn blinked. This was happening. "When the hell did you get that thing?"

Shane stood and moved in front of her. "Yesterday. Sincere ask. Yes or no, Cynthia."

His voice was low; the gravelly tone vibrated over her skin and arrowed right between her legs. She gazed up at him. "You're sure?"

"One hundred percent." He took her left hand in his again and paused, ring hovering above her finger.

Cyn glanced down at it and then back to his eyes. *Yes!* On

a complete overload of the feels, Cyn couldn't speak, but Shane could read her mind, right? *Yeah, right. Freak.* Giving herself a mental slapping, she rose up and pressed her lips to his. Shane gripped her hand as he delved his tongue into her mouth and slid the ring on her finger.

She felt the cool of the metal on her skin and was amazed it fit so perfectly. But then again, it was Shane. Of course, it fit. He'd probably measured her finger while she was asleep weeks ago... She pulled from his lips and glanced at her finger. "Good, because I'm sure too."

"Is that a yes?"

"Bet your sweet ass it is." She smiled, gazing at him, and pressed her lips to his again.

Shane wrapped his arms around her waist and raised her off the floor. God help her, this man...she'd never get enough of him. After what felt like forever, but never long enough, Shane broke the kiss and set her down on her feet. He cupped her cheeks in his big hands, and his gaze wandered over her face. And Cyn felt every moment of it as a physical touch. She also saw the love in his eyes—saw it as clear as the moon shone on a cloudless night.

"Told you it wouldn't be enough."

Cyn frowned. "What wouldn't be enough?"

"One kiss. The night all of this started." A smirk arched his lips.

Cyn barked a laugh. "This is the one time I'll let an 'I told you so' slide. Go for it, gloat all you want, Sergeant."

"You are *sooo* gonna be the death of me." He smiled and traced her lips with the edge of his thumb. "But I love you, so you go right ahead."

"I love you, too." Cyn's heart melted in her chest, and her pulse kicked up about a thousand notches.

Shane Conlon: Her grade- and high-school crush. Her unattainable dream. He was everything and then some. And he wanted her for always and forever. Guess he showed that picker of hers who was boss. As she gazed up at him and drowned in his endless eyes, Cyn knew she wanted Shane forever and always, too, and it was likely she'd never stopped wanting him.

Maybe she was just finding her way to him the whole time. All those bad choices had been because Shane would be coming for her, and as corny as it sounded, sometimes a girl had to kiss a few frogs to find her dream come true.

Yeah, Shane Conlon was her dream come true. Shane was her everything.

And he always would be.

ABOUT THE AUTHOR

Dorothy F. Shaw lives in Arizona, where the weather is hot, and the sunsets are always beautiful. She's a self-proclaimed sex scene snob and is proud of it. When she's not writing, she's thinking about writing.

With her ever-open heart, bright red hair, and many colorful tattoos, she truly lives and loves in Technicolor!

Get in bed (and read) with your favorite redhead!

Newsletter sign-up: Yes, please!
Join *Dorothy's Ruby Readers* on FB:
http://bit.ly/DFSRubyReaders
www.dorothyfshaw.com
DorothyFShaw@Gmail.com

facebook.com/AuthorDorothyFShaw

instagram.com/authordorothyfshaw

bsky.app/profile/dorothyfshaw.bsky.social

tiktok.com/@authordorothyfshaw

threads.net/@authordorothyfshaw

goodreads.com/dorothyfshaw

amazon.com/stores/author/B00DPRI5HK

bookbub.com/profile/dorothy-f-shaw

ALSO BY DOROTHY F. SHAW

Head to my site to find all links to my available backlist:

www.DorothyFShaw.com

Next in the Donnellys series:
Jaded Heart

The Donnellys Book 4
© 2022 Dorothy F. Shaw

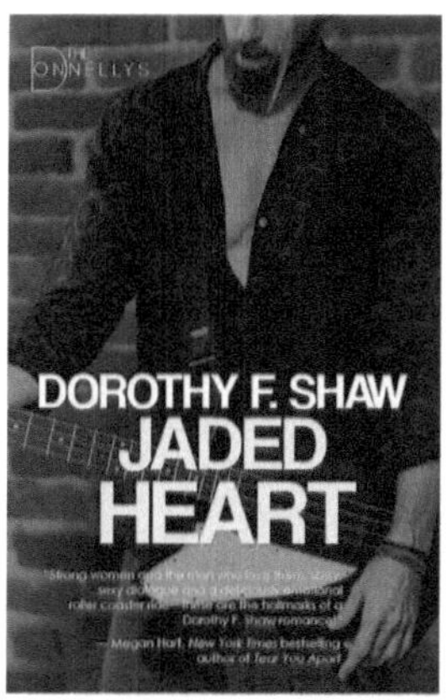

Even jaded hearts can be tempted into trying again.

When Angela Donnelly heads to Arizona for a family event, she meets older and hotter-than-hell, Garrett James.

Garrett runs a small concert venue on the outskirts of Phoenix…and that's about as close as he wants to come to the music biz. His hey-day in the late 90s, playing bass and singing with his band, Copper Seven, is long gone. Far from the lime-light and willingly single, the only woman Garrett wants or needs in his life is his daughter.

That is until he meets the way too young for him, Angie. Long dark hair and long legs have always been his downfall and Garrett can't keep his eyes, or his hands off of her.

Angie might be young, but she's no fool. She knows a good thing when she's found one—Garrett is a once-in-a-lifetime good thing for her.

But Garrett can't seem to convince Angie that he's not her once-in-a-lifetime anything. As far as he's concerned, he's absolutely the wrong man for her with nothing to offer someone as promising as Angie.

Angie recognizes that Garrett has his heart fully guarded. But when he gives her everything she wants, except his heart, she knows this will be the fight of her life.

And Angie won't back down. Or give up.

Turn the page for a sneak peek…

Jaded Heart

Chapter One

"Which side? Wait, wait, wait." Angela Donnelly spun around and stared up at the signs above the exit doors of Terminal Four at Phoenix Sky Harbor International Airport…sweating. To. Death. "Okay, yeah. I'm on the south side. Door number six."

"Perfect. I'm on my way."

Angie closed her eyes as the familiar dinging from the key entering the ignition came over the line, which was promptly followed by the distinct sound of the engine starting. *Really?* "*Ohhhmygahhhd, Celia.* You haven't even left yet, have you?"

"Sorry, *sorrysorrysorry.* I'll be there in fifteen. I swear."

"Seriously?" Angie dropped her purse on top of her suitcase. "Ugh. I'm already sweating my ass off. In fact, I can see it. It's melted on the sidewalk. And it's fucking gross."

"Ewwww. That *is* gross. And graphic. Okay…*loveyousorryloveyousorry*…be there in a few. Hanging up now so I can drive. Bye!"

"Fine, but don't get a spee—" Angie pulled the phone away from her ear and stared at the home screen. "Speeding ticket," she said to no one because her younger sister, Celia, had already hung up. "Okay then."

Angie pushed her long hair off her shoulders. She should go back inside and buy a water from the Starbucks she spotted while waiting for her bag. Ooh! Or maybe a Caramel Frappuccino. She frowned. She might appreciate the caramel yumminess, but her ass and thighs wouldn't. Oh well. She didn't much feel like lugging her suitcase back inside, anyway.

Pulling the hair tie off her wrist, Angie gathered up her hair and twisted it into a knot on top of her head. She cocked her hip to the side and fanned her face. Scrolling through her phone, she checked the weather app. Ninety-eight degrees out? Yeah, no.

Lugging her suitcase was exactly what she was going to do. Okay, maybe not lug since it was on wheels. But whatever. Who cared about semantics when a person was melting? Not her. That was for damn sure.

By the time she made it back outside to the curb—half-drunk water bottle stuffed in her purse and a tall Caramel Frappuccino in her hand—her phone was vibrating her ass cheek to the point of numbness. After dumping her purse back on top of the suitcase, she slipped the phone from her back pocket and answered.

"Hello?"

"Where are you? I'm circling. You went to the south side, right? Door six?"

"Mmhmm." Angie sipped from the straw. Whoops. She hadn't meant to take that long, but there was a line. "I didn't see you."

Her sister let out an exasperated-sounding sigh. "Coming around again."

"All right. I'm here. Waiting. Still sweating, by the way." She grinned, then took another sip and focused on the oncoming line of cars. "What color is your car again?"

Her sister laughed. "It's silver. And it's a truck, you goof."

"Oh, yeah. I forgot. Ooh! Is that you?" She raised her sweet, ice-cold beverage in the air. "I think I see you."

"Yes, that's me."

"Yay!" Angie took the phone from her ear and shoved it in her back pocket as her sister pulled her truck up to the curb.

Celia came around the front of the vehicle, grinning. "Starbucks? Really?"

"Well, can you blame me? It's hot out." Angie grinned and tried to look innocent. "I got thirsty."

"Poor baby." With a laugh, Celia gave Angie a quick hug before muscling Angie's suitcase off the ground.

Angie opened the passenger door. "It has wheels, you know."

"No shit, really? Get in before you melt, princess." Celia hefted the suitcase into the back seat of the truck with a grunt. "Good God, what's in this thing?"

"Oh, you know, everything." Angie shrugged before hopping inside the cab to the blessed AC, and then Celia slid behind the wheel. In the next minute, they were navigating out of the airport and heading for the freeway. Angie tilted the plastic cup in her sister's direction. "You want some?"

"I'm thinking you should just give it to me as payment." Celia took the drink and sipped from the straw. "Mmm. Especially because you didn't get me one. And while you weren't getting me one, I had to drive in circles waiting for you."

Angie laughed. "Fair enough. It's all yours. My ass doesn't need it anyway."

"This is why I opt for sugar-free." Celia grinned, sucked some more from the straw, and then set the drink in the cup holder. "Welcome to Phoenix in the spring. We're having a bit of a heat wave. But only a small one."

"A small one, huh? My body's in shock. It was seventy-five degrees when I left Burbank an hour and a half ago."

"It's the desert. Plus, climate change is real, sis. Pretty much anytime starting mid-May to mid-October is summer now." Celia turned up the volume on the radio.

Angie gazed out at the mountains in the distance and then looked back at her sister. "Yeah, it's hot as hell, but it's a beautiful hell."

"That it is." Celia glanced over and smiled before focusing back on the road. "Glad you're here, Ang."

"Me too. A month-long vacation is just what I need. My dating moratorium is over, and I am *so* ready to hit the clubs and stretch my legs!"

"Clubs?" Celia groaned. "There goes my social life."

Angie frowned. "Ohhh, right. No worries. We can go to

some gay clubs, too. You know I'm all down for that." She turned the AC dial up and adjusted the vent closest to her. "Aside from that, I'm confused. I thought you were dating someone."

"I was." Celia merged onto another freeway. "Past tense."

"That sucks. Sorry, honey." Angie reached over and squeezed her sister's forearm. "When did that happen?"

"A couple of weeks ago. No need to be sorry. It just wasn't working out."

"Yeah, I know how that goes. Still sorry, though." Angie swiped a stray hair away from her eye. "Maybe you should try a moratorium like me?"

"Uh, no, thank you." Celia visibly cringed, and Angie laughed. "I'm still surprised you followed through with a whole year."

"Shoot, you and me both." Angie looked back toward the mountains. She'd spent a year single, committed to a real deal, no relationship, no dating, no one-night stand, moratorium. Before making the commitment, there'd been a steady stream of guys in and out of her life. None of them were worth bringing home to the parents. There'd been a couple she liked, sure, but she'd never gotten attached to any of them.

Angie sighed and glanced over at Celia. "If you recall, it wasn't my idea. Cyn and her brilliant plans. Then along comes Shane, and boom, they're all happy ever after now."

"I do recall." Celia chuckled. "She tried and failed in the best way, I suppose. But not you. I give you props. No way I could've followed through like you did."

"Honestly, it wasn't as hard as I thought it was going to be." Angie shrugged. "I'm glad I did it. I focused on work, reevaluated my goals, and set some new ones."

"New ones?"

"Yep. New ones." Angie grinned and played with the tendrils of hair hanging down at the base of her neck.

"Are you going to share or leave me in suspense?"

Angie laughed. "Time to put my degree to better use, little sister. My focus is still music, of course, so I'm shooting for Rolling Stone Magazine. I don't know if it'll happen, but I'm going to try."

"That's awesome!" Celia glanced at Angie, her smile big and bright. "I know you can do it, Ang. You just gotta put your mind to it."

"Aw, thanks, Celia. Don't get me wrong, I love writing indie music reviews for that small press in L.A. But…" Angie shrugged again. "I want more. But not until *after* this nice month-long vacation, though."

"You got this. It all starts right now." Celia grinned and turned the music up louder.

Angie tapped her thumb on the armrest to the beat of the song. "Country, huh? Who is this?"

"Yes, country. Ashley McBryde."

Angie grinned. "You never cease to amaze me."

"What's wrong with country?" Celia rolled her eyes. "Whatever."

"Nothing, just never took you for a country girl. Wait, is she singing about one-night stands?"

"She sure is." Her sister grinned.

Angie laughed, shaking her head. "Perfect."

She'd meant what she said; Angie really did need to stretch her legs, and she was glad to be back in Arizona. It'd been a few years since she'd been there. She missed her sister and her brother, Mark, but more than that, she needed a change of scenery.

Life was unfolding around her, moving forward, and she'd been standing still. Or at least that's what it felt like. Her younger brother Mark was graduating from ASU in a couple of weeks, and he'd go on to whatever it was he was planning to do with his life. Angie was excited for him.

Mark's graduation was the perfect opportunity to get out there and have fun…and do it with her brother and sister around her. They could be the three musketeers for a month.

Donnellys on the loose in Sin City…aka Tempe, Arizona. Perfect.

Garrett James stood on the loading dock at the back of the building he ran his small concert venue out of and signed the bill of lading for the delivery of booze that had just been unloaded.

He handed the clipboard back to the driver. "Thanks, man. Have a good day."

"You too, Garrett." After a brief handshake, the guy stepped away and made his way to his truck.

Garrett ducked inside and pulled down the steel garage door. For now, the building was quiet as a church, and he was alone. But not for long. The three bands he had lined up for the night weren't due to arrive for another five hours.

Once they got there, the building would turn into what could only be called "managed chaos" as they got set up, and his mixing engineer took them through their soundcheck. Truth be told, the real chaos would happen when patrons started arriving. But he loved it, every minute of it.

He'd have plenty of time to update the liquor inventory, catch up on paperwork, answer a couple emails, and then get ready to open. Perfect. Garrett took the back stairs up to his office two at a time and then settled behind his desk.

Two hours had come and gone before the sound of his cell ringing drew his attention. After picking up the phone, he swiped the screen and put it to his ear. "Who's this?"

"Knock it off, Dad. I'm totally running late. As usual, you didn't answer my text."

"What text?" Garrett leaned back in his seat and smothered a chuckle. He'd seen the text but hadn't replied yet.

"Ugh, give me a break. I know you saw it. Anyway, do you want something from Starbucks?"

"Ah, yes. Your daily caffeine run."

"You're one to talk. You live on coffee *and* chips. Makes no sense to me—hold on. Yeah, can I get two tall coffees—okay, I'm back."

"What's wrong with potato chips?"

"Uh, how about the fact that you're getting older and eating healthy is a tad important?" His daughter laughed.

"I don't know what you're talking about. I'm fine. Leave my diet alone."

"Someone has to pay attention to it. It's a well-known fact that married men live longer, you know? Honestly, with the hours you keep, I'll never understand how you aren't asleep at your desk the majority of the time." Chassidy laughed again. "So, before I pay, you want anything else?"

Garrett rolled his eyes. "Funny girl. You trying to set me up with someone, or did you mean something else besides coffee?"

His daughter barked a laugh. "I know better than that. Too many gold diggers out there. Ooh, they have those birthday cake pops you like so much. They look fresh, too. You want one? Two?"

"Sold! Bring me two." He shifted a stack of papers to the side for filing. "See? Who needs a wife when I can have cake!"

"Sick, sick man. Although, you're right. Cake is probably better than a gold-digging stepmother."

Garrett grinned and shook his head. "I'm so glad we agree."

"Well, I am a chip off the old block."

"Calling me old again, kid?"

"What's that?" His daughter laughed again. "You cut out. See you in twenty, Dad."

"Smartass." Garrett chuckled as he hit the "end call" button and set the cell back on his desk.

Glancing at the picture of Chassidy when she was five years old on the corner of his desk, he let out a breath and ran his fingers through his long hair.

She worked for him at the club for the last five years—handled all the bookings and was fantastic at it. All things considered, their relationship was rock solid, even though he drove her insane, and sometimes they fought—though that'd lessened significantly since she moved out of his house two years ago.

She was stubborn, just like he was, but Garrett couldn't say he was upset he'd passed that little trait onto her. Actually, except for his self-destructive ones, he'd passed a lot of good traits on to her. Considering he'd missed the majority of the first ten years of her life, that was saying something.

After one too many tragedies, Garrett finally hit rock bottom, cleaned himself up, and attempted to be a father for the first time in his life…and as far as he was concerned, Chassidy was all he needed to make a new beginning. It wasn't an easy road by any stretch, but they'd done okay.

He and his little girl. Chassidy was the only thing from his past he *didn't* regret.

The office line assigned to Chassidy rang. Instead of letting it go to her voicemail, he answered. "Copper Halo, bookings. How can I help you?"

"Hey, yeah, this is Josh Chasen. Manager for Gothic Princess? Is Chassidy available?"

Garrett looked over the lineup for the night. Gothic Princess was their opener. "Chassidy isn't available right now. Did you try her cell?"

"Yeah, but no answer. Hate to do this, but I need to pull the girls out of their spot tonight. Lead singer's got the stomach flu."

"Fuck sake, okay." Garrett sat back and let out a frustrated sigh. Damn musicians could be total flakes. Stomach flu likely translated to being too hungover to perform. He cringed at how jaded his thinking was, but honestly, back in his heyday, he'd used that same excuse a million times. It was the nature of the beast. "You got anyone that's any good you can refer?"

"Not off the top of my head. I'll ask around, though. Again, sorry. I feel real bad, man."

Garrett leaned forward and pinched the bridge of his nose. "Appreciate it. Thanks for letting us know. Take care of your girl."

Setting the receiver back in the cradle, Garrett grabbed his used coffee mug and headed into the bathroom to rinse it out. Filling a slot last minute could be easy, but often, the takers you got weren't very good. Sadly, just because a group of people got together that could sing or play instruments and called themselves a band didn't mean they actually could perform worth a damn. Likely, Chassidy had someone on the back burner she could call to fill the spot. He hoped.

Taking a deep breath, he reminded himself not to get too worked up. This was his life, a life he'd chosen. He owned his own business. Answered only to himself. But owning a business came with the good and the bad. In his case, it was music, musicians, people and lots of booze—though he didn't partake anymore.

Garrett took his seat again and leaned back in his chair. Letting his head fall back, he closed his eyes and let his thoughts wander back to Chassidy.

Lately, she'd been dropping comments about him being single. He wasn't sure why. He preferred being single. Not that there wasn't the occasional hook-up or someone he casually dated. There were. It was just Chassidy wasn't exposed to them when she was young, and why should she have been?

Most women he met, even after all these years, proved to not be truly interested in him as a person, so why bother keeping them around?

As a single father, Garrett wasn't interested in disrupting the stable life he'd finally given his daughter. Her life had been far too unstable before she lost her mother, and then before he'd gotten cleaned up.

Memories broke through, and Garrett shuddered. He didn't like to think about his ex-wife, Amanda. Or her death. Or how he used to live, either. Really, any part of his life from that time.

It was ugly. He had been ugly, and as far as Garrett was concerned, that ugly needed to stay right where it was, in the past.

Want more?
Head to my site to find all links to my available backlist:
www.DorothyFShaw.com

Available from all major e-sellers in digital and print.

Start at the beginning of
The Donnellys series with:
Unworthy Heart

The Donnellys Book 1
© 2019 Dorothy F. Shaw

Opposites not only attract, sometimes they spontaneously combust.

Ryan Donnelly's past relationship may have failed, but he's determined to make single fatherhood and his career a resounding success. He's got his eye on the top of the ladder at an L.A. marketing firm when his gaze snags on co-worker Maiya Rossini.

She's a feisty, witty, tattooed redhead who's nowhere near his type, but she pushes every one of his hot buttons.

Maiya clawed her way out of her dysfunctional, trailer-park childhood to earn a college degree and establish a promising career. Her future dreams are big, bright and packed with full-throttle fun, but when it comes to matters of the heart and men—especially stuffy corporate types like Ryan —her past slams on the emotional brakes.

In the office and in the bedroom, Maiya and Ryan rub each other in all the *right* ways. Though Maiya is everything Ryan didn't know he wanted, he's got his work cut out for him convincing her she's worthy of love—or the bright light she's brought to his life could slip through his fingers.

Defensive Heart

The Donnellys Book 2
© 2019 Dorothy F. Shaw

***Uptown girl, tattooed bad boy. Think you know which
one is wild? You'd be wrong.***

Greenwich Village is home to successful artist Jimmy
Donnelly, and the world is his playground. A broken heart in
college left him with zero interest in being tied down. But
when he meets a sexy, quick-witted Manhattan attorney, he
reconsiders his bad boy ways.

Sonja Martin's life is filled with work, an ex-husband who
refuses to stay gone, and a teenage daughter who won't follow
the rules. Jimmy, with his myriad of tattoos and piercings,
looks more like one of her clients than a potential lover. But
when every argument between them feels more like foreplay,
she can't seem to stay out of his bed.

The heat burns through whatever defenses Sonja thought
she had. And Jimmy finds his every fantasy fulfilled—and

exceeded—by a woman whose fire burns as bright as her fiercely guarded vulnerability.

But his case for breaking her out of her self-imposed mold might just be dismissed. And he'll lose the best thing he's ever found.

Dorothy F. Shaw
Phoenix, Arizona
SHATTERED HEART
Copyright © 2020 by Dorothy F. Shaw
ISBN-10: 0-9978310-3-0
ISBN-13: 978-0-9978310-3-0
Draft2Digital ISBN-13: 978-0-4637309-6-6
Edited by Tera Cuskaden
Cover by Kanaxa

Red Queen Publications electronic and print publication: April 2020

Publishing History
Digital/Print 1.0 edition / January 2016
Digital/Print 2.0 edition / March 2017
Digital/Print 3.0 edition/ April 2020

Red Queen
Publications